praise for
GREEN GRASS, RUNNING WATER

"Impressively ambitious and funny." —*The New York Times Book Review*

"With this brilliant, enduring novel, King has demonstrated an apparently effortless mastery over narrative." —*The Globe and Mail*

"King is equally at home with his vivid, often comic characters and with the vibrant natural world in which their dramas are played out." —*People*

"With this clever, vastly entertaining novel, King establishes himself firmly as one of the first rank of contemporary Native American writers—and as a gifted storyteller of universal relevance." —*Publishers Weekly*

praise for
TRUTH AND BRIGHT WATER

"A storyteller of the first order. . . . [*Truth and Bright Water*] is a world only Thomas King could create, whimsical and contemporary and smart, rooted and knowing and sad." —*The Globe and Mail*

"A sparkling triumph." —*Toronto Star*

"The dialogue crackles with intensity and wit, and the story is littered with radiant objects that reflect the lives of the characters. . . . [King] has mixed the banal and profound to create something like life—only more startling and truthful." —*The Gazette* (Montreal)

THE BACK OF THE TURTLE

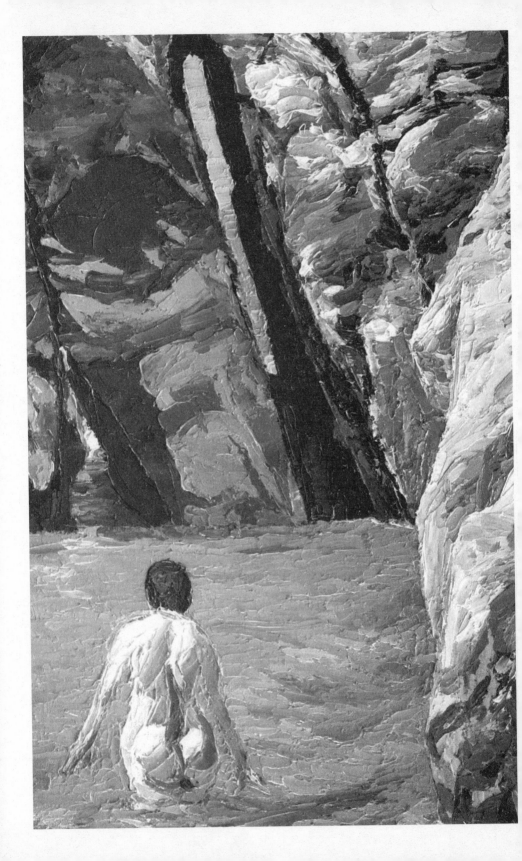

THE BACK OF THE TURTLE

A NOVEL

THOMAS KING

HarperCollins Publishers Ltd

Published by HarperCollins Publishers Ltd

First paperback edition

HarperCollins books may be purchased for educational, business,
or sales promotional use through our Special Markets Department.

HarperCollins Publishers Ltd
2 Bloor Street East, 20th Floor
Toronto, Ontario, Canada
M4W 1A8

www.harpercollins.ca

Library and Archives Canada Cataloguing in Publication
information is available upon request

ISBN 978-1-44344-646-4

Cover art (also shown on p. iv), *Interlude* © Helen Hoy

Printed and bound in the United States of America
RRD 9 8 7 6 5 4

For the songs and the singers

Prologue

FIRST LIGHT.

The shore in shadows, the fog banked on the horizon. Water, land, and the line of the tide.

So it would begin.

THEY sat together on the bluff overlooking the water and waited for the dawn. Crisp pulled an apple from his pocket, split it with his knife, held out the fatter half to the dog.

"'Tis the stuff of creation," he said, "and a remedy for the bowels."

The dog sniffed at it cautiously.

"See there!" Crisp leaned forward and squinted into the gloom.

Far below, at the bend in the trail, a figure emerged from the trees and began the final descent to the beach.

"There he be, as ye predicted."

The dog growled and struggled to his feet.

"Did ye know that a fortune may be read on a face and a fate found in a query?"

The dog raised his head and tested the air, opened his mouth and began a soft, low keening.

"Fine, fine," said Crisp. "But just remember, this be your idea."

And then the dog was away, loping across the flat, dropping onto the slope, picking up speed as he hurried to close the gap.

Crisp lay back in the grass to await the sun. "Aye, Master Dog," he whispered, to no one in particular. "I am well, if ye be well, too."

1

THE MAN STOOD AT THE BOUNDARY OF THE BEACH, IN THE shadows of the hanging cedars, and listened to the heavy surf run in from deeper water. The beach pitched up sharply here, the high sand soft and dry. Farther down, the shore was firm and wet, and footprints vanished with each step.

He didn't hear the dog until it came bursting out of the ferns and the underbrush. It raced past him, cut a wide arc in the sand and seagrass, and galloped back, snorting and trembling.

"There you are."

He could build a fire to chase away the cold and the damp. A fire would ease the ache in his hands, and he could warm the drum, turning it over and over until the heat pulled the hide tight against the wood frame.

"What about it? Would you like a fire?"

On the far bluff above the beach, the motel star blinked pale blue. At one time, perhaps when the motel had been fresh and crisp, the neon sign had read, "Ocean Star Motel" and "Vacancy" and "Welcome," but the damp fog and the corrupting salt air had made the sign undependable.

He imagined that people strolling the solitude of the beach might find such a sign an irritating presence, but as he made his way across the sand, the four letters that remained seemed oddly reassuring.

As though the old motel might mark a place of shelter and safety.

He stopped and knelt. The sand was dark and fine. Thick. More like clay. He picked up a handful and squeezed it as hard as he could. Then he set it down and watched as it slumped and melted away.

"*Post hoc*," he said to no one in particular, "*ergo propter hoc.*"

Behind him, he could feel the sun roll out of the mountains like a bright wave. He touched the sand again and tried to remember which of the diving animals had brought up the first lump of earth.

"Muskrat," he told the dog. "Or maybe it was otter."

He stepped into the lapping surf and waited. It would not be long now. And then the waters would part, the sand flat would rise out of the receding tide, wet and dark, like the hump of a massive sea creature, and the path to the lonely cluster of rocks in the distance would clear, straight and narrow.

The Apostles.

During much of the tidal cycle, they were little more than a low-lying cluster of bleak crags, beaten by the waves. But when the moon turned to face the earth, the sea would pull back to reveal tall columns of basalt smoothed and sharpened by wind and water, slanting into the sky, and braced against the racing currents.

The dog moaned and looked back to the high sand.

"It's okay," said the man, "you don't have to come."

At one time, the lower reaches of the Apostles had been covered with orange starfish, black mussels, and purple urchins. Crimson crabs had scuttled in and out of the crevices and cracks, and green sea anemones had fluttered against the rock like grass.

But not now.

Now all that remained of that community were the bleached bodies of barnacles still bound to the rock. As they had been in life.

It was impossible to avoid the brittle shells, and, with each step, they shattered under his feet. The rock itself was smooth and slick at first, but, as the man climbed, the basalt turned ragged by degrees, scored with deep channels and razor flutes. Near the top, he found the narrow saddle, a tentative refuge, a place from which to watch the tide come in and cut off any escape.

He had been here before. And each time he had retreated to the beach before the sea swallowed the rocks.

Not this time.

He turned towards the eastern mountains, angled the drum to catch the rising sun, and began a memorial song. But the elk skin was too soft now, too damp. The beats slid off, and his voice was drowned in the rushing water. In the distance, he could see the dog laid out on higher ground.

And in that moment, in that moment, he thought about retreating once again.

But the path back was only a memory now, all safety choked off as the sea ringed the Apostles in ink and foam.

He began the song anew, picking up the beat and raising the pitch, so that his voice carried above the slicing surf. The sun was full in his face now, the sky blue and polished. It was going to be a good day.

But as he turned back to the ocean to encourage the tide, the drum died in his hand.

"No!"

The fog had come out of nowhere. Dank and dark, its mouth gaping, it raced across the water and swallowed the dawn whole and complete.

"No, no, no, no!"

He slumped against the side of the saddle. So this was how it was going to be. No sun. No blue sky. No last view of the forest and the mountains. Just a wet abyss and the pounding thump of the waves.

Wonderful!

He had wanted sunshine, had no intention of dying in shadows. He had lived his life that way. He wasn't asking for much. A low tide, so he could get to the rocks. A high tide, so he couldn't get back. A little privacy and some light, so he could see the world at the moment he left it.

But here was that wizard fog again, and, as he watched, the trees and the mountains and the dog on the beach disappeared without a trace.

Okay. No sun.

So be it. If that's the way it was, so be it. He took off his jacket and laid it on the rocks. A soft, cloth-and-leather jacket, black and tan, with "Crow Fair" stencilled across the back above a panorama of tipis, with a banner that read, "Powwow Capital of the World." It was a special jacket, strong and powerful, and even Sonny, with his endless babble about salvage, didn't bother him when he wore it.

The photograph was in his shirt pocket. He didn't need to look at it again. He had looked at it countless times.

He removed his glasses, stripped off the rest of his clothes, and took up the song once more, stronger this time, aiming his voice into the heart of the fog. But the breakers were having no truck with ceremony. They surged over the Apostles and sent him sideways. The drum was soaking now, but it had never sounded better. He had never sounded better. Maybe singing in the fog was like singing in the bathroom. Maybe the acoustics were always better in wet places.

The rising tide tugged at him, tried to pull him in.

"Soon enough!" he shouted, breaking off the song and wedging himself tighter into the rock. "But not yet!"

And then he felt it.

Something in the water touched him, grasped his leg for a moment and then was gone. A small fish probably or a piece of debris. Or maybe something larger. Something looking for a meal. He pulled his feet further up the rock and watched the ocean roil below him.

At first he didn't see it. Saw only the vague shadows of the running tide. And then it was there. A hand thrust out of the water, then an arm, fragile, a slender branch caught in a flood.

And then a pool of black hair, floating around a child's face.

He quickly shifted his weight and reached for the arm, just as a wave broke over his back and sent him sprawling, the salt rising in his nose and mouth like blood, the water burning his eyes. Two more waves broke against him before he found the child again, closer this time, almost at his feet.

"Hang on!"

He caught the arm, awkwardly, his own shoulder twisting with the strain as he waited for the water to float the child closer to the rocks. Then he arched his back and pulled hard in one long motion.

A young girl.

Thin as tin. Cold and naked like him.

"It's okay." He gathered her in his arms, so she wouldn't slip away. "It's okay."

He could feel her shaking, and he wished he had something warm to wrap her in. But his clothes were gone. Washed off the rocks.

Except for his jacket.

It had been driven into a crevice. The leather was sopping and cold, but he draped it over her anyway, hoping it might provide some protection from the wind and the spray.

He rocked the girl gently, trying to comfort her. "It's okay."

The waves came faster now with hardly enough time between each surge to catch a breath. And in that moment, the girl turned and tried to break free, holding her arms out as though she wanted to return to the water.

"No," he said softly, pulling her back. "No."

She pushed away again, reached down into the foam, just as another wave slammed into the Apostles and flung both of them backwards.

"Sonofabitch!"

The basalt cut into his shoulder and thigh, and he could feel the blood run warm on his skin. He had only one arm around the girl now, but as he struggled to regain the saddle, he saw a second body rise out of the swirling water.

"Stay here!" He lifted the girl onto the saddle, forced her arms around the rock, and quickly slid down the side of the shaft, searching for a ledge he could stand on.

"Here!" he shouted. "I'm here!"

And suddenly the sea was alive with people. He caught a young boy by the hair and dragged him to the rocks. Then a young girl and an older woman. Another wave and an old man. Two young men. All naked and cold. Their mouths filled with water. Their eyes wild with life.

Patiently, his arms and back in agony, he caught each one in turn, until there were a dozen souls clinging to each other, as the surf thundered around them.

And then for no reason other than exhaustion and exhilaration, he began to sing again. Not the memorial song. A grass dance this time. A fierce song. A song for warriors. For now he knew these people. They were the sea people. The first people. The ones who had come from the ocean when the world was new. The long black hair. The fierce eyes. They had heard his song, and they had come to be with him at his dying.

Or perhaps he had summoned them. Perhaps it was time for a new beginning. Perhaps it was time for the twins to walk the earth again and restore the balance that had been lost.

He quickened the beat and imagined that the song alone had brought them forth, that his singing alone could hold the ocean back. And then very slowly, one voice at a time, beginning with the girl who had first reached out to him from the water, the people began to sing with him, their voices higher and sharper than his.

Until the tide turned again, and the fog began to clear.

Then as the melting light revealed the shore and the trees, the sea people touched his hand in turn and slipped back into the calming water.

He stayed on the saddle. And when the sun returned and the sky was high and cloudless, he waded to shore, watching the while for the young girl with the long, black hair, hoping she would appear to greet him.

But the only person waiting for him, when he limped back to the beach, was the dog.

2

DORIAN ASHER RELAXED IN THE QUIET COMFORT OF THE limousine and watched the world glide by. Ice continued to form near the breakwaters, but the remaining trees along Toronto's lakeshore had finally begun to come green. Winters in Toronto were never as cold as they had been in Ottawa nor as long as they had been in Edmonton.

Or at least, that's the way they used to be. Before the influx of fresh water from the melting Arctic ice cap had begun to slow the ocean's thermohaline conveyor, and global weather patterns had begun to shift.

It wasn't a surprise.

It had been predicted, the matter studied until the public had gotten tired of being told what was going to happen. Yet now that it was happening, everyone was indignant and annoyed, as though the longer, colder winters, the lost springs, and the tentative summers were somehow an unexpected personal affront.

Still, spring had finally arrived. A dark, cold spring, to be sure, but spring nonetheless.

And wet.

That's what Dorian noticed the most. The chilling dampness.

Even from the warmth of the back seat, he could feel the cold tumble over the car, like a glacial stream flowing across bedrock.

A glacial stream flowing across bedrock?

Where had that come from? Of late, Dorian found his imagination running away from his intellect, turning the ordinary and the mundane into vivid metaphor. He had always been a calm, organized man. Not like Winter, of course.

No one was like Winter.

It was probably the damn drugs. Lately, the nausea had been more of a problem, the ringing in his ears more pronounced. In the last little while, he had noticed a slight loss of concentration as well, coupled with a propensity to see catastrophes in canaries. It could be the pain, of course. Or maybe these breezes of melodrama had come from simple exhaustion.

There it was again. Catastrophes in canaries. Breezes of melodrama. Before long he would be standing at the corner of Yonge and Dundas, predicting the end of the world.

Dorian pulled the new issue of *Luxury Home Magazine* from the seat pocket and thumbed through the offerings. There was a pleasant-looking Florida property at Cape Harbour for a little under five million and a larger house in Port Royal for just under eight.

He dog-eared the page so he could find it later.

Last month, there had been a lovely six-bedroom home in Hualalai on the Kona-Kohala coast. He had shown the listing to Olivia.

"Twelve million?"

"Hawaiian oceanfront."

"We already have two homes."

"One home," Dorian had corrected. "One condo."

"And we don't need the condo."

He and Olivia had had this conversation any number of times. Yes, the condo was an expense, he would always concede, but it was a business expense, so it really wasn't an expense at all.

"There are times when I have to stay in the city overnight."

"Get a hotel room," Olivia would tell him. "No maintenance fees and you can still write it off your taxes."

"I need a kitchen."

"You don't cook."

"I don't want to be checking in and checking out all the time."

"You just like the status of having a condo in the city."

"I like the view."

Yes, Olivia would agree, the views past Toronto Island and across Lake Ontario were splendid.

"You can't just make money," Dorian would tell her softly, as though it were a secret. "You have to spend it."

Of course, Olivia was right about Hawaii. Twelve million dollars was really too steep for a third house. Still, knowing that he could buy any of these if he really wanted to was comforting. His only regret in terms of luxury homes and properties was not buying lot number six at Rosie Bay, near Tofino on Vancouver Island.

Four acres set on the side of a cliff, with a flat, one-acre building site perched above a private beach, a sea cave, and a 180-degree view of the western Pacific.

The day that he and Olivia had walked the boundaries, a black bear sow and two cubs had appeared out of the fog and then slipped away, primordial ghosts come back to see what had happened to their forest.

Dorian had seen the bears as a good omen, a ceremonial passing by the old order to the new. Olivia saw them as a potential nuisance.

"They'll get into the garbage," she had said. "There'll be no end of bother."

DORIAN closed the magazine and began counting the barren trees along the lake, trees that would never come green again. It was our own damn fault, he reminded himself, not that finding blame in the obvious was of any value.

Or consolation.

The car left the lakeshore and turned onto the access road to Tecumseh Plaza, world headquarters of Domidion. At ground level, there wasn't much to see, just a bunkered arrangement of concrete low-rises that was supposed to resemble a circle of Native longhouses.

Unlike the other corporate monuments that dominated the skyline of the reclaimed waterfront, Domidion had been built down, ten storeys into the earth, accessible only through a series of long, angled tunnels that led to the underground parking levels.

All part of the new world protocol.

If you were supposed to be in Tecumseh Plaza, you knew where to go. Otherwise, you had no business being there at all.

The limousine dropped into the tunnel reserved for upper management. Dorian took the pass out of his jacket. Even the head of Domidion had to run the gauntlet of security checks and retractable crash barriers. On occasion, he would time the process and was always reassured by the delays. It was an illusion, of course. Fear had made us cautious, even paranoid, Dorian acknowledged, and it had made us vigilant.

It just hadn't made us safe.

Aristotle had said that we make war so we may live in peace. Dorian wondered if the old Greek had ever realized just how wrong he had been. We make war so that we may destroy our enemies. We make war so that we may control resources and markets, and make money.

WINTER Lee was waiting for him when Dorian stepped off the elevator. Winter was the perfect corporate executive. Educated. Constrained. Precise. Youthful. No matter what time Dorian arrived at the office, Winter was there, ready to go to work.

"A new outfit?"

"Yes, sir."

Dorian appreciated Winter's attention to style. Today she was wearing a white cotton blouse, a black wool and raw silk skirt, and matching jacket. On her lapel was a jet brooch with thin alabaster diagonals.

Winter's psychological profiles continued to be mildly disturbing, but Dorian knew that, while successful people and the insane often wandered off into dark areas, the Winters of the world could always find their way home.

"What do you know about Tecumseh?"

"Shawnee. Late eighteenth, early nineteenth century," said Winter, without breaking stride. "Organized an Indian confederation to oppose European expansion. He was killed in the War of 1812, when the British deserted him on the battlefield."

"And the plaza is named after him."

"It is," said Winter.

"Ironic, don't you think?"

"There's a peace prize named after Alfred Nobel," said Winter.

"Touché," said Dorian.

"Dr. Toshi's office called," said Winter. "They want you to ring them back at your earliest convenience."

"The market?"

"Down," said Winter. "New York, Toronto, London, Tokyo. Oil has dropped to ninety-six."

"Good news would be appreciated."

"Noted," said Winter.

THE fourth subfloor of Domidion was a geometric arrangement of heavy glass partitions. There were no windows to the outside, because at over fifty feet below grade, there was no outside. But neither were there interior walls, at least not in the conventional way. All the offices were glass boxes. You could see everyone and everyone could see you. The only rooms that had any privacy were the bathrooms, and even here, strategically placed cameras recorded who came and went, though not what they did.

At least that was what everyone was told.

～～～

DORIAN sat down at his desk and brought up *The Globe and Mail*, *The New York Times*, and *The London Times* on separate monitors.

"The Zebras? Again?"

"Yes, sir," said Winter.

Dorian scrolled down the lead story in the *Globe*. "They're circulating personal and corporate credit card numbers on the Internet?"

"Along with names."

"Are we affected?"

"We're looking into that."

"This Zebra thing is getting out of hand." Dorian entered his password into the computer. "I need a PAM environment."

"PAM is running," said a compliant, female voice. "Please confirm."

"Confirmed." Dorian turned away from his computer and faced Winter. "So, aside from anarchists in stripes, what else do we have?"

"Three items." Winter touched her tablet. "An American army recon unit found a 'Chinese laundry' near Chaman."

"Another one?" Dorian took a deep breath and let it out slowly. "What the hell did the French do, give away franchises?"

"Anthrax. Botulism," said Winter. "Several nasty flu cultures."

"Don't suppose it was a Class A lab? Just a plastic tent with a sink and a microwave?" Dorian could feel the beginnings of a cramp in his left leg. "Maybe we should give these assholes the proper equipment, so they can do the job right."

Winter stood in front of Dorian's desk, her skin glowing like soft wax in the low light. Her lampblack hair, pale-blue almond eyes, and wire glasses made her look like a university student.

Or a sociopath.

And not for the first time, Dorian had the curious feeling that he was looking in a mirror.

"Are you telling me that the cultures were ours?"

Of course, there was really no way Domidion could keep track of every virus and bacterium that the corporation shipped around the world. Cultures sold to the Japanese for research might be resold to the Italians, who might trade them to the Saudis for oil, and from there no one knew where they went. Not the corporation's fault that product occasionally fell into the hands of madmen.

Certainly not the corporation's responsibility.

"The second item?"

"Yes," said Winter. "That would be the *Anguis*."

Dorian had only seen pictures of the *Anguis*. It was one of a dozen heavy-capacity barges that Domidion ran under a Bolivian registry and flag. Six months ago, the ship had left Montreal on a routine run to dump a mountain of toxic waste and incinerated biohazards into the ocean.

But before the *Anguis* could drop its load, the bright lights in Ottawa passed a law that prohibited the disposal of hazardous waste in this manner. So the barge turned around and came chugging back to Montreal.

Where provincial officials refused to let it land.

Quebec, as it turned out, had no objection to garbage leaving the province, but had strict laws prohibiting it from coming in, and the *Anguis* was ordered to vacate the St. Lawrence Seaway and find another port of call.

"The ship's been found?"

"No."

"I thought we had decided to stop looking for it."

"Yes, sir," said Winter. "At the January meeting of the Board."

By the time the barge cleared the headlands at Gaspé, the newspapers and networks had picked up the story. In a media minute, there wasn't an anchorage on the Eastern Seaboard that would give the ship safe haven, and the *Anguis* became a ship without a country.

It should have been a relatively easy matter to find someone who would take the waste. In the past, the corporation had always been able to find poor countries and desperate governments who needed money.

"Then what's the problem?"

"The crew," said Winter. "There's the question of a compensation package."

"Filipinos? Russians?"

"Taiwanese."

Domidion had initially struck a deal with Haiti. But by the end of the first week, the barge had become such a powerful symbol of what was wrong with North American culture that not even the Haitians were willing to take it. Up and down the coast the *Anguis* went, an orphan looking for a home.

The barge had been off the coast of Brazil when a rare subtropical cyclone punched its way out of the Caribbean. Subtropical Storm Nora did only minor damage to the coastline, but when the storm finally settled down into a series of cranky squalls and tropical depressions, the *Anguis* had vanished.

"I suppose we could announce some kind of package."

Winter looked at her tablet. "Shall I have accounting put the figures together?"

"Let's start with the announcement," said Dorian. "We can revisit compensation itself at a later date."

"Yes, sir," said Winter. "Revisit at a later date."

The only thing that had really mattered was that, when the barge broke apart and sank with her load of biologicals, she be as far away from Canada and the U.S. as possible. Off the coast of Cuba, though that was a little too close to Florida and the Gulf. Argentina or Chile perhaps. Or any of the other Central and South American countries that had not supported North America's trade and peace initiatives.

An accidental sinking was the best possible outcome. The *Anguis* was insured, and its mountain of waste would wind up at the bottom of the ocean, where it belonged.

"And the last matter?"

Winter shifted slightly. "Dr. Quinn."

"Quinn?"

"Dr. Gabriel Quinn," said Winter. "Head of Biological Oversight."

"Ah, you mean Q." Dorian waited to see if Winter recognized the reference. "From *Star Trek*? The television show? There was a character named Q, who knew everything there was to know about the universe. In Biological Oversight, they call him Q."

"I see," said Winter.

"Man's a genius with bacteria and viruses."

"He's gone."

Winter was precise. Dorian liked that about her. No frills. No adornments. No sound bites. No platitudes. No half answers.

No guesses. In many ways, Dorian imagined that Winter could well be the prototype for artificial intelligence.

"Gone?"

"Disappeared."

Dorian glanced at the monitor to make sure the Passive Audio Masking system was still running.

"Dr. Quinn was to have returned from vacation on the twenty-fourth," said Winter. "That was a Friday. On Monday, he failed to show up for work."

Dorian closed his eyes and tried to bring the biochemist's face into focus. There was an enormous aquarium that stood in the main foyer. At one time, there had been a single turtle in the tank, and, each day, Gabriel would eat his lunch and watch the turtle as she swam back and forth in the long rectangle of water.

Dorian had never asked Quinn about the tank and the turtle, but he supposed that sitting and watching was somehow soothing.

"The twenty-fourth was over three weeks ago."

"Yes, sir."

"And no one noticed that Quinn was missing?"

"There was some confusion," said Winter.

"Is there anything to suggest that we have a problem?"

Winter blinked once. "Domidion scientists aren't supposed to disappear."

No, thought Dorian, Domidion scientists were definitely not supposed to disappear. They're supposed to be brilliant, and Dr. Gabriel Quinn had not disappointed. Under Q's tenure, Domidion had developed several bacterial and viral strains that had changed the face of agribusiness.

And of warfare.

It was one of the small ironies of biology that an organism designed to increase crop production could also be modified to destroy nations.

"I sent you a file," said Winter. "There are images you'll want to see."

Dorian leaned back in the chair. "Is this going to complicate my day?"

"Yes, sir. I expect it will."

Dorian moved his mouse and opened a folder marked "Quinn.addendum."

The file contained photographs. The first image was of a small, nondescript house. Dorian remembered that his grandfather had owned such a house.

"Postwar bungalow."

"Yes," said Winter. "I believe it is."

Dorian smiled. "Are you trying to depress me?"

"This is the house Dr. Quinn was renting."

"Quinn was renting?" Dorian scrolled through the photographs. "And these are?"

"As I understand," said Winter, "these are the rooms in the house. The walls, to be precise."

"Quinn did this?"

"Every wall," said Winter. "The landlord called our Community Liaison office to complain."

Dorian remembered the day the turtle disappeared. A large sea turtle, as Dorian recalled, with a strange indentation in its shell, as though it had spent its life bearing a heavy load. Along its neck was a dark red slash. When Dorian had first seen the mark, he thought the turtle had been injured. But it wasn't blood. Just a colour abnormality in the rough skin near the creature's head.

The reptile wasn't of any value. Still, things weren't supposed to vanish from Domidion. Security had investigated, had issued a memorandum concluding that the turtle had somehow climbed out of the tank, wandered off somewhere, and died. It was the only explanation that made any sense, the only explanation that satisfied everyone.

Gabriel, Dorian recalled, had continued to eat his lunch in front of the empty tank with its blue water, thin green plants, and bright white sand, as though he expected the turtle to return.

Dorian stared at the images on the monitor. "He wrote on all the walls?"

"We think it's a list," said Winter.

"A list of what?"

"We're not sure," said Winter.

"Chernobyl. Idaho Falls. Chalk River." Dorian read the names on the screen. "Pine Ridge, South Dakota?"

"It's an Indian reservation," said Winter. "It was used as a bombing range during World War II."

"Rokkasho and Lanyu?"

"Nuclear and biological waste dumps."

"Renaissance Island." Dorian's face softened, as though he had run into an old friend. "The Russian anthrax facility."

"Yes, sir."

"Has Security seen these photographs yet?"

"Security took the photographs."

Dorian tapped the screen with his finger. "This is disturbing."

"Yes, sir," said Winter. "It is."

The image on Dorian's monitor showed a four-burner electric stove and a green refrigerator. On the wall above the sink, Gabriel had written "Bhopal" and "Grassy Narrows."

"Do we know what any of this means?"

Winter's eyes remained passive. "The Board was hoping that you might have some ideas."

The fatigue had returned. Dorian rubbed his neck and dug his thumbs into the muscles at the base of his skull. Perhaps a little pain would chase the weariness away.

"If you scroll to the end of the photographs, there's one that you should see."

"I'm supposing that this isn't going to be good news either."

"No, sir," said Winter. "I don't believe it is."

Dorian worked the mouse. Each new photograph was of another wall on which Dr. Quinn had written. Except for the final photograph. That photograph wasn't of a wall at all.

"That's the front door," said Winter.

Dorian sat up in his chair. Suddenly the fatigue was gone.

"The front door?"

"So far as we can tell," said Winter, "this is the last thing that Dr. Quinn wrote before he disappeared."

Dorian stared at the monitor. "Who's Quinn's number two in Biological Oversight?"

"Dr. Warren Thicke."

"All right," said Dorian. "I want Thicke in my office at ten tomorrow. I want to know where Quinn went on his vacation. And I would like us to find him as quietly and as quickly as possible."

~~~~~

FOR the rest of the morning, Dorian worked his way through the papers on his desk. Yet try as he might, he couldn't work up any enthusiasm for the jobs at hand. He had had days like this before, days when even the optimism of science and business couldn't carry him past the suspicion that the world had somehow slipped through his hands. Such concerns would pass, of course.

They always had.

Maybe it was time to do something about the empty aquarium in the lobby. There had been talk about fish. He had even ordered an illustrated catalogue, had been tempted by the colour plates of the salt-water species. But, each time Dorian tried to imagine schools of blueface angelfish, cinnamon clowns, green chromises, flame hawkfish, and black tangs all swooping and darting about, the thought of all that motion and flash left him feeling disquieted and anxious.

The turtle had been trouble enough.

He never understood what Gabriel had seen in the turtle. The animal had spent its life bump-bump-bumping against the glass, as though it expected to find a way to escape.

Then somehow, unexpectedly, it had.

And it was only after it had vanished that Dorian realized just how much he appreciated the simplicity and silence of empty water.

3

SONNY STANDS BY THE POOL, THE TOOL POUCH HANGING ON his hip, and looks out over the beach. On a clear day, you can see all the way to eternity. That's what Dad says. From here to eternity. Right now Sonny isn't trying to find eternity. He's watching the old guy lying on the beach.

Pretending to be dead.

Again.

The first time the old guy pretended to die on the beach, Sonny had raced down to collect the salvage.

Pants.

Shirt.

Shoes.

The jacket with the feathers and the tipis stitched across the back.

But then the dead rose up and went forth.

No salvage.

Wham-wham!

There are rules. If you want to play on Sonny's beach, that's okay. If you want to die on Sonny's beach, that's okay, also.

Play. Die.

Okay. Okay.

But pretending to die on the beach is not okay. It's against the rules. And what has happened to the old guy's clothes? Why is he naked? Has someone else taken Sonny's salvage? That wouldn't be fair. That wouldn't be right.

The pouch with the hammer and the wire cutters and the multi-head screwdriver jig-jig-jiggles against his thigh. Salvage is mine, Sonny reminds himself. I will be paid.

Sonny looks at the sky and the ocean. It's another beach day. Another day of ocean smells and ocean noises. Another day at the Ocean Star Motel. With the blue neon star that goes blink, blink, blink all day and all night.

Follow the Star.

That's the motel's motto.

Follow the Star.

Maybe today will be a good day. Maybe someone will stop by the motel and rent a room. Maybe today will be the way it used to be, with honeymooners and families and long-haul truckers and sports stars all flocking to town to see the turtles.

Before the turtles left.

Before That One Bad Day.

A famous actor stopped by the motel once and told Sonny a funny story about a duck who went into a pharmacy looking for grapes. "Got any grapes?" That's what the duck said. "Got any grapes?"

The Ocean Star Motel. Twenty-four rooms. Cable television. Video rentals. Free Internet.

The Ocean Star Motel. Pool. Ice-making machine. Laundromat. Vibrating beds.

The EverFresh vending machine.

Sonny stands on the patio in front of the EverFresh vending machine and considers the day. Maybe the ocean has brought new salvage ashore. That's what Sonny likes about the ocean.

Salvage.

I have looked to the water, whence cometh my salvage. Verily, I say, my salvage is at hand. Sonny didn't think these sayings up by himself. They all come from Dad, and Dad has had him repeat them over and over.

In the beginning was the salvage.

THE man hasn't moved. Sonny considers going down to the beach, in case the man is really dying and is in need of encouragement. Maybe Sonny could tap him on the head with his hammer, just to get his attention.

If the man is dead, Sonny could take a picture with his digital camera and sell the story to a newspaper in Vancouver.

"Body found on beach by Sonny."

Wham-wham, hammer-hammer!

Sonny shields his face with his hand and squints hard. The man on the beach is moving his toes. So much for the picture. So much for the story. So much for the salvage.

Sonny has a thought. He's had it before, but it's a good thought and worth thinking more than once. Maybe he should go back to school. Better yet, maybe he should sign up for cable. The deluxe package with the movie channels, the technical training programs, and the nature shows.

Sonny is trying to decide between going back to school and signing up for cable, when he hears something sharp and quick, lonely and far away. Sonny isn't at all sure what the sound is. At first he thinks it might be the raven that used to sit on the motel sign and yell death threats across the parking lot.

Throw rocks at that bird, Dad used to tell Sonny. Aim for the beak. No point in being subtle.

In the distance, on the far side of the bay, Sonny can see the warm vapours hanging above the hot springs. Perhaps someone has wandered into the wrong pool. Perhaps that was what he heard.

Sonny rests his hand on the head of the hammer and waits. But the sound doesn't come a second time.

4

GABRIEL LAY ON THE BEACH AND SLOWLY WIGGLED HIS TOES.
Now the sun was out. The inconsistent, unreliable, derelict sun.
Back from its morning holiday. Where was it when he needed
it? Where was it when he was on the rocks?

And what of the people he had pulled out of the ocean? Who
were they? Where had they come from? Where had they gone?
Had he really sung them out of the depths?

Ridiculous, of course. He understood physics, understood
the intricacies of the universe. The people in the water weren't
mythical beings. He had no responsibility for them. His only
concern was with dying, and that should have been a simple
matter.

In the distance, Gabriel could make out a figure moving
along the shore. The young girl he had rescued? Maybe she was
returning his jacket. He should have kept his glasses. That had
been a mistake. Now he couldn't see the world, couldn't see what
was coming at him.

THE day he arrived in Samaritan Bay, Gabriel had stopped at the
Co-op market and rummaged through the community bulletin

board. Under rentals, next to a faded "Stop the Pipeline" poster, he had found a posting, handwritten on a piece of lined paper. "Land and trailer," it said. "See the surf, sitting down. Nicholas Crisp, Finder-Minder."

He imagined that Nicholas Crisp would be short and thin, with translucent skin and a soft chin, but the man who walked into the Tin Turtle was tall and lanky with a bald head, sharp blue eyes, and a red beard that floated about his face like a cloud on fire. Seeing Crisp for the first time, Gabriel was struck by the odd fancy that the fellow had somehow got his head on upside down.

"I believe you have a trailer." Gabriel placed the flyer on the table and smoothed out the edges. "Is it for rent or for sale?"

"Them's the choices in life, to be sure." Crisp broke off a piece of banana bread and held it out. "The milk or the cow herself."

Gabriel tried the bread. It was dry, days stale with the oily flavour of something left too long under plastic.

"Not to your liking, is it?"

"It's not very good."

"Not much in life that is," said Crisp, "but we eats it up anyway, crumbs and all."

THE figure was getting closer. He could make out what looked to be a woman in jeans and a blue shirt, wading in the surf. Perhaps she would pass without noticing that there was a naked man lying in the sand. Not that he cared if she found him. Not that he cared in the least. But you could never count on people.

Sometimes they avoided things that were out of the ordinary, and other times their curiosity would float them into deep water.

He watched as the woman left the surf and came towards him.

"Hello."

Gabriel propped himself up on his elbows, scooped sand onto his groin, and tried to look stoic and fierce. "I'm naked," he shouted. "Just so you know."

"Yes," said the woman, sounding neither curious nor concerned, "I can see that."

He couldn't make out her face, couldn't tell if she was beautiful or plain, or if she was young or old, kind or cruel.

"I found this on the beach," she said, holding up a shirt. "Is it yours?"

"I was on the rocks."

"Yes," she said, "I've seen you out there several times."

"I'm trying to kill myself."

"You're not very good at it." The woman gestured at his groin. "And you missed a spot."

Gabriel rummaged in the pockets of the shirt. The photograph was still there, soggy and soft. So were his glasses. He wiped them off, put them on, and the world leapt into focus.

"I'm Mara," said the woman. "Mara Reid."

The shirt was wet and heavy and cold, but he slipped it on anyway, trying not to disturb the pile of sand on his lap.

"Gabriel," he said. "Gabriel Quinn."

THE trailer was an aluminum lump parked hard against a stand of Douglas fir and hemlock. It had been silver at one time, but the salt spray had skinned it grey. Gabriel wondered whether, if you rubbed the sides, a genie might pop out.

"Flying Cloud, she be," Crisp said, as they walked around the trailer the next morning. "Bath with a shower, stove and fridge, dinette, television with selected videos, and a bedroom with a view. Ye know trailers from trawlers?"

"No."

"Nothing much to know. Simple they are, not like a house. Now there's a pox. A house, ye see, don't want to move. Once she's built, she figures to stay put. A trailer's more compliant. Ye doesn't likes where ye have come ashore? Well, just drop the hitch on the ball and away ye go. Trailer's the better companion. Happy on the road or off. All love for ye and your caprices, and no complaining."

Through the quartering fog, Gabriel could see a blue glow twinkling in the distance.

"Ocean Star Motel," said Crisp. "The boy's poorly lit, but a sweet neighbour."

He waved a hand over the water, as though he expected the sea to part.

"The Apostles is good exercise at low tide, if ye have no aversion to climbing about on carcasses and bones. But watch your back. The sea's a shifty slut. She'll tide in behind and suck ye up in a salty slurp."

"I'm not sure how long I'll stay."

"There's wisdom enough in that for shirts and pants to fit us all." Crisp ran a hand through his beard, and it crackled and flashed in the pale light. "Will ye be needing a chair?"

"Chair?"

"For the deck," said Crisp. "So ye can sit and imagine to have some say in creation. Would ye object to such an assembly?"

"No, a chair would be nice."

"And what will it be?" Crisp clapped his hands together. "One for solitude, two for friendship, or three for society?"

Gabriel tried to remember if Thoreau had had a preference. "One should be enough," he said.

"Then I'll do that. Nothing illustrious or imposing. Won't charge for the improvement, and I'll still give ye the fugitive rate."

"Fugitive rate?"

Crisp stepped in close and lowered his voice. It came with the smell of garlic and wet wool.

"Folks used to come to the Bay for all manner of reason. Vacations, festivities, family, friends. All that before The Ruin, of course. Now, most of what gets washed up on this parcel of purgatory were a fugitive. Broadsided, blistered, and beached."

"It's a fine trailer."

"Course it's impolite to ask a man what's disturbing his shadow, and sometimes a man don't know precisely what set him on the hurry. But when he gets here, when he gets here, he's clean out of run. For here be the land as we stand, and there be the water as we see."

"I'll take it."

"Birds," said Crisp, holding his arms out so that his coat caught the wind. "We might have prospects for an escape, if we be birds."

～～～

CRISP came by the next morning.

"If ye must have a chair, a rocker is what's required," he said, as he dropped the tailgate of his pickup. "Like riding an ocean swell or resting safe in your mother's arms."

"You made this?"

"We used to sit on the ground," said Crisp. "And we used to walk on all fours.

"This is a nice chair."

"And for all the good truth will do us, we were happier then." Crisp walked to the edge of the deck. "Have ye a name some-where about your person?"

Gabriel nodded. "Several."

"A name for every occasion," said Crisp. "The Indians do such a thing, I'm told. Collect names as they're earned or as they appear. In that, I'm a poor man with but one name to drag about."

"Nicholas is a fine name."

"It covers a territory, it does. St. Nick. Old Nick. Christmas and hell. And all the bleeding nicks of life in between."

"Gabriel. Mostly, I'm called Gabriel."

"Gabriel!" Crisp's voice rushed through the trees like a truck in a tunnel. "Now there's thunder and storm. The best-loved of the four angels. The one chosen to announce the birth of John the Baptist and to reveal the Qur'an to Muhammad. It's Gabriel what tells Mary about the road ahead."

Nicholas shook his head with delight.

"Dante made Gabriel the chief of the angelic guards placed at the entrance to paradise. Did ye know that? And if the creative arts

35

are your butter and jam, there's a movie called *Constantine* what has a Gabriel who betrays heaven and joins forces with the Dark Lord."

Crisp's eyes flashed in the fading light and his lips curled away from yellowing teeth.

"And now, at the meridian of the world, on this seal-piss and foggy-dog of a day, here stands another Gabriel, rigged for battle and havoc. It surely takes my breath away."

"I'm not that Gabriel."

"Yet here ye are," said Nicholas, grabbing Gabriel firmly by the shoulders. "Here ye are."

"GABRIEL," said Mara, pausing on each syllable. "Like the left-handed twin?"

The dog came shuffling back, dragging Gabriel's pants with him. They were colder than the shirt and full of sand.

"Why do you want to kill yourself?"

Putting the clothes on was a mistake. The chill sank into his bones, and the sand rubbed at his skin with every movement. The sun was weak, the wind off the ocean fresh and brittle.

The dog leaned up against Mara's leg and began testing her ankle with his tongue.

"Sold," Gabriel told the dog, "no licking."

Mara smiled. "His name is . . . Sold?"

The dog whined and looked up at her, his face bright with expectation.

Gabriel rubbed the dog's neck and fingered the weather-worn collar. "The tag is corroded," he said. 'Sold' is all you can make out."

"So, he's not yours?"

Gabriel could feel his clothes tightening around him. "He likes to follow me."

"You need to find him another name," said Mara.

Gabriel wanted to ask Mara about the sea people. Had she seen them? Had they washed ashore with his clothes? Had she found his jacket? If he had to live, he'd like the jacket back.

And the drum as well, for that matter.

Mara kneeled down beside the dog and looked into his eyes. "Sold . . . Solder . . . Soldering . . . Soldier . . . how about . . . Soldier?"

The dog began humming happily and came to his hind legs.

"See," said Mara, "he likes that name."

"Sure." Gabriel shrugged. "If that's what he wants."

The dog rolled over in the sand and farted.

"Are you alone?" said Mara. "Is that the reason?"

"Everyone is alone," said Gabriel.

Mara wrapped her arms around herself and turned her back to the wind. "Are you going to try to kill yourself tomorrow?"

Gabriel looked out across the sand, watched the water rise and fall as though the ocean were breathing.

"If I were going to kill myself," said Mara, "I'd do it when the sun was shining."

BY the time Gabriel got back to the trailer, Soldier was already splayed out on the deck. The woman on the beach had been somewhat disconcerting. She hadn't been put off by his abruptness or his lack of clothes or his suicidal intentions. If anything, she had seemed . . . disappointed.

Gabriel took out a black marker and wrote "SS *Mont-Blanc*" on the edge of the deck. Next to it, he wrote "SS *Imo*."

"1917," he told the dog. "Over two thousand people killed. Nine thousand injured. The pressure wave bent iron rails and demolished buildings."

The dog struggled to his feet, hobbled over to the chair, and put his head in Gabriel's lap. Wisps of high fog began floating through the trees. Gabriel understood the hydraulics. Warmer inland weather sucked the moist air from the ocean in across the land, and the differences in temperature caused condensation to form.

"Okay," he said to the dog, "you pick one."

Soldier sat up and grumbled.

"West Anniston creek?" Gabriel took the marker out again. "Yes," he said, "that's a good one. That's certainly one of my favourites."

But the dog had lost interest in the game. He limped away and lay against the door of the trailer.

Gabriel stayed on the deck and tried to remember how many people had died in the Benxihu Colliery disaster in China, while below on the beach, the fog moved back across the waves and turned the world the colour of soft lead.

5

DORIAN SAT IN HIS OFFICE SPEED-READING A JAPANESE study that measured toxicity in furniture, and wondered, once again, if his health issues might be related to the bed that he and Olivia had purchased.

"You'll sleep like babies," the sales associate had told them. "The foam moulds to your body and eliminates any pressure points."

They had taken off their shoes and stretched out on the mattress. It had been a pleasant enough experience, much like sinking into warm custard.

But when the new mattress arrived and the plastic wrapping was removed, their bedroom immediately filled up with a violent odour that irritated their eyes and set the both of them to coughing.

Olivia opened all the windows, but the room remained unbearable, and they were forced to take their books and pillows upstairs and sleep in the guest quarters.

The next morning, Dorian called the store.

Yes, the sales associate told him, off-gassing was quite common. Yes, all the emissions were within government regulations and did not pose a health hazard. Yes, in rare cases, the fumes might irritate eyes and cause some minor coughing. No, the guarantee only covered manufacturer's defects. But there was no need to worry, the man assured Dorian. In most cases, the problem would resolve itself.

Two months later, Dorian and Olivia were still in the guest suites. By then the smell had disappeared, but each time they tried sleeping on the mattress, they would wake up in the morning with headaches and sore throats.

The store manager was sympathetic. "Aside from that, how does the bed feel?"

"It's comfortable," Dorian admitted. "A little warm for my liking, but comfortable."

"And that's the most important thing, isn't it."

As a token of the company's commitment to customer service, the manager gave Dorian twenty percent off on a special mattress cover that protected the bed from moisture but still allowed the foam to breathe.

"We recommend this cover for people with heightened sensitivities, and it reduces the incidence of dust mites."

Dorian put the cover on that evening, and, over the next two weeks, the headaches did go away.

The sore throats continued for a while longer.

THROUGH the glass partitions, Dorian watched Winter step off the elevator and come along the corridor towards the office. The woman had the unsettling ability to move through the physical world as though it didn't exist.

"Do you know anything about organic mattresses?"

Winter tilted her head to one side, as though she had been asked a question for which there was no good answer.

"Olivia and I have to get a new mattress. We're thinking we might try natural latex."

"I spoke with Dr. Thicke." Winter adjusted her glasses and consulted the tablet. "He'll be here tomorrow."

"Probably thinks I want to talk to him about the biofuels position."

"Yes, sir," said Winter. "He did mention biofuels."

Dorian snorted. "Cold day in hell."

"And it appears that Dr. Quinn didn't go anywhere for his vacation."

"He stayed in town?"

"Archives," said Winter. "Dr. Quinn spent his vacation in archives."

Dorian rubbed his eyes. The ringing in his ears was back.

"Our archives?"

"Yes, sir."

"Access to archives is restricted."

"It is," said Winter.

"Did I authorize such access?"

"No, sir," said Winter. "You did not."

"Then how the hell did he get in?"

"Archives were reorganized in the last restructuring." Winter slid a finger across the tablet several times. "Currently, we have no staff in archives."

"Security footage? Computer records?"

"We're going through everything now," said Winter. "An initial assessment indicates that Dr. Quinn was interested in the files on *Klebsiella planticola.*"

"*Klebsiella planticola?*"

"The SDF 20 variation."

Dorian turned to the monitor. "PAM environment," he said, speaking clearly and distinctly. "I'd like a PAM environment now."

KLEBSIELLA *planticola*, or SDF 15, was a naturally occurring bacterium that grew in the root systems of every plant in the world. In the 1990s, a German company genetically modified the original bacterium to allow it to accelerate the decomposition of plant litter and produce alcohol as a by-product.

SDF 20.

Dorian remembered how the first reports had electrified the agribusiness community. But while SDF 15 was a beneficial bacterium, the genetically modified version, SDF 20, turned out to be an environmental nightmare. It was about to be approved for general use, when a team of scientists at Oregon State University ran independent tests and discovered that SDF 20 killed all plant life. Had it been sprayed on fields and then spread by the wind and birds and irrigation runoff, it could have meant the eventual destruction of all plant life on the planet.

"HE might have been reviewing laboratory notes," said Winter. "I understand that he was quite dedicated to his work."

Dorian pressed a finger against his temple. The ringing in his ears was more pronounced now. He had spoken to Toshi about this at the last visit. He would have to mention it once again.

"Would you spend your vacation in archives?"

Winter took a moment to process the question. "No, sir," she said. "I don't believe I would."

SDF 20 was one of those mistakes that gave agribusiness a bad name and got the public up in arms about genetically modified organisms. What the average family didn't know was the extent to which genetic modifications were already a part of the products that they found on grocery shelves.

Nor did they know that it was much too late to turn back.

Dorian had seen the studies. Most of the soil in the world was exhausted. In California's central valley, on the northern plains, and in the Midwest, it was dead. Years of pesticide use and agricultural stress had stripped the land of all its nutrients and its disease-suppressing bacteria, fungi, protozoa, and nematodes. The only way these soils could support any kind of growth was through the extensive use of artificial fertilizers.

Like it or not, without the initiative and vision of companies such as Domidion, the world would starve.

What the average family did need to understand was that research and innovation in maintaining food production was expensive and that companies had the right to expect a reasonable return on their time and investment.

DORIAN came out of his chair and paced the room. "I want Q's house sealed."

"Already done."

"I want a full biography back to the day he was born. I want Security to review all footage for the month before he disappeared. I want to know why he was in archives and exactly which records he accessed."

Winter stood as still as a statue, her finger flying across her tablet.

"And I want Quinn found."

"Find Quinn," said Winter.

"I want him found now."

DORIAN watched Winter walk down the glass hallway. Then he turned back to the screen and brought up the photographs of Quinn's house. The writing on the walls was neat and organized, the penmanship exemplary.

He scrolled forward to the bedroom. A small, dark dresser stood against one wall. There was a bed, a nightstand, and a reading lamp. The mattress and the box spring looked thin and uncomfortable. Not natural latex.

Just a fugitive from a big box store.

Dorian magnified the end of the bed to see if the thing even had a brand name, but all he got for his efforts was a screen filled with black and white pixels.

6

MARA HAD RISEN EARLY THAT MORNING TO GO DOWN TO THE
river. It was an old ritual. Her mother and grandmother had
begun each day in this manner, standing on the bank, touching
the water, sprinkling tobacco on the current. It was a reminder
of the relationship that human beings had with the world, as
well as a practical routine for ensuring that everyone got out of
bed in good order.

In the last year of high school, her English class was assigned
to write something interesting about their family, and she had
described the practice. The teacher had liked Mara's essay, had
given her an A.

But at the bottom of the last page, the teacher had written,
"Is this the way Indian people send prayers to their water god?"

Mara had not known what to do about the question, so she
took it home. That night her mother and grandmother made a
pot of tea and a bowl of popcorn, and considered the paper on
the table between them.

"Didn't know we had a water god," said Mara's mother.

"News to me," said her grandmother.

"What am I supposed to tell my teacher?" said Mara.

"Is she a good teacher?" her grandmother asked. "Is she kind?"

"She's okay," said Mara. "She gave me an A on my paper."

"What do you think will make her happy?"

Mara had shrugged. "I don't know. I think she likes the idea of a water god."

"What about that story that Rose Sampson likes to tell," said her mother. "'The Woman Who Fell from the Sky.' There's water in that one."

"Done that already," said Mara. "Lilly and I told that story last year. Remember? The group project? You guys had to go in and talk to the principal."

"That's right," said her grandmother. "He had bad breath."

"And he was rude," said her mother. "Told us that stories about women falling out of the sky were inappropriate in an educational setting."

"Pregnant women falling out of the sky," corrected Mara's grandmother. "Rose was always specific about that detail."

"Then he went and told us about that naked couple in that garden," said her mother.

Mara's grandmother pursed her lips. "After that, it got ugly."

In the end, Mara decided to tell her teacher the truth, that the women in her family had always gone to the river at dawn to lay tobacco on the water. It wasn't a ritual or a ceremony, so much as it was a long-standing custom, a way of welcoming the day.

"That's it?" her teacher had said.

"Pretty much."

The rest of that year, Mara got nothing more than B-pluses on her work.

~~~~~

IN those days, there had been a family of weasels that owned the opposite bank of the river. Mara remembered how the runt of the sneak would stop his foraging to watch the women rub the tobacco in their hands. It would dash back and forth over the rocks, trilling happily, as the brown strands floated in the air and settled on the water.

Mara had worried that the animal might think the tobacco was food and jump into the river, and she would clap her hands to warn the kit of the danger. Over that summer, it had become a game. Mara would clap, and the weasel would leap straight up into the air, as though it had been shot, tumble back into the ferns, and disappear in the undergrowth.

The weasels were gone now, along with the birds and the fish and the other animals.

And the turtles.

Each year the turtles had returned to the beach to lay their eggs, and each year baby turtles had crawled out of the sand and raced the gulls and the terns and the hawks to the surf and the safety of the salt.

All gone.

Still, the Smoke was running clean again, and you could reach into the water and draw your hand back without incident.

THE house waited on the edge of the town, a single-storey yellow shiplap that she rented by the month. It wasn't the home in which she had been raised, but it suited her mood. Not the reserve and not the Bay.

A rest stop. A middle ground. A temporary shelter.

Mara started a fire and put on a pot of coffee. She wasn't expecting anyone. Hardly anyone ever came by. Nicholas Crisp would drop in on occasion, and there was Sonny, of course. At least once a week, he would come up from the beach with his hammer and his bag of salvage, and wander the edges of the town like a phantom. Several times, she discovered him standing behind the house, near the cedars, but when she came out to say hello, he would flee into the trees without a word.

Like the weasel.

There was something sad about the boy. He had no friends, and the only person he ever talked to was himself.

Mara looked out the window. Where had the morning gone? It was almost noon. She should get to painting but felt more inclined towards a nap. Yes, that sounded like an excellent plan. A nap.

Maybe she would dream.

When they were alive, her mother and grandmother would talk for hours about dreams and how problems that vexed a person could be sorted out in sleep. Mara hadn't found this to be true. Before that day in March, her dreams had been no more than pleasant collages of sound and sexuality, devoid of any wisdom.

In the aftermath of The Ruin, she had stopped dreaming altogether.

Mara took her cup out to the porch, along with a quilt in case the day turned damp and cold, and sat down in the white wicker chair. She could see Samaritan Bay laid out in the light. The church, the stores and shops along Station Street, the wharf, and the Ocean Star Motel off in the distance. Some days, when the fog was in, the town would disappear and all you would be able to see was the top of the church spire and the neon star of the motel.

It was a scene she might have painted.

She could remember the days when tourists flocked to the Bay for the season, could remember how the town had swelled with activity and noise. The endless festivals had been fun, but she didn't miss the press of people surging through the streets, pouring out onto the beach in search of driftwood and shells, the more adventurous individuals hiking up to the reserve to bother the band with their cameras and incessant questions.

There had been jugglers then, fire eaters, acrobats, magicians, and musicians, who set up shop along the boardwalk each evening and entertained the multitudes who came down to the water to wait for the turtles and to watch the sun set.

All gone.

And now, after all this time, there was a man on the beach. Gabriel, that was his name, wasn't it? Curious. That was the name Lilly's mother had used when she told the story "The Woman Who Fell from the Sky."

Gabriel.

Gabriel had been the left-handed twin, the one who had brought chaos to the perfect world that his twin had created. So that there would be balance. What was the right-handed twin's name? Or was Gabriel the right-handed twin?

Where had he come from? People didn't arrive in Samaritan Bay anymore. They left. And if by some chance someone *did* find their way to this place, they didn't stay. Yet here was this Gabriel. Mara smiled as she remembered finding him naked

on the beach. Was he really trying to kill himself or just looking for attention?

Mara held the cup in both hands. The warmth felt good.
Perhaps if this Gabriel stopped by for coffee, she would ask him.
Or better yet, she would ask Soldier.

All things considered, the dog looked to be the smarter of
the two.

7

SONNY WALKS ALONG THE BEACH, SWINGING THE HAMMER BY his side.

One, two, one, two, one, two, one, two.

Sonny loves the wide open spaces of the beach. He loves the soft sand, the wind, the water. He misses the seals that used to flop about in the surf, and sun themselves on the rocks. He misses the fish that played at the mouth of the river. He misses the crabs that clattered along the waterline.

That One Bad Day.

Each day on the beach, the world begins anew. Fresh. Clean. Full of salvage. Sonny bends down and rakes the hammer through the sand. He likes the designs that the claw makes, and sometimes he finds things people have lost.

Eyeglasses.

Rings.

Baby soothers.

Car keys.

So far today, Sonny has found several metal spoons, a plate, and a cup. Right at the water's edge, he's found a trunk buried in the sand.

Wham-wham!

There are labels on the trunk with writing that looks like the writing you see in martial arts movies. Both Sonny and Dad like this kind of movie. Sonny remembers the evenings when the two of them would sit together in the dark with a bowl of popcorn and watch people smite each other.

The trunk is very exciting, and Sonny tries to dig it out with his hammer and his hands.

Dig, dig, dig.

Hammer, hammer, hammer.

But the trunk is stuck fast, and Sonny will have to wait for the next high tide to float it free.

In addition to the trunk, Sonny finds a number of turtle skeletons and shells—big turtles, medium turtles, baby turtles. Sonny leaves these where he finds them. Finding dead turtle pieces on the beach is easy. Turtle pieces are not proper salvage.

Sonny walks the shoreline until he gets to the wide channel where the Smoke cuts through the sand on its way to the ocean.

The river is looking better now.

It's the colour of water again.

Sonny shakes his sack. Not a good salvage day. Maybe he should check the trail. Maybe today is a good day to check the trail to the hot springs.

Beatrice Hot Springs.

Nine descending pools of varying temperatures. There's one just right for you. That's what the brochure at the motel says. There's one just right for you.

Other than the beach, the best place to find salvage is along the sides of this trail. The trail to the hot springs is steep, and Sonny has seen people stumble and fall, and when they stumble and fall, they can lose things. Wallets, cameras, towels, water bottles, cellphones. The list of things that people can lose on the trail is long and exciting.

While Sonny likes the prospect of finding salvage on the trail, he doesn't care for the knotted shadows of the deep woods, and he doesn't like the disturbing sounds that follow him up the path. Wailing sounds. Scratching sounds. Hissing sounds. Rocks running wild. Ferns whispering to each other.

Roots spreading lies about Dad.

Sonny follows the river back up the beach, and, when he gets to the large spruce tree that guards the trailhead, he stops dead in his tracks.

Leaning against the tree is a drum.

Sonny rocks back and forth on his feet. It's a drum for sure. An old drum that has seen better days. An Indian drum. Sonny has never found an Indian drum before.

Sonny picks up the drum and wipes off the sand. It feels damp, as though it's been under water, and when Sonny taps on the hide, it makes a soft *dub-dub-dub* sound that reminds him of his heart when he tries to go to sleep at night.

Dub-dub-dub.

Sonny holds the drum to his nose and discovers that it smells like bacon. Not exactly like bacon, but something tasty that has smoke and fat in it. He can't wait to show Dad the drum. When Sonny shows Dad the drum, Dad will surely take him in his arms and say, Behold my beloved son, in whom I am well pleased.

Wham-wham, hammer-hammer.

But while Sonny is savouring the certainty of Dad's love, he discovers he has fallen into curiosity. Where did the drum come from? Who left it here? What might the drum signify? Sonny knows that Dad isn't terribly fond of curiosity. Sure, Dad is a proponent of free will, and Sonny is reasonably sure that curiosity is one aspect of free will, but Sonny also knows that curiosity can lead to questions, and Dad has been firm about questions.

Questions, Dad has told Sonny on numerous occasions, are the consequence of uncertainty and can lead to doubt. Doubt can turn into confusion, confusion can foster disbelief, disbelief can provoke anger, anger can find its way to revolt, riot, and revolution, and from there the world will quickly fall into calamity and chaos.

Sonny is sad when he realizes that he has fallen into curiosity, and he has to sit down and wait for the sorrow to pass.

Okay. All better.

Sonny hits the beach with his hammer.

Wham!

He likes the way the sand leaps up as though it's been startled out of a nap.

Suddenly, Sonny has a thought, though it could actually be a revelation, now that he thinks about it.

The Indians have returned.

That's what has happened. That's the answer to the question of the drum. The Indians have come home. That which was lost is found. This is good news. Sonny has missed the Indians.

Of course, there's that Indian in the yellow house. She's still here. Maybe the drum is her drum. Maybe she lost it. Maybe she left it behind by mistake.

Sonny could take the drum to her house. Here's your drum. Found by Sonny.

Then again, it might not be her drum at all. Sonny can feel uncertainty and doubt creeping into his thoughts, again, and he begins to experience the first stirrings of confusion. This is not good.

Not Good!

What is he thinking? What has Dad told him? In the face of uncertainty, have faith. That's what Dad always says. Have faith. That which is to be, shall be. Life is a mystery. The only way to understand existence is through faith, not curiosity.

Have Faith.

Dad has said this over and over again, but Sonny cannot remember Dad ever saying have curiosity.

The wind blusters in off the ocean. Sonny likes the damp salt air on his face and the sensation of his hair fluttering out in flags and streamers. Sonny starts back along the beach to the motel. Asking questions is not only dangerous, it is also strenuous, and Sonny realizes that he is hungry.

Out on the water, Sonny sees a dark shape slouching along the horizon. A solitary ship, perhaps, moving at the edge of the world. Ships come and go all the time. Some come close to shore. Maybe one day a ship will wind up on Sonny's beach. Now that would be exciting, Sonny tells himself.

A ship on the beach.

On that day, there would be no end to salvage.

8

THE ABSENCE OF WINDOWS IN THE DOMIDION COMPLEX HAD always made it difficult for Dorian to gauge the time, and when he looked at the icon in the lower right-hand corner of his computer, he was surprised to see that it was after five.

Dorian took off his glasses and closed his eyes. Tonight would be a quiet night. Dinner with Olivia. He might even watch the football game. He couldn't remember who was playing. Not that it mattered.

So long as it wasn't Buffalo.

Most of Toronto followed the Bills, but Dorian had no time for that team. No matter how they started off, they always came up short. Dorian wondered if Buffalo itself had something to do with the team's failures. The city had a palpable stink of depression and need. Perhaps failure was in the air. In the water.

He checked the Internet. The Arizona Cardinals were playing the Houston Texans.

Terrific.

All right. Dinner with Olivia and then a movie.

Dorian looked up to find Winter at his door. He had already seen enough of his assistant today. Then again, Winter never came to his office unless it was necessary.

"The car will pick you up at six," she said. "Lobby level. They're updating security protocols in the garage."

Dorian tried to keep his face passive and open.

"The Walper Lecture at the university."

"That's tonight?" Dorian slumped slightly in his chair. "Wonderful."

"You're giving the keynote on public-private partnerships." Winter handed Dorian a tablet. "You can review the talk on the drive to the university. There'll be a teleprompter."

"Fine."

"You should spend some time with the president and the board of governors."

"Am I bearing gifts?"

"A major partnership with the Humanities," said Winter. "The Domidion School of Business and Media Communications. Physical plant, start-up costs, endowed chairs. The plan is to fold English, Sociology, and Psychology in to the new school."

"What about Philosophy, History, and Fine Arts?"

Winter waited as though she had not understood the question.

"Are we concerned about those disciplines?"

"No," said Winter. "Remember to emphasize the benefits of university-corporate co-operation in an increasingly competitive world."

Dorian looked at the phone. Winter would have already called Olivia to tell her that her husband would not be home until late.

Winter touched the side of her glasses. "There'll be a delay in compiling all of Dr. Quinn's background information."

"A delay?"

"Many of those records are in archives," said Winter.

"And there's no one in archives."

"That's correct."

Dorian was sure that somewhere in his talk this evening would be a mention of the efficiencies of contemporary business and the capacity of multinational corporations to outperform their public sector counterparts.

"You're familiar with archives."

"Yes, sir. I am."

"Supervise the search yourself," said Dorian. "I want those records by morning."

Quinn would be found. Dorian was sure of that. They'd have a chat about his interest in classified files, about his sudden disappearance. Everything would get straightened out, and that would be that.

"The school colours are red, gold, and black."

Dorian frowned.

"You might want to wear an appropriate tie."

What was particularly curious was the writing. When they found Q, that's how Dorian would start the conversation. "The writing on the walls," he'd say, "tell me about the writing on the walls."

Winter stopped at the door. "You might encounter a rally."

"A protest?"

"A small demonstration is what we've been told," said Winter.

"Zebras?"

"Possible," said Winter. "I can arrange a security team if you like."

Dorian waved a hand. "Bad PR."

"Yes, sir," said Winter. "Enjoy the evening."

DORIAN walked through his office to the executive suite. He opened the closet and ran a hand along the rack of ties. Red and gold and black. Not exactly subtle colours. He chose a silk Brioni, a soft crimson with gold flecks.

As he stood in front of the mirror, working the tie into a compact knot, he noticed a dark spot on his temple. He touched the mark. It felt strange and somewhat numb. This was new. Or perhaps he just hadn't noticed it before. He had been able to avoid the signs of age, but now, here was a blemish, a distinct and unmistakable sign of decay.

No doubt there would be others.

The lobby was empty. As he walked by the aquarium, Dorian remembered the turtle. The reptile had vanished. Just like Quinn. It had gone somewhere, and it had never been found. Maybe Quinn had taken it.

Maybe the two of them had run away together.

The limo was waiting. Dorian settled in the back, took *Luxury Home Magazine* from the seat pocket, and opened it to the dog-eared page. The idea of Quinn and the turtle lighting out for the territories amused him beyond expectations, and he found himself inexplicably laughing out loud.

Tomorrow he'd have his medications checked.

9

GABRIEL LAY ON THE DECK AND WATCHED THE SUN BRIGHTEN the tops of the waves. For no reason in particular, the light reminded him of the year that an American bomber had developed engine trouble over the St. Lawrence River and jettisoned a Mark 4 nuclear bomb a few kilometres downstream from Quebec City.

1949? 1950?

The pilot exploded the bomb at an altitude of 2,500 feet. The plutonium core wasn't in place at the time, so there was no nuclear detonation. But the blast rattled windows and scattered uranium-238 over the area.

Now he remembered: November 10, 1950.

No one knew what to do with the radioactive dust that settled on the water and along the shoreline, or what the long-term effects might be. And since not asking was deemed to be better than knowing, no one asked.

GABRIEL pressed the pillow against his face. It felt as though it were made out of laundry parts—socks, underpants, T-shirts, small towels—all stuffed into a bag. The thing was lumpy and had a stale odour to it that was not so much unpleasant as it was old.

He wondered if you could actually smother someone in this manner. The pillow would have to be foam, he reasoned. Feathers would be too leaky. He pressed harder, wrapped his arms around the pillow and squeezed. Yes, a pillow would probably do the job, but it would take a fair amount of effort and will. Still, Gabriel could feel his heart picking up speed, could feel his lungs running out of air.

"Be ye aboard?"

Soldier barked once and dove off the deck. Gabriel peeled the pillow from his face and got to his feet.

Nicholas Crisp was kneeling at the corner of the trailer, roll-ing Soldier's head back and forth in his hands.

"Master Dog here tells me ye be slack in the doldrums."

Gabriel looked at Soldier.

"Exhaustion can be a perilous companion on the open seas." Nicholas laughed and shook his head. "But I'm a meddlesome creature, always sticking an oar in between strokes."

"Would you like something to eat?"

"I've commerce in town," said Crisp, "but it's a sorry soul what turns down groceries."

"Chicken's not ready yet," said Gabriel. "But there's coffee and some bread and jam."

"Not much for the sinew and bone," said Crisp. "Still, it'll wake the garrison and rally the troops for the manoeuvres ahead."

Soldier began a long, low rumble in his throat as he rubbed himself against Nicholas's leg.

"Aye, Master Dog," said Crisp, "they're back."

"Back?"

"The Jabberwoks," Crisp cried out, his beard trembling. "No doubt bearing idle gifts and sweet-water words."

"Jabberwoks?"

"The destroyers of worlds."

Gabriel considered Crisp for a moment. "Now I am become Death," he said, letting the words roll out like a wave, "the destroyer of worlds."

Crisp's eyes twinkled. "So it's a learned man ye be. A personage of the spoken word. Ye know the Bhagavad-Gita then. Perhaps even in the original Sanskrit?"

"Oppenheimer," said Gabriel. "I know the phrase because of Robert Oppenheimer."

"Los Alamos," said Crisp. "The Holy Trinity."

"July 16, 1945, August 6, 1945, and August 9, 1945." Gabriel set a jar of jam on the table. "Years later, Oppenheimer was asked how he felt about the tests, and he quoted that passage from the Bhagavad-Gita."

The fur on Soldier's neck rose up like the edge of a knife, and he began stalking the borders of the deck, shaping a slow circle around the two men.

"But he was wrong," said Crisp, "for it ain't the vanities of physics what'll do us in, but the vulgarities of our own greed."

"Cream?" asked Gabriel. "Sugar?"

"Neither," said Crisp, "for it's the dark of a thing what sets its worth."

~~~~~

GABRIEL stepped into the trailer and came out with the Bodum and two heavy ceramic cups.

"Bread's from the bakery in town."

"Webb's," said Crisp, tearing off a piece and putting it to his lips. "I recognizes the tug and pull. Family what makes the tack. They was to catch the tide a while back and sail off with the rest of the privateers, but decided that staying at anchor was wiser than running before the wind."

"Jam's apricot."

Crisp painted a ragged edge of bread. "A treasure unto itself."

Gabriel cradled his cup between his hands. "So, tell me about . . ."

"Not much to tell," said Crisp between chews, "for they've the same names and faces. Burbling foes, with eyes aflame. They appear and disappear as they're needed. Some years back they came and tried to sell us heaven and all the stars."

Gabriel couldn't help the smile. "So you're going to . . . snicker-snack them with your . . . vorpal blade?"

"Indeed, indeed." Crisp threw his head back and roared. "There's no telling what the slithy toves be flogging this time! The Girdle of Hippolyta, perhaps, or the Seal of Solomon. But betwixt the threes of us, I'm supposing that they want to pick up where they left off. Negotiating the right of way once again."

"Right of way?" said Gabriel. "For a road?"

"In a manner of speaking," said Crisp. "It were a bad idea then, and it were a bad idea now. So it must be stopped."

"Can I help?"

Crisp put a hand over his heart and turned to Soldier. "Did ye hear that? An offer so full of grace it would make money weep."

"I've nothing better to do."

"No, no," said Crisp. "Ye be both genial and generous, but such a crusade on your part is not required. I only disturbed your meditations to drop off complimentary passes to the hot springs. Ye and a friend, if one can be found. If not, then come twice and bring the dog, if that be your pleasure."

"Soldier," said Gabriel. "Evidently his name is Soldier."

"Soldier, is it?" said Crisp. "Raising an army, are we?"

"It's just a name."

"Yet there be much in a name." Crisp stepped off the deck and gave his pants a quick brush. "No, no, stay here. Enjoy your day. Come by the pools at the full moon, for the waters will be in riot with insomnia and lycanthropy."

"I don't have a swimming suit."

"Then ye be in luck," said Crisp, "for we don't require that the loins be clad."

GABRIEL took the dishes and the cups back into the trailer. Soldier found his bowl and pushed it around the kitchen, banging it about between the stove and the refrigerator.

"So, what do you want to do?"

Soldier continued pushing and banging.

"We could jog to the beach." Gabriel let the water drain from the sink. "Did you know that exercise is supposed to release hormones that make you feel happy?"

Soldier stayed with the bowl.

"I could throw a stick, and you could chase it. I could try to destroy the world. You could try to stop me."

Soldier licked his chops, sat back on his haunches, and waited.

Gabriel ran a hand across his face. Maybe he'd grow a beard. He didn't have much in the way of facial hair. Not like Crisp. But it might be fun to try. He could let his hair grow long, stop taking baths, start talking to himself. He could run in the woods with the dog and howl at the moon.

Or he could just lie on the deck by himself and give the pillow another try.

10

BY THE TIME SONNY GETS BACK TO THE MOTEL, IT IS LATE afternoon, and now he is very hungry. The Ocean Star Motel is famous for its fish. Poached fish, baked fish, fish fingers, fish and chips, fish chowder, fish balls.

Fish, fish, fish, fish.

Sonny doesn't like fish. Fish tastes like the ocean. Fish has thousands of little bones in it. Fish has slimy scales. Sonny likes toasted cheese sandwiches.

Sonny goes into the motel café. He sits at the table with the best view and studies the menu.

Toasted cheese sandwich for Sonny, Sonny shouts to the kitchen.

Sonny takes the drum out of his salvage bag. The skin is drier and the sound is deeper now, full of muscle and authority. Sonny taps out Dad's favourite Native song, the one from the old Hamm's beer commercial.

"From the land of sky-blue waters . . ."

Sonny puts the drum down, goes to the wait station, and gets himself a glass of ice water, along with a knife and fork wrapped up in a white napkin. He arranges these in their proper order on the table, just the way Dad has shown him.

The kitchen is deserted. Sonny goes to the cupboards and opens all the doors.

Empty.

He goes to the refrigerator and opens the door.

Nothing.

Wham-wham.

Toasted cheese sandwich for Sonny, Sonny shouts into the empty refrigerator. With mustard.

There are marks on the shelves of the refrigerator where food used to be. There are crumbs in one of the crisper drawers and green stains in another where something has rotted away.

Sonny gets a plate from the sink, rinses it off, and goes outside to the EverFresh vending machine with its individual compartments and clear plastic doors. Sonny puts his money in the coin slot, and when the machine makes its *jingle-jingle* sound, he opens the door and takes out an egg salad sandwich. He puts in more money, opens a second door, and takes out a small bunch of grapes. More money, a third door, and a piece of pound cake. Then he carries everything back to the table with the good view.

Sonny's supper.

The egg salad is tasty, but the bread is somewhat stale and hard at the edges, and, as Sonny debates sending it back or reducing the tip, he realizes that he may have a problem. There are any number of musical instruments of which Dad approves, instruments that Dad has deemed to be appropriate accompaniment for joyful singing and dancing. Trumpets are a great favourite, as are kinnors, nebels, pipes, and cymbals.

But no drums.

Dad has never mentioned drums. Drums do not appear any-where on Dad's list of approved melodic devices.

Of course.

Drums are cruder instruments favoured by cruder people with a limited understanding of salvage. Such as Indians and Africans. Sonny remembers a show he watched on the Discovery Channel, where little Asian men beat out perplexing rhythms on enormous drums the size of oxen.

Why hasn't Sonny thought of this problem with drums?

Perhaps Dad won't be as pleased with his beloved Sonny after all. Sonny tries to put this dilemma out of his mind, but by the time he gets to the second half of his sandwich, he has lost his appetite.

Wham-wham.

Sonny cautiously holds the drum up to the light and immedi-ately recoils at what he sees. It's all there. The pallid veins run-ning through the body of the skin, the ominous checks in the wood frame, the twisted sinewy strands that hold the drum head in place. He can even feel the heat of the fire and smell the stink of the smoke on the hide.

Wham-wham, hammer-hammer.

What is he going to do with the drum he has found? Perhaps the drum is a test. Dad has always been fond of tests. Tests to gauge Sonny's resolve. Tests to measure Sonny's endurance. Tests to evaluate Sonny's devotion. Maybe the drum is a test to determine Sonny's intelligence.

That's it. The drum is an intelligence test.

But if Dad left the drum by the trailhead to test him, then this would mean that the Indians have not returned as Sonny had originally thought. This would mean that the reserve is still silent and deserted.

However, if Dad *didn't* leave the drum, then it's possible that the Indians *have* come home. And this pleases Sonny a great deal, because he has never done well with tests.

When Sonny was much younger, Dad had taken him for ice cream and told him he could have whatever he wanted.

Use your best judgment, Dad told him. Use your best judgment.

Sonny spent a great deal of time looking at all the tubs of ice cream. Chocolate, strawberry, rocky road, peach, raspberry, root beer, praline, butterscotch, cherry jubilee.

Forty-two flavours!

Whatever you want, Dad told him. Use your best judgment.

And on that day, Sonny had made the wrong decision. He did not use his best judgment. He had been tempted by all the colours, seduced by all the flavours. He had been tested and found wanting. That afternoon, Sonny went back to his room, crawled into the closet, and cried. He was sick for days after.

Shamed and repentant. Lactose intolerant.

Wham-wham.

Sonny looks at the drum. It's the colour of French vanilla. This time Sonny *will* use his best judgment. This time he *will* make the right decision. This time he will *not* spend any part of eternity in his closet.

Wham.

Sonny taps the hammer on the table, and the strikes make the plate and the silverware and the glass jump about. The sound of the hammer hitting the table helps Sonny concentrate. The feel of the hammer in his hand helps Sonny think.

Wham-wham, hammer-hammer. Wham-wham, hammer-hammer.

The vibration runs up his arm into his shoulder and then into his neck. Each time he hits the table, the vibrations rise a little higher until he can feel his brain begin to quiver.

Any time now, the solution will come.

11

MARA SAT ON THE VERANDA IN THE SUN, ENJOYING THE late-afternoon warmth. The coffee was cold, but she had no intention of coming out from under the quilt. In the old days, her mother or her grandmother would have brought her a fresh cup as well as a cookie, would have tucked the blanket in around her.

They had fought, of course, the three women. Generational battles over jurisdiction and control. Sometimes, the older women would skirmish between themselves over something as simple as a recipe, or go to war to settle the details of a long-forgotten dispute. Mostly, though, they would double-team her.

The worst times were when she started dating boys from the town. She'd bring them home to the reserve, and the two older women would descend on the hapless youths like hawks hunting rabbits. Mara would have to sit on the sofa, embarrassed and angry, as her mother and then her grandmother would explain just how fierce the People were and what a poor sense of humour the clans had when it came to inappropriate behaviour.

At fifteen, with Lilly's encouragement, Mara had taken the offensive. Over dinner one evening, she announced that she was old enough to make her own decisions, and that she didn't need her mother's advice or her grandmother's approval, for that matter.

"Mara's thinking about having sex," her mother told her grandmother.

"With whom?" her grandmother had wanted to know.

Mara realized her mistake immediately. "No one," she had said.

"I've always wanted a great-granddaughter."

"I'm not having sex."

"She's thinking about having sex," her mother had corrected.

"We could name the baby after your great aunt, Thelma."

"I'm not thinking of having sex."

"If you need any technical guidance," her mother had said, "all you have to do is ask."

The two women had giggled back and forth for a while, and then collapsed into raucous laughter, cackling and screeching like a conspiracy of ravens.

Mara couldn't remember if her grandmother had actually used the word "penis." Mercifully, there were parts of her adolescence that she did not remember with complete clarity.

But how she missed them. She would give anything to hear her mother tell her, once again, that she didn't want her only child to date fast boys, Indian or white, and for her grandmother to chime in that, if Mara was fast herself, she shouldn't be dating at all.

MARA slid a hand out from under the quilt. A soft wind was coming in off the ocean, but the sea was flat and tranquil, the line between sky and water almost invisible. The day was mostly over, and she hadn't done a thing.

Wake up.

Walk on the beach.

Sit and stare at the world.

Breakfast was most often a piece of toast and some cheese. Lunch was yogurt with banana. Dinner was peanut butter on a spoon. Mara flinched as she ran through the meals and what they might suggest.

Depression, of course.

So why was she so sanguine with such a diagnosis? Because there was no one left who cared. That was it. Not even her.

Through the window, she could see the canvas on the easel. She had started the portrait as a way to climb back into life. Each morning she had tried to gather the energy to work on the painting, and each morning she had failed.

Not miserably.

Simple failure.

How could she be so vulnerable? She had friends. Somewhere. But when her mother and grandmother died, her world had taken a tumble, cracked apart, much like that egg on the wall. And there seemed no putting it back together again.

Mara wondered about the man on the beach. He didn't seem to be in any better condition, but he was trying to do something about it. Suicide wasn't a choice she would have embraced, but at least it was a choice. She hadn't even gotten to the point of choosing.

On the plus side, this Gabriel had someone. This Gabriel had a dog.

Curious.

Tomorrow she'd go to the reserve. It might be therapeutic to stand on her grandmother's porch one more time, walk through the townsite, and remember the families who had died on that day and in the days that followed.

Not that memories would save her. She already knew that. She knew that there was nothing left to see. The abandoned houses, the empty trailers, the deserted community centre, the solitary water tower. Without the people, none of these places had any meaning.

In the end, they were little more than gravestones in a grave-yard.

12

IT WAS AFTER ELEVEN WHEN THE LIMO PULLED UP IN FRONT of the restaurant. The speech at the university had gone well enough. Winter had been right about a demonstration. Somewhat larger than anticipated, though not all that well organized. As Dorian watched the students mill about with their signs—"End Corporate Greed," "Tax the Rich," "Redistribution or Revelution," "GMOs Have Got to Go"—he had had the inexplicable urge to push his way into the protestors and counsel them on how to organize an effective rally. Focus, he would have told them. Organize around a single theme. Send the scruffy folk to the back where the television cameras couldn't find them, put some money into more professional-looking placards, and for God's sake, learn to spell.

THE restaurant was surprisingly full, but Fernando was able to find him a quiet table in a corner.

"Is Mrs. Asher joining us tonight?"

Until Fernando had asked the question, Dorian had forgotten that Olivia was in Florida. How had he not remembered that?

"No," he said. "She's in Orlando. With friends."

"And will you be joining *her*?"

DORIAN had been to Orlando once. Olivia had talked him into the trip.

"You need to relax."

"Going to Orlando doesn't sound relaxing."

They had booked a suite at the Waldorf Astoria, worked their way through the better restaurants and nightclubs in the area, and had finished off several evenings with inordinately good sex.

Dorian's libido had been missing in action. He wasn't sure if his poor performance and general malaise were the result of the drugs he had been taking or the onset of impotency, so, without telling Olivia, he had had a word with the hotel concierge and came away with a discreet supply of blue pills that were purportedly the first choice of considerate lovers and professional athletes.

They had worked.

Or to be exact, the pills had allowed him to maintain an erection through the course of lovemaking. While Dorian's potency and stamina had been a pleasant surprise for the both of them, he found the overall experience mixed. The drugs had kept him hard, but they had also made his penis feel like a wooden dowel he had strapped on for the occasion. And whatever was in the pills gave him a headache. It was, he supposed, a small price to pay for a resilient boner, and Olivia had been impressed.

"My God," she said, giving it a squeeze. "Orlando certainly seems to agree with you."

The second day, they had gone to Pura Vida Plantations to see a house that Olivia had found. It was large with vaulted ceilings, a grand staircase, marble and granite countertops, designer appliances, a movie theatre in the basement, an enormous master with separate bathrooms and his-and-her walk-in closets.

With views of the lake.

"The owner is motivated," the real estate agent had told them.

Dorian was surprised how little $4.5 million bought. It was waterfront property, but the lake was too shallow for a dock or a boat. The kitchen had a climate-controlled wine cabinet, but there was no wine cellar. The deck was ample enough, but it was already beginning to fray at the edges, and there was no hot tub or built-in barbecue. The house did come with a three-car garage, but one of the bays was half the depth of the other two.

"The short stall is for your golf cart," the agent told them.

More than anything, the house felt sticky and tired, as though it had just come home from a bad date.

"The Orlando area is a wonderful place to raise a family," the agent had assured them. "All the amenities are within easy driving distance. Disney World, SeaWorld, Universal Studios, Wet 'n Wild."

"We don't have children."

The agent gave them her card along with coupons for Gatorland and Ripley's Believe It or Not. "I can write an offer today," she said. "This property won't last long."

"No tennis court," Dorian reminded Olivia.

"These days," said the agent, "everyone plays golf."

In the end, Dorian concluded, once you pushed past the expensive facades, the glossy brochures, and the television ads, Orlando was nothing more than a collection of theme parks, golf courses, and malls, all floating on a humid landscape of wetlands and sinkholes.

At the airport, he had taken time to stop in the men's room, where he dropped the coupons in the trash and washed his hands until he could no longer smell the house on his fingers.

FERNANDO removed the second place setting. "Isn't Disneyland in Orlando?"

"No," said Dorian. "Disneyland is in California. Disney World is in Orlando."

"Ah," said Fernando.

"There's also a Disneyland in Paris and one in Tokyo."

"Such a clever mouse," said Fernando. "May I start you off with something from the bar?"

There was no reason why Dorian should feel antagonistic towards another corporation. Disney was substantially smaller than Domidion, but ever since the problems with the French had been worked out, the company had been a solid producer. Dorian had followed Disney stock shares, had even considered buying a block.

What he couldn't get past was the fact that the Disney corporation didn't produce much of anything. They sold tickets on rides. They made movies. What kind of work was that for an adult?

WITH Olivia out of town, there was no point in going home. The house in Bridle Path was only a thirty-minute drive, but he'd stay in the city tonight.

Fernando was back. "The usual?"

The usual was *Poulet Rôti Croustillant*, always an excellent choice, but tonight Dorian wanted something more solid than chicken.

"This evening's *gibier du moment*," said Fernando, "is Wild Boar *Daube* with Mushrooms, Chestnuts, and Corsican *Nielluccio*."

"I'll have that."

"And for the wine?"

AFTER his talk, during a short question-and-answer period, Dorian had been asked if agricultural research pursued solely for profit would inevitably lead to environmental disasters. It was a question he was always asked, and he answered it as he always did.

"Everything we do, all of us," Dorian told the audience, "is in pursuit of profit."

This had led, predictably, to a series of animated arguments that the audience had with itself and, when that fire burned out, Dorian thanked everyone and left the stage.

"THERE is only one serving of crème brûlée left."

"Could you set it aside?"

"Of course," said Fernando. "The boar will be here shortly."

~~~~~

79

AT the reception afterwards, Dorian had chatted with the president and told him how excited Domidion was to be a partner in the new School of Business and Media Communications. The proposal was before the various committees, the president told Dorian, but the restructuring and the renegotiation of union contracts would take time.

"That is where the private sector has the advantage," the president told Dorian with a smile. "You can make mistakes more quickly."

"Yes," Dorian countered, "but our mistakes don't waste as much time and money."

The wine selection was limited to a thin Chablis and a grapey Merlot. The cheese was white cheddar squares, with brightly fringed toothpicks stuck through their hearts. The red pepper spears and broccoli crowns had held the most promise.

He was standing by the vegetable arrangement when a young woman came by and asked him if had ever read John Maynard Keynes.

"The British economist?"

"Keynes said that capitalism was the extraordinary belief that the nastiest of men for the nastiest of motives will somehow work for the benefit of all."

"Keynes also erroneously believed that government intervention could mitigate the adverse effects of economic cycles."

The woman wasn't unattractive, though somewhat severe, with wide hips and no apparent appreciation for cosmetics.

"I would guess," said the woman, "that you don't have children."

"Neither did Keynes."

One of the vice-presidents performed the obligatory ceremony of giving him several books written by faculty members, presenting him with a coffee mug that had the university's logo imprinted on its side, and thanking him for his insightful comments.

By the time Dorian walked out to the waiting limo, the pro- testors had vanished, and the stars were bright in the heavens. He settled into the back seat and glanced at the three books that had been tied together with thick vanilla yarn. He checked the titles, hoping that there might be a biography on someone interesting such as Bill Gates or a history of the North American Free Trade Agreement.

The first book was a novel.

"HOW was the boar?" said Fernando, pouring Dorian another glass of wine.

It had had a somewhat gamey taste, a wild fragrance that was smoothed out nicely by the earthy flavours of the chestnuts and mushrooms.

"Delicious." Dorian sipped the wine and let it wash around his mouth. "Tell me, Fernando," he said. "What are your views on the rich and the poor?"

Fernando shrugged. "There appear to be too many of both."

DORIAN lingered over dessert. Even Le Cinq in Paris didn't make a better crème brûlée. As he sat at the table and watched the staff clear the restaurant, he tried to remember if the condo had a forty- or a forty-eight-inch television. Not that it mat- tered. Tonight he'd sit on the balcony and enjoy the view and the quiet. He'd get a good night's sleep and wake to the sun brightening the lake. And then he'd go back to his glass office and the work that sustained him.

FERNANDO returned to the table, his face ringed with regret.

"A small difficulty," he said, keeping his voice low. "Your credit card. They wish me to apprehend it and break it apart."

"My Black AmEx?"

"With scissors."

"They said to cut it up?"

"Yes," said Fernando. "Someone has made a terrible mistake, of course, but I am powerless in this matter."

Dorian sat back and rubbed his forehead gently with his fingers. "Zebras."

"Is there another credit card we could use?"

"I'll pay with cash."

"I'm very sorry for the inconvenience," said Fernando. "I hope you and Mrs. Asher will be able to join us again soon."

"We will," said Dorian. "Tell me, Fernando, do you read?"

"I do," said Fernando. "Thank you for asking."

DORIAN waited until Fernando had disappeared into the kitchen. Then he stood, set the books at the edge of the table, slipped a hundred-dollar bill under the yarn, and walked out of the restaurant and into the night.

13

NICHOLAS CRISP TOOK OFF HIS CLOTHES AND SLID INTO THE last of the pools. Here, the water was bitter cold, threatening, at any moment, to seize up into ice. But after the fury and temper of the town-hall meeting, he welcomed the biting chill.

So that was their game. After all this time, after all the sorrows, here they were again, bent on gnawing the bones and sucking the marrow. Crisp took a deep breath, plunged under the water, and came up spitting.

"Bubbling cheeses!" he shouted, flinging the water from his beard. "But ye wouldn't want to do that for an eternity!"

Crisp climbed to the top of a rock. From here he could look, over the trees, at the tops of the buildings in the town below. Most of the homes were deserted now, some already fallen into various states of disrepair, but the scene still had a painterly quality to it, something that a Cézanne might have considered.

Or a Moses.

Or a Constable.

Crisp's eyes sparked as he remembered the moment at the meeting when the Jabberwoks had unveiled their economic charts and their artistic renderings for the proposed oil pipeline and deep-water terminus.

Opportunity, they blithered. Salvation, they blathered.

"Pale promises," Crisp had howled from his front row seat.

They had spent the better part of an hour with an audiovisual presentation on the benefits that such a project would bring to the area and to every person in the Bay.

Wealth. Prosperity. Economic security.

Cuban vacations.

Sign here.

Carol Miller reminded everyone of what had happened the last time the project had been proposed, and the Jabberwoks had magically pulled a young man out of their hat who thanked Carol for her excellent question, assured everyone that those oversights had been corrected, and insisted that this proposal was a completely new proposition.

"It looks exactly like the old proposal," Terry Collins had offered.

Whereupon the Jabberwoks made the young man disappear and replaced him with a pleasant young woman, who encouraged everyone to look to the future and not dwell on the past.

CRISP climbed over the rock and dropped into the next pool. The water was mercifully warmer, and he could feel his blood as it found its way home. He pushed away from the edge, floated on his back with his arms stretched out from his sides, his legs crossed at the ankles.

"When a strong man, fully armed, guards his own house," Crisp whispered to himself, "his possessions are safe."

He drifted, leisurely enjoying the cedars framed against the sky. When his head finally nudged the rock wall, he rose up. And with the water shimmering about his body like chain mail, he stepped into the next pool.

For the first time in a very long while, Crisp felt alive. They were all here now. Mara, Soldier, and this Gabriel.

So, it had begun.

At last, it had begun.

14

THE MORNING TRAFFIC WAS HEAVY, AND THE LIMOUSINE WAS reduced to drifting along with the schools of cars and lumbering pods of delivery vans and transport trucks, everyone jammed together fin to gill, in a sea of diesel fumes and exhaust.

Dorian used the time to return Benjamin Toshi's call.

"This is Dorian Asher. I'm a patient of Dr. Toshi."

"Yes," said the woman, "do you need to make an appointment?"

"Dr. Toshi called me. I'm returning his call."

The woman put him on hold, and he was forced to listen to Wayne Newton singing "Danke Schoen."

"Dr. Toshi would like to see you at your earliest convenience."

Dorian didn't like the sound of that. "There were blood tests," he said. "Is that why Dr. Toshi wants to see me?"

"I'm sure the doctor will discuss that with you when you come in."

Come in? Surely Toshi understood that Dorian had better things to do. The doctor was a busy man. Dorian was a busy man. There was no need for this archaic physician-patient dance and certainly no need for an appointment, if all Toshi wanted to do was to tell him about the test results in person.

You're fine.

You're sick.

You're dying.

It was pretty simple stuff. Dorian had never liked the way the medical industry tried to mystify the process of living. The human body was quite capable of taking care of itself. Sometimes it needed a little help, and that's where doctors were useful. But most of the time, it didn't require their services at all.

"I'd like to speak with Dr. Toshi."

"Dr. Toshi doesn't do that."

Doesn't do that? Doesn't talk to his patients? Dorian tried to explain to the woman that he wasn't really a patient, that his relationship with Dr. Toshi was that of one professional to another.

"I can fit you in later this week."

It was a most unsatisfying conversation, and he could see that he would have to get this matter straightened out with the good doctor.

WINTER Lee wasn't waiting for him when Dorian stepped off the elevator, but his assistant had clearly been at work. There was a selection of muffins and fresh fruit, along with juice and coffee, tastefully arranged on the long table in front of the sofa. Dorian expected Winter would have left him a message with an update on Quinn, but the only new email was from Olivia, who said she was having a good time in Orlando and that she had found a house they might want to consider.

Olivia had attached the listing. A California bungalow. Five bedrooms, six full baths, a screened pool and patio, six thousand square feet on just under three-quarters of an acre. Golf course, lake, helicopter pad. All in a gated community for $5.2 million.

There was something terribly familiar about the place, and Dorian was about to write back when he saw Dr. Warren Thicke get off the elevator and shuffle his way down the hall in short, jerky steps, as though he had been hobbled for an evening of grazing.

"Mr. Asher," said Thicke, filling the doorway with his frame. The man had a deep, jolly voice, which he used in a generous way to remind Dorian, once again, that Thicke had a doctorate and Dorian did not.

"Dr. Thicke," said Dorian. "Please come in."

"Thank you for seeing me."

Dorian waved a hand, as though he were shooing a fly. "It's always good to see you."

Dr. Thicke squeezed himself into one of the two wingback chairs. "I'm pleased we have the opportunity to talk about biofuels."

"Actually," said Dorian, "I want to talk to you about Dr. Quinn."

"Dr. Quinn? Not biofuels?"

Dorian could feel his patience leaving the room. He glanced at the monitor. The price of the house wasn't outrageous, and lakefront property was seldom a bad investment. But why did it have to be Orlando? What was wrong with the Guanacaste coast of Costa Rica or Golden Bay on the South Island of New Zealand, or one of the many seaside resorts in the south of France?

"Remind me," said Dorian. "How many years have you worked for Dr. Quinn?"

"With," said Thicke, his jolly voice icing up at the edges. "I work *with* Dr. Quinn."

Thicke was a breakfast buffet. Hash brown hair, egg yolk eyes, soft butter lips, and a short stack of pancakes for a chin.

"Of course, Dr. Quinn is the *official* head of Biological Oversight," said Thicke, "but we work as a team."

"Most commendable," said Dorian. "Teamwork is critical in scientific endeavours."

"And as you'll recall," said Thicke, his attention drifting to the food, "when Dr. Quinn went to India several years back, I was asked to head the division."

Dorian fabricated a smile. "Where are my manners," he said. "Please. Help yourself."

Thicke heaved himself out of the chair and hovered over the tray, before taking one of everything. Dorian was surprised at the dexterity and speed with which the man was able to get to the food and reseat himself, a cup of coffee balanced on one knee, a plate of muffins and fruit on the other.

"I understand the two of you were friends."

Thicke looked up from his plate. "Friends?"

"Yes."

"I wouldn't say that we were friends."

"No?"

Thicke shifted in the chair. "Dr. Quinn tended to keep to himself."

"So, you don't know where he might be?"

"No idea." Thicke pulled a muffin apart and stuffed the larger piece in his mouth. "And I must say that his absence is creating problems for the division."

Dorian forced a thin smile past his lips. "I appreciate your concern."

"I thought you should be aware of that."

"But what I need to know is if there have been any problems at work. Did he seem upset in the last little while?"

Thicke stuffed the other piece of muffin in his mouth. "There was the folder."

Dorian waited.

"A few months back, I noticed a folder on Quinn's desk. A rather thick one."

Dorian continued to wait.

"Of course, that's not unusual," said Thicke. "We all have files and folders on our desks, but when I asked him about it, he got quite angry and told me to mind my own business."

"Why?"

"Why did he tell me to mind my own business?"

"No. Why did you notice the folder?"

"The colour." Thicke wiped a muffin crumb off his lips. "The file folders we use in Biological Oversight are light tan. The folder I saw was green."

"Green."

"Dark green. I thought it might have been a personal file of some sort."

"Because it was green."

"And because of what Dr. Quinn had written across the face of the folder." Thicke licked his fingers. "'The Woman Who Fell from the Sky.' In block letters."

"'The Woman Who Fell from the Sky'?"

"Frankly, he could be somewhat eccentric."

"Was there anything else?"

Thicke's eyes wandered around the room, as though they

were trying to find something they had lost. "Well, he was more talkative of late."

"More talkative?"

"He even bought me coffee at the cafeteria. That was unusual."

Mr. Muffin Mouth.

That's who was sitting in Dorian's chair, making important noises, and blowing brown crumbs all over his Mashad.

Not Dr. Warren Thicke. Not the biologist and genetics engineer. Mr. Muffin Mouth.

"What did the two of you talk about?"

"*Klebsiella planticola.*" Thicke picked a strawberry off his plate. "The variation on SDF 20 that we developed."

Dorian could feel his body tighten. He took a deep breath and let it out slowly. "GreenSweep," he said, his voice calm and flat. "The two of you talked about GreenSweep."

Thicke nodded and bit the strawberry in half. "Several times, actually. It seemed somewhat odd, since that project had been cancelled."

Dorian rubbed his eyes. "Thank you for your time. I really appreciate your help," he said. "But I should let you get back to your laboratory."

Thicke struggled to his feet, knocking food off his pants as he stood. "I was hoping we might have a conversation about biofuels."

"Right now," said Dorian, shaking the scientist's hand, "my immediate concern is finding Dr. Quinn. I'm sure you understand."

"Of course." Thicke held his plate up. "May I take this with me?"

15

GABRIEL LAY IN BED AND CONSIDERED HIS RECURRING dilemma. It was morning, and he didn't want to get up, could not think of a good reason to do so. Most days he would wait until hunger or bodily functions forced him from beneath the covers.

Today it was the latter, and today he had waited a bit too long to reach the bathroom in good order. Not an accident really. Merely a fender-bender.

He stood in front of the sink and peered in the mirror. Scruffy. Very scruffy. The "running with the dog in the woods and howling at the moon" scenario that he had considered the night before had lost most of its appeal. A shave was in order. Deodorant. Remove ear hairs. Flatten the shark's fin of hair sitting on his head. Take a shower.

Scrub off the melancholy. Wash away the past.

Gabriel padded into the kitchen in a fresh shirt and clean underwear. He tossed his pants over a chair. He'd put those on when they became necessary. He had had to wear pants in the laboratory, of course, but now that that life was behind him, he saw no reason to rush into trousers when he had nowhere to go and no idea what he wanted to do.

Why was fresh underwear always so stiff?

The photograph was on the refrigerator door. He had taped it there the night before to keep it from curling. It was mostly dry now. Gabriel stepped back to make sure it was straight, and there she was. His sister. Smiling at him. As though she were happy to have found him at long last. That hadn't changed. Each time he looked at the picture, Little was smiling.

The baby wasn't smiling, but Gabriel wasn't sure if babies, at that age, smiled much or if they smiled at all.

It was strange to see his sister all grown up. And holding a child. The baby had Little's eyes, full of marvel and pleasure. Gabriel tried to imagine having a child of his own, wondered whether it would come to know the world as he had or if it would be spared that sorrow.

Gabriel propped the door open and let in the day. Soldier was lying on the deck, a fine coat of dew on his fur.

"Good morning."

The dog got to his feet, shook himself off, and limped into the trailer. He went directly to his bowl and pushed it to the centre of the room with his nose so Gabriel could see that it was empty.

"Hungry?"

Gabriel filled Soldier's bowl and stood back as the dog did his impression of a vacuum cleaner.

"Slow down."

The sun was out. The morning air was cool and, from the look of the waves, the tides had decided to take the day off. Gabriel walked out onto the deck and sat down in the chair. Maybe something would happen today, something that would move him in one direction or another.

Behind him, he heard the dog making strange noises in his throat.

"No puking."

More noises.

Gabriel leaned out of the chair and turned around.

The dog had his pants. Soldier had Gabriel's jeans stuffed in his mouth, the legs dragging along behind him.

"Cute."

Soldier stuck his hind end up in the air like a stubby flag, his body alive with energy.

"How about we drop the pants."

Instead, Soldier exploded off the deck, the pant legs flapping around his head, as though he had somehow caught an ill-tempered albatross.

"Bad dog!"

For a moment, Gabriel thought the dog might just roll about in the ferns and the underbrush until he got tired or bored, but, instead, Soldier turned and trotted up the trail.

Towards the headlands and the reserve.

Gabriel shook his head. He wasn't about to play the game. He had all day. He would just sit on the deck and wait for Soldier to come to his senses and slink back full of remorse and apology.

His wallet.

His wallet was in the jeans.

FOR the first kilometre or so, Gabriel tried to pretend that he had signed up for one of those health-and-fitness vacations where speed walking after an opinionated dog was part of the spa's daily exercise offerings. He hadn't expected to be so short of breath, was not at all pleased with the sensation. The trail was pleasant enough, and, as he struggled along, Gabriel tried to push past the discomfort by humming in time with each stride.

Trees, rocks, ocean, sky. Trees, rocks, ocean, sky. Trees, rocks, ocean, sky.

Not much different from Toronto, when you got right down to it. Except for the traffic. And the pollution. And the noise. The city had trees. Not as grand as the cedars and the firs, but trees nonetheless.

And rocks.

There was an enormous granite boulder in Yorkville that had been brought down from the Canadian Shield in pieces and reassembled as the centrepiece of a small but tasteful park.

No ocean, of course. Still, Lake Ontario was large enough to fool the casual eye. It had certainly duped European explorers, who expected that the lake would lead them through the continent to the Pacific.

And he knew that there had to have been a sky over Toronto, but when you lived in a city, you didn't spend much time looking up.

THE trail came out of the trees for a moment, and Gabriel paused at the edge of a steep drop to watch the colours of the ocean shift and change, as the waves formed and broke apart on the rocks below.

Okay, so it wasn't much like Toronto after all.

Gabriel took a last look at the water and then began the climb to the reserve. He felt foolish traipsing about in just a shirt, a pair of socks, and shoes.

At least the underwear was clean.

It wasn't a charitable thought, but he found himself hoping that he would find Soldier around the next turn, lying in the dirt, dying of exhaustion, sorry that he had started this nonsense in the first place.

GABRIEL had never had a pet, and Gabriel's father had been clear about animals.

"We got enough to do taking care of ourselves," Joe told Gabriel and his sister.

His sister had ignored her father's directive, had brought home any number of puppies and kittens, some strays, some that had been given to her by neighbours and friends. And, in turn, each one had been sent back. But Little hadn't been discouraged. Instead of arguing with Joe, she began cutting out pictures of animals and taping them on the walls of her bedroom.

"This is my pet monkey, Merlin," Little explained. "And this is Shadow. She's my golden retriever."

Gabriel enjoyed his sister's pets. They didn't make noise. They didn't have to be walked. They didn't have to be fed. And they didn't grow old and die. Even Joe approved. One day he brought home a page from a magazine that had a picture of two baby seals cavorting on a beach.

"They look like you and your brother," Joe told his daughter.

"Which one is me?" Little had asked.

"The one causing all the trouble."

Joe. That's how he had known his father. Gabriel wasn't sure how it had come about. He couldn't remember his father ever insisting that his children call him by his first name. Gabriel's mother called her husband "Joe," so that might have been it.

He got along with his father just fine. They simply didn't live in the same universe. Joe was an RCMP officer, and he understood the world through its sins. Gabriel understood the world through its mysteries.

Late one evening, when he was twelve or thirteen, he overheard his parents talking in the kitchen.

"What are we going to do with him?" Joe had asked. "He's smarter than the both of us."

"I guess we'll do what we can."

"Don't know if it's a good thing," said his father, "being that smart."

"He'll find his place," said his mother. "I just hope he'll be happy."

THE entrance to the Smoke River Reserve was blocked by a derelict school bus. Next to the bus was a large wooden sign bolted to posts set in the ground.

"Restricted Access Area," the sign said. "Authorized Personnel Only. By Order of the Minister of Indian Affairs."

There was a series of official-looking documents, from a variety of government agencies, affixed to the bus itself—warnings and prohibitions—and its long, yellow flank had been spray-painted with graffiti.

Gabriel stopped at the bus to catch his breath. And to read the messages. They were the usual assortment of Bible verses, declarations of love, profanities, protest slogans, and phone numbers. Across the bus's windows, someone had scrawled "Indians Go Home" in white paint.

He wasn't sure what the bus was supposed to do. It wasn't much of a barricade. The only thing it blocked was the view.

One of Gabriel's shoes was untied, and as he bent down to tie it, he saw Soldier. Under the bus. Lying on his pants.

"There you are."

Soldier didn't move.

"Come here, boy. Come on."

Gabriel lay down on his side and scooted forward. He could see Soldier's eyes now. They were open, full of sin and sedition.

Perfect.

"What are you doing?" Gabriel reached out for Soldier's collar. The dog backed farther under the bus, dragging the pants with him. "Do you know what you're doing?"

"Not sure someone lying under a bus in his underwear should be asking that question."

The voice startled him. Gabriel jerked his head up and cracked it on the undercarriage. "Damn!"

"Sorry."

Gabriel tried to hold his shirt down as he wiggled out.

"Hi."

Mara was standing by the front wheel well. "You were on your back the last time I saw you."

Gabriel stood and brushed himself off.

"Do you always go sightseeing in your underwear?"

"Sightseeing?"

"Smoke River. Beyond the fence is the reserve."

Gabriel picked a twig out of his hair.

"But as you can see," said Mara, "it's closed for the season."

Soldier pushed his way from under the bus and trotted to the fence, dragging the pants behind him. Mara watched the dog for a moment.

"I take it those are your pants?"

"They are."

"I don't suppose you gave them to him."

"No."

Soldier rolled over on his back. Mara walked to the fence and knelt down. She rubbed the dog's belly and gently pried the pants from his jaws.

"Good boy."

"Matter of opinion."

Mara stood up and shook the jeans. "So who are you?"

Gabriel pulled his shirt down as far as he could. "Gabriel."

"Which Gabriel is that?" said Mara. "Depressed Gabriel? Hopeless Gabriel? Miserable Gabriel? Mysterious Gabriel? Stop me when I'm close."

"Just Gabriel."

Mara's eyes darkened.

"Okay, let's try something simple. Why here? Of all the gin joints in all the towns in all the world, why here?"

"Vacation," said Gabriel. "It started out as a vacation."

"Then you need to fire your travel agent." Mara was smiling, but her voice was hard. "Course, we do have an authentic Aboriginal Ghost Town." Mara extended an arm, as though she were leading a tour. "Indians. See where they died. Tour their homes. Relive their last moments. That could be fun."

"I just want my pants."

Mara gave the pants a second shake and tossed them to Gabriel. "And here they are."

Gabriel stepped into the pants and pulled them up. The crotch was sopping with slobber.

"I should get back."

"To what?" Mara pushed off the fence. "No, you stay. This is your vacation. You don't want to miss anything."

"Why are you angry?"

"And the turtles. Everybody comes to see the turtles." Mara brushed past Gabriel and started down the trail. "When you get to the beach, make sure you check out the turtles."

GABRIEL waited until Mara disappeared into the trees. Then he walked past the bus and stood by the sign. There were houses in the distance and some trailers. Off to one side was a small water tank that had been painted a robin's egg blue. The colour was faded and chipped, but you could still read the words.

Smoke River.

On a trailer next to the tower, someone had painted an upside-down Canadian flag. Gabriel leaned against the cyclone fencing and cupped his hands in an effort to bring the townsite into focus.

But he didn't see anything that felt familiar.

16

ALL DONE. THE DRUM PROBLEM SOLVED.

Sonny walks along, enjoying the morning sunshine and the sense of accomplishment that comes with having avoided an error in judgment. Now he won't have to tell Dad about the drum or his moment of temptation.

Although he could.

He could tell Dad how he had been tempted and how he had fought and fought and how he had finally been able to overcome his desire. That would make Dad happy. Another vindication of free will.

The town square is empty, and there is no one in the park. Sonny walks around the square and counts the deserted stores. He gets to eight before he is distracted by a naked mannequin standing in the window of Fee's Surf Wear. The last time he had come to town, the shop had been open. Now it is closed. There is a sign on the door that says, "Out of Business."

When did Margery leave? Did she forget her mannequin?

The mannequin in the window has breasts, so it is not really a mannequin. Sonny stands next to the window and tries to think what a mannequin would be called that is not really a mannequin. "Womanequin" has too many syllables and "ladyquin" sounds like "late-again" and could be confusing. The mannequin in the window is too old to be a girl, so "girliquin" won't work either.

"Heriquin."

Wham-wham.

"Heriquin" sounds like "hurricane," and this reminds Sonny of Hulda Krause, who drove the school bus when the school was open. Ms. Krause was a large, powerful woman, who spent much of her time yelling at unruly children who would not sit in their seats. Sometimes Ms. Krause would stop the bus and huff and puff up and down the aisle, spraying everyone with gales of saliva.

Jimmy Turner and Bobby Thornton called her Hulda the Hurricane. Sonny liked Ms. Krause, and he was sorry when she died on That One Bad Day.

"Heriquin."

Sonny wonders if he has come up with a new word. If the library were still open, he could go there and look up "heriquin" in the dictionary. And if he couldn't find it there, then it could be a new word, and Sonny might get his photograph in the newspaper.

"Heriquin."

New word discovered by Sonny.

But then "mannequin" should be "himiquin"?

Wham-wham, hammer-hammer.

Two new words discovered by Sonny.

SONNY misses the stores that have closed. He misses the art shows and the music festivals and the fish fries that filled the square. He misses the tourists who used to rent rooms at the Ocean Star Motel. He misses the families who would flock to the beach to see the turtles, and he misses the salvage that fell out of their pockets when they shook the sand from their clothes and beach towels.

Then again, there were times when the noise in Samaritan Bay was quite loud and bothersome. There were times when the sounds of glee and merriment were so loud that Sonny couldn't think. There were times when he wanted to march into the park, ascend the gazebo, and speak to the town.

Quiet, he would cry out. Sonny is trying to think.

Now, the town is very quiet, and Sonny has no trouble thinking.

Sonny cups his hands and peers in through the window of the Samaritan Bay Tourist Information Centre. The centre used to be open seven days a week, but now it is only open on weekends. Inside, he can see the racks of colour brochures and the big turtle meter on the wall. Sonny feels sad for the information worker who has to stand behind the desk on Saturdays and Sundays waiting for the Laytners of Bracebridge, the Warltiers of Penticton, and the Hodges of Toronto to come in to get their plastic bags filled with free brochures.

Sonny wonders if he should go to the centre in disguise. He could pretend to be a tourist and take every brochure the information person offers. Good job, he could say in an encouraging voice. Good job.

Sonny looks around the square once more and pretends that the town isn't dying, that it is just resting.

And then, there it is. The power jacket. The jacket with the tipis. Sonny sees it for only a second at the entrance to the alley that runs behind the Co-op market. Strange, Sonny thinks to himself. Strange. It isn't the old guy from the beach who is wearing it. It's someone else. Someone moving quickly. Someone moving quickly with long black hair.

An Indian.

A young Indian girl in the alley.

First the drum and now this. Sonny can feel his whole body tremble with excitement as he realizes what it means.

The beginning of days.

The Indians have arrived. Soon the birds of the air and the fish of the sea and the animals, big and small, will come home, two by two. And then the people. All the people who had left will return with glad tidings of comfort and joy.

And in his mind, Sonny can see everyone together, gathering on the beach to await the second coming of the turtles.

And he is pleased.

17

MARA WAS IN SIGHT OF THE HOUSE BEFORE HER ANGER BEGAN
to subside. There was no reason for it. This Gabriel hadn't done
anything. He had simply chased down his pants. He hadn't even
crossed the barrier. Not like the tourists and transients who had
tramped through the reserve, invaded homes, scavenged for
souvenirs, and marked the buildings.

Not at first, of course. Not when the people were dying. No
one came then.

Mara tried to remember how long it had taken before curiosity had overcome fear. She had chased more than one gawker
off the reserve. At the height of the invasion, she had hidden
herself in her grandmother's house and waited for the trespass-
ers to focus their cameras. Then she would shake her hair into
seaweed and snakes, fling open the front door, and leap onto the
porch, screaming and shrieking.

She was not particularly proud of those moments, and she
had only done it three or four times. Okay, maybe more.

MARA saw him as she came out of the trees. Nicholas Crisp.
Sitting in the wicker chair on the veranda. The man appeared

to be snoozing in the afternoon sun. On his lap was a small hand drum.

"Hello," she called out, so as not to startle him.

Nicholas's eyes slid open, and a smile flooded his face. "Mistress Mara. It's a fine figure ye carry around. And with fashion."

"Mr. Crisp, but aren't you the silver-tongued devil."

Nicholas clapped his hands together and rubbed his thighs. "I'll hope ye will forgive the audacity of my having commandeered this fine chair."

"The chair's there for that very reason." Mara mounted the steps and sat down on the matching sofa. "Have you taken up the drum?"

"This?" Crisp held the drum out. "No, no. I've no such thing, though I fancy I might have a voice for such scales. No. It be here when I arrived. Sitting on this chair, as I am now."

Mara took the drum and turned it over. It was well made, with time and skill. "It was here?"

"Aboriginal, I would guess," said Crisp.

"Yes," said Mara. "So it would appear."

"Then I take it, it's not one of yours."

"I've not seen it before."

"And ye hadn't anticipated its arrival." Nicholas stroked his beard. "Perhaps it's from a secret admirer, for who else would leave such a fine piece of craftsmanship behind with no explanation but the gift itself."

Mara struck the drum with a fingertip. The skin was tight and full of sound.

"Of course, the suggestion of an admirer is mere speculation on my part, and, to be prudent, ye might wait to see what floats up in its wake before ye puts the wind in your sails."

"Would you like some coffee, Mr. Crisp?"

"It's such generosities as what sparkles a day," said Crisp. "I put a pot on every morning for courtesy's sake and in hopes of luring passing souls into critique and conversation. But I didn't stop by for a cup, blessed though it would be. I'm here on an errand."

"An errand?"

"Two, to be precise." Nicholas leaned forward in the chair. "The first is to invite ye to a festivity."

"A festivity?"

"Aye, at the hot springs. Tomorrow evening at the full moon."

"Ah," said Mara. "It's your birthday."

"It's a nimble memory ye has." Crisp ran a fingernail along the wicker. "I celebrate it then, I do, for it's a fine excuse for delight and revelry."

"And just how old are you, Mr. Crisp?"

"Old." Crisp laughed and rubbed the side of his nose. "Old and worn to an edge, if it's the truth ye wish."

"What can I bring?"

"Hope and charity." Nicholas eased himself to his feet. "The rest will be provided."

"You're welcome to stay."

"Pools to be tended," said Crisp. "The boatman paid. Guests to be greeted, should any appear."

"What was the second thing?"

"The second thing?"

"You said there were two errands."

"Of course, of course." Crisp scratched at his head, as if he hoped to start a fire. "I'd almost forgotten. The smoke! I was to mention the smoke."

"Smoke?"

"On my way here," said Crisp. "Floating above the reserve. As though someone were raising up a meal."

"I was just there," said Mara. "I didn't see any smoke."

"Well, then it was the fog and the mist playing mischievous tricks on these old eyes." Crisp stepped off the porch and filled his lungs with the afternoon air. "And wishful thinking, for I was hoping that perhaps your relations had come home."

Mara wrapped her arms around herself. "No one's coming home."

"Everyone comes home," said Crisp. "Trust an old traveller on that. In the end, we all comes home."

18

DORIAN HAD TO WASH HIS HAND SEVERAL TIMES TO GET THE muffin slick off his fingers. When he came out of the bathroom, Winter was waiting for him with a box.

"You just missed Thicke."

Winter glanced at the chair and the floor.

"It was disgusting," said Dorian.

"Your replacement AmEx Black is here. I took the liberty of sending Mrs. Asher's card directly to her in Orlando."

"Zebras?"

"We believe so," said Winter.

"How the hell did they get our credit card numbers?"

Winter set the box on Dorian's desk. "These are all of our files on Dr. Quinn."

Mr. Muffin Mouth?

Where had that come from?

Thicke was a fool, to be sure, but there was no need for that sort of assassination. Mr. Muffin Mouth. God, but that was funny. Dorian didn't catch the giggle in time.

"Sir?"

"Nothing. I just thought of something amusing."

Dorian could feel his emotions settle down. Mr. Muffin Mouth. Yes, now he could think it without going silly.

"So, what do we know?"

Winter took a file out of the box and placed it on Dorian's desk. "This is the background check that was done when Dr. Quinn came to work for Domidion."

Dorian opened the folder and began reading. "Born in Lethbridge, Alberta, 1970. University of Minnesota. Stanford Ph.D. Never married?"

"So far as we know," said Winter.

Dorian paused on a page. "His father was in law enforcement. What did his mother do?"

"Teacher."

"A sister?" Dorian looked up from the file. "Gabriel has a sister?"

"Younger."

"Q never mentioned his family. What do you make of that?" Dorian turned a page. "Father and son moved to Minnesota? Mother and sister stayed in Lethbridge? A divorce?

"No record of a divorce," said Winter. "The father was originally from Minnesota. A place called Leech Lake."

"Sounds charming."

"It's a reservation."

"Indian?"

"Anishinabe."

"Q's Indian?"

"Yes, sir," said Winter. "It appears that he is."

"He doesn't look Indian."

"I understand that such things are not uncommon," said Winter.

"I suppose that might explain a great deal."

Actually, it explained little. Dorian was embarrassed to have said it out loud, and he hoped that Winter hadn't noticed.

"Let's talk to the father."

"Deceased," said Winter.

"The mother?"

"We haven't been able to locate her yet."

"And the sister?"

"We're looking into both the mother and the sister."

"Look harder." Dorian closed the file and settled into the chair. "So we have a mystery on our hands."

"Sir?"

"A palpable mystery, my good Laertes."

Dorian could feel his whole body begin to tingle. It was a pleasant enough sensation, and he hoped that it was the result of enthusiasm and not drug toxicity.

"A man disappears for no reason. The walls of his house are covered with strange writing. Secret files have been accessed. It's almost Shakespearean, don't you think?"

"Shakespearean."

"Actually, Shakespeare didn't do mysteries," said Dorian, warming to the task. "A drama. That's what's going on. A drama. Before you know it, we'll have twins separated at birth. Girls disguised as boys. Mistaken identities. Long-lost siblings reunited . . . "

Dorian caught himself. Now that had been bad. Worse than usual. What had he called her? Laertes? Not good. Not good at all.

"So what else do we have for today?"

"A mystery," said Winter. "As you say."

"Really?"

"The *Anguis*."

Dorian pressed a key on the computer. "I need a PAM environment." He waited until the icon on the monitor popped up.

"It was lost in a storm."

"Yes, sir," said Winter. "That was the assumption."

"But?"

"We've just received word that the *Anguis* might have been spotted off the coast of Argentina. Two months ago."

Dorian did the math in his head. "So, it didn't go down in the storm."

"It would appear."

"Which means the damn thing could still be floating around. Have we been able to confirm that it was the *Anguis*?"

"No."

"Then I think we should assume that the ship off the coast of Argentina was *not* the *Anguis*."

"Yes, sir."

"Anything else?"

Winter picked up the television remote. "This is footage that was shot early this morning."

The image on the screen was of a wilderness river. Dorian knew he was supposed to recognize the area, but he couldn't place it.

"North of Fort McMurray," said Winter.

"Ah," said Dorian. "The Athabasca River."

"The tar sands," said Winter. "As you know, Domidion has a sizable interest in Alberta's energy sector."

Dorian remembered arguing against tar-sands oil as an investment opportunity. The process required to extract bitumen was complicated and expensive. It used enormous amounts of fresh water and produced four times the greenhouse gases of oil extraction from wells. More troubling was the proximity of the processing plants to the river and the danger that the tailing ponds posed.

"A spill?"

"No," said Winter. "But evidently there has been some seepage. Possibly from one of our ponds."

"Didn't we fund an environmental study that tied pollutants in the river to fluctuating water levels and natural erosion?"

"Do you recall the problem with the ducks?"

In 2008, more than 1,600 ducks had been killed when they landed on one of the tailing ponds. In 2010, another 350 ducks died in the same manner. These were the public figures. In actual fact, Dorian knew, the numbers were much higher.

"There's been another waterfowl kill?"

"Fish," said Winter. "Dead fish have started appearing along the banks of the river."

Dorian watched the video. So that's what those white dots were.

"But none of our dams have failed?"

"No," said Winter. "The dams are holding."

"Then this might not be our problem."

"The level in one of our tailing ponds has been dropping rapidly for the past two weeks."

"Don't we have emergency protocols in place to handle situations such as this?"

"We do," said Winter. "We're pumping fresh water into the pond to keep the level where it's supposed to be."

"Our exposure?"

"Syncrude, Imperial, Royal Dutch Shell, Suncor all have holding ponds along the river," said Winter. "There are over sixty companies in the immediate area."

"So it will be difficult to determine where the problem originated." Dorian turned away from the screen. "Do we have a Rapid Response Team on site?"

"We do," said Winter. "They're keeping the media away."

"Who's taking point?"

"Public Relations. They're considering a press release."

Dorian felt his face flush. He touched his cheek and discovered that he was sweating.

"Are any of the other companies issuing press releases?"

"No."

"Then neither should we."

It wasn't a serious sweat. Just a thin film of moisture that lay on his face like a mist and felt cool to the touch. The condition wasn't new. It had happened before. It would go away in a while.

"I'm going to the gym."

"An excellent idea," said Winter.

Dorian wondered if Winter worked out. She didn't look as though she did free weights. Jogging perhaps, or more likely yoga. Dorian had tried yoga once but had been put off by the mystical overtones and the godawful positions that the instructor wanted everyone to assume.

Downward dog.

No matter what the health benefits, Dorian couldn't see the point of lying on a mat with your butt stuck up in the air.

"Tell me," said Dorian, "do you exercise?"

"Dance," said Winter.

"Commendable," said Dorian. "Olivia plays tennis."

DORIAN was in the elevator before he realized he was humming. "Danke Schoen."

Great. Sweating and humming.

He'd grab a couple of towels from the attendant, have a swim *and* do a circuit on the machines. Maybe two. Force all the tensions and toxins from his body. But it would take him the rest of the day to get that stupid song out of his head.

19

HE HAD EXPECTED TO FIND THE DOG SPLAYED OUT ON THE
deck, waiting to be fed. But when Gabriel returned to the trailer,
Soldier wasn't to be found. Of course, the dog could be anywhere. He could have snuck onto the reserve to nose around the
deserted houses. He could have run down to the beach to chase
waves. Or he could have followed Mara home. She was certainly
someone who would flatter a stray.

The dog had come with the trailer. More or less. When
Gabriel opened the door that first morning, there Soldier was,
his ears up, his tongue bouncing out of his mouth as if it were
fastened to a spring.

"Whose doggy are you?"

He was reasonably sure that he did not want a pet. His sister
would have taken Soldier, no questions asked.

"It's my sister you want," he had told the dog. "Don't count
on me."

Gabriel didn't know much about dogs. There were big dogs
and small dogs. Friendly dogs and mean dogs. Dogs of many
colours. What he did know about dogs was that they liked to
bark. All the dogs he had ever known had barked. Barked at
cars, barked at people, barked at each other, barked at shadows,

barked at barking. Gabriel suspected that, aside from licking themselves, barking was what dogs did.

Soldier seldom barked. The dog moaned and groaned, growled and snorted. He spent more time than necessary farting, but he seldom barked. Gabriel wondered if it was because the dog was old.

Maybe old dogs were quiet dogs.

Instead of barking, Soldier spent a good deal of time humming to himself. Or at least that's how it sounded. Something between a wheeze and a buzz, a rattle and an asthma attack. Still, there was a melody to the noise, a rhythmic rise and fall of sounds, and more than anything, it reminded Gabriel of the Clay Pigeons.

GABRIEL'S father had been a singer with the Clay Pigeons, and during the summer months, Joe had taken the family to the powwows around southern Alberta.

A Metis from Fort Qu'Appelle had started the drum. Jerry "Digger" Dumont had come up with the name after watching a movie in which rich white people shot at clay discs that were tossed into the air.

"Jesus, all that shooting," Digger told everyone, "and there was nothing you could eat. I was laughing so hard, they threw me out of the theatre."

One evening, when the men had come by the house for a meal and a practice, Digger had passed out red T-shirts with "Clay Pigeons" written on the front and a bull's eye target printed on the back.

"Rich man's sport," he told the boys. "Good enough for them, good enough for us."

GABRIEL sat in the chair and rocked back and forth. Somehow he had annoyed Mara, had made her angry. It hadn't been his idea to go to the reserve. From now on he would just stay put and wait for the next high tide. He'd read, watch one of the videos that had come with the trailer, wander the town, and look in the empty storefronts. He might even go to the hot springs. Crisp was a peculiar duck, but agreeable, and the man seemed willing to keep his curiosity to himself.

Or he could walk the tide line, one foot on the beach, the other in the ocean, and lose himself in the divide between land's end and water.

If Soldier were here, Gabriel might consider sending him to Mara's and having him explain how he had taken Gabriel's pants as a joke, how it was Soldier's fault that Gabriel had been at the reserve, how he was sorry he had caused a problem.

Who could resist an apology from a remorseful dog?

WHEN Gabriel was eight or nine, Joe had taken him to a drum practice, put him at his right hand, gave him a stick, and told him to pay attention. The stick was heavy and clumsy, and Gabriel had had to hold it with both hands, as he banged the drum at odd angles. It had been impossible to keep the beat, but the other men had been good-natured about it.

"When he's done hacking at that skin," Narcisse Blood told Joe, "I got a pile of wood needs cutting."

It had been slow, but by the time he was twelve, Gabriel could sing most of the songs, and he could hold the beat as well as the next man.

"Boy sings better than you do," Narcisse would tease Joe. "Hear he's a better lover, too."

"This from a man with a fondness for sheep."

"Just a rumour started by the goats."

The family had gone to Indian Days each year, and there was always room for them in Narcisse's lodge during Sun Dance. Wilton Goodstriker had let Gabriel and Lilly ride his horses, whenever Joe had time to bring them out to Wilton's camp. And they had spent evenings at Leroy Littlebear's house, listening to Leroy's endless supply of stories and bad jokes, while Amethyst First Rider rolled her eyes and made disparaging noises in her throat.

Those were the good times.

NOT that Soldier was particularly remorseful.

The dog was more contrary. Obstinate even. Gabriel had never heard of a dog who would not fetch. Gabriel had tried several times to interest Soldier in the game.

"Here we go," he'd say, waving a stick over his head. "Here we go."

And he'd throw it out in a long, floating arc.

"Fetch the stick!"

Gabriel had seen dogs so fast that they would catch the stick before it landed, dogs so fixated on getting to the stick that they would crash through any obstacle that was in their way, dogs so happy to have found the stick that they would chew it into pieces before they remembered to bring it back.

Soldier simply sat down and waited for the stick to land, and then he would wait for Gabriel to pick it up.

"How about we try this again."

But Soldier had no interest in chasing a stick. It was almost as though he had more important things to do and wasn't about to waste his time with such a silly activity.

"Come on, this is a fun game."

What the dog did do was follow Gabriel around. Gabriel didn't know why the dog found him so interesting, but everywhere he went, Soldier would go as well. Each day, when Gabriel came out of the trailer, the dog would be waiting for him, and every night when he went to bed, Soldier would prowl the edges of the deck, as though he were guarding the perimeter from a surprise assault.

GABRIEL had liked singing at the powwows, had liked being with his father. But he was never comfortable. He knew that, when other people saw him at the drum, they didn't see an Indian. His skin was pale. His hair was brown. His features were soft and delicate. He didn't look like his father. Or his mother. Or his sister for that matter. And he had gotten tired of having to explain.

Once, in the middle of an intertribal, Digger had motioned for Gabriel to take the lead, and Gabriel had shook him off. He wasn't ready, he told the other men afterwards. He didn't want to mess up the song.

"Hell," Digger had laughed, "I mess up songs all the time. You don't have to be perfect, you just have to try."

Joe didn't say anything, but Gabriel knew his father was disappointed.

That summer he went to all the powwows, and when the singing was strong, there would be a moment when Gabriel was tempted to lean forward and catch Digger's eye, raise a finger to signal that he wanted to take the lead.

And each time he had let the moment pass.

SO where was he? Soldier hadn't disappeared like this before. Not that it was a big deal. Gabriel was just curious. The dog could have injured himself dragging Gabriel's pants up the trail, or he could have wandered off into difficulty. Soldier was ancient, and there was something about the way the soft coastal light played on the dog's body that made Gabriel wonder if Soldier wasn't already dead, if what was following him around this dreary landscape of water and wind was a ghost.

IT was a clear evening, and from his chair, Gabriel could see the deserted streets of the town and the shifting shoreline all the way to the river. He settled back and waited for the sun to set.

And when the light disappeared and the stars showed themselves overhead and the dog had not returned, Gabriel retreated to the trailer and went to bed.

20

SONNY OPENS THE EVERFRESH VENDING MACHINE, EMPTIES the cash box, and puts the money in his pocket. Then he wipes the green plastic front with the soft towel, so the machine is shiny and clean. The EverFresh vending machine, with its blinking lights, tinkling sounds, cheery colours, and the tempting products that wave at you through the glass doors.

In the days before the turtles and the Indians went away, Magic Mel, the vending-machine man, would come by every other week to fill the machine's compartments. Magic Mel had been a magician when he was younger, and, if he had time, he would show Sonny a magic trick.

"People are easy to fool," Magic Mel would say. "People like to be tricked."

Sonny has practised several of the tricks that Magic Mel taught him, but now there are no people to mislead.

The sun has disappeared into the ocean. Sonny likes this time of the evening, when all the colours are soft and there are no hard edges to bump against. The cash boxes of the Scrub-A-Dub vending machine and Lava Java hot drink machine are empty, as is the box of the Toy Chest vending machine. The Toy Chest vending machine is Sonny's favourite, because you can keep grabbing at prizes with the metal claw until you get one.

As he checks the vending machines, Sonny wonders if the Indian woman liked the drum. He had considered leaving a note, "Salvage from Sonny," so she would know whom to thank. Sonny had also considered waiting in the trees, so he could see the expression on her face when she found the drum on the chair. And if the gift pleased her, if she held the drum up to the sky and cried out joyfully, then Sonny would burst from his hiding place and run across the field to the house, shouting, It was me! It was me!

Of course Dad has warned him about taking credit for good deeds. Be patient, Dad has told Sonny any number of times. Patience is better than pride.

Still, Sonny would like to see the woman smile. He would like to hear her laugh.

Off in the distance, he can see the steam from the hot springs rising into the night sky, and he imagines how lovely it would be to sit in water as warm as you please and never have to come out.

Sonny tries not to think about the hot springs, for Dad has decreed that thinking is the handmaiden to doing. And while there are many prohibitions in Dad's inventory of edicts, the ban on the hot springs is near the top of forbidden activities.

Thou shalt not go to the hot springs.

Sonny likes that Dad has set these rules down in a clear and organized fashion, because it makes it easier to avoid indiscretions and mistakes. But sometimes Sonny wishes that Dad didn't have so many.

Sonny reaches down and touches the water. Cold. No floating

in the pool tonight, but he could sit in one of the lounge chairs. That would be pleasant. Sonny cannot recall any prohibitions against this, so he drags the chair with comfortable cushions to the centre of the patio.

And as he sinks into the cushions, as he settles back to enjoy the stars in all their glory, he sees the dog.

21

CRISP'S VISIT HAD RAISED MARA'S SPIRITS, AND SHE FELT
more energetic than she had in ages. She stood in front of
the easel and considered the sketch she had begun. Then she
uncovered her palette and began to paint.

Nothing dramatic. The light was too weak for any major
adventures. She fixed small areas of Lilly's face and roughed
in the background with the larger brushes. She had originally
planned to keep the portrait simple, but now she knew she
would incorporate parts of the reserve into the painting.

A building or two. Perhaps a section of the water tower.

Mara stepped back from the easel. She and Lilly had been
teenagers together, young girls on the threshold of a new fron-
tier. To boldly go where no man has gone before is how Lilly had
described puberty.

Hormones, failed relationships, betrayals, reconciliations.
More hormones.

They had run wild on the reserve, especially on weekends
when they weren't hobbled by school and homework. They'd
take off in the morning with a sandwich stuffed in a jacket and
stay away until hunger drove them home.

Mostly they'd go down to the tidal pools and chase small

fish and crabs. Other times they'd hide out in the caves that the waves had carved out of the rocks and plot revenge on the town girls, who liked to strut about in their new clothes every year on the first day of school.

What Mara had liked best about Lilly was that she was always there. Good times and bad, she had always been there. Someone you could count on. Someone you could find at all times simply by reaching out.

And now she wasn't.

MARA had been in Toronto, getting ready for a major show at the Roberts Gallery when the letter arrived. Inside was a photo-graph of Lilly and her newborn son.

Riel.

"Here I am, Auntie Mara," Lilly had written in a cartoon balloon above the baby's head. "Hurry home and change my diaper."

Mara had been stunned by the picture. She hadn't realized that Lilly had been pregnant. How could that have happened? Where had the time gone? How had she lost track of her best friend? Lilly with a child. It was impossible to imagine. And wonderful. Auntie Mara. God, it sounded like something you would put on a wound.

Maybe Riel could call her something else.

MARA added cerulean and ochre to the board as she tried to remember the evenings the two of them had walked to town and back, talking about the futures they imagined for themselves. Lilly was going to raise horses in Alberta. Mara was going to go to France and become a world-famous artist.

Those were their dreams.

But even then, realities had begun to hem them in.

Lilly's mother had injured herself in a fall. The recovery had taken longer than anticipated, and, along with the pain, there had been unexpected moments of forgetfulness and sudden rages.

"Mum's not well," Lilly had told Mara. "It's not just the hip."

By the time Mara was fifteen, it was clear that Rose wasn't going to get better.

"I can raise horses anywhere," Lilly had told Mara. "But you have to go to Paris. Don't even think about staying."

THE light vanished, and the colours dimmed and died on the canvas. Mara put the brush down. She hadn't accomplished much, but tomorrow she would do a little more. And, after that, a little more. Until Lilly and Rose and baby Riel came back to life.

Life.

There it was.

Standing at the easel, looking at what she had created, Mara realized that she might have found a purpose, something that would help her push past the numbing sorrow, something that would help her make the world whole again.

22

AS IT TURNED OUT, DORIAN DIDN'T GET TO THE GYM UNTIL well after seven. Miscellaneous conference calls, a disagreement with the agricultural ministers of several European Union countries over seed-licensing agreements, news that Silhouette, a weight-loss product Domidion had released three years ago, was being linked to kidney failure in teenage girls and young women, and a less than encouraging report on the corporation's expansion efforts into China.

Domidion's health club was on the ground floor of the complex. Dorian tried to spend at least an hour in the facility each day. Thirty minutes on the rowing machine, an assortment of free weights, followed by twenty minutes on one of the elliptical trainers. When he had time, he would swim laps in the salt-water pool as well.

He was on the elliptical trainer when an older woman carved her way through the barbells and the machines. Dorian was sure he recognized her, but he couldn't place the face.

"Mr. Asher."

Dorian maintained his speed.

"Victoria Lustig. Public Relations," said the woman. "Your assistant said I might find you here."

Dorian glanced at the monitor. "Three minutes. I'd like to finish my workout."

The woman looked around the gym as though she had just realized where she was. "Certainly," she said. "We can do that."

The monitor had his heart rate at 142. He would like to get to 150 and hold it there for twenty minutes, but that would have to wait until next time. Dorian shortened his stride and began slowing the pace, allowing his body to cool down.

Victoria Lustig from Public Relations waited patiently, working the cellphone with her thumbs.

Dorian glided to a stop, wrapped the towel around his neck, and stepped off the machine. "All right, Victoria Lustig, what can I do for you?"

"The major networks are lining up, and they're being quite insistent."

Dorian wiped the sweat off his face. "They don't waste any time, do they."

"They do not."

Lustig was a tall woman with broad shoulders and stout legs. She was neither pretty nor handsome, but looked quite capable of bringing down large antelopes and small deer all on her own.

"Let's find a celebrity who can go on camera and talk about our efforts to preserve wilderness habitat. Somebody sympathetic. Someone the public likes."

"This isn't about the fish kill," said Lustig. "It's about an employee."

Dorian could feel his heart pick up speed, as though he were still on the machine. "An employee?"

"One of our scientists," said Lustig. "A Dr. Gabriel Quinn."

~~~~~

WINTER had rearranged Dorian's office so that the three of them could watch the television at the same time.

"CBC's *En Garde*," said Lustig, as she worked the remote. "The topic is genetically modified foods."

Dorian watched as the host of the show, a stunning dark-haired woman named Manisha Khan, introduced her guest, a middle-aged man with glasses and a bald head that glistened under the studio lights.

"Thicke?"

Manisha started the discussion by asking the perennial question. Were genetically modified foods safe for consumers?

"Well, Manisha," said Thicke, leaping in with no encouragement. "Humans have been modifying their food for centuries. It's nothing new. The Egyptians created hybrid varieties of wheat."

"So Domidion is doing the same thing the Egyptians did."

Dorian wondered if anyone had ever told Thicke that when he smiled, he looked like a dolphin.

"Not exactly, Manisha. We've come a long way since the Egyptians."

"But are industry safeguards sufficient to protect the crops we depend on?"

"Absolutely," said Thicke, smiling his goofy dolphin smile. "Nothing leaves our research facilities until it has been thoroughly tested."

"What about *Klebsiella planticola*? Wasn't that modified with disastrous results?"

Dorian resisted the urge to strangle the armrests on the chair.

"Yes," said Thicke, without breaking stride. "That's the example critics always dredge up. *Klebsiella planticola* is a beneficial and benign organism, and, yes, one of the modified versions did have *potentially* unacceptable side effects, but the important thing to remember, Manisha, is that because of the safeguards the industry imposes on itself, that virus never got out of the laboratory."

"A bacterium," said Dorian, under his breath. "A bacterium, you idiot."

"But isn't *Klebsiella planticola* a bacterium?"

"Absolutely," said Thicke, his voice going thin and reedy. "Slip of the tongue. Yes, of course, it's a bacterium."

"And it wasn't the industry that recognized the danger the bacteria posed, was it? It was the work of an independent team of scientists at a university that saved the day."

"All part of the safeguards, Manisha. All part of the safeguards."

"We're talking with Dr. Warren Thicke, a senior scientist with Domidion's Biological Oversight. After the break, we'll continue our talk with Dr. Thicke about genetically modified foods."

Dorian stared at the screen. "How long is the show?"

"Half an hour."

"When he smiles," said Dorian, "he looks like a damn dolphin."

"That's good," said Winter. "People like dolphins."

Lustig held up the remote. "Shall I fast-forward through the commercial break?"

The colours jumbled and flashed across the screen, and then the show was back, Manisha sitting alertly in the easy chair, Thicke relaxing on the sofa.

"Today we're talking with Dr. Warren Thicke, a senior scientist at Domidion, about the dangers of genetically modified foods."

Thicke nodded his head and chuckled. "That will be a short conversation, Manisha, because the dangers are almost non-existent."

Dorian saw it immediately. The flash in Manisha's eyes, the look of a cat who'd come across a chubby rodent.

"Still, a year ago, when *En Garde* talked with Dr. Gabriel Quinn about this same subject, he told us that genetically modified foods were not being adequately tested."

Thicke reddened and sat up straight. "That's a matter of opinion, Manisha."

"But isn't Dr. Quinn the head of Biological Oversight at Domidion?"

Dorian could see the sweat bead up on Thicke's head.

"You have to understand, biogenetics is a field that changes daily."

"So, Dr. Quinn is . . . out of date?"

"'Out of date' is rather harsh, Manisha." Thicke relaxed again. Dorian watched as the man leaned back against the sofa, his legs drifting away from his body. "I think the kinder explanation is that he was just tired."

"Was?"

"What?"

"You said 'was.'"

"Well, he did . . . disappear."

Dorian was on his feet. "Has this been broadcast yet?"

"At six this evening," said Lustig. "It was live."

"Disappear?" said Manisha, looking directly into the camera. "The head of Domidion's Biological Oversight has disappeared?"

Even now Dorian could see that Thicke didn't realize that he was circling the drain.

"Biological Oversight is a team effort, Manisha." Thicke wagged a finger at his host. "Team effort."

"Have the authorities been notified?"

Thicke's dolphin smile vanished. "The authorities?"

"I mean," said Manisha, "this must be troubling."

"What?"

"That Domidion's top scientist has gone missing?"

"Dr. Quinn is not Domidion's top scientist. I . . ."

And then Thicke was gone and the camera was on Manisha. The show's theme music began playing in the background.

"A breaking story," intoned Manisha, as the credits scrolled on the screen. "A major scientist at one of the world's largest biotech corporations is missing. Stay tuned to CBC for *Wheel of Fortune*, which follows immediately. I'm Manisha Khan, and you can stay current with *En Garde*."

It took a minute for the air to find its way back into the room.

"Is that all of it?"

Lustig put the remote on the table. "Yes."

Dorian kept an eye on the bright blue screen, in case Thicke reappeared to shoot himself in the other foot. "Has the Board seen this?"

Winter straightened her glasses. "I would imagine."

Lustig retrieved the DVD. "All of the networks have asked us to comment on our missing scientist."

"He's not missing," said Dorian. "We simply don't know where he is. At present."

"Several reporters have suggested that we're hiding him or that we have flown him to another country to keep him from talking to the press."

"About what?"

"We have several options," said Lustig. "We can stand behind our confidentiality policy and say that we cannot comment on a Domidion employee."

"That won't get the genie back in the bottle," said Dorian.

"Does Dr. Quinn happen to have a wife who died recently?"

"He wasn't married."

"Any hospitalizations for anxiety or stress?" asked Lustig. "Any prescription or recreational drug abuse?"

"He kept to himself."

"So he was anti-social." Lustig paused for a moment and took a deep breath. "Do we know where Dr. Quinn is?"

"No." Dorian held up a hand. "What I want to know is, does his disappearance present us with any potential problems?"

"Legal or civil?"

"Either," said Dorian. "Both."

"We don't know yet," said Lustig. "But in the meantime, I'd recommend invoking employee confidentiality. It doesn't tie us to anything that can come back on us later."

"All right. Employee confidentiality it is." Dorian turned to Winter. "Make sure that no one, and I mean no one, talks about Quinn on the record or off."

"I'll speak to Dr. Thicke personally," said Winter.

Lustig stood up and straightened her skirt. "There's an upside," she said with a flick of her head. "So long as the press has a missing scientist to chase, we might be able to keep the Athabasca off the news."

23

WHEN GABRIEL STEPPED ONTO THE DECK THE NEXT MORNING, he found that a weather front had sailed in from the northwest. The sky was high grey and hammered steel, and a flotilla of rain clouds was holding formation on the horizon, looking for a reason to come ashore.

Soldier was nowhere to be seen.

Gabriel had discovered an old waffle maker at the back of one of the cupboards. The results had been mixed. Even though he had oiled the iron, the waffle stuck to the top and bottom plates, and he had had to pull the two halves off with a fork. The presentation was scrappy, but the taste was fine.

The second waffle had been better.

However, the result of an all-carbohydrate, butter-and-syrup breakfast had been a general lethargy. Gabriel remembered reading that exercise helped to reduce blood sugar and increase alertness. He had never had an interest in organized exertion and compulsory sweating. But a walk along the shore had much to recommend it. Fresh air. The calming voice of the surf. The soft sand beneath his feet.

The chance that a rogue wave might come along and crush him when he wasn't looking.

He stepped off the deck, took the marker from his pocket, and wrote "Turkmenistan" on the wood skirt and "The Gates of Hell" next to it.

Then he started down the trail to the beach.

THE first time Gabriel saw the ocean was when he went to Stanford University to check out their graduate program. He had been offered a full scholarship, and one of the conditions was that he first come to Palo Alto to see the place.

"We like to have our scholarship students visit the campus before they make their decision," the voice on the phone told him. "Stanford will pay all your expenses."

It took Gabriel most of the first day to convince himself that Stanford was actually a world-class university. It was the architecture. The University of Minnesota had had an abundance of old, ivy-covered, brick-and-limestone buildings, and even the newer glass and steel high-rises had an austere dignity to them that maintained the aura of academic excellence.

Stanford, with its sprawling acreage of low-slung adobe stylings, tile roofs, palm-tree-lined boulevards, gardens, and fountains, looked more like an affluent housing development. Or an upscale, open-air shopping mall.

And there was a casualness to the place that left Gabriel feeling apprehensive. Maybe it was the extra sun that fell on Palo Alto or maybe it was the Bay Area's history of counterculture enthusiasms. Whatever the reason, students and faculty alike tended to dress as if they were on an extended vacation at an all-inclusive resort.

Floyd O'Neil was the graduate student assigned to show Gabriel around. "Don't let the place fool you," Floyd told him. "School's world class."

Gabriel's concerns were quickly dispelled with a tour of Biology, Chemistry, and Applied Physics. While Stanford might not have lived up to his visual notions of a university, the faculty and the research facilities in the hard sciences more than made up for any reservations.

On the third day of the visit, Floyd suggested a trip to Santa Cruz. "Have you ever seen the Pacific?"

"No."

"Before I came here," said Floyd, "neither had I."

THE sea was flat with hardly any roll, and the waves struggled to make it to the land. Gabriel took off his shoes, hung them around his neck by the laces, and walked along with the tide at his ankles. The water was sharp and unpleasant, colder than he had expected, but he could feel a new alertness as his body began burning through breakfast.

The Apostles were still there, waiting for him. Set against the high water, with only the tops of the spires showing, they looked frail and insignificant.

He considered going back to the reserve. By himself this time. Without Mara and certainly without the dog. He didn't need company. He should do that. Before he died, he should do that.

Or not.

Either way, there was no salvation, no forgiveness, no hope for redemption. Not that he believed in such abstracts. If he believed in anything, he believed in the laws of chemistry and biology and physics. He could see these gods, negotiate with them, anticipate what they would do. He liked that kind of certainty, liked knowing that if you mixed twelve atoms of carbon with twenty-two atoms of hydrogen and eleven atoms of oxygen, you got sugar. Or that beans from the castor plant could be processed into a deadly gas.

If you were so inclined.

An organized and regulated world. He had been happy in that universe.

BY the time they got to Santa Cruz, Gabriel was sure that he would never voluntarily make that drive again. Highway 9 through the Santa Cruz Mountains had been an evil twist of a road. Floyd had stayed below the speed limit, but even so, the drive had been harrowing. Bungee jumping off a roller coaster would have felt safer.

"You get used to it."

To his credit, Gabriel hadn't thrown up, and he hadn't tried to jump out of the moving car. And, as they made the final winding drop to the coast, he had to admit that getting to the ocean had been worth it.

"So," said Floyd, as they stood on the beach below the boardwalk. "What do you think?"

AT first he thought it was the wind freshening off the ocean, but as Gabriel came away from the surf line and moved to higher ground, he heard it again.

Someone singing.

Ahead the beach was darker and humped up, and before Gabriel could put the pieces of the puzzle together, something large rose out of the sand and shook itself with a bellow.

"Master Gabriel!"

Nicholas Crisp was on his knees in a hole, next to a wooden trunk that was buried in the sand.

"Do ye know the words?"

"No."

"Well then," said Crisp, "we'll manufacture verses as we go."

"What are you doing?"

"Retrieving a lost soul." Crisp jammed the shovel under the box. "Grab the neck and give a wiggle, for we'll not johnny-bolt this clam from its hole but will needs coax it with rough harmony and leverage."

"You want me to pull on it?"

"She's a grip, she is," said Crisp, "and not about to smile on us any time soon."

"Okay."

"And ye must sing as ye pulls, for no good can come from silence and brute strength."

Crisp repositioned the shovel, began the song anew, and Gabriel followed as best he could.

"Again," cried Crisp. "Put your back into the chorus."

It took another twenty minutes to work the trunk free.

"Aye," said Crisp, "but ain't she a beauty. Have ye ever seen such a box?"

The trunk was made out of several kinds of wood, with slats at the seams for strength. The lid was hinged, and the hasp secured with a bent iron rod. All along one side was a series of marks and designs.

"Kanji," said Crisp. "Asian pictographs what tells a story, reveals the contents, or names the owner."

"It's a trunk."

"Scratch the wood." Crisp ran a fingernail along one of the slats. "Can ye smell the history it contains?"

"What are you going to do with it?"

"Exactly," said Crisp, "for rescue's the easy matter, ain't it. And in that rescue lies the burden, for now we be responsible for its well-being."

"I suppose we should look inside."

"Why?"

"I don't know," said Gabriel. "Curiosity?"

"Ah," said Crisp, shaking the sand from his beard. "Curiosity indeed. It don't just kill cats, ye know."

GABRIEL had expected that the Pacific would resemble a large lake. It didn't. It didn't look like a lake. It didn't sound like a lake. It didn't smell like a lake.

"You have to see the sea lions."

They spent much of that day walking the beach, wandering the boardwalk, and talking.

Floyd was from Roseville, a small railroad town at the eastern edge of California's Central Valley. "You believe it," he said. "I was born and raised a couple hundred miles from the coast and never got out here before Stanford."

"Where'd you do your undergraduate work?"

"Utah," said Floyd. "But I escaped."

Gabriel's favourite moment was standing at the end of the pier and looking at the horizon. In all directions, as far as he could see and beyond that, there was nothing but water.

"Stinks a bit," said Floyd, "but it's one hell of a view."

That evening, as they drove back to Stanford, the two impressions that stayed with Gabriel were that the ocean was vast, and that it was alive.

"SPEAKING of curiosity and cats," said Gabriel, as he stood by the edge of the hole, "have you seen Soldier?"

Crisp turned away from the trunk. "The dog's gone?"

"He ran off last night."

Crisp's voice dropped, and his face darkened. "Not like a messenger to desert his post. He must have had serious business what required his attendance."

"Soldier?"

"Aye," said Crisp. "Dogs are the messengers of the universe. Did ye not know that?"

The last time Gabriel had seen the dog, Soldier had been lying on his back with his tongue hanging out of his mouth.

"He's a messenger?"

"He is." Crisp pointed his chin at the mountains. "On the morning of The Ruin, it were Master Dog what set the alarm, barking and howling for all the good it did. On that day, the Smoke ran green and sparkling down to the sea. On that day, everything died."

The clouds in the distance were moving towards shore. The fog would be back before dark.

"He'll come home," said Crisp, "for his employment ain't done."

Gabriel smiled. "Employment?"

"Stories to tell, wrongs to right, worlds to save." Crisp cocked his head. "Do ye know the story 'The Woman Who Fell from the Sky'? I imagined ye might, what with the records ye be keeping on the deck."

"I should stop doing that."

"No, no," cried Crisp, "for it's well and proper to write what must be seen and to speak what must be heard."

"It's a hobby."

"Tonight," said Crisp, in softer tones, "ye must not miss the party. And if the stars are still in the sky, we'll have Mara tell the story, for she's a gentler hand with words than myself."

"At the hot springs?"

"It's my birthday, Master Gabriel. Will ye help me celebrate it?"

"Sure."

Crisp picked the trunk up with one hand, as though it were of no weight whatsoever, and set it on his shoulder like a perched parrot. "Heed the hound," he called out as he strode off through the beach grass. "He's a wise soul. Don't be letting his looks fool ye."

FLOYD took him to the airport.

"You know what you're going to decide?" Floyd had asked, as the two of them stood in line at the check-in counter.

"I'll probably take the offer."

"Did you notice," said Floyd, as they walked to the security gates, "all the campus washrooms have three-ply toilet paper."

GABRIEL waited until Crisp disappeared into the dunes. Then he stepped into the hole and squatted down.

Now he could see the ocean as the beach saw it.

He wedged his shoulders against the walls and drew his legs up to his chest. Intriguing. Too deep for a bed. Too shallow for a grave. Still, the space was surprisingly comfortable.

The tide was a slow roll, and the shoreline was edged in sea-foam, soft white meringues and frothy creams that made Gabriel think of pies and coffees. He leaned back, closed his eyes, and listened to the desolate sound of the surf as it spread out across the sand, searching the beach for friends and strangers alike.

24

WHEN SONNY GETS UP THE NEXT MORNING, THE DOG IS GONE. But what a wonderful time the two of them had.

Wham-wham.

When Sonny first saw the dog standing on the patio by the pool, he was concerned, for Dad has spoken of dogs on numerous occasions.

Don't throw food to dogs.

Dogs vomit a lot.

Dogs have mighty appetites.

Sonny tries to remember if Dad has had anything good to say about dogs. He's sure that if Dad met this dog, he would feel differently.

First, this dog is a good listener. Sonny told him all about the motel and the town and the turtles and the tourists who don't come to Samaritan Bay anymore, and the dog did not interrupt once.

Second, this dog is a good swimmer. Sonny and the dog braved the cold water, jumped in the pool, and swam laps, and Sonny won five out of seven times. Sonny the winner!

Wham-wham, hammer-hammer.

Third, this dog knows stories that Sonny has never heard,

strange stories about women who fall out of the sky, about creatures similar to dogs who can change their shape, about birds who steal fire, and hero twins who fight monsters.

Some of these stories sound like the stories that Dad tells, but most of them don't.

After they got out of the pool and dried themselves, Sonny showed the dog the nails that were popping out of the siding on the motel and how fast he could hammer them flush with the wood.

Wham-wham.

Watch Sonny, he would tell the dog, and then Sonny would snatch the hammer from his tool belt, line the nail up, and sink it with one swing.

Watch Sonny again.

Sonny could tell that the dog was impressed with Sonny's strong stroke.

Snatch, line, swing. Snatch, line, swing. Until all the nails had been driven home.

Wham-wham, hammer-hammer.

And, when he ran out of nails, Sonny showed the dog how easy it was to hammer other things. Afterwards, he lay on the lounge chair with the dog curled up at his feet. They watched the stars together, and, for the first time in a long time, Sonny did not feel lonely.

BUT now it is morning and the dog is gone. Sonny is sad. He liked having a friend, and if the dog were still here, Sonny would suggest that they go to the beach. They could run up and down the shoreline, chasing each other, searching for salvage, doing the things that Sonny has seen good friends do on television.

But when Sonny stands up and looks around, he sees the problems that can come from high times. Hasn't Dad told him that virtue is more important than fun, and that only fools think simply of having a good time?

More than once.

Wham-wham.

The EverFresh vending machine doesn't look so good. The plastic face of the machine has been cracked in several places, and a number of the dispenser doors have been broken.

Was Sonny too energetic with his hammering? Was he trying too hard to impress the dog? Is this what happens when Sonny runs out of nails to hit?

How is he going to explain this to Dad? How could he have been so imprudent?

"Hello, Sonny."

Sonny doesn't think that this voice belongs to a tourist come to rent a room. He doesn't think this voice belongs to the naked guy on the beach. He doesn't think this voice belongs to the Indian woman in the yellow house.

He knows this voice.

"Business still adrift in the latitudes, I see."

Sonny spins around, snatches the hammer from the belt, and looks for a nail to hit.

Wham!

"Peace, lad, for I've not come to run ye aground," says Crisp, and he hoists the trunk off his shoulder. "I've brought ye a gift, a bit of salvage what washed up and buried itself deep in the shore."

Sonny glances at the Lava Java machine. It has hammer marks on it as well.

"It's your beach, of course, and I'm only about a small service in bringing it to you along with an invitation."

Sonny holds his hammer at the ready and tries to look calm and fierce.

"As ye know," says Crisp, "tonight's my birthday, and I'm to celebrate it with a small gathering of friends at the springs." He pauses and waits. "I'm hoping that ye might slip your anchor and join us, for there's nothing so fine in the known world as firm friends and warm water."

Sonny looks at Room Number One, and he hopes that Dad will hear the commotion and come out to see what's wrong. Dad will know how to deal with this predicament. Dad will know what to say. Dad will know what to do.

Dad will have extra nails.

"All right, then. I must be off." Crisp takes one step back into the shadows. "Think on the offer, lad, for I'd like us to be the friends we once were."

Sonny waits until he is sure that the predicament has left. That was close. That was very close. However the trunk is still here. The predicament didn't take the trunk with him, and when Sonny looks at the chest closely, he recognizes it.

This is the trunk he had found. The trunk with the martial-arts writing on it. The trunk that was stuck in the sand on his beach.

This is his trunk.

Sonny carries the trunk to the pool. He puts it on the table with the pop-up umbrella, carefully removes the bent rod from the weathered hasp, and takes a deep breath.

Then he opens the lid.

25

MARA HAD GOTTEN UP BEFORE FIRST LIGHT AND SET THE
water to boil. The sun was shining, but she knew this wouldn't
last. These were the days when the fog came and went as it
pleased. She debated packing a lunch, in case she stayed on
the reserve longer than expected. Not that she could afford an
extended visit. She needed to get back and finish the portrait.

Tomorrow she would start the underpainting for the others.

MARA had always dreamed of going to Paris to study art. The
Samaritan Bay library had had several books on the city, and
she had devoured them. The galleries, the cafés, the parks, the
monuments. Everywhere she had looked, history had looked
back.

One of the books had a fold-out map. She and Lilly had followed the streets past La Conciergerie, where the Revolutionary
Tribunal had sent thousands to the guillotine during the French
Revolution, and had traced out the borders of the Place de la
Concorde, where Louis XVI and Marie Antoinette had been
beheaded. There had been a picture of the Arc de Triomphe,
the monument that Napoleon commissioned to commem-

orate French soldiers fresh from their victory at the Battle of Austerlitz, and another of the Seine as it flowed under Pont Neuf, the oldest bridge in the city.

Mara had been mesmerized by the images of the Crypte archéologique, the third-century Roman ruins that lay beneath Notre Dame, and she had promised Lilly that, when she got to Paris, she would send her a photograph of the Pont des Arts with the thousands of locks that desperate lovers had fastened on the wire fencing to celebrate their grand romance.

"They leave locks on a fence?"

Mara had opened the book to the page. "It's about love."

Lilly had spent several minutes looking at the photograph.

"So, what do you think?"

"Dead bodies? Love locks?" Lilly had rolled her eyes. "If you ask me, Paris looks kinda creepy."

THE school bus was still parked in front of the entrance to the reserve. Mara didn't know why someone hadn't driven off with the vehicle. So far as she knew, it was operational. Surely the authorities hadn't pulled the motor out and left a yellow shell to guard the entrance to the townsite.

All of the tires were low. Two of them were completely flat, but anyone with a pump could fix that. Maybe the bus had just been forgotten.

But having asked the question, Mara had to see for herself. She released the locks and raised the hood. Indeed, the motor was still there. So it could be driven. Now that would be a sight. The old bus with its panels covered with graffiti, proclamations, and warnings come floating down Station Street, looking for the world like a ghost ship out of a horror novel.

The Bus.

Mara pulled the doors open and stepped inside. It looked like the same bus that had taken her and Lilly to the school in town. The two of them had sat near the front, Lilly at the window, Mara guarding the aisle, fending off Eddie Bull and Leo Thom with their quick smiles and stupid jokes.

Two of the bench seats were missing. The metal around the support bracket was shiny and raw, as though the theft had been recent. If anyone was going to drive off with the bus, they had better do it while it still had most of its parts.

Mara eased herself into the driver's seat and worked the wheel back and forth. She stepped on the clutch and tried to pull the shift into second. Yes, she thought. It would be fun to drive the bus into Samaritan Bay. She could paint her face in morbid colours and designs, hold a flashlight between her thighs so that the light caught her at a creepy angle, roll down all the windows, and shriek and shriek and shriek as she careened through town.

Not that anyone would hear her. The Bay was almost as deserted as the reserve.

Or she could drive the bus across the headlands and send it plunging over the cliffs into the ocean. That had appeal as well.

Instead, she stepped off the bus and shut the doors. Another time. Another time for that.

~~~~~

MARA'S mother and grandmother had been guarded about her plans to go to Paris.

"You don't speak French," her mother had told her.

"I'll learn."

"If you want to marry a French guy," her grandmother offered, "try Quebec. I hear the place is lousy with them."

"I don't want to get married. I want to study at the École des Beaux-Arts."

"You should go to Vancouver and become a nurse."

"I don't want to be a nurse."

"Your auntie Belle is a nurse in Victoria," her grandmother told her. "You should talk to Belle."

"Who's going to look after the river," her mother had asked.

"I'll come back."

"That's what everyone says," said her grandmother.

Lilly had been more supportive. "If you want to go to Paris, go to Paris."

"You said it looked creepy."

"It does," Lilly had said, "but that's no reason not to go."

Mara had stopped by the Blue Skies travel agency and asked Mr. Webster about the cost of airfare to Paris.

"France?"

"Yes," Mara had said.

"You'll have to go to Toronto first." Mr. Webster gave her several brochures. "From there you can fly to Paris."

"Okay."

Mr. Webster had written the airfare on a yellow sticky. Mara had taken it home and stuck it to the wall of her bedroom.

That afternoon, Lilly had come by and they had sat together on Mara's bed with the brochures spread out between them.

"Course, you don't *need* to go to Paris," Lilly told her. "You're already a good artist."

"I want to be better."

"That drawing you did of the weasel was really good."

"I don't want to draw weasels the rest of my life."

"We got lots of turtles." Lilly had pushed the brochures out of the way and flopped back on the bed. "Why don't you draw turtles?"

THE reserve was wrapped in fog. The water tower had vanished somewhere in the weather, but her grandmother's house was waiting for her.

In the first year after the spill, vandals had invaded the reserve and had taken anything they could carry, anything of value, anything that could be sold as macabre souvenirs to the sick and the wealthy. Her grandmother's quilts, the cedar hope chest that her grandfather had finished just before he died. The family photographs that had sat on her mother's dresser. The trash container from the kitchen.

Who would steal a trash container?

All gone.

Except for the orange plastic chair with its bent leg and the thin crack in its seat. Mara's grandmother and mother had reserved this chair for special guests, for government agents, school officials, and other people who came at them sideways. If you didn't know about the chair and weren't careful, you'd get a nasty pinch when you sat down.

"Serves 'em right," her grandmother would say. "They've always been a pain in the butt."

The orange chair had sat in the corner of the room for as long as Mara could remember, and now it was the only thing that remained.

MARA'S mother had rescued a five-pound Tenderflake lard pail from the community-centre garbage, and Mara's grandmother had stuck a piece of tape on the side with the word "Paris" printed in capital letters. Whenever they could, the two women would throw change into the pail. They called the container the "bank," and the rule was that once money was deposited, it could not be withdrawn.

Mara found part-time jobs waiting tables at the Tin Turtle and stocking shelves at the Co-op. You couldn't see how much money was in the lard pail, but that didn't keep Mara and Lilly from guessing.

"Got to be at least a couple of hundred by now."

"More than that."

The pail had sat on the bookshelf gathering dust and collecting cash. Every so often, when her mother and grandmother were off playing bingo, Mara would take it down and shake it gently, just to listen to the coins shuffle against the paper money.

The day after she graduated from high school, Mara opened the yellow and blue container and spread the money out on the table, so she and Lilly could count it. Then they counted it again.

"Okay," Lilly had said, finally breaking the silence. "Now what are you going to do?"

MARA went to the kitchen window. The fog was swirling in off the headlands, smouldering between the houses like smoke, and, for just a moment, she thought she saw something. A figure moving quickly in the greyness.

Mara waited.

It had been a girl. Mara was almost sure of that. But the longer she looked into the fog, the more she began to doubt that she had seen anything except shifting shadows.

She zipped the jacket up to her neck and went outside. Crisp said he had seen smoke. Maybe he had. Mara had always expected that there would be problems with squatters, but so far the grisly stories that had attached themselves to the reserve had kept everyone away.

Except the looters, of course.

But those ghouls had already picked the place clean. Mara searched the fog for a sound, for a smell.

Squatters?

The rage was sudden and unexpected. She had been calm one moment, and now she was furious. The stripping of the homes had been bad enough. She had been helpless to do anything about that. But she'd be damned if she was going to allow the land to be stolen as well.

After the spill, the government had forced the surviving families off the reserve. For their own safety, the officials had said. And for their own safety, the families had been relocated to Saskatchewan and Manitoba, to communities as far away from Samaritan Bay as possible.

But the reserve was still band land. The families would return. Over time, they would find their way home. Mara was sure of this. And when they did, their homes weren't going to be occupied by a bunch of cowboys trying to rustle free real estate.

Not if Mara could stop it.

She'd come back when the fog lifted and search the houses. Maybe she'd bring Soldier and Gabriel with her. The dog looked fierce enough. And, if that didn't work, she'd get Gabriel to take off his clothes.

Again.

That would scare anyone out of Dodge.

The fog had thickened. Someone else might have gotten lost, but Mara's feet knew the path. Even in the dark, she could travel the land on the rhythms of the ground and find her way there and back.

The bus was still parked in front of the fence. Here, the fog began to disperse and the air was warmer. She unzipped her jacket and started jogging down the trail, setting an easy pace. And when she arrived on the beach, she was once again in sunshine.

26

THERE WERE STRANGE RUMOURS AFOOT IN SAMARITAN BAY.
As Crisp wandered through town on his way back to the springs,
each business he stopped at told much the same story. Things
were missing.

Webb's Bakery was missing bread. Carol Miller's second-
hand clothing store was short shirts and pants. Terry Collins
over at the Co-op market told Crisp that someone had removed
flour and bottled water from a storage room.

"Doors open onto the alley, so it wouldn't be hard to do,"
said Terry. "But who the hell steals bottled water?"

Peter Canakis, who owned the old dry-goods emporium just
down from the church, reported that at least three blankets had
vanished.

"Not even nice ones," Canakis told Crisp. "Me, I wouldn't
steal blankets like that."

As Crisp walked the streets, he was saddened by the empty
storefronts. It seemed as though every month someone else
would leave. Souto's doughnuts, Vigneux's hardware, Tupholme's
used books and DVDs, Antaeus's beauty salon, Virone's furniture, and Cort's pet supplies. Except for the Ocean Star Motel,
the hotels and motels and B & Bs had closed their doors long

ago. The businesses that were still hanging on were doing so in the hope that, eventually, the town would come back from the dead. Crisp was sure it would.

He just didn't know when.

It would depend on the turtles. Crisp was sure of this. If the turtles returned, so would the people.

No one had been able to explain why the turtles had decided to nest so far north in the first place. Crisp knew that they normally frequented nesting beaches in places like Florida, Puerto Rico, Costa Rica, and Mexico. A number of the scientists who had studied the phenomenon of the Samaritan Bay turtles had concluded that the unusually warm currents, the temperature of the sand, the slope of the beach, and the deep water just off shore duplicated the necessary conditions for a breeding habitat.

Crisp liked to think that a turtle had landed on the beach in a storm, liked what she saw, and told her friends.

"It's not bad," Crisp imagined her telling the other females. "Warm sand, deep water, lots of jellyfish and squid just off shore. And ye don't have to put up with the commute."

Whatever the reasons, the turtles had come. And they had stayed.

Until The Ruin.

After The Ruin, the turtles had not returned. No eggs hatched. No baby turtles burst through the sand and raced for the open ocean. Now, the only sign that the turtles had ever been to the bay were the bleached skeletons that piled up on shore after each storm.

And Crisp had seen nothing on his morning swim out to the horizon and back to suggest that anything had changed. He had looked hard and long between breaths and strokes, and all he had found were shadows and empty water.

He stopped in front of the Shamrock Pharmacy and cupped his hands against the glass. Crisp could see the empty display cabinets and the rows of shelves that used to be home to Aspirin, shampoo, Band-Aids, toothpaste, tampons, greeting cards, chewing gum, and breath mints. Ed Lueders had stayed well after The Ruin, had kept the store open as a community service, but there had been family problems.

"I'd like to stay," Ed told Crisp, "but our girl out in Manitoba isn't doing all that well, and the wife wants to go back and be with the grandkids."

Crisp had helped Ed close the store.

"I'd give it to anyone who was fit to run it," Ed had said. "But there isn't anyone left who knows cough drops from condoms."

The closing of the pharmacy had been a blow. Even Crisp had felt the loss. He wasn't sure what people who needed prescription drugs were going to do. Move, he guessed. Move to another town. To another town that wasn't dead.

As he looked into the empty store, he wondered if the bread and the clothes, the flour and the water, and the blankets had actually been stolen. Maybe, in the end, they had just given up. Maybe, like the rest of the town, the staples had packed their bags and hit the road.

Crisp didn't think this was the case. You could always count on bread and blankets, he reasoned. It were people what let you down.

The walk back was pleasant, and Crisp took his time, checking each storefront, saying hello to any survivors that could be found. When he got back to the springs, he'd check to see if anything was missing. He didn't think there'd be. There wasn't much to steal.

The only items of any value at Beatrice Hot Springs were the warm water and the steam.

27

AS SONNY LIFTS THE LID ON THE TRUNK, HE HOPES THAT IT
will contain items that are on Dad's list of approved acquisitions.

Hope, hope, hope.

As Sonny opens the trunk, he closes his eyes and thinks of
England. This is not something that Dad has mandated. This
is rented-movie advice, so it's almost as good. Close your eyes,
the woman in the movie had said. Close your eyes and think of
England.

Sonny doesn't know what this is supposed to mean. If
Tupholme's were still open, he'd go there and ask. But the
store is closed and empty, and now the only movies Sonny gets
to watch are the ones on television, the ones with the exciting
commercials and the starving children for sale.

Wham-wham.

What if he had heard the woman wrong? What if she hadn't
said "England." Close your eyes and think of . . . what? What else
could you think of? What rhymes with "eyes"? Sonny runs up
and down the alphabet.

"Lies"? No. But "guys" would work. So would "pies."

"Thighs."

Wham-wham, hammer-hammer.

Okay, all done. No more rhyming.

Sonny takes everything out of the trunk and arranges it on the table. There are several books with strange writing. There are tools, some of which Sonny recognizes. There are bottles of leaves and powders. And there are photographs. Photographs in a plastic bag.

No gold. No frankincense. No myrrh.

Sonny enjoys photographs. He's always wanted a photograph of himself with Dad. The two of them. Together.

Wham-wham.

The photographs in the trunk are of a family of six. They aren't smiling, but they look happy, and as Sonny holds a picture up to the light, he recognizes one of the girls. It's the same girl he had seen in town.

The Indian girl in the alley.

Now Sonny understands. This is an Indian trunk. The markings on the trunk are Indian markings. Indian drum. Indian trunk. Yes, Sonny tells himself, now it all makes sense. The Indian girl has lost her drum and her trunk. That's why she's wandering about town. Trying to find her misplaced items.

That's what happened to the jacket the old guy was wearing.

Okay, okay. How many times has Dad said, Let us not grow weary of doing good. And what could be doing good any better than returning the trunk to the girl? Dad has been very clear about the restoration of sheep and coins, and Sonny is sure that trunks are covered as well.

Sonny puts everything back into the trunk. He is especially careful with the photographs, which look old and fragile. Sonny shuts the lid and locks it with the iron pin. He wishes that he hadn't given the drum to the Indian woman in the yellow house, but perhaps she and the girl are related.

Sonny hoists the trunk on his shoulder and heads off to do the first truly good deed that he's done in a very long time.

"Fries."

That's what the woman was trying to say. Close your eyes and think of fries.

28

WHEN GABRIEL WOKE AND LOOKED OVER THE RIM OF THE hole, the tide was still trying to push waves up the beach. But there was little danger that they would reach him. At least not today.

Maybe tomorrow.

The sand in the hole was warm. Gabriel tried to shift his weight and discovered that he couldn't feel his legs. Not a serious issue since he had no particular reason to stand up. He had nowhere to go. He might spend the night if he felt like it.

He heard the footfalls and the voice at the same time.

"Not something you see every day."

Gabriel turned his head to the sound and found he was looking at running shoes. Vivid blue shoes with sharp red lines and yellow laces.

Mara squatted down next to the hole. "Are you trying to kill yourself, again?"

"It's comfortable. The sand is warm."

"The hot springs run underground throughout the area."

"But I don't think I can stand up."

"Would you like some assistance?"

Gabriel's legs weren't simply asleep. They were dead. He had lost all feeling from the waist down.

Mara grabbed his hands and leaned back. "You're going to have to help."

"I am helping."

"You're going to have to help more."

In the end, Gabriel had to brace his shoulders against the sides of the hole and wedge himself out with his elbows. He remembered watching a gymnast do a similar routine on the parallel bars.

The guy had won a bronze medal.

Gabriel rolled over on the sand and waited for his legs to come back to life.

"That was an impressive imitation of a crippled seal."

The blood was finding its way home. The sensation was electric. Gabriel clamped his teeth together and tried to keep from screaming.

"Okay," said Mara, "what were you doing in that hole?"

"Are you hungry?" asked Gabriel. "I'm really hungry."

DURING his second year at Stanford, Gabriel found himself in a required class on the ethics of science. The professor, Dr. Eugene Harden, was a tall, skinny man, with a storm of white hair and a baritone voice that filled the lecture hall like summer thunder. His clothes were too large for his frame, and they rattled as he stalked the floor between the board and the lectern. More than anything, Harden reminded Gabriel of a scarecrow on loan from a cornfield.

That first day, Harden had gone directly to the board and had written "BRUNO."

"Class dismissed," he announced when he had finished. "Come back when you know more than you do now."

And he gathered up his jacket and his briefcase and left.

The class had sat there for a while, thinking that this was one of those jokes professors liked to play on unsuspecting students. Gabriel was sure the man would burst through the door at any moment and continue with the class.

But Harden hadn't reappeared. And after twenty minutes of sitting and fidgeting nervously, the class broke into parts and slipped away.

That night, Gabriel had stayed in the library until it closed.

GABRIEL stood on Mara's porch and tried to decide between the wicker sofa and the wicker chair.

"Try the chair," Mara shouted from the kitchen. "It should be more comfortable than your hole."

The wind was off the water, soft and warm. Not warm perhaps, but not cold. He sat back and tried to relax, but he found himself wanting to take out his marker and write "Aral Sea" on the railing.

"You want coffee."

"Sure."

His pants were damp. He had brushed the sand off as best he could, but he knew that the finer particles were still embedded in the cloth. When he got up, he'd try to remember to clean the cushion.

"I've got coffee. And muffins."

"Sounds wonderful."

"I wasn't expecting company."

"I wasn't expecting to be company."

Mara put the mug on the small table.

"This is a nice house."

"It's temporary," said Mara, curling up on the sofa. "Until I can move back to the reserve."

"The reserve."

Mara swirled cream into her cup. "I may move back tomorrow."

"Tomorrow?"

"Why not? You see anyone stopping me?"

Gabriel took a bite of the muffin. It was dry and crusty at the edges with a peculiar taste that reminded him of old clothes left too long in a hamper. He wondered if a quick turn in a microwave with some butter would help.

"Delicious," he said.

"My mother and grandmother were the cooks," said Mara. "My job was to eat."

Gabriel could see an easel through the living room window. "So, you're an artist?"

"No," said Mara. "I'm a nurse."

"A nurse?"

"Family joke."

The muffin had been sitting in a refrigerator for a while. Gabriel could make out the lingering trace of onion along with something else, something mouldy.

Mara cupped her coffee in her hands and leaned forward. "So," she said, "what is it exactly that you do."

Gabriel put the muffin on the plate and licked his fingers. "Worlds," he said. "I destroy worlds."

~~~~~

THE second day the class met, Harden strode into the room and wrote "BRUNO" on the board once again. Then he pulled out the class list.

"Hume, D."

"Here," said a student in the back row.

"'Here' is not the answer," boomed Harden. "Locke, J."

"Not sure what you want," said a young woman a few rows in front of Gabriel.

"That's painfully evident," said Harden. "Quinn, G."

Gabriel took a deep breath and held it for a moment.

"Well?"

"Giordano Bruno," Gabriel had begun. "He was an Italian monk who was sentenced to death and burned at the stake in 1600."

"Why?"

"He believed in science."

"Do you believe in science, Mr. Quinn?"

"Yes."

"That's reassuring," said Harden, and he wrote "Katheryn Kousoulas" on the board. "Next week," he said, "Mr. Quinn will lead the discussion."

MARA put her lips to the rim of the cup and blew across the coffee. "And they pay you for that?"

"They did."

Mara stretched out on the porch sofa, assuming the pose she had seen in any number of preposterously romantic paintings.

A Modern Olympia.

Nude Looking over Her Right Shoulder.

Female Nude Reclining on a Divan.

Nude Woman Reclining.

She even slipped a cushion under her side so that one hip was thrust into the air. Like a muffin.

Cézanne, Modigliani, Delacroix, Van Gogh. The masters and their muffins.

"Were you any good?"

"What?"

"At your job."

Gabriel took another bite of the muffin. Definitely onion.

"What about sex?"

Gabriel stopped eating. "Sex?"

"Do you have any interest in sex?" Mara removed the pillow and lowered her hip. "In general."

Gabriel took a sip of coffee. "For . . . procreation?"

Mara waved him off. "No, for comfort. For pleasure."

"You mean . . . for the hell of it?"

"Yes," she said. "For the hell of it."

GABRIEL spent several long evenings at the library, locating the reference, copying the salient details, and organizing the information into a series of points that he put on a transparency. That morning, when he arrived in the classroom, Harden had waved him to the lectern, marched up the steps to the back of the lecture hall, and sat down in the last row.

"Begin!" he barked.

Gabriel was surprisingly calm as he put the plastic sheet on the overhead projector. He was confident that Harden couldn't ask him a question about the incident that he couldn't answer.

Dr. Katheryn Kousoulas was a neurologist and research fellow at University Hospital in Tucson, Arizona.

In 1961, the pharmaceutical giant Bush International contracted with the university to conduct clinical trials for a new drug called Lucror, which would, according to the company, revolutionize the treatment of migraines.

Kousoulas led the study. Halfway through the trials, she discovered that, while Lucror was remarkably effective in the control of migraine pain and nausea, the medication also appeared to trigger gliomas in the brain stem.

"For whom did Kousoulas work?" Harden called out from his aerie.

"The university."

"Did she have a contract with Bush International?"

"She did."

"Did that contract have a non-disclosure clause?"

"It did."

"So," said Harden, raising his voice so that it filled the room, "what did Dr. Kousoulas do?"

"She shut down the trials and informed her patients of the potential risk."

"In violation of her contract with Bush."

"I suppose."

"Don't be supposing, Mr. Quinn. There's no need for that."

"Technically, she was in violation of the non-disclosure clause," Gabriel said. "But it was the ethical decision."

Harden leapt out of his seat and marched down the aisle. "Was it indeed?"

Gabriel held his ground. "It was. There were other drug groups available to treat migraines. Triptans, opioids, gluco-corticoids."

"But none of them as effective as Lucror."

"The side effects were unacceptable."

"To whom?"

The question had caught him by surprise. "What?"

"Sit down, Mr. Quinn," Harden said. "We have a great deal to cover in the semester."

THE MASTERS AND THEIR MUFFINS.

Now there was a title for a painting. Mara thought about the women artists whose work she knew and how they handled the same subject matter in their work. Romaine Brooks's *La Marquise Casati* came to mind, her defiant nude, thin as a knife. Or Gwen John's melancholic portrait of her friend Fenella Lovell. And Frida Kahlo's disturbing *The Broken Column* or her *Henry Ford Hospital*.

"I'm not asking you to take me to bed."

"Okay."

God, why had she said that. Take me to bed? As though she couldn't get there on her own.

"Let's start again."

Gabriel nodded. "Okay."

"I was just curious if someone who is trying to commit suicide has any interest in sex," said Mara.

Gabriel picked up the muffin and held it out like a shield. "I hadn't thought about it."

"You don't have to tell me."

"No. I hadn't thought of it."

"Well then," said Mara, sitting up straight. "I suppose that's the answer."

29

DORIAN SAT ON THE EXAMINATION TABLE, HIS LEGS DAN-
gling over the side, and thumbed through the latest issue of
Sports Illustrated. There was a story on football stars and their
salaries, but as he read the article, he discovered that the football under discussion was actually soccer.

The top salary belonged to some teenager who reportedly
received over €44 million a year in salary and bonuses. On top
of that, the kid made another €20 million in endorsements.
Dorian didn't know the exchange rate off the top of his head, but
anyone who got that kind of money for kicking a ball around a
field was paid too much.

And what the hell did this child do with his money? Dorian
had heard stories of athletes who blew their windfalls on high-
ticket items. Houses, jewellery, cars, designer clothes, and
drugs. One guy had gone to Las Vegas, and, in one evening,
dropped over half a million on the tables.

Stupid.

A little restraint. Some intelligent investment. Most people
couldn't imagine spending that kind of money in a lifetime.

Dorian was just starting an article on the ten greatest Super
Bowl scandals, when there was a knock on the door.

"Decent?" Dr. Benjamin Toshi slipped into the room, a folder in his hand. "How are you feeling?"

"Great."

Toshi wheeled a stool to the table. "Nausea?"

"Minor."

"Headaches? Dizziness? Ringing in the ears?"

"Nothing I can't manage."

"Any changes in mood? Any emotional distress?"

"Nope."

"Okay," said Toshi. "Let's take a look."

It was the same routine. Blood tests, poking and prodding, the promise to get together at the club. This time, Toshi was slower and more thorough.

"I think we need an MRI."

"I hate those things."

"I know, but we want to see what's going on."

"We had an MRI six months ago."

"We did, but we need to do it again," said Toshi. "And as soon as possible."

Dorian had never been fond of the royal plural, especially when it came to medical chit-chat. "And by 'we,' you mean me."

"Doctor's privilege." Toshi wrote out a prescription. "And let's give this a try. It's an older drug, but it might prove effective."

Dorian gestured at the folder. "Something wrong?"

Toshi shook his head. "Some elevated levels. Probably nothing, but you want me to be thorough."

"I do, do I?"

Toshi stood. "Yes," he said. "You do."

~~~~~

DORIAN took the *Sports Illustrated* issue with him, and he settled into the back seat of the limo with the Super Bowl article. The number one Super Bowl scandal, it turned out, was the 2004 Janet Jackson halftime show. Evidently another singer had pulled part of Jackson's costume off, revealing a partially cloaked breast. The incident had set off a fury of viewer outrage. Jackson was admonished. The network was fined.

A breast.

World hunger can't make the back page of *TV Guide*, but an almost bare breast can destroy the morality of a nation. Dorian shook his head. No wonder democracy and Christianity had been such failures.

So Toshi knew. He hadn't told the good doctor that the nausea and the dizziness had gotten worse. That would have just opened the door to even more tests, and, before he could stop it, Toshi would have him in a hospital bed, flat on his back.

Dorian stuffed the magazine into the seat pocket and leaned forward. "Have you driven me before?"

"I have."

"It's Thomas, isn't it?"

"Kip, sir."

Kip? What the hell kind of name was Kip? What parent in their right mind would call a child Kip?

"Do you know Rosen's? On Bloor?"

"A very fine men's store," said Kip.

Kip. Kipper. Kippy.

"I'd like to stop there."

Toshi had found something, but the cautious son of a bitch wanted to wait for the MRI to confirm it. A benign tumour?

An aneurysm? Some nasty brand of cancer? Who the hell did Toshi think he was dealing with? Some mattress salesman? A limo driver named Kippy? A dime-a-dozen rock star with an unfettered breast?

"Are you all right?"

"What?"

"You were shouting."

Shouting? Was he? Not good. His skin felt as though it was on fire. Not good at all.

"You were driving too fast."

"Very sorry, sir."

The rage had passed. Now he was exhausted, raw and bruised, as though he had been in a fight. He put his hand to his forehead and discovered that he was sweating again.

DORIAN was surprised to find Robert waiting for him when he arrived at the store.

"A gentleman named Kip called to say that you were on your way."

"Just a quick visit," said Dorian. "I don't need anything."

"If need was all I sold," said Robert, as they took the escalator to the second floor, "I'd be out of a job."

Rosen's had been extensively remodelled, and Dorian still wasn't sure if he liked the new interior. Marble floors with dark wood borders, nickel-plated suit racks, and steel and bamboo tables. "Professional" is how Robert had described it. Dorian would have thought "austere" or "sleek" to be the better choice of words.

There was a small but elegant cappuccino bar near the escalator. Dorian helped himself to one of the polished wood stools.

"How have you been?"

"Fine."

"And Mrs. Asher?"

"In Orlando."

"Florida," said Robert. "Many of our clients go there in the winter."

"I don't see the attraction," said Dorian.

"Nor I," said Robert, "but someone has to go."

Florida. Dorian was sorry that the subject had popped up. They weren't buying a home in that state, no matter how many luxury houses the real estate industry threw at them. Why was Olivia wasting her time?

"We've just received some new Brioni ties," said Robert. "Enjoy the cappuccino, and I'll bring a few over that I think you might like."

Dorian left his drink at the bar and wandered through the suits. Zegna, Brioni, Kiton, Canali, Ford, Valentino, Kos. They were all here.

Dorian looked at a dark blue Zegna and an olive Brioni, but there was no excitement in either. There was more to see, of course. Shirts, shoes, belts, sweaters. Instead, he wandered back to the bar and finished his drink.

He was dying. That was it. Toshi didn't need to see another MRI. He was just going through the motions. Doctors were probably taught this kind of crap at medical school. If a patient is dying, don't tell him he's dying. That could depress him, and depression will only worsen his condition.

It could even lead to suicide.

Tell him that further tests are needed. And when the tests come back, talk to him about the various options that he could pursue, and the new treatments that are being developed every day, and how a positive attitude is the best medicine.

Fuck!

Fuck, fuck, fuck!

"They're not that bad," said Robert, smiling.

"What?"

"The ties."

"Did I say . . . something?"

"You did." Robert had three ties on a black velvet tray. "But as luck would have it, we have the floor to ourselves."

"My apologies."

"Nonsense," said Robert. "We have pressures. That's why we shop."

"I'll take the gold one."

"That would have been my choice as well. Is there anything else I can help you with today?"

Maybe the new interior wasn't so bad. It was bright. It was clean. It was unemotional. Perhaps the idea was to create a space that would take nothing away from the clothes.

"I have a friend who is dying."

"I'm so sorry," said Robert.

A young man stepped off the escalator. He looked familiar. Television. A comedy series or a news program.

"And I was wondering," said Dorian, as he watched the man head back to the Armani room, "what you would suggest I might buy for him to raise his spirits."

30

IT'S A SONNY DAY IN THE NEIGHBOURHOOD.

Sonny likes to sing, especially when he is on the beach. Or in the shower.

It's a Sonny day in the neighbourhood.

The day is warm, the sand is soft, the ocean waves go lap, lap, lap. The trunk isn't very heavy, but Sonny switches it from one shoulder to the other and then back again on every third verse.

It's a Sonny day in the neighbourhood.

As Sonny walks the beach, he tries to think up a plan. Sonny finds thinking up plans quite challenging, in the same way that getting the right answer on tests or remembering rules is difficult. Walking on the beach helps him think, and right now he needs all the help that he can get.

Sonny starts just below the motel and walks towards the river in time with the waves.

Lap, lap, lap.

Step, step, step.

In the good days, Sonny would walk the turtles up the beach as they came out of the ocean.

Step, step, step.

And when the babies hatched, he would walk them into the sea.

Lap, lap, lap.

It's a Sonny day in the neighbourhood.

Those were the days of miracles and wonder. The babies would break out of the sand and run for the water.

But where were the mothers?

Wham-wham.

Why weren't the mother turtles there when their children needed them, for as soon as the hatchlings were loosed upon the beach, the birds would fall upon them like lions to lambs.

Wham-wham, hammer-hammer.

Mayzie-bird mothers.

But not Sonny. Sonny is faithful, one hundred percent.

In the days before That One Bad Day, Sonny would strap on his tool belt. He would find a long stick. And with his hammer and his staff, he would protect his flock.

Wham-wham.

Hammer-hammer.

Just like in the stories that Dad tells.

Sonny misses walking the turtles up the beach. He misses protecting the babies. If he were a baby turtle, he is sure that he would want to be protected.

Who will protect Sonny?

Sonny shouts this at the wind and the water. He shouts this at the sand and the bleached turtle shells.

Who will protect Sonny?

Sonny is shifting the trunk from one shoulder to the other when he sees something in the sand. What is this? What is this on Sonny's beach? Sonny puts the trunk down and moves forward cautiously.

A hole?

A hole on Sonny's beach?

Wham-wham!

Sonny can hardly contain his excitement. There have been holes on his beach before. In the good days, tourist children and tourist dogs used to dig holes on Sonny's beach. But this hole is different. This hole is larger. This hole is deeper.

So, who has dug this hole? All the tourist children are gone. All the tourist dogs have fled.

As Sonny walks around the hole, he realizes that here is the perfect answer to his perfect plan, and he knows that if he had thought of it earlier, he would have dug the hole himself.

Hammer-hammer.

Sonny steps into the hole and sits down. Perfect. A perfect hole for Sonny. Deep enough, but not too deep. Wide enough, but not too wide. Long enough, but not too long.

Sonny reaches up and drags the trunk across the opening of the hole so that it blots out the light.

The perfect plan.

Now all he has to do is wait.

31

BY THE TIME GABRIEL GOT BACK TO THE TRAILER, HE WAS starving. And somewhat shaken. Had Mara asked him to have sex with her? He tried to replay the conversation, but the only thing that he could recall with clarity was the muffin.

He grabbed the cereal from the cupboard, milk and peaches from the refrigerator, a banana off the counter, and some raisins out of the bag, and dumped everything into a bowl. Ham and eggs would have been the better choice, something with protein, but what was needed right now was speed.

He had handled the moment poorly. "For procreation?" Had he actually said that? Mara had asked him if he was interested in sex, and he had said, "For procreation?"

Gabriel swallowed the bowl whole and set it to one side.

"Yes," he should have said, "I could be interested in sex." And why not. From a strictly pragmatic perspective, sex was just another activity. Like jogging with a friend. Or walking along the beach with a stranger you happened to meet.

And given his current plans, there wouldn't be the need for awkward conversations around commitment.

~~~~~

GABRIEL had given up on most forms of intimacy long ago, had replaced them with research. Even before his father had been killed, Gabriel had been at one remove from his family, one remove from the world. He had loved his father and his mother. Especially his sister. He simply didn't feel as though he was a part of their lives.

Nor they a part of his.

His world was a world of facts, of equations, of numbers. His family's world was made up of connections and emotions.

GABRIEL was still hungry. He didn't want another bowl of cereal, and there was little else in the refrigerator that could be turned into a quick meal. A lone chicken thigh was hiding in the crisper, but he wanted to save that for later. Nothing in the freezer besides ice cubes and frozen fish.

Now, there was a disgusting thought. A fish-sicle. Not even Soldier would go for that.

Speaking of the dog, where had he gone? Not that Gabriel had a hold on the animal. They weren't friends particularly. Acquaintances. That's what they were. Still, it would have been nice to have someone with whom he could talk.

And what about the sea people? Gabriel hadn't thought of them much since that morning on the Apostles. The young girl he had pulled from the sea. The men and women who had followed. What had happened to them?

The sea people.

Except they weren't. In the world of applied physics, such a thing was impossible. One human being didn't sing other human beings up out of water. Their appearance in the high tide was unexpected, but there was a scientific answer for every anomaly.

Stories were stories. They were not the laws of the universe.

Soldier and the sea people. Maybe they had found each other.

WHEN his sister was nine or ten, she came home and told the family that she had a boyfriend. Joe told his daughter that if she couldn't have a pet, she sure as hell couldn't have a boyfriend. Gabriel remembered the tears, the screaming, the slammed doors. Later that evening, he had gone to his sister's bedroom to offer some comfort.

There were more boys in the world than girls, Gabriel told her, so statistically she had nothing to worry about. He even drew a diagram to show that this particular boy had little chance of being the perfect boy for her.

He had spent some time thinking through the logic and double-checking the math, and had not been prepared for her reaction.

"It's not about math," his father told him.

"She's a young girl," said his mother. "You're not going to find a formula for that."

Two weeks later, his sister announced that she had a new boyfriend. After boyfriends three and four, Gabriel stopped trying to keep count, and he never mentioned probability theory to his sister again.

~~~~~

GABRIEL was seriously considering defrosting the fish, when he remembered that tonight was the party. Crisp's birthday party. At the hot springs. Crisp would have food. He was too conscientious a host not to feed his guests.

Gabriel shoved the fish back into the freezer.

Why did everyone put so much stock in relationships? People were like the universe. Expanding. That was the human condition. Moving away. Babies moved away from mothers. Children moved away from their parents. Lovers moved away from each other. The dying moved away from the living.

At the end, like a failing star, you collapsed into yourself and disappeared.

Gabriel shut the refrigerator door. He tried to think whether he had anything to wear that resembled a swimsuit. Stretchy black underwear might work. Once he was in the water, no one would notice.

Sex with Mara. He'd have to think about that.

In case she bothered to ask again.

32

WHAT THE HELL WAS SHE THINKING?

Mara stood at her easel and worked the paint onto the canvas with a palette knife. The technique was harder and bolder than using a brush, but the effect fit her mood.

"Do you have any interest in sex?"

Had she really said that? It wasn't what she had meant to say. She didn't want to have sex with anyone. Sex in general? For comfort? For pleasure?

Sex for the hell of it?

That's what she had said. Sex for the hell of it.

Mara loaded the knife and pressed it against the canvas with enough force to draw blood.

SHE and Lilly had spent countless hours talking about boys and sex. Lilly was the bolder of the two, and one afternoon, she had shown Mara a men's magazine she had rescued from a trash can at school.

"I saw Eddie ditch it just before Mr. Pratt went through his locker. "It's all in Spanish."

Mara had never seen so many men and women with their clothes off. And not just with their clothes off.

"That is gross."

"Yeah," said Lilly. "It is."

It was also fascinating, even a little erotic. Especially the stills of the couples.

"She looks like Cindy."

"Cindy's heavier."

"Sure," said Lilly. "But take off fifteen pounds, and it's Cindy."

The initial flush didn't last very long. As Lilly flipped through the photographs, as everything ran together in a repetitious assembly line of body parts, Mara began to feel bored. Before long she and Lilly were howling with laughter, as yet another couple appeared on the page in a more complicated position than the last.

"Eight and a half," Lilly would shout.

"Not good enough for a medal."

And then the comedy gave way to unease and, from there, to repugnance and revulsion. Is that what she and Lilly were going to look like under the bodies of men?

"You think guys are going to want us to do that?"

"I guess," said Lilly. "Looks really gross."

Mara wanted to ask Eddie or Leo or any of the boys at school if this is how they imagined women, how they imagined sex, but she knew if she or Lilly let slip that they had looked at the magazine, there would be no end to the trouble.

After the encounter with the magazine, Mara and Lilly made a pact that they would never do any of that stuff. It was an idle promise, of course, but in all the years as an adult, whenever she had sex, Mara couldn't help but remember those images and wonder if that was who she became every time she took off her clothes.

MARA stepped back from the painting. It wasn't finished. But it was done. She had never considered any of her paintings finished. There were always changes that could be made. What Mara looked for was a place where she could stop, the moment when, for the first time, a painting held its own.

She had liked that about art, the notion that nothing was ever done, that art was fluid and continuously full of potential.

She set the painting against the wall and put a fresh canvas on the easel. Mara was pleased to have hit upon this project. She could already feel her creative energies returning. Maybe that was it. She hadn't asked Gabriel about sex. She had asked him about life.

"Are you interested in life?"

That's what she should have said. That's what she meant to say. Are you interested in life?

Mara stared at the canvas, trying to decide who to do next. Mrs. Rice probably. Edna and her son had lived next door, had been mainstays in the community. Maybe that was Gabriel's problem. Maybe he didn't have a community, didn't have anyone to anchor him to life. People weren't single, autonomous entities. They were part of a larger organism. When her mother and grandmother were alive, Mara had flourished. Now that they were dead, she was diminished.

Living was a process of losing parts of yourself. That couldn't be helped. But the hope was that, in the end, you'd still have pieces left, that you wouldn't die alone, that you'd have family and friends at your side to see you off.

But what if you lost everything? What if you lost everyone? Mara had come home to that reality.

You could start again. Mara had told herself that any number of times. You could move forward, find new opportunities, cultivate new relationships.

If you wanted to.

That's what she had meant to ask this Gabriel. Not whether he was interested in sex, but whether he was interested in new possibilities, whether he was interested in living. She had just phrased it badly, and she wasn't sure he was smart enough to figure that out.

If there was a next time, she'd be more explicit.

33

ROSEN'S HADN'T BEEN ENOUGH.

Even after he left the store, Dorian could still taste Toshi's office in his mouth. He should have returned to Domidion. He had more than enough work. Instead he walked up and down Bloor Street, touring the other high-end shops and adding some twelve thousand dollars to his credit card.

It hadn't been difficult. Along with the Brioni tie, he had found a pair of Ferragamo shoes, a couple of Eton shirts, a bottle of cologne, and a Rolex Milgauss. The Glace Verte model with its distinctive green-tinted sapphire crystal, orange lightning-bolt second hand, and black face. In the world of fine watches, the Rolex wasn't an expensive piece. A Jaeger or a Patek would have made a larger dent in his expense account— and he had seen a very nice Jaeger—but he liked the casual look of the Milgauss.

The watch was the perfect sports accessory for a winter getaway, and he was looking forward to wearing it the next time he and Olivia went to Bali or Monaco.

He had taken his time with each purchase, allowing the salespeople to confirm the value of quality and the pleasures of status. But none of it had cheered him. Twelve thousand dollars, and he was still depressed.

Maybe he hadn't spent enough.

WINTER Lee was waiting for him in the garage. Dorian had hoped to have a quiet and uneventful afternoon, but seeing Winter standing in front of the executive elevators put an end to that.

"Good news would be appreciated."

"I'm sure it would," said Winter.

Dorian inserted his card in the slot and pressed the button for the fourth level. "All right, then, the bad news."

"Manisha Khan," said Winter.

Dorian frowned. "Khan?"

"The broadcaster. *En Garde.*"

Dorian waited.

"She called looking for a comment on a story that will air this evening."

"What story?"

"The Athabasca," said Winter. "There's been a new development."

They rode the rest of the way in silence, and neither spoke again until they reached Dorian's office.

"PAM environment." Dorian hit the Enter key harder than was necessary. He waited for the electronic-voice confirmation, and then he turned to Winter. "A new development?"

"There's a problem with our holding pond."

"The one that we thought might be leaking?"

"Evidently," said Winter, "it is leaking."

"Are we still pumping water into the pond to keep the level up?"

"We are. But the levels are continuing to drop."

"And Khan knows this?"

"Yes, sir," said Winter. "We believe she does."

DORIAN tried to remember if the Jaeger Reverso had been $23,000 or $24,000. It was a handsome piece of craftsmanship. A rose-gold case and band, with reversing black and white etched faces.

The salesperson had been a woman. Arlene. And she had insisted that Dorian try on both the Rolex and the Jaeger. They were two completely different watches, she had explained. The Rolex Milgauss was a functional piece, like driving a Mercedes E-Class, while the Jaeger Reverso was akin to sitting behind the wheel of a Maserati.

"It's not about money," Arlene assured him, "but how you feel about yourself."

Given the way his day had gone so far, Dorian wasn't sure that was the question to ask.

"Are you a Rolex or a Jaeger?"

"Right now," said Dorian with a smile. "I'm feeling like a Citizen."

Arlene had a good laugh about that, and Dorian obliged her by trying on the two watches again. They're exquisite, she told him, and the intelligent decision might be to buy both.

DORIAN rubbed his head harder, pinching his temples with his thumb and fingers. The nausea was back. So was the dizziness.

"No comment for Khan. She's fishing."

Winter nodded. "She also asked after Dr. Quinn."

"Are we any closer to finding Q?"

"Mother and sister are no longer in Lethbridge."

"And the father?"

"Shot and killed in the line of duty."

Dorian frowned and waited for Winter to finish the sentence.

"In Minneapolis," said Winter. "The transcript of the trial is on your desk. I believe you'll find it interesting."

"So the family is in Lethbridge. Then the father and son go to Minneapolis. The father is killed, and Dr. Quinn . . . ?"

"Stays at the University of Minnesota. And then he goes to Stanford."

"He doesn't go back to Lethbridge?"

How could anyone get so far into life so unmarked, so unattended? No wife. No children. No rumour of friends. There was not even a name on the "next of kin" portion of the original employment contract. Had Dorian ever had Quinn over for dinner? Had he ever invited the man to the club for a round of golf? Dorian seemed to recall that Quinn had been with him on that fishing junket to Key West. Or had that been the weasel from the Prime Minister's Office?

Dorian put more pressure on his temples. "I find that strange. Do you find that strange?"

"That he doesn't go home?"

"Yes."

"He may have gone home," said Winter. "At this point, we don't know."

The writing was disturbing. Dorian could think of no easy explanation for why Quinn would write on the walls of his house, other than the obvious.

Which raised the question.

How had a mentally unbalanced scientist been allowed to work with some of the world's most deadly pathogens?

Dorian gave up the rubbing and began whacking his head with his hand. "The family is our best lead."

"Are you all right, sir?"

Dorian hit himself again. The pummelling seemed to help him focus. "Find the mother and sister," he said. "Find the mother and sister, and we find Q."

DORIAN spent the rest of the day reading through the trial transcript. Not the bits and pieces of legal debris that littered the document, but the basic plot of the case. At five-thirty, he put it aside and called for the limo. Enough was enough. Time for a quiet dinner and a good night's sleep. Everything would look better in the morning. It always did. As he waited at the elevator that would take him to the garage, Dorian wondered what Toshi hadn't told him. And, now that he had had time to think about it, he realized that Arlene had been right.

He should have bought the Jaeger as well.

34

SONNY SITS IN HIS HOLE AND WAITS.

Wait. Wait. Wait.

Sonny likes his hole. It's dark and quiet, and, when Sonny is in his hole, he is at peace. There's nothing to do. There's nothing to think about. There's nowhere to be.

Sonny wonders if this is how baby turtles feel. At peace. Sonny wonders if baby turtles ever think about staying in the sand and never coming out. Outside are the birds and the ocean and the things with teeth in the ocean. In the sand, the turtles are safe.

Why do they come out?

Sonny tries to think of the reasons he would come out of his hole.

One, he'd have to come out to eat. Two, he'd have to come out to go to the bathroom. Three, he'd have to come out to clean the pool and to empty the coin box in the EverFresh vending machine. Four, he'd have to come out to watch his favourite television shows.

If Sonny were a turtle, he wouldn't have to worry about three and four.

Eating is the answer. Whether he is a turtle or whether he is a Sonny, he'd have to eat. That's why the babies leave their perfect world.

Food.

Wham-wham, hammer-hammer!

Sonny is all tingly from getting the answer right, and he imagines how much fun it would be to burst onto the beach with the baby turtles.

But there are no baby turtles. Not anymore.

Sonny sits in the hole and thinks of fries. Fries and a toasted cheese sandwich.

Wham.

Sonny can feel the day drifting by. How long has Sonny been in the hole? How long will he have to wait? Be patient, Sonny tells himself. Be patient in tribulation. Dad has told him this numerous times. Have patience with all things. Dad has said this, too.

Sonny reaches up and begins tapping out the Indian song on the bottom of the box.

"From the land of sky-blue waters . . . "

Sonny is about to swing into the chorus when the box moves. Sonny stops tapping and singing.

Patience.

The box moves again.

Patience.

And then the chest is pulled away from the top of the hole, and now, where there was darkness, there is light. Too much light. Very bright light. Sonny stays in the hole and waits for his eyes to adjust.

Patience.

Sonny wonders if baby turtles think about patience as they scamper to the sea.

Sonny's eyes have adjusted now, and as he looks out, he sees the Indian girl with the old guy's power jacket, standing at the edge of his hole.

Along with the dog.

The girl is holding the box, and she looks surprised to see Sonny.

The dog looks surprised, too.

Hello, says Sonny. I'm Sonny.

The girl doesn't say anything, but Sonny knows that some-times when people are surprised, they become speechless.

Welcome home, says Sonny. Welcome home.

As Sonny is trying to think of something else to say, the dog jumps into the hole and begins to lick Sonny's face. At first, Sonny isn't sure how he feels about being licked by a dog, but the dog's tongue is soft and warm.

Nice doggy.

Sonny tries to remember the last time someone touched his face. Dad doesn't believe in touching. Dad believes in rules. Sonny can't remember any rule against touching, but neither can he remember one that encourages it.

Thou shalt touch. Thou shalt not touch.

The dog's tongue makes Sonny happy, and he begins to laugh, and the Indian girl with the Indian box begins laughing, too.

Wham-wham!

What a wonderful day. Sonny on the beach with friends.

But before Sonny can say anything, the light softens, and the fog begins moving in, and the Indian girl and the Indian box slowly disappear. The dog stops licking and jumps out of the hole, and, before Sonny can cry out and tell them not to go, they vanish in the mist.

And Sonny is alone.

Wham.

Where did she come from? Why didn't she speak? How could she disappear like that? Why did the dog follow her?

And then he understands. As Sonny sits in his hole, staring out at the fog, he has a revelation.

The girl is a ghost.

She's one of the Indians who died. A lost Indian. A sad ghost who is trying to find her way home. And the dog is her guide.

This is not what Sonny had asked for. He had wanted live Indians returning to the reserve. Sonny isn't sure what can be done with ghosts.

Still, it's a start.

Sonny stays in the hole. He wraps his arms around himself and sings as he rocks back and forth.

"Hamm's the beer refreshing . . . "

Patience.

Surely, the ghost girl and the dog will return. Surely, the naked guy who is trying to die will come along. Surely, the Indian woman from the yellow house will appear.

But no one comes.

Sonny. The first and the last.

In the beginning there was nothing. Just Sonny.

Okay. Enough patience. Sonny grabs the sides of the hole and pulls himself out of his nest. Now that he is standing, he realizes that he is hungry.

Hungry, hungry, hungry.

Wham-wham!

Dad has said that all good things come to those who wait, but Sonny isn't sure that Dad was talking about supper.

And then Sonny has a second revelation.

The hot springs.

As soon as Sonny thinks about the hot springs, he tries to put that temptation behind him, for Dad has been very specific about the clearing in the woods.

Go not into the lakes of fire.

Still, Dad would not want his only begotten son to starve. Sonny wonders if this is another of Dad's tests. He hasn't passed many, so he'd really like to pass this one. But he also needs to eat.

Ask and it shall be given.

Seek and you shall find.

Knock and the door will be opened to you.

Free will. Of course. Free will.

That's the answer he wants. That's the remedy he was hoping would come along. That's the beauty of Dad's rules. They forbid all and allow all.

At the same time.

"Free will," Sonny shouts at the incoming tide. "Free will."

And he hurries up the slope of the beach and into the trees.

35

NICHOLAS CRISP STOOD AT THE ENTRANCE TO BEATRICE HOT Springs and surveyed his handiwork. All of the decorations and festive arrangements were in place. Tiny lanterns swayed on wires above the water, towels of many hues were stacked at the edge of each pool, and soft music floated down from speakers hidden in the trees.

And the food. Crisp was particularly pleased with the array of things to eat and drink. Fruits, cheeses, vegetables with dip, hummus, baba ghanouj, cold cuts and condiments for the unadventurous, breads of several varieties, two soups, a vegetarian lasagna, a spicy meat chili, along with wine and beer, and lemon squares and chocolate brownies for dessert.

Crisp looked out over the pools, and he was pleased.

Yet in spite of all the delights, the merry-making would have a bittersweet edge to it, for many of the people who had come to his birthday party in years past would not be here tonight. In fact, Crisp wasn't sure who would come. When he had gone through town renewing his invitation, he had sensed a new level of defeat in the voices, as though his neighbours and friends had reduced themselves to prisoners in their homes and businesses, as though they no longer had the energy to walk the streets of Samaritan Bay.

Or the courage to wander the beaches or roam the woods.

Before he had gone to the motel, Crisp had been hopeful that he and Sonny could put the past behind them, that they could sit down and talk, forge a new beginning. He had expected that the trunk would provide the occasion and the moment for such a reunion. The boy did love his salvage.

Perhaps he should have called in advance and not just shown up out of the blue. Had he frightened Sonny with his sudden appearance?

Existence, Crisp reminded himself, was a game of Snakes and Ladders, where life twisted and turned with how you rode the dice and where you landed. Perhaps the boy would come tonight. Perhaps after the initial shock, Sonny would find curiosity more powerful than fear.

Crisp cocked his head. There were voices in the woods.

Excellent.

He clapped his hands, and the lanterns brightened. The fog had spread over the springs like a blanket, thick and cozy, and tucked itself around the trees. But Crisp wasn't concerned. When the time was right, he'd pull the gloom back to reveal the stars and the heavens in all their majesty and splendour, for the pleasure and entertainment of his guests.

36

GABRIEL FELT SOMEWHAT SILLY WALKING ALONG THE TRAIL
to the hot springs with a pair of black stretchy underwear
stuffed in his jacket pocket. Of course, he didn't have to get into
the pools. He could lounge around the edges, eating and making
polite conversation. He had even considered not coming, but
Crisp was an interesting character, and Gabriel had never been
in an actual hot springs.

The closest he had come to such an experience was at Stanford.
His third fall on campus, he had been invited to a party that the
head of the Physics department had thrown. Gloria Levinson was
a big name in biophysics, and she had a Spanish-style adobe in
Los Gatos with a swimming pool and a hot tub in the backyard.

At first, Gabriel could hardly stand the temperature of the
water, but Dr. Levinson's husband, a blockish man named
Parker with vacant blue eyes and wet lips, told him that if he
stayed long enough, he'd get used to it.

"Of course you know about frogs and hot water."

"That you can put them in a pot of cold water and heat the
water slowly until it's boiling, and the frogs won't try to get out?"

"Same thing is true of the poor," said Parker. "We don't need
scientists to tell us why this happens."

Dr. Levinson had come over. "Is my husband boring you?"

"No, ma'am," said Gabriel.

"He's a consultant," said Dr. Levinson. "Did he annoy you with his treatise on humanity?"

"It's not a treatise," said Parker. "It's a fact."

"All Parker believes in is power and wealth."

Parker's face was bright red, and his eyes had started to water. "They're one and the same," he said. "Wealth is simply an attribute of power."

Dr. Levinson shook her head and laughed. "Would you believe that my husband gets paid to travel the country and spew this nonsense?"

"Either you're the frog in the pot," said Parker as he sank deeper into the hot tub, "or you're the frog who controls the heat."

THE fog had come in hard and thick, and Gabriel had some difficulty staying to the path. Several times he found himself stumbling about in the undergrowth and had to feel his way back to level ground. He should have brought a flashlight, though he didn't think any amount of light would help.

As a child and as a young man, Gabriel had been in the woods any number of times, and what he remembered most was the noise. The night woods were noisy. Large animals moving around, the sharp cries of the night hunters, small things scratching in the earth.

These woods were especially dark and silent, and Gabriel felt as though he had wandered into an ancient church. He wasn't frightened. A little anxious perhaps, and as he shuffled along, he began to sing. He started with a flag song but couldn't find the lead, kept getting it mixed up with an honour song, so he switched to a round dance.

Which was more appropriate.

Tonight was a social, a two-step, a chance for people to get together and enjoy each other's company. Gabriel hadn't been company in a very long time. Maybe he'd finally get around to asking the questions that had brought him here. Maybe Crisp had the answers. He didn't want to ask Mara. He shouldn't care, but he didn't want her to know who he was. Not yet. Perhaps not ever.

GABRIEL had been standing by the food table, when Parker caught up with him. Out of the water, the man looked shorter and stouter.

"Hello, froggy," he said. "Gloria tells me you're a genius."

Gabriel kept his attention on the food, hoping that Parker would go away.

"So what do geniuses do?"

"Nothing special."

"Genetics and biology. Right?"

Gabriel took his food to a table at the far end of the pool. Parker followed him.

"Here's a question for you. Which would you rather discover? A revolutionary weight-loss product or a protocol to restore hair?"

Gabriel had held his disdain in check. "I'd rather work on something that matters."

"What matters is profit." Parker fished a card out of his pocket. "I recruit for major biotech companies. We have summer intern programs available for geniuses. Pay is good. Experience is even better. Cutting-edge research facilities, yada yada yada."

Suddenly, Parker didn't sound quite so stupid or arrogant.

"You interested?" Parker wrote on a napkin. "Check them out. That's my number."

Gabriel looked at the name on the napkin.

Domidion.

Parker picked up his plate and started back to the hot tub. "When you're ready to get out of the pot," he said, "give me a call."

UP ahead, the fog thinned. Gabriel could make out a clearing in the distance and the soft glow of lights. He was stepping along with the song now and enjoying himself. It had been a lifetime since he had been to a powwow. He didn't miss it. Particularly. It was just a memory that still had value, a memory that he hadn't discarded yet.

"That's a round dance."

Gabriel almost tripped over his feet.

Mara stepped out of the trees. "I recognize that one."

"You startled me."

Mara had changed out of blue jeans and into a dress. A green cotton print with yellow and white flowers. The result was start-ling. "So you decided to come to the party."

"I was hungry."

"I fed you."

"No, you didn't."

Mara chuckled. "My mother was the better cook."

"The muffin was fine."

"Liar."

"A little dry."

"Fine? Dry?" Mara put her hands on her hips. "Make up your mind."

Gabriel could feel himself smiling. "Dry," he said. "Definitely dry."

"Did you bring a swimsuit?"

Gabriel touched the pocket of his jacket. "No."

Mara started up the trail. "Neither did I."

Gabriel waited until she reached the clearing, and then he followed her into the light.

37

THE AFTERNOON HAD BEEN A FLURRY OF CREATIVE ENERGY. Mara had done the underpainting for four new canvases and had finished the preliminary sketches of Elvin Grunes and Thelma Walker. Thelma had been one of the elders on the reserve, a woman in her seventies who still spoke the language and divided her time between the women's shelter and the elementary school in town.

She had been at the river that day.

Elvin had saved over a dozen of his neighbours, piling everyone into his pickup and driving like hell to the hospital in Kimi, two hundred kilometres and three mountain passes away. He had accomplished this rescue on half a tank of gas, gliding down the hills in neutral with his foot off the accelerator and letting the truck run out across the flats before he got back on the gas.

Once he was sure everyone was safe, Elvin had filled the tank and raced back to the reserve.

Death hadn't played favourites that day or in the days that followed. No one could have imagined the loss of such a beloved woman or predicted the uncommon courage of an unemployed drunk.

The party. She had almost forgotten about the party.

"Shit!"

And now she was late. Mara dumped her brushes into the cleaner and wiped her hands on the cloth. What the hell was she going to wear? Jeans and a nice blouse. No, the only jeans she had were the ones she was wearing and her last good blouse was in the laundry basket. Okay, the dress, the green one with the flowers. She hadn't washed her hair in two days, though once she was in the pools, that wouldn't much matter.

Mara didn't want to stop working. Now that she had finally started, she hated to pause for even a moment. But it was Crisp's birthday, and a soak in the hot springs would do her a world of good. And, unless he had found a way to kill himself in the last while, this Gabriel would be there. Maybe they could amend their earlier conversation. She didn't want him to think that she was loose.

Or incoherent.

MARA had gotten more than one lecture on promiscuity. When her grandmother first cautioned her about "loose women," it had made Mara laugh, as though the answer was to tighten them up.

"Don't get me wrong," said her grandmother. "Sex is fun."

"Granny!"

"But it don't do you no favours. Just ask your mother."

So Mara did.

"She said what?"

"Granny said that sex is fun, but that it doesn't do women any favours, and that I should ask you about it."

Mara's mother didn't say a word for several minutes, and Mara wasn't sure that she was going to say anything at all.

"Okay," said her mother. "Listen up, cause I'm only going to do this once."

"Sure."

"If you're a guy and you have sex with a woman, you're a big shot." Her mother paused. "You got that part?"

"Yeah, I already know that."

"If you're a woman and you have sex with a man, you're a slut."

"Yeah," said Mara, "I know that, too."

"That's mostly for single women," said her mother. "If you're married, it can get worse."

Mara wanted to tell her mother just how out of date she was.

"And if you get pregnant and you're not married," said her mother, "well, that's the worst of all worlds."

"Like you."

"That's right," said her mother. "Like me."

"But you got me."

"Not the point," said her mother. "Now go back and bother your grandmother."

Mara was tempted to ask her mother about women having sex with women and men having sex with men, but she knew she wouldn't get as much pleasure out of annoying the woman as she imagined.

THE fog had returned, and as she started for the springs, she could barely see the trees. Some people found the gloom oppressive. But not Mara. Even as a child, she had taken comfort in the calm that the fog brought and its trick of making the world vanish.

Tonight was one of those times.

Halfway up the trail, she stopped. Somewhere off to the left in the woods, someone was singing. Mara stepped off the path. There was some stumbling, and suddenly Gabriel popped out of the fog.

"That's a round dance." Mara was delighted to see him jump. "I recognize that one."

"You startled me."

"So you decided to come to the party."

"I was hungry."

Mara tried not to think about the muffins. She had made them according to her mother's recipe. It wasn't the first time a dish hadn't turned out. Mara could follow the directions easily enough, but nothing seemed to taste as good as the food that came from her mother's hand.

"I fed you."

"No, you didn't."

That was at least the fourth time she had tried the muffin recipe. She wouldn't try it again.

"My mother was the better cook."

"The muffin was fine."

"Liar."

"A little dry."

Mara put her hands on her hips and blocked the path. "Fine? Dry?" she said. "Make up your mind."

Gabriel was smiling. Mara's mother had warned her about men who smiled. A little smile is okay, her mother had told her. Just watch out for the ones who are nothing but white teeth.

"Dry," said Gabriel. "Definitely dry."

"Did you bring a swimsuit?"

"No."

Mara wondered if he had forgotten to bring one or if he was just trying to shock her. She had seen him naked. Well, mostly naked. No mystery there. Still, the thought of skinny-dipping with this Gabriel was mildly arousing.

"Neither did I."

Mara headed up the trail. Let him stand there and think about it. He'd be along soon enough. Up ahead she could see the clearing, and she walked through the fog and into the light.

38

BEFORE HE LEFT THE OFFICE, DORIAN CHANGED INTO ONE OF his new shirts and slipped into his new shoes. He hadn't planned on wearing the Rolex just yet, but once it was on his wrist, it felt good. The purchase hadn't been a mistake.

The nausea and the dizziness had abated, and he was left feeling hungry and somewhat adventurous. There was a new restaurant in Yorkville that he had been meaning to try. He debated calling ahead for a reservation, but there was a chance he would be told they were full. Better to show up in person and negotiate a table.

It wasn't Kip this time. The limo driver was a larger man named Vernon, a more appropriate name for a chauffeur in Dorian's opinion, and he had Vernon drop him off in front of the restaurant.

"I hear the food is good," said Vernon.

Dorian wondered if chauffeurs were required to read restaurant reviews. "Stay close," he said. "I'll call when I'm ready."

The restaurant was busy. There were several vacant tables, but Dorian suspected that they were reserved.

"Do you have a reservation?"

"Dorian Asher," said Dorian.

The maître d' consulted the computer. "I don't seem to have a reservation for you, Mr. Asher."

"It might be under the corporation's name. Domidion? I'm the CEO?"

The maître d' went back to the computer. "Domidion," the man said. "Yes, I believe we will be able to offer you a table tonight."

The table wasn't the best in the house, but Dorian wasn't trying to impress anyone tonight. He scanned the room. No familiar faces, but it was somewhat early for the A-list to show up.

It wasn't until he looked at the menu that he wondered if he had made a mistake. The prices seemed rather low. Dorian watched as servers brought food to nearby tables. Everything was professionally plated. Good. All the parts artistically arranged. Excellent. One table that was about to move from the main course to dessert was being tidied up by a server with a silver crumber.

Dorian had always appreciated that particular touch of elegance. Very European.

It was only when the server came to his table to discuss the menu that Dorian realized he had been looking at the prices for the appetizers. After a brief discussion, he decided on the crispy black cod with organic shrimp, along with a bottle of Carneros della Notte Pinot Noir from California that was recommended as a perfect pairing with fish.

WINTER had been right. The trial transcript was interesting.

Joseph Quinn had been shot and killed by one William Church. Church was an unremarkable man, a manager at a local

Walmart. Gabriel's father and his partner, Rosa Martinez, had gone to Church's home on a domestic disturbance complaint. Quinn had knocked, announced himself as a police officer. Church had opened the door and shot him three times point-blank with a large calibre semi-automatic. Before Martinez could draw her weapon, Church shot her twice as well, once in the shoulder and once in the leg.

Quinn had died on the way to the hospital. Martinez had survived her wounds.

Church had been charged with murder. Martinez testified that the man had shot Quinn without provocation, had simply opened fire as soon as he saw the two officers.

Church's attorney argued that his client had fired in self-defence, that at the time of the shooting, the Walmart manager had feared for his life.

DESSERT was a hazelnut chocolate mousse with clotted cream. Dorian opted for a cup of coffee instead of a digestif. Halfway through the mousse, he saw Franklin and Lillian Wakefield being escorted to a table, and shortly after that, Reid Sloan came in with three other men Dorian didn't recognize.

He debated visiting Sloan's table, but he wasn't really in the mood for socializing, and the man tended to be a snob. Another time. When he was better dressed and more appropriately accessorized.

Instead, Dorian stayed at the table and lingered over his coffee. The food and the service had been excellent, and seeing other captains of industry in attendance made his choice of restaurant seem all that more astute. He'd have to bring Olivia here when she returned from Orlando.

ACCORDING to Church's testimony there had been an altercation at the Walmart where he worked. Church claimed that a Mr. Spencer Powless, whom he described as a "drunk Indian," had assaulted him and threatened his life.

DEFENCE: *What did Mr. Powless say?*
CHURCH: *I'm going to kill you, you white piece of shit.*
DEFENCE: *Were you frightened?*
CHURCH: *Absolutely.*
DEFENCE: *Did Mr. Powless say anything else?*
CHURCH: *He said he would find me and kill me.*
DEFENCE: *Had you injured this man in any way?*
CHURCH: *No.*

The prosecution had told a different story. According to several witnesses, Church had started yelling at Powless for no apparent reason.

PROSECUTION: *So Mr. Church started shouting at Mr. Powless?*
WITNESS: *He was angry.*
PROSECUTION: *What did he say?*
WITNESS: *He was yelling about how Indians were nothing but drunks and welfare bums.*
PROSECUTION: *What was Mr. Powless's response?*
WITNESS: *He told Mr. Church to go to hell.*

PROSECUTION: *Did you hear Mr. Powless threaten Mr. Church's life?*
WITNESS: *No.*

Ever since that day, so Church claimed, he had feared for his life. And when Officer Quinn and Officer Martinez arrived at his house, Church said he thought it was Mr. Powless and another Indian come to make good on the threat.

DEFENCE: *But Officer Martinez was a woman.*
CHURCH: *It was dark. She was dark.*
DEFENCE: *So you couldn't tell.*
CHURCH: *That's right. I couldn't tell.*

Throughout the trial, Church repeated the same phrase over and over again, that he was in fear for his life. Church's attorney had hammered home the fact that police uniforms were relatively easy to rent and that his client had no reason to believe that Officer Quinn and Officer Martinez were, in fact, police officers.

VERNON, the limo driver, wasn't answering his cell. Dorian tried several times. Then he called the service that Domidion used. The woman spoke with a heavy South Asian accent that Dorian found frustrating to follow. Evidently, someone had cancelled the car for the rest of the evening.

"Who cancelled my car?"

"Mr. Dorian Asher."

"I'm Dorian Asher."

"You cancelled the car."

"No, I didn't," Dorian told the woman. "I did not cancel the car."

"I am looking at the log," said the woman. "The car was cancelled."

"But not by me."

"No," agreed the woman. "It was cancelled by Mr. Dorian Asher."

Dorian carefully explained the situation again. Halfway through the third try, he gave up and hailed a cab.

He felt foolish standing there, his new shoes rubbing his heels, the Rolex sparkling on his wrist in the crackle of city lights, and he hoped that Franklin and Lillian, or Sloan, for that matter, wouldn't come out of the restaurant and catch him at the curb with his arm out.

39

BEATRICE HOT SPRINGS WAS MARKED BY DARK PILLARS OF dry-fit stones, with a heavy header of rough timbers. Even with the light from the lanterns, the entrance looked like the mouth of a cave.

Gabriel had to hurry to catch up to Mara. "You move pretty good."

Someone had carved words into the face of the timbers that spanned the pillars. Gabriel had to stand at an angle and fight the shadows to read them.

Aeterna Sustineo.

"It's Latin," said Gabriel.

"Of course it's Latin," said Mara. "Come on. I smell food."

THE entrance was dark and narrow, but the path immediately opened onto a broad garden, framed by a cathedral of tall trees. Mist had settled over everything, and, while Gabriel couldn't see the pools clearly, he could hear the sound of water moving.

"Welcome!" Crisp strode out of the fog, naked, with an enormous smile on his face. "The table's set, the fare anxious for approval, and damned be him what cries, hold, enough."

The man looked to have been put together from unrelated parts. Bald head, flaming red beard, smooth muscular chest and stomach, trim waist, and thin, sinewy legs that were covered with hair and reminded Gabriel of a goat.

"Nine pools in all," said Crisp, "and each available, though I'd sail clear of the alpha and the omega."

"Happy birthday, Nicholas," said Mara, and she gave Crisp a hug.

"Happy birthday, Mr. Crisp," said Gabriel, extending a hand.

"Sweet words," cried Crisp. "Sweet words! But come! Let's be about the waters. There's places there in the shadows to change if ye have an issue with modesty."

"No issue here." Mara slipped out of her dress and turned to Gabriel. "What about you?"

"I'm going to look at the food first."

"Suit yourself."

GABRIEL wandered along the tables and helped himself to some cheese and crackers. He passed on the thick sausages, which reminded him of Crisp's penis, and went with the sliced ham instead. He could always eat more later.

Somewhere in the fog, he could hear voices and splashing. Mara and Crisp were in the water together. Gabriel could feel an unwelcome energy surge through his body, and suddenly he was no longer hungry. He set the plate on the table, pulled the underpants out of his jacket pocket, and folded his clothes on a chair.

He quickly slipped into the first pool he could find. As far as he could tell, the springs meandered through a broad meadow.

Wooden boardwalks followed the pools, and there was a large deck where you could sit and enjoy the natural surroundings.

"Master Gabriel!"

"Here."

"Stay where ye are," shouted Crisp.

There was more splashing and laughing, along with the sound of bodies pushing through water.

"Be ye here?"

"Yes," said Gabriel, "I'm here."

Crisp appeared out of the mist first, in the pool just above Gabriel.

"There ye be."

"Here I am," said Gabriel.

Crisp leaped and dropped into the lower pool with a splash. Mara was right behind him. Gabriel sank a little lower in the water and quickly removed his underpants.

"Did ye get your fill?"

"I did."

"Then it's time to begin the celebration." Crisp climbed out of the pool and onto a large rock, his disparate parts glistening in the lantern light.

"Bring me my Bow of burning gold," he shouted, holding his arms out to the night. "Bring me my Arrows of desire. Bring me my Spear. O clouds unfold!"

Mara floated towards Gabriel. "Bring me my Chariot of fire!" she whispered.

"Aye, girl," roared Crisp, with such force that ripples spread out across the water. "That's the line all right. But it must be said in thunder. 'Bring me my Chariot of fire!'"

Crisp shook his beard and stamped his foot as though he expected the rock to split. And then he leapt into the air, curled up in a tight ball, and hit the water with the force of a comet.

"Mercies!" he bellowed. "But you've got to love Blake."

"'Jerusalem,'" said Mara. "The man likes his poetry."

"Indeed, I do," said Crisp. "But even Blake don't hold a candle to 'The Woman Who Fell from the Sky.' We tell that story here each year as a reminder."

"A reminder?"

"Indeed, Master Gabriel." Crisp lowered his voice and sent it skipping across the water. "As a reminder."

Gabriel's mother had told the story any number of times, but he couldn't remember if she had ever given a reason. Gabriel and his sister had taken turns cheering for the various animals who dove down to the bottom of the ocean, betting cookies on who would be the first to try to find dirt. Gabriel suspected that his mother varied the outcome, so that neither of her children got too far ahead of the other in the overall standings.

"Do ye know the tale?"

"No," said Gabriel. "I don't think I do."

"Well, then," said Crisp, "'tis time ye learned it. And since there are but the three of us, I'll call on Mistress Mara to do the honours."

"You're a better storyteller, Mr. Crisp."

"True enough," said Crisp, "but it's not my story to tell. I only do so when there's not a proper human being in the assembly."

"He means an Indian," said Mara.

"It's a story that comes with the land, and the two are forever wedded," said Crisp. "Do ye not agree?"

"I suppose," said Gabriel.

"Don't be supposing in the pools," said Crisp, "for they'll not tolerate indecision or arrogance."

"Be that as it may, no one's been here longer than you, Mr. Crisp," said Mara. "As well, it's your party, so you must tell the tale tonight."

The fog hung in the air like gauze. Mara floated in front of him, the swell of her breasts breaking the water. Somewhere in the shadow of the trees, something moved. Gabriel wondered if it might be Soldier and was about to call out when Crisp began.

"'Tis flattery I smell," cried Crisp. "But I do love the tale and so will succumb to my base instincts."

"It was on a night such as this," Mara began.

"Aye," said Crisp, jumping in without further encouragement. "It could have been night or perhaps it was day. No difference, no difference, and somewhere high above this plane, somewhere in the black realm of space, on another world, a woman was digging for tubers. And where do we find the best of the tubers?"

"Under old trees," said Mara.

"Exactly!" shouted Crisp. "So our woman searches until she finds the oldest and largest in the forest and she sets to digging her hole. She's a strong woman, she is, and she digs and she digs and she digs, until . . . ?"

"She digs a hole into the sky," said Mara.

"Put your back into the telling!" howled Crisp. "For it's an uncommon dig by an uncommon woman."

"She digs a hole into the sky," shouted Mara, and she reached across and poked Gabriel in the thigh with her foot.

"And what's a woman to do when faced with such an aperture? Why she looks into it. That's what she does. She looks and leans in. She looks and leans in further. She looks and leans in even further. And then . . . "

Crisp paused and waited. Mara poked Gabriel a second time.

"She falls in!" Mara's and Gabriel's voices filled the meadow.

"She falls in!" Crisp raised himself out of the pool until you could see his penis floating on the surface and the tops of his goat thighs. And then he fell back into the water and disappeared.

Mara and Gabriel waited, while the water calmed and softened, until there was nothing to mark Crisp's plunge.

"He's okay, right?"

"I guess it's just the two of us."

"I thought I heard Soldier in the trees."

"I wonder," said Mara, "if this is what Eden was like."

"The fortunate fall," shouted Crisp, as he burst from the water, "for our woman was falling through time and space, tumbling, tumbling, tumbling through the blackest night, down, down, down, she comes, and off in the distance at the edge of reason and sight, what does she see?"

"A small blue dot."

"Such clever children," hissed Crisp. "For indeed it is as you say. A small blue dot. A blessed plot, a magic realm, this earth. But at that time, it was nothing but . . . "

"Water," yelled Mara and she began splashing Gabriel.

"Manners," trumpeted Crisp. "But ye are correct. The world towards which our woman was falling was a world with naught but water."

"She's going to get wet," said Gabriel, and he splashed Mara back.

"We all fall into the world wet." Crisp raised his arms and let the water flow off his palms. "Yes, it were a water world, but it weren't *terram vacuam*. It were filled with water creatures."

"Water birds," said Mara, holding up the necessary fingers, "and water animals."

"Quite so," said Crisp. "All that and more. The birds be the first to see her, for they possess the gift of sight. So, down our woman comes, picking up speed as she clears the moon, and the birds can see that if she hits the water at flank speed, there'll be nothing but trouble."

"Trouble." Gabriel splashed more water at Mara. "Hell, at thirty-two feet per second, per second, she'll destroy most of the planet."

"A scientist," cried Crisp. "I knew ye were no ordinary castaway. Yes, it's true, and the birds knows this to be true as well, and they fly up into the sky, beat their wings to great effect, and catch her on their backs. Then slowly, very slowly, they lower her to the surface of the water."

"But there's no place to put her," said Mara.

"Just dump her in the water," said Gabriel.

"She's not a water creature."

"Quite so," said Crisp. "Our woman is no water creature, and, if the water creatures abandon her to the sea, she'll drown." Crisp paused and sank into the pool until his beard appeared to float free of his face. "What to do, what to do?"

"I know," said Mara. "I know."

"Let's be giving the other children a chance to shine," said Crisp.

When Gabriel's mother had told the story, she always liked to draw this part out and let Gabriel and his sister guess. His sister favoured whales and walruses. She had never been happy with a turtle. "They're too small," she had told her mother.

Gabriel shrugged. "I don't know. Maybe a turtle?"

Crisp squinted at him. "Are you sure ye have not heard this tale before?"

The noises in the woods were back. Gabriel was sure he could make out voices now, low and indistinct.

"You hear that?"

"Softly," said Crisp. "For they don't wish to be acknowledged."

Mara rose out of the pool, the water sliding off her body. Gabriel had seen breasts before. Movie breasts, television breasts, magazine breasts. Just not that many in-person breasts.

"Miller, Webb, Canakis, Collins." Crisp kept his voice low. "The ones who survived, the ones who stayed. Tragedy has a trick of bringing folks together."

"Or it can separate them from the world," said Mara, "isolate them from their families and friends."

"Ye have it whole," said Crisp. "Each year on my birthday, I set the table and open the pools, and they come and go as they please, alone and in darkness."

"But they survived," said Gabriel.

"And that's the sin they live with," said Crisp.

"So what are we supposed to do?"

"Finish our story," said Crisp. "There ain't nothing to do but finish our story. Now where were we?"

Mara slid back into the water. "On the back of a turtle."

"Aye," said Crisp, and he clapped his hands together. "On the back of a turtle."

40

SONNY SLIPS OUT OF THE TREES AND MAKES HIS WAY THROUGH the fog to the long table. He is very stealthy, and he is very hungry, and he wastes no time filling a plate with food. He can hear happy voices in the pools behind him, and he is bewildered once again.

Why would anyone come to such a place? How could anyone find pleasure bathing in lakes of fire and ice.

The food. Of course. Sonny doesn't know why he didn't think of this sooner. This is where the food is. This is the lure that leads the unwary into the trap. Come for the food, stay for the sulphur.

Wham-wham.

Sonny piles the plate as high as he can. He slips several sausages in a pocket and stuffs vegetable bits into the other. He has no intention of staying.

Watch me, Dad, watch me.

The voices slide through the fog, along with the sound of splashing, and then someone shouts, "Water." Sonny peers into the mists that boil off the pools, and for an instant, he can see three grey shapes in the gloom.

Sonny turns back to the food and discovers that he's forgotten about the desserts. His plate is full, and there is nowhere in his pockets to put the lemon squares and the chocolate brownies. Which means only one thing.

He'll have to eat the desserts on the spot.

Sonny selects a lemon bar and finishes it in one bite. Excellent. Sonny likes lemon bars, especially the ones that are tart and don't have too much sugar. He picks up a brownie, and just as he's about to take a bite, he realizes that he's not alone.

Someone else is at the table with him.

At first Sonny thinks that the people in the pool have gotten out, but he can still hear them talking and splashing. The people at the table are different people.

Samaritan Bay. Of course. The people at the table with Sonny are from town. The people at the table with Sonny are the ones who stayed. They must be hungry just like Sonny.

And then the ghost Indian in the power jacket steps out of the fog.

Wham-wham, hammer-hammer!

Not the town. Not the town at all.

Behind the Indian girl are more people. All Indians. Black hair. Flinty eyes. Sonny watches as they float about the table, taking small portions of everything. Ghost Indians. More ghost Indians than Sonny could have imagined.

The Indian girl doesn't have much on her plate. Sonny supposes that ghosts, even Indian ghosts, don't eat all that much. Perhaps they don't eat at all and are only taking food to be polite.

Sonny puts a lemon square on the Indian girl's plate. She smiles at him and nods her head. Sonny nods back, and he wonders if Dad has any rules about being friends with a ghost. But before Sonny can examine such a proposition, the ghost Indians with their plates of food step off the deck and vanish into the trees and the night.

And Sonny is alone again.

41

WHEN CRISP RETURNED TO THE STORY, HE RETURNED WITH passion and fury. He moved about the pool, climbing on the rocks, leaping into the water, plunging beneath the surface, and then slowly rising, his back breaking water first to simulate a turtle shell.

"It were the birds," he boomed. "The birds what brought our woman to safety and sanctuary on the back of the turtle."

Mara had heard Lilly's mother tell the story any number of times. Rose was more delicate and particular in the telling. Crisp was bold and bombastic.

"And sanctuary was what were needed, for when the water creatures placed our woman on the back of the turtle, they discovered that she be pregnant."

Rose had spent time on why the woman was digging in the first place and how her clothes were torn off as she fell through the sky, how she arrived on the water world cold and naked, how the water creatures gathered around to keep her warm, and how the labour had been long and hard.

Crisp had none of that in his telling.

"Twins," he shouted, tossing the details to the side. "She gives birth to twins."

Rose said that she had heard the story from her mother, and that sometimes the twins were two boys and sometimes they were two girls and sometimes they were one of each. Rose said she guessed her mother varied the gender based on her audience. But in every case there was a right-handed twin and a left-handed twin, a light twin and a dark twin.

"Boys they were. Left-handed and right-handed, one cold, one hot. And now there's not room on the back of the turtle for the family."

Mara had always enjoyed the next part.

"So our woman calls all the creatures together and announces a contest," sang Crisp, as he treaded water. "A diving contest and all are welcome to participate. The first to reach the bottom and bring up a ball of mud wins! The line forms here!"

Lilly's mother had always started with the pelican.

"First up is the beaver." Crisp smacked the water with his hand. "Down he goes, down into the depths. But he ain't got the breath for it and he floats up scarce alive."

Mara stretched out and floated on her back. She knew her breasts were exposed, and she caught Gabriel glancing in her direction. She wasn't sure what he could see through the mist with fogged glasses, but there was unexpected pleasure in the mystery.

"Next is the loon, then the grebe, and after that the cormorant." Crisp held his arms out from his sides and glided about in a circle, the water swirling around his waist. "But none of them could dive deep enough."

Mara never understood why whales and dolphins weren't part of the story. Whales, in particular, could hold their breath for long periods and dive to great depths. They'd be able to get to the bottom and bring up the mud. But, in the telling, Rose had never mentioned them. And neither did Crisp.

"One after the other, the creatures tried, and one after the other, they failed."

Rose had generally made the otter the hero of the story.

"Until there weren't no one left. Save muskrat. None of the other creatures had any faith that muskrat could do what they could not, for muskrat weren't the biggest nor the swiftest. She couldn't run fast or dive deep. But muskrats is cranky and stubborn, and this one weren't no exception."

Mara floated against the side of the pool and tried to imagine what it would have been like to ride on the back of a turtle with two babies.

"So down muskrat goes, down to where all light is gone, and nothing moves in the black. Down into the freezing depths what drops into eternity.

"And she don't come up." Crisp took a deep breath, and, without another word, he dove underwater.

Mara waited for the water to settle. "How long can you hold your breath?"

"I don't know," said Gabriel. "A minute. Maybe two."

"Used to be able to hold my breath for three," said Mara. "Are you wearing a suit?"

"What?"

"A swimsuit," said Mara. "Are you wearing a swimsuit?"

Crisp broke the water between them. "Then up she comes! Belly up, that is. Dead. Well, almost dead. All the creatures gather round and there in muskrat's paws is a ball of mud. Like this."

And Crisp sucked in another breath and dove underwater again.

"I'm not wearing a suit."

"Okay."

"Why did you want to know?"

"Just curious." Mara took a step forward and hooked her foot on something soft and stretchy. At first she thought it was a lump of pond vegetation, but as she drew it out of the water, she could see that it was a pair of dark underwear. She held the underwear up to the light of the lanterns.

"Yours?"

"Nope." Gabriel dipped his glasses in the water and shook them clean. "Never saw them before."

"Must be from another party."

"Mud!" shouted Crisp, as he broke the surface. He held one arm aloft with his fist clenched. "The universal glue!"

Crisp opened his hand. It was mud all right, dark and slimy with a somewhat putrid smell, and Mara hoped that the woman who fell from the sky had had something better to work with than this.

"Mistress Mara," said Crisp. "Do ye know any songs appropriate to the moment? For now our woman puts the mud ball on the back of the turtle and commences to sing."

Mara had been daydreaming: fragmented flashes of sausages and wet underwear. "What?"

"A song, girl," said Crisp. "Do ye know a song for our occasion?"

"No," said Mara, shaking the pieces out of her head. "But our Gabriel does."

"Does he?" said Crisp.

"He was singing a round dance on the way to the springs."

"That'll do," said Crisp, "for it's a social song, as I recall, and it ain't hard to imagine all the creatures grabbing hands and two-stepping about the turtle."

Gabriel opened his mouth to object.

"Nay, nay," scolded Crisp. "Now's your time, Master Gabriel. Quickly. Help us call the world into being."

Mara drifted next to Gabriel. "Take the lead," she said. "I'll sing behind you."

"We don't have a drum."

Mara touched Gabriel's shoulder. "Use the water."

THE surface of water, Gabriel discovered, would never take the place of a stretched hide, but he slapped out a rhythm anyway and sang the song. Mara came in at the turn, her voice pitched higher and stronger than his, while Crisp danced his way around the edge of the pool.

"A fine melody," Crisp sighed, when Gabriel had brought the song to an end, "for now that small ball of mud has grown into the world as we know it."

"See," said Mara, tapping Gabriel on the hip with her hand. "That wasn't so hard."

It had been a while since he had sung like that. In front of people. For a purpose. And he had to admit, it felt good.

"But our world ain't naught but mud. So now our twins go to work on it."

Mara closed her eyes. So this Gabriel had been telling the truth. He wasn't wearing a suit.

"The right-handed twin makes the mountains nice and low with easy slopes, so the walking about is pleasant, and he smooths out valleys, so all are broad and flat. The left-handed twin comes along and grabs those mountains with his hands and pulls them into the sky, chips off the sides, makes them craggy and inhospitable. He stomps on the valleys, so some be deep and narrow and trapped by the terrain."

Crisp paused for a moment to catch a breath.

"The right-handed twin makes medicinal plants what will cure all manner of malady. The left-handed twin fixes it so some of those plants will cure while some will kill."

"You were lying," Mara whispered to Gabriel.

"I'm not wearing a swimsuit."

Crisp forged on ahead. "As for the rivers and the streams, the right-handed twin made them languid and running in both directions at the same time. Then that rascal of a brother came along and turned them to one ways only, tossed rocks in, and conjured up rapids and falls."

"No," said Mara. "The story. You've heard this story before."

"And on they went. The right-handed twin creating a world of ease and convenience, the left-handed twin complicating the parts, until the world were complete and perfect."

Crisp slid into the water, exhausted. "'Tis a hard story," he said.

"It's long," said Gabriel. "That's for sure."

"Not the length," cried Crisp. "But the sadness of the thing."

Gabriel nodded. "Sort of like the Garden of Eden."

"Nothing like it," roared Crisp. "For in that story we starts with a gated estate and are thrown into suburbia, because we preferred knowledge to ignorance. In our story, we begins with an empty acreage, and, together, the woman, the animals, and the twins creates a paradise what gets pissed away."

"Free will."

"True enough, Master Gabriel," said Crisp. "You've nailed me there. And in the end, whether we was tossed or whether we was the architects of our own ruin, the end's the same."

Mara held up a hand. "Might we continue this conversation over food?"

"Clams in custard," shouted Crisp. "What manner of a host am I? Ye must be staved in at the ribs. Come, come. Let's leave the waters and attend to the tables."

Crisp bounded out of the pool.

Mara smiled at Gabriel. "You first, please."

THE food glistened under the lanterns.

"Do ye see!" said Crisp. "Do ye see! They've come and gone, eaten the food, and in that they do me honour and celebration."

"They didn't say anything." Gabriel looked over the table. There were three lemon squares left. "They ate your food without a word."

"'Twas why it was there," said Crisp. "Food's for the belly, and I'll feeds the silent as certain-sure as the noisy, with no expectation of praise for him what sets the table."

Gabriel was thankful that Mara had put on her dress. And disappointed. He climbed into his own clothes as quickly as he could. Only Crisp remained naked.

Mara picked up a plate and helped herself to the vegetables and the hummus. "There's lots of food left."

Only Crisp's plate remained empty.

"You all right?" said Gabriel.

"Fine," said Crisp. "Fine. A bit sodden, if truth be the point, for I had hoped that the boy would bend the rules this fine evening and join us."

Mara looked up from the food. "Sonny?"

"The kid from the motel?" Gabriel helped himself to the tomatoes. "The kid with the hammer and the talk about salvage?"

"A sweet lamb," said Crisp, "with a brutish burden to bear and no whereabouts in his head to carry it."

"He's a little . . . different," said Gabriel.

"As are we all," said Crisp. "My brother's boy, so I adjust for tolerance."

"Brother?" Mara set her plate on the table.

"Did ye not know?" Crisp suddenly slapped the side of his head. "But of course ye wouldn't, would ye? Before your time. Not even your grandmother would carry that tale."

"Sonny's dad is your brother?"

"Twins we were," said Crisp. "Just like in the story. I was the oldest, but nought by more than a breath and a bellow. Me feeling my way along and him pushing from behind."

"So, Sonny's your nephew."

"Aye," said Crisp, squeezing the water out of his beard. "Blood of my blood."

Mara stepped into the light of the lanterns so she could look into Crisp's face. "I can see a story."

"Ye has a raptor's eye," said Crisp. "We weren't always from the Bay, ye know. In another time, Dad and me were loose in the world, astride the universe with grand designs, him with his assurances and admonishments, me with my appetites and adventures. We believed we was elemental and everlasting."

Crisp sighed and shook his head. "Wondrous," he whispered into the night. "It were wondrous."

Gabriel set his plate on the table next to Mara's. "What happened?"

"What always happens to such fantasy and enterprise." Crisp helped himself to a slice of apple. "And then there were the cruel words what can't be retrieved, expectations thwarted, convictions undone, dreams collapsed. Rough seas followed, and here was where we was washed ashore."

"The Bay."

"The Ocean Star Motel," said Crisp. "My brother took Room Number One, even though I was the oldest and should have had the first sitting, but arrogance and inflexibility had followed us, so, for the sake of goodwill and tranquility, I took the third room along, and we put Sonny in between. And when that didn't succeed, I came here."

"That's sad."

"Heart-rending," said Crisp.

"You could still reconcile."

"Ah, Mistress Mara, 'tis a sweet thought, but not one that will bear any weight, for there's no one with whom to reconcile."

"Sonny's dad is . . . "

"Gone," said Crisp.

"The Ruin?"

"Nay. Dad was gone long before that black day."

"What happened?"

"But ye have had your own losses," said Crisp, "and Master Gabriel as well, for you can hear it in his voice and see it in his stride. There's none here tonight but what's not been cut and bled."

Crisp wiped his face. "Listen to me. Blubbered up like a beluga. 'Tis a party we're at, and I'll not have melancholy corrupt the water nor sorrow foul the food. Eat up. Sing if ye have a mind. Dance if ye have a will. As for me, I'm back in the bath to warm the bones and ease the heart."

And Crisp sprang off the deck, disappeared with a splash into the depths.

Mara and Gabriel stood by the table with their plates.

"I guess it's just the two of us."

Gabriel held up a brownie. "You like chocolate?"

It was at the end of the table, just beyond the lemon squares. Folded neatly as though it had just been cleaned and pressed.

"Is that your jacket?"

Gabriel picked it up and held it out. The tipis were sharp and bright. "Didn't expect to see this again."

"Someone from town must have found it," said Mara. "Tonight's your lucky night." She turned away from the pools and the darkness of the forest. "You know what I'd like?"

"More desserts?"

"No, I'd like to go home." Mara twisted her wet hair into a knot. "And while you're at it, Muskrat," she said, "I'd like some mud."

42

SONNY SITS IN ROOM NUMBER TWO AT THE OCEAN STAR MOTEL
and watches *The Sound of Music* on the classic movie channel.
Sonny likes all the singing and dancing and people being kind
to each other. Sonny especially likes the children, who start off
wilful and wild, but who become obedient and well behaved.

He doesn't like the German soldiers, and whenever they
come on the screen, Sonny mutes the sound.

Most of all he likes the father, who protects his children and
keeps them from harm. Whenever the father is on the screen,
Sonny whispers, You're a good dad, to the television set.

Sonny likes most of the songs. He especially likes the song
about the deer, and sometimes he dances along with the children as they sing about needles pulling thread and tea you eat
with jam and bread.

Tonight Sonny doesn't dance with the children. Sonny is busy
eating the food from the hot springs, and he knows that if he tries
to dance, it will just hurt his stomach. But Sonny sings along with
the songs. Eating and singing doesn't hurt his stomach.

When Sonny watches *The Sound of Music*, he wonders what
it would be like to have brothers and sisters. Sonny has mentioned this to Dad on a number of occasions.

Sonny would like some brothers and sisters.

Sonny looks up from one of the sausages. The German soldiers are back. He wipes his hands and hits the mute button. Bad things aren't nearly so bad when there's no sound.

One of the special songs in the musical is about all the favourite things Maria can think up. Raindrops and sleigh bells and wild geese in mittens. Ponies with wings and cream-coloured kittens. Sonny likes to sing along with the song, and sometimes he makes up his own favourite things.

Tourists and turtles who come in the summer.

Movies with heroes and four-wheel-drive Hummers.

Mothers and fathers and children who sing.

These are a few of my favourite things.

The hummus is very good. Sonny especially likes the fresh vegetables and the soft cheeses. You wouldn't have to melt these cheeses to make a good toasted cheese sandwich. You could just spread the cheese on bread and put the sandwich in the microwave for twenty seconds.

The soldiers are still on the screen, doing unfortunate things. They don't sing or dance, and Sonny believes that this is one of their problems. Maybe if they sang the song about the goatherd, they wouldn't be so mean.

But as Sonny watches the musical, he finds himself thinking about the ghost Indians. He had thought there was only the girl, but now he knows that there are many more, and he's not sure what to make of this. He had tried to count exactly how many ghost Indians there were, but the fog kept messing up the total.

So tomorrow he'll go to the reserve. That's where the ghost Indians will be. On the reserve. Sonny is sure of this.

The soldiers are gone now, and everyone is singing and dancing, so Sonny turns the sound on. The family is all together again. Everything is okay now. Everyone is safe.

And this makes Sonny very happy.

43

CURIOUS.

Crisp sat on a rock, his haunches drawn up to his chest, and considered the situation. The party had been a rousing success. He was sure that Mara and Gabriel had enjoyed themselves, and an audience, no matter how small, was a gift to be treasured. The story had gone well, maybe not as well as in past years, but he had told it with energy and snap. He had always liked the part where the animals dive for the mud, for that moment allowed all manner of theatrics.

He might have stayed underwater longer. He might have exploded out of the pool with greater effect, but those gymnastics were best saved for larger groups, where such displays were necessary to hold the attention and dazzle the eye of the congregation.

And the song. That had been a fine moment. Crisp would have preferred something with backbone, but the round dance had been full of rhythm and community, and Gabriel had sung it well and with conviction.

Mara finding Gabriel's underpants was an added delight.

Clever girl.

He hoisted his body out of the water and shook himself like a great dog. The people who had come in the night had made good work of the food. Crisp sat down at the edge of the water, raised his face to the sky, and drew a long breath in through his nostrils.

Curious.

"Ye are not from the Bay, are ye, for ye have not the stink of the place on your person."

Curious, curious, curious.

"From somewhere else," Crisp whispered to himself between bites. "From somewhere farther out."

Sonny had come, and that was an encouraging sign. Not officially of course. Not in the open. But it was a start. Perhaps a reconciliation was possible. Crisp had been tempted to call out, but he knew that any word of acknowledgement would have run the boy to a rabbit.

What had Sonny made of the gift? Crisp wasn't sure what he made of the trunk himself. Perhaps the people in the night and the trunk were related. Much in the world was. And if that were the case, then the lad would sniff it out, for he was as good a hound as any and could follow a scent to the moon and back.

And Mara and Gabriel. What was Crisp to make of them? Mara had come back after The Ruin. That had not been a surprise. But in the aftermath of the disaster, Mara had stayed. That had been a proper startle. Crisp half expected that he would wake up one day to find her gone.

That hadn't happened.

She had rented the yellow house at the end of Station Street and had stayed there, floating in place, as it were. Still, he could taste change on the winds that came across the headlands.

Wait and see. Wait and see.

Gabriel was the easier of the two. Crisp had known him from the first, knew why he had come, knew the sharp secret that be wrapped up in his skin. By now, Crisp had expected that the man would be departed and unlamented, the trailer swept and scrubbed and readied for the next soul what needs sanctuary. But somehow this Gabriel had tricked him, had sailed through destruction, and found safe harbour where there should be none.

Wait and see. Wait and see.

As for the strangers, whoever they be, they was frightened and lost. There had been misgivings on the mist and fear in the fog.

Crisp rubbed his belly and let loose a tremendous belch that buried itself in the night.

"I endure eternal!"

And then he eased himself off the rock and slid smoothly into the water, without leaving so much as a bubble or a ripple to mark his passing.

44

THE CANVAS WAS WAITING ON THE EASEL, WHERE MARA HAD left it. Gabriel stood back and considered the image.

"Who's this?"

"Elvin Grunes," said Mara.

There was a second canvas leaning against the wall. "And this one?"

"Thelma Walker. She was one of our elders. She and my grandmother were close."

"You're not using brushes."

"Palette knife," said Mara. "It's a bolder effect."

"You should paint Crisp," said Gabriel. "He'd be an interesting subject."

"You mean nude?"

Gabriel tried to imagine how Mara would manage the bald head, the flaming red beard, the hairy legs. "I was thinking head and shoulders."

"I've painted naked men before," she said. "They're not all that interesting."

They had walked from the springs in silence. Gabriel wasn't sure why he had followed her home. Maybe this was the sort of thing one did while waiting for a sunny day and a low tide.

247

"Are you using photographs?"

"Memory. I'm painting from memory."

"The Ruin?"

Mara nodded. "You've been talking to Nicholas. 'The Ruin' is his name for what happened. Sounds monumental, doesn't it. Biblical even."

"Actually, he hasn't said much."

"He hasn't told you how the river ran bright green that morning? How the people sickened and died? How they continued to die in the weeks and months after? How the turtles and every living thing in the river's path were destroyed?" Mara hunched her shoulder around her neck. "It can be quite a production. Every bit the equal of his version of 'The Woman Who Fell from the Sky.'"

Gabriel touched the edge of the canvas.

"I was in Toronto." Mara looked past Gabriel.

Gabriel put his hand behind his back and tried to rub the paint off his finger.

"By the time I got home, everyone was dead." Mara folded her arms as if she had caught a chill. "Well," she said, "aren't I a happy host."

"No problem."

"Hardly. I invite you back to my house. You probably thought that sex was in the offing and, wham, I dump this on you."

"I didn't think . . ."

"Sure you did." Mara started to laugh. "Maybe I should paint you."

"Me?"

"I could add you to my collection of dead people."

"Nude?"

"Course, you're not dead yet. But I suppose I could make an exception." Mara stopped and shook her head. "I've freaked you out, haven't I?"

"No."

"Sure I did." Mara ruffled her hair and dropped her voice for dramatic effect. "I paint dead people!"

"Bruce Willis, Haley Joel Osment. *Sixth Sense.*"

"Scared the hell out of me," said Mara.

"So you came home."

"I came home."

"And you stayed."

"That's why they call it home." Mara smoothed her hair. "But you don't have a home, do you?"

"No."

"You'll have to tell me about that some time."

Gabriel tried to stop it, but the yawn got away from him.

"Aha," said Mara. "Crazy woman. *And* boring."

"I guess I'm tired."

"Of living?"

"Sometimes."

"Now?"

"No," said Gabriel. "Not now."

"You can stay if you want."

"Here?"

"It's a long walk back to your trailer," said Mara. "It's dark. You'll just get lost."

"It is dark."

Mara turned to Gabriel. "Were those your underpants in the pool?"

Gabriel couldn't keep himself from smiling. "They were."

"I would like someone to hold me." Mara glanced at the canvas. "Is that something you might be willing to do?"

"Sure."

"I'm not talking about sex."

"No."

"Just two people under a quilt, keeping each other warm."

MARA checked her brushes. She turned out the lights and went to the bedroom. Gabriel was already there, lying on the covers, trying to look casual.

"You can take your shoes off," said Mara. "And your jacket."

"This is a nice bed." Gabriel got up and pulled the covers back. "The one in the trailer is lumpy."

"Which side do you want?"

"Doesn't matter."

"Good," said Mara. "I want the right side."

Mara slipped off her shoes and climbed into bed with her back to Gabriel. She waited, hoping that he would pull the quilt over the both of them without her having to ask.

He did.

Mara lay there, rigid and tense. There was something about having someone that close to you and so far away. She realized that her breathing was quick and shallow. She'd never get to sleep this way. "Are you tense?"

"A little."

"Would it help if you held me?"

"It might."

"Okay," said Mara, "why don't we give that a try."

Mara held her breath as she felt the bed shift. And then Gabriel's body touched hers, and it was as if she had been struck by lightning.

"You okay?"

"Fine." Mara could feel her nipples stiffen and her groin begin to glow. "But I don't want this to get out of hand."

"No," said Gabriel.

Mara's breathing was returning to normal now. Gabriel's arm felt surprisingly good. He had buried his face in her hair, and that felt good as well. She wasn't sure she could sleep in this position, but having someone in bed with her was comforting, something she hadn't felt in a very long time. She moved back into Gabriel, pressing herself against his body and drawing his hand to her breasts.

"This is nice," she whispered to herself.

GABRIEL stayed awake most of the night, listening to Mara snore. Nothing horsey. Just a soft, gentle murmur. At first he had been aroused, and, in spite of his efforts to think of sheep and hockey, he had remained aroused. It didn't help that Mara's hair smelled like flowers or that his hand was up against a breast. Though that didn't last long. After a short while, the arm had gone to sleep, and his fingers had gone numb.

But he didn't move, didn't want to disturb the moment and have Mara shift away. He liked being in bed with this woman. He liked holding her.

He liked being alive.

And as he eased into sleep, he thought about the woman who fell from the sky, how it would have been to have seen her streaking through the heavens like a falling star, plunging towards earth.

And how different the outcome might have been if the birds hadn't caught her.

45

THE DRIVER DROPPED DORIAN OFF IN FRONT OF THE CONDO. It had been a while since he had been in a taxi, and he hoped not to repeat the experience any time soon. The interior of the cab had felt bored, as though it had lost any interest in the job at hand. He hadn't been able to see what was on the floor, and that was just as well. The seats had a tacky feel, and there was a cloying smell to the vehicle that reminded him of the blue discs used to disinfect urinals.

The driver had been pleasant enough, asking Dorian where he was from, whether he was in town on business or pleasure, and pointing out the various sights as they drove towards Queen's Quay. Dorian decided to play along and told the man he was from San Francisco, that he was in Toronto for a major agribusiness conference.

"Have you heard of Domidion?"

"No," the driver had said, "but it sounds important."

"Yes," Dorian had told him, "it is."

The driver was duly impressed. He praised San Francisco as a place to live and offered his services if Dorian needed a driver during his stay.

When Dorian paid the fare, he added a twenty-dollar tip, holding the bill out at arm's length, so the man could enjoy the Rolex.

"You call, any time," the driver had said, as he handed Dorian his business card. "Twenty-four hours, no problem. We businessmen must stick together."

Yes, Dorian had agreed, businessmen should stick together.

"A wonderful watch," said the man. "It must make you very happy."

DORIAN went straight to the liquor cabinet and poured himself a glass of the forty-year-old Laphroaig that he and Olivia had bought at Cadenhead's in Edinburgh, when they toured Scotland with Ray and Meredith.

"Smoke and peat, with sweet licorice root and seaweed," the man at the store had told him. "If you like the taste of fine cigars and can afford the pleasure, then this is the Scotch for you."

Dorian settled on the sofa in front of the windows that overlooked the lake and called Olivia. He let the phone ring, and when no one answered, he hung up and dialed the number again, carefully this time, in case he had made a mistake.

"Dorian?" Olivia's voice sounded distant.

"Are you all right?"

"It's midnight."

Dorian consulted the Rolex. It was actually three minutes after midnight.

"Sorry."

"Have you been drinking?"

Dorian put the glass on the side table. "No," he said, "I was just wondering when you were coming home."

"Haven't you seen the weather report?"

"For Orlando?"

"No, silly," Olivia said. "Toronto. There's a big snowstorm on its way."

"That's Sudbury," said Dorian. "Weather's great here. All the snow is gone. It's not even that cold."

"Two days," said Olivia. "It's supposed to be there in two days."

"Jennifer and David have invited us to come up to Jackson's Point this weekend. Dinner at The Briars."

For a moment, Dorian thought he had lost the connection.

"Olivia?"

"I'm here."

"I thought I lost you."

"I'm going to stay in Orlando a little longer."

"Longer?"

"Just another week," said Olivia, "maybe two."

Dorian began tapping the arm of the chair.

"What's that noise?"

"Nothing," said Dorian. "I don't know if that's a good idea."

"Pardon?"

"Staying in Orlando."

"You're sweet."

"What?"

"That you miss me."

"Of course I miss you."

"And I'll be home before you know it."

~~~~~

THE jury had deliberated for three days and returned a not guilty verdict.

Dorian had been surprised. How did you kill a policeman and get away with it? Church's contention that he feared for his life seemed weak. He must have noticed the patrol car parked in front of his house. He must have seen that both Quinn and Martinez were in uniform. He would have heard Quinn identify himself. But he had come to the door with a pistol in hand and had shot Quinn before the officer could say another word.

And then he had turned the gun on Martinez.

The prosecution hadn't asked Church why he didn't kill Martinez. If the man had feared for his life, why hadn't he finished the job? If Church had believed that Quinn and Martinez were assassins, why hadn't he shot her a third time as she lay wounded in his front yard?

Dorian wished that the transcript had contained photographs of both the officers. Maybe Church had been frightened by Quinn's appearance. That might have been the tipping point for an angry man with a loaded gun.

DORIAN stared at the phone. So Olivia wasn't coming home. Jackson's Point was one of her favourite places, but even the promise of a visit to The Briars hadn't swayed her. So far as Dorian could tell, all Orlando had to recommend it was sun. Toronto was a world-class city. It had the better restaurants, the better theatres, the better shopping.

Orlando was a tourist trap.

Now that he thought about it, Olivia hadn't sounded sleepy so much as she had sounded annoyed. As though he had been an interruption to her evening.

Dorian picked up the remote and flipped through the channels. *Duck Dynasty* was on. He had watched parts of previous shows, had found them mildly amusing. Rich rednecks in Louisiana who made duck calls. Or was it Arkansas. He checked the Turner Classic Movies channel.

The Sound of Music.

Dorian took his drink with him to the windows overlooking the lake. But in the dark, the glass acted like a mirror, and the only thing he was able to see was himself.

46

GABRIEL AWOKE THE NEXT MORNING TO FIND HIS ARM hanging over a pillow. He tried lifting his hand.

Nothing.

He tried moving his fingers.

Nothing.

He dragged the arm free and waited for the pain to begin. Not pain exactly. More an ache, an excruciating pricking that bordered on arousal, without any of the pleasure. All he could do was bury his face in the bed and wait for the sensation to pass.

His last clear memory was of being pressed up against Mara, his hand on her breast. Now her side of the bed was empty. Most likely she had realized her mistake and slipped away in the night.

Just as well.

If she were still here, he would have had to come up with something to say, something to mark the moment. Something wise and gentle. Something that didn't sound like the inside of a greeting card. It wouldn't need to be profound or apologetic. They hadn't had sex. They had simply slept together.

The blood had returned to his arm now. Gabriel flexed his hand and drew it to his mouth, tried to find her taste on his fingers.

~~~~~

THE morning that they left Lethbridge for Minneapolis, Gabriel had helped his father pack the truck, while his sister stood on the sidewalk and watched.

"I don't want you to go."

"We're all going," he had told her. "As soon as Joe finds a place and we get settled, you and Mum are coming down."

His sister had kept her eyes on the ground the whole time. "Mum doesn't want to go," she said, "and you'll never come back."

"It's an RCMP exchange program, Little. Three years. Then we'll all come home."

Little had taken an envelope out of a pocket. "Here," she said. "This is for you."

Inside was a laminated picture of a turtle.

"Turtles carry their houses on their back," his sister had said. "Everything they need, they carry with them."

"Cool."

"That's what you are. A turtle."

"I like it."

Little had started to cry then, and she wrapped her arms around his waist. "I'm not a turtle."

"No," Gabriel had told her. "You're my little sister, and we'll all be together again in no time."

THEN again, maybe Mara had gone to the bathroom to pee or brush her teeth. His own mouth felt slippery and treacherous.

Gabriel rolled over and was debating what to do next, when he noticed an unfamiliar dresser and realized that he wasn't in his trailer. Mara hadn't gone home. She was home. He was the intruder.

Okay. That was embarrassing.

So, he was going to have to come up with something thoughtful after all, and he was never at his best first thing in the morning. If Mara wasn't in the bathroom, maybe he could get there undetected.

He got as far as the doorway.

"Down the hall. First door on the right."

"Bathroom?"

"Down the hall. First door on the right."

He looked worse than he had imagined. His shirt was wrinkled, and his hair was pushed to one side, as if his head had been caught in an avalanche. He found the toothpaste and debated the social and hygienic implications of using someone else's toothbrush, before settling on his finger. If he had had his razor with him, he might have shaved, but that wasn't urgent.

Last night had been perplexing, the signals confusing at best. Mara had invited him to share her bed. She had been clear about not wanting sex. However, she had been open to being held. They had lain against each other. She had moved his hand to her breast. He had been aroused and might have considered something more intimate, if Mara had indicated a firm interest.

That hadn't happened.

Gabriel stood by the sink and soaked his hair. He took in a deep breath, wondered whether last night's adventure had left a residue of sexuality behind, something that might suggest possibilities.

But if such a trace was in the air, he couldn't find it.

GABRIEL'S mother hadn't come out of the house to see them off.

"Your mother's not feeling well," his father had told him. "Your sister's going to stay with her."

"Mum's angry, isn't she."

"She has to wrap up some things here, and then they'll join us in Minneapolis."

"That's not true."

"Sure it is," his father had said. "She just needs a little time."

"But what if she doesn't come."

Joe had smiled. "You got a lot to learn about women."

MARA was in the living room at her easel. The painting had been little more than a sketch when they had gone to bed. Now, it was all but finished.

Gabriel checked his hair with his hand. "Good morning."

"You want coffee?"

"Sure."

"In the cupboard." Mara stayed at the easel. "You want eggs?"

"Okay."

"In the refrigerator."

He had used a bit too much water on his hair, and now it was dribbling down the sides of his face. "Scrambled?"

"Sunny side up would be nice," said Mara. "Potatoes are in the drawer."

Gabriel had tried to come up with something intelligent and thoughtful to say. He had stood in front of the mirror and practised a series of banalities.

"Bacon," said Mara. "Freezer. Extra crispy, please."

Why did he feel responsible? Mara had invited him home. She had been the one who suggested that they share a bed. He had simply been . . . co-operative.

"Last night was nice."

"There's some onion in a glass container on the top shelf," said Mara. "You like onion in potatoes?"

"I do."

"Did you know you snore?"

"Really?" Gabriel found the grater in the drawer by the stove.

"Not bad. Rusty gate stuff." Mara stepped away from the canvas. "So what are your plans for today?"

"My plans?"

"Tide isn't low enough to get to the Apostles. I was wondering if you wanted to give me a hand."

"Sure."

He put oil in the pan and turned the burner to medium.

"I have to go up to the reserve, and I can't carry everything by myself."

"You don't have a car?"

"I don't have a car." Mara took the canvas off the easel and set it against the wall with the others. "It's nothing heavy. Just awkward."

"Sure," said Gabriel. "We could look for Soldier along the way."

Mara angled her head. "You lost Soldier?"

"More like he lost himself." Gabriel dumped the shredded

potatoes into the hot oil. They made a satisfying sizzle. "He ran off."

Mara set a new canvas on the easel and loaded her knife with paint. "He'll come home," she said. "Unless someone else is feeding him."

Gabriel worked the bacon under hot water, peeling off the strips in order.

Mara wiped her palette and set it on the easel. "Did you know that Crisp is Sonny's uncle?"

"Nope."

"Neither did I."

"He's a little strange."

"Crisp or Sonny?"

Gabriel set the eggs on the counter. "Both, now that you mention it."

"Are you going to cook the eggs in butter?"

"Is that a problem?"

"No," said Mara. "I like butter."

"Is there anything else you'd like?"

"Coffee," said Mara, stretching her arms over her head and leaning to one side. "I'd like some coffee."

HIS father had eased the pickup away from the curb, and his sister had followed, keeping pace with the truck, calling out, trying to get their attention. Joe had kept both hands on the wheel, his eyes straight ahead.

"Don't look."

At the corner, Joe turned left and headed for the river valley and the east side of town. All the way down to the river and up the other side, Gabriel had watched the road behind them in the side mirror, but the only reflection that he had been able to find was the bright sky arching over the dark land.

LAST night had been perplexing. Mara didn't know what had possessed her, inviting a virtual stranger into her home and then into her bed. They hadn't done anything, but that hadn't been Gabriel's fault. She had been poised, had gone so far as to move his hand to her breast. The manoeuvre had inadvertently brushed a nipple, which set off a minor riot in her body.

She had stayed there in the bed, frozen in position, with Gabriel pressed up against her, and it was all she could do to keep from pushing back. She had felt his arousal and knew that all he had to do was to grasp her hip and pull her into position.

Instead, he had held to his place and went to sleep, while she was left wide awake with a body in flames.

Strange. She wasn't particularly attracted to this Gabriel. He wasn't handsome or even rugged. He was, in most respects, ordinary. All the damage and pain were in his eyes.

Mara hoped that this Gabriel didn't think she was easy. Or worse, weak. Did he think that she was one of those women who needed a man to complete her? If they were going to spend any time together, she'd have to make short work of that fantasy.

The chances of a relationship were slim. He had the Apostles and this on-again, off-again death wish. Frankly, she wasn't sure he knew what he wanted to do, and, for her, indecision in a man was in the same category of defects as smoking and religious zeal.

She could just have sex with him and walk away. She'd done that before with no ill effects. But what she had felt last night had not been simple passion, and Mara was curious to see if she could find it again.

47

SONNY WAKES TO A FARAWAY SOUND THAT REMINDS HIM OF aluminum cans being crushed. In the good days of plenty, when there was an abundance of tourists and turtles, Sonny had flattened a great many shrieking cans with his feet, so he knows that they don't like being mistreated.

It is a disturbing sound, a sound that Sonny has never trusted, and he rushes out the door, past the injured vending machines, his hammer at the ready.

Make way for Sonny!

But when he looks down on the beach, all he can see is fog.

Once, Sonny found a definition of "fog" in a dictionary. "Droplets of liquid water suspended in air near the earth's surface." That's what the book said. Sonny laughed when he read the definition.

Everyone knows that fog is smarter than that.

The ghost Indians.

That could be what he heard. Ghost Indians singing. Now that Sonny thinks about it, Indian singing sounds a lot like aluminum cans being stepped on.

~~~~~

SONNY goes back to the room and brushes his teeth. He washes his face. He combs his hair. He puts on clean socks. There is still sausage and cheese left over from the night before. Sonny puts these in a plastic bag and fills his water bottle at the sink.

Now he's all set. Time to check the beach for salvage. If Sonny runs into the ghost Indians, he'll let them know that it's okay to sing on his beach. Maybe they'll invite Sonny to sing with them.

Sonny shakes the plastic sack. He's sorry he doesn't have more food. If he had more food, he would be able to share it with the ghost Indians. Dad knows a trick to deal with such situations, but Sonny hasn't learned it yet.

SONNY starts down the hill to the ocean, and as he slips and slides on the steep slope, he decides that today he is going to do something important. Today, he is going to do something that will impress Dad. Today, he is going to show the world that he can be about his father's business and be a good son as well.

What would Dad expect?

What would Dad demand?

What would Dad do?

These are the questions Sonny always asks himself when he runs out of answers.

WHEN Sonny gets to the beach, he stops and stands very still. Maybe the answers to these questions can be found in the stories that Dad likes to tell. One of Dad's stories has a garden in it. Several feature walls, while others mention boats. Sonny concentrates as hard as he can. Gardens, walls, boats. Gardens, walls, boats.

Towers.

Wham!

That's the answer. Towers.

Sonny dances around, his feet kicking sand into the air. Dad is very fond of towers. There are any number of towers in Dad's stories. A tower would be less work than a boat but would be more satisfying than a wall or a garden. A tower would take a certain amount of skill but not too much.

But why would it be important? What could a tower accomplish that a wall or a garden or a boat could not? And now Sonny finds his thoughts running into one another.

Not just any tower.

Sonny stops dancing and concentrates on thinking.

A beacon. A tower beacon. A lighthouse. More or less. A symbol of hope. A guiding light. A monument to perseverance.

That's what Sonny will build. Right here on the beach. A tower. A bright tower that will stand against the dark sky and bring the turtles home.

48

AT SIX IN THE MORNING, DORIAN FOUND HIMSELF STARING AT the ceiling, his body crackling with energy. Given the night before, he shouldn't even be awake.

The Sound of Music.

He had stayed up and watched the entire movie. Worse, partway through the film, he had begun singing along with all the songs. At one point, he had actually come off the couch and danced around the room like an idiot.

Three in the morning.

That's when he had finally gotten to bed.

All right. So, he was awake, and the first thing that came to mind was exercise. When he had been a student at the University of Toronto, he had started out each morning with a routine of push-ups and sit-ups. He had done one hundred of each in five sets of twenty on the floor of his apartment.

Could he still do that? Only one way to find out.

The floor felt cold against his chest, but he did the first set of push-ups and sit-ups with relative ease. By the time he got to the third set, he was breathing hard. The fourth set was a strain, and the last set required determination.

But he had finished. He had finished the routine, just as he had done when he was twenty-two. And it had felt good. Terrific, in fact. As though he had been able to turn the clock back and recapture all the vigours and enthusiasms of youth.

It was probably the medications.

He stripped off his sweaty clothes, stepped into the shower, and discovered that he was fully erect.

Nice.

Dorian couldn't remember when water had felt this good. And soap. What genius had invented the stuff? Magic, really. What a way to spend a day. Standing under hot spray, getting all lathered up with a bar of slippery soap.

How long could a person stay in a shower?

God, but he felt alive.

Dorian took his time with the bath sheet that Olivia had bought at the Pottery Barn on Bloor. It was large and soft, and when he had finished, Dorian wrapped it around himself in the manner of a Roman senator. In the fogged mirror, he could have mistaken himself for a latter-day Caesar.

Even shaving was a pleasure.

As he got dressed, he was struck by an intriguing idea. Why not take the morning off? Why not reprise one of those mornings he had spent as a student? Out of bed early. Exercise. Shower. Breakfast.

The Bluebird.

The Bluebird Café near Church and Wellesley. A hole-in-the-wall greasy spoon pinned between a convenience store and a tattoo parlour. The menu had been limited to the usual suspects, but the Bluebird also served a thick, spicy sausage that

Gus Mavrias made himself. Two eggs scrambled, toast, fried potatoes, sausage, and Dorian had been good to go.

Dorian wondered if the café was still there, if Gus was still turning out the sausages for a newer and younger troop of students.

That's what he would do. Forgo the limo, or a taxi for that matter. Catch a streetcar. Or the subway. Dorian tried to remember how to get to the Bluebird using public transportation and was delighted to find that he could remember the route with no difficulty at all.

He folded the tie and slipped it into the pocket of his jacket. Casual was the order of the day. Slide under the radar. Dorian Asher, CEO incognito.

The streetcar from Queen's Quay to Union Station was crowded. The subway from there to Wellesley was a crush of warm, perfumed, and sweaty bodies, all of them standing much too close to one another. But none of this interfered with Dorian's feeling of euphoria, and he stepped off the subway just as cheery and hopeful as when he left the condo.

The walk along Wellesley was a stroll through his past. Most of the businesses were still there. Some had been replaced. There was a McDonald's where a bookstore had stood, and some clever developer had torn down half a block of brick fronts and thrown up a residential-commercial condo. But that was to be expected.

Nothing to get upset about. Nothing to mourn.

Progress was a celebration of life.

~~~~~

THE Bluebird was still there. The sign was the same. The exterior the same. But when he walked in the door, Dorian could see that changes had been made. The old Bluebird had been a tacky arrangement of chrome, Formica, and red Naugahyde. The new Bluebird was creamy white counters, black and white tile floors, cherry wood booths and dark green upholstery, with a flat-screen television hanging near the register, and another on the back wall. Dorian missed the older decor, but he had to admit that the new, upscale look was an improvement.

Gus must have died or sold the place. Or both.

A young man, slender with perfectly groomed stubble and an earring in one ear, seated him.

"Our special today is Red Tofu with Ho Fun Noodles and Scallion Pancakes."

"When Gus had this place, he made his own sausage."

"Your first time here?"

"I used to be a regular," said Dorian. "When Gus Mavrias made his own sausage."

"We don't have sausage."

Dorian glanced down the menu. "I don't see eggs."

"No eggs either," said the young man. "You might try our Sweet Potato Oatmeal Breakfast Casserole."

"No eggs?"

"We're a vegan restaurant."

"Ah."

The young man cocked his head and frowned. "Has anyone told you that you look like James Coburn?"

"Really?"

"When he was younger," said the young man. "Are you into old movies?"

"Sure."

"*The Great Escape*," said the man. "Coburn was hot in *The Great Escape*."

"Didn't he play a psychiatrist?"

"*The President's Analyst*." The young man put a hand over his heart and worked it back and forth. "He was so much fun in that. The scene with the family and the station wagon and the guns?"

Dorian couldn't recall the scene, but he smiled and nodded.

"You're not vegan, are you?"

"No," said Dorian, "I'm not."

"Then why don't you try the Raw Buckwheat Breakfast Porridge."

THE Raw Buckwheat Breakfast Porridge was not what came to mind when Dorian thought about breakfast. It had walnuts on it and tasted like something he might have stumbled across in a field. Who would think of putting walnuts on porridge? Evidently vegans.

The coffee was excellent.

"Could I get a side of toast with butter."

"We don't serve butter."

"Honey?"

"We have apple butter."

Dorian was almost afraid to ask. "Muffins?"

"Blueberry," said the man, "and oatmeal raisin."

"Blueberry," said Dorian. "I'll take a blueberry."

THE café had filled up since Dorian had sat down. He was surprised that so many men found the food appealing. He could understand the attraction for women. Olivia was always looking for something new and healthy to try.

"How was the porridge?"

"Just fine."

"I'll get you more coffee, Mr. Coburn."

The television on the back wall was showing a soccer game, and Dorian wondered if the overpaid kid in the sports magazine was playing. He watched the players as they loped up and down the field, but he didn't see the point. Try as he might, he found soccer slow and boring.

Unlike hockey, which he found fast and boring.

He was relaxing over coffee and the muffin, when he noticed that the café had gotten remarkably quiet.

"The fuckers!"

Dorian looked up. The soccer game was gone, replaced by a news broadcast. The sound was off, but the picture showed a woman in a yellow trench coat standing by the bank of a river. The screen was too far away, but there was something familiar about the reporter.

"Turn the sound on!"

One of the servers aimed the remote at the screen and the woman's voice sprang to life.

" . . . reporting from the Domidion tar-sands facility on the banks of the Athabasca," said the woman. "I'm Manisha Khan for *En Garde*."

A heavy-set man was out of his seat. "Fucking Domidion!"

Dorian turned, so he could see what the man had ordered. If that was the Red Tofu special, it didn't look bad at all.

"The bastards!" the man shouted. "The fucking bastards have destroyed the Athabasca."

The action on the television had switched back to CBC's main broadcast studio, where Peter Mansbridge was going over the particulars of the story.

"Early this morning," Mansbridge began, "an earthen dam at Domidion's oil-sands facility gave way and dumped thousands of gallons of toxic sludge into the Athabasca River. A spokesperson for the corporation has told CBC that a cleanup crew is on site and that the spill does not constitute an immediate hazard to local communities or to the environment."

Dorian put the coffee down and quickly checked his phone. Shit.

He had turned it off the night before and had forgotten to turn it back on.

The protest group that had met him in the parking lot of the university had had an almost festive air to it. The gathering in the café felt more murderous. Dorian looked around. There was no easy exit. Many of the men were on their feet, and some of them had even started chanting "Domidion" in four distinct syllables.

"Do-mi-di-on! Do-mi-di-on!"

Now the image on the television was of Tecumseh Plaza and Domidion corporate headquarters. Superimposed in one corner of the screen was a picture of . . . him.

"CBC has tried to speak with Dorian Asher, the CEO of Domidion International," Mansbridge was saying in a calm monotone, "but a spokesperson tells us that Mr. Asher is currently unavailable for comment."

It wasn't an up-to-date photograph. He had had longer hair then, and he had been a fraction slimmer. But it was Dorian Asher, and if anyone in the Bluebird looked hard at the image on the screen and at the man in the booth, things could get out of hand.

Dorian ran a hand through his hair to muss it up. The sleeve of his jacket slid up and there was the Rolex, a lightning rod in a room of storm clouds. He dropped his hand into his lap and worked at the clasp. It wouldn't open.

Great.

He kept the Rolex arm below the table and raised the other one.

"Do-mi-di-on," he chanted, his voice blending in with the other men. "Do-mi-di-on."

And then it was over. The chanting stopped. Everyone took his seat, and the business of breakfast resumed. The server brought the coffee by, but Dorian waved him off.

"I have to get to work," he told the man.

"Man, is that stock going to take a hit," said the server.

Domidion headquarters and Dorian's picture were still on the screen. Why the hell couldn't they go back to images of the river?

"Fuckers," said Dorian.

"Damn straight," said the server. "This will rip the lid off the garbage can."

Dorian had no idea what that was supposed to mean, and he

didn't ask. He paid the bill, left a reasonable tip, and was at the door when the server stopped him.

"You know," the man said, gesturing towards the back wall, "he looks like him, too."

Dorian quickly glanced at the television. He was still an insert on the screen.

"James Coburn," said the man. "Both of you look a lot like James Coburn."

49

WHEN THEY GOT TO THE OLD BUS, THEY STOPPED AND LEANED the paintings against the front fender.

"Is it always foggy like this?"

"It's the coast," said Mara. "If you want sunshine, move to Florida."

Breakfast had been marvellous. This Gabriel had surprised her with his culinary skills. The eggs had been soft and buttery, the bacon crisp, the toast hot. And everything had arrived on a warm plate at the same time.

Of course, he might have gotten lucky, and Mara decided that she would have to see him cook a couple more times before she was convinced.

MARA had set wide strips of cardboard along the edge of each painting and wrapped everything in butcher paper to protect the canvases from accidental bumps and the antics of the coastal winds. The brown packages looked like pizza boxes about to be mailed. All that was missing were the stamps.

She had considered waiting until she had completed all the portraits, but having finished the first four, Mara found herself anxious to take them to the reserve.

"Did you remember the hammer?"

"I remembered the hammer." Gabriel patted his pocket. "And the nails."

Mara looked through the fence. She had hoped the sky would be clear today so she could see the reserve all at once, the houses, the trailers, the community building, the water tower. The land stretching up to the mountains.

"So, why did you come?"

"You asked me if I would help."

"You could have said no."

Gabriel shrugged. "I thought you might like the company."

"It took them two days to put the fence up." Mara kicked at the wire. "No one came to help when people were dying. But they came to string the wire."

Gabriel pushed on a post. "They did a good job."

"Seven hundred and twenty steps," said Mara. "From here it's 720 steps to my grandmother's house."

"You've counted the steps?"

"We'll start there," said Mara.

MARA was right. More or less.

"Seven hundred and nine," Gabriel said, as they walked onto the porch.

"You take longer steps." Mara pushed the front door open. "I grew up here. Two bedrooms, one bath. There used to be a chair right about here. One of those recliners with a footrest. My grandmother slept in it."

"In a chair?"

"Said it was easier to get out of than a bed. All she had to do was lean forward, and she was on her feet."

Gabriel tried to imagine what the house had looked like when it was filled with furniture and people.

"There used to be a wood stove over there, but someone took it."

"Took it?"

"Stole. Everything they could carry," said Mara. "A family drove in with a trailer. B.C. plates. Mother, father, two teenage sons and a ten-year-old daughter. I caught them looting the community centre. Chairs, dishes, flatware, napkin holders, a coffee urn."

"Napkin holders?"

"The father was indignant when I told him to put everything back and get off the reserve. He said there were laws that covered abandoned buildings and goods, and that he had as much right to what was here as the next man. One of the boys had a camera. He took photographs of each item his parents carried out of the building."

"Photographs?"

"Provenance."

Mara could feel the anger creep in at the corners. "Genuine Aboriginal ghost-town souvenirs. Own a piece of creepy misfortune. Hear the cries of the dying in every teacup. Feel the cold hand of death on every place setting."

Gabriel took a step backwards.

"An eBay special. Bid early, bid often. Use the security of PayPal." Mara went to the window. "The father had a knife that he waved at me. I think his son photographed that, too. When they drove off, I took down the licence plate and called the police."

"So they got caught."

Mara pulled her lips back, thin as razors. "Oh, sure," she said. "Quick, quick, there's a dreadful family, with a trailer, stealing priceless cafeteria trays from a condemned Native reserve."

She unwrapped one of the paintings. "Bet that went right to the top of the crime docket."

Gabriel tried to imagine the kind of person who would steal from the dead. Ordinary. They were probably perfectly ordinary.

"It's cold." Mara rubbed her arms. "And damp."

"WHERE do you want to hang it?"

"Not here," she said. "It feels dead in here."

Gabriel followed Mara to the porch.

"I'll take the hammer and nails," she said. "Hold it up next to the door, so I can see how it looks."

Gabriel held the canvas by the wire. Mara was right. The painting had more life out here in the open.

"Okay," she said. "Put it down and get out of my way."

Gabriel retreated to the railing and waited. The fog was thick and still. Mara drove the nail into the wood with two strong strokes, as though she had done this all her life.

"Martin Luther," said Gabriel.

"The sixteenth-century monk?"

"He nailed stuff to doors, too."

Mara slipped the portrait over the nail. "As I recall, he was a pain in the ass."

"He was," said Gabriel.

"So am I." Mara stepped off the porch and walked into the fog. "Grab the other paintings, and try to keep up."

50

DORIAN STOOD ON THE SIDEWALK OUTSIDE THE BLUEBIRD and tried to relax the muscles in his neck. Winter would have called him as soon as the dam had collapsed. What had Mansbridge said? Early in the morning? Was that Alberta morning or Ontario morning? He checked his watch.

Eight-twenty.

Dorian took a deep breath. Stupid. Turning off the phone. How the hell was he going to explain that? A dead battery?

No. The damn thing was fully charged.

The spill would have sent shock waves through the corporation. What he needed to do was get to the office.

Right now.

Stock prices would be in free fall, and there was always the chance that one of the vigilantes in the café had recognized him from the news broadcast and was organizing a breakfast mob to chase him down. He had heard of such a thing happening in Texas.

Thank God this was Canada. At least they wouldn't be armed with anything more lethal than forks.

He was debating how long it would take to arrange for a car, when a cab pulled up alongside him and the driver touched his horn. Dorian didn't hesitate. He pulled the door open and slid in, glancing back at the Bluebird only to make sure that no one was gaining on him.

"Tecumseh Plaza," he told the driver.

"Tecumseh Plaza," the driver repeated.

"Yes."

"You businessman?"

"I'm in a hurry."

"Sure," said the driver, "all business is rush-rush."

Dorian tapped the phone on his knee. Olivia had a friend who was famous for destroying cellphones. Every time a new model came out, her old phone would have an accident. Dorian hadn't thought cellphones were that delicate.

"What's that?" said the driver.

"I dropped my phone."

"My wife drops her phone," said the man, "and boom, it's gone."

Dorian checked for a dial tone.

"You drop your phone again?"

The phone bounced off the door and onto the seat. "Yes," said Dorian. "I dropped it again."

Dial tone.

The third time he dropped the phone, he dropped it with authority. It ricocheted off the ceiling of the taxi and banged off the headrest.

"You okay?"

No dial tone.

"Yes," said Dorian, settling back into the seat and closing his eyes. "I'm fine."

~~~~~

THE cab dropped Dorian off at the front entrance to Domidion. As he paid the driver and started across the plaza, he realized that he had never used this entrance before.

Unsettling.

The public lobby was slick and austere. Stone-coloured walls. Stone-coloured floors. Stone-coloured guards controlling access to the elevators. The only colour in the foyer was the blue-green water in the empty aquarium.

"I'm Dorian Asher."

The young woman behind the counter tapped at the computer. "Could you spell that?"

Dorian smiled. "I'm not here for an appointment."

"You need an appointment."

Dorian smiled harder. "No, I don't. I'm the CEO."

The woman smiled back. "Of . . . ?"

"Domidion!"

THE waiting room was a stone-coloured box, a continuation of the lobby. Spartan, but not especially depressing.

Austere. That's what it was. Austere.

The delay was annoying. Dorian had shown the guards his credentials, and that should have done the trick, but, having started off on the wrong foot, he had been forced to wait until his identity could be verified.

Dorian spent the time enjoying the second hand on his new Rolex as it swept effortlessly around the dial. It took Winter six minutes and thirteen seconds to reach him.

The taller of the two guards remained somewhat skeptical.

"You're sure this is the CEO?"

"Yes," Winter told the guard, "I'm sure."

"Executives don't use the front door."

"It's all right," said Dorian. "You did what you were supposed to do."

"They use the executive tunnel."

NEITHER Winter nor Dorian spoke until they were on the elevator. Dorian fished the phone out of his pocket and handed it to Winter.

"It's broken," he said. "I dropped it."

"Public Relations is waiting," said Winter. "They'll brief you in the conference room."

"And last night someone cancelled my car." Dorian slipped the tie out of his pocket and knotted it around his neck. "I had to take a cab home. Find out what the hell happened."

THE conference room was arranged around an oval table that took up most of the space. The table was designed to seat twenty-four comfortably, but today there were only three other people in the room.

"You remember Victoria Lustig from Public Relations," said Winter.

"I do."

Lustig gestured to the two men who were standing on either side of her. "This is Dr. Jeremy Wang from Engineering and Jonathan Weisman from Legal."

"Tell me."

There were three flat-screens on the far wall. Weisman picked up the remote and aimed it at the middle screen. "At 3:30, Alberta time, the earthen dam at Holding Pond Number Four gave way, and the contents spilled into the Athabasca River. This is the network footage of the spill, taken from a CBC helicopter."

"What about the no-fly zone?"

"Quite right," said Weisman. "The news crew shouldn't have been there."

"But?"

"But they were."

"And we couldn't stop the broadcast?"

"It was a live feed," said Weisman. "We were able to clear the airspace shortly after this was shot." He aimed the remote at the left screen. "And this . . . this is footage from our containment crew."

Dorian's eyes moved back and forth between the two screens. "It's not the same spill."

"That's right," said Weisman. "We've had two dams collapse. Right now, the networks don't know about the second one. But they will."

"What the hell happened?"

The second man cleared his throat. He was Asian, slight, in his late fifties or early sixties with black hair and enormous glasses. "I am Dr. Wang from Engineering."

"All right, Dr. Wang from Engineering," said Dorian. "What the hell happened?"

"The dams were not meant to hold liquids for an extended

period," said Wang, his voice ringed with anxiety. "They were supposed to be evaporation ponds."

"Explain."

"The water used to process tar-sand oil is pumped into the ponds. The idea is that once a pond is full, the liquid is allowed to evaporate and the toxic residue is removed and processed."

Wang paused for a moment. Then he continued. "But production has kept the ponds at capacity, and there hasn't been an opportunity for evaporation to run its course."

"Because we keep pumping new effluent into the ponds."

"Yes," said Wang. "As soon as levels in a particular pond drop, we pump in more waste water."

"And the ponds are not designed for this kind of use."

"No," said Wang. "They're not."

Dorian watched the toxic waste pour through the dams and into the river.

"How many ponds do we have?"

"Seven," said Wang. "Four at 160 acre feet each and three at 500 acre feet. The first breach was at one of the smaller ponds."

"Holding Pond Number Four."

"Yes," said Wang. "The second breach was at Holding Pond Number Two."

Dorian returned to the left flat-screen. "And this is a larger pond."

"It's the largest at the facility," said Wang, "585 acre feet."

Dorian nodded and raised his fist. "Do-mi-di-on," he chanted. "Do-mi-di-on."

Wang and Weisman glanced at Lustig.

"That's what you're going to hear," said Dorian, "if we don't get control of this. 'Do-mi-di-on.' Give it a try."

Lustig looked stunned. "Sir . . ."

"Do it!"

"Do-mi-di-on." said Winter. "Do-mi-di-on."

"All of you," shouted Dorian. "Do-mi-di-on!"

WHEN Dorian got back to his office, he poured himself a very large Scotch.

"So, how bad is it?"

"Compared to what?"

Dorian finished the Scotch in one swallow and poured himself another. "Deepwater Horizon."

"It's worse," said Winter. "The 2010 Gulf of Mexico spill dumped more than five million barrels, or 210 million gallons, of oil into the ocean."

"But it was oil, and it was the open ocean."

"That was BP's contention," said Winter. "Our spill has dumped about 242 million gallons of toxic waste into a river system."

"So our screw-up is more concentrated."

"The spill will kill everything in the river. In less than a week, the toxins will reach Lake Athabasca. From there the toxins will join the Mackenzie River system and everything will wind up in the Beaufort Sea."

Winter ticked off the information as though she were reading items on a grocery list.

"How long?"

"To the Arctic Circle?"

"Yes."

"A month," said Winter. "Within a month, the pollution will reach the Arctic Circle."

Dorian put his glass down. "Is there a cleanup plan in place?"

"Yes."

"Will it stop the toxins?"

"No."

"But we'll be seen to be trying."

"PR is sending two full camera crews."

Dorian brought the drink to his desk. "I bought a new watch yesterday," he said, holding out an arm. "What do you think?"

"A Rolex is always a good choice."

"I assume the Board is upset."

Winter raised a fist and smiled. It was the first smile that Dorian had ever seen on the woman's face. "Do-mi-di-on," she said. "Do-mi-di-on."

51

IT HAS TAKEN SONNY ALL MORNING TO COLLECT THE NECES-
sary materials. There will be more to collect, but for now, at
least, he can begin. Sonny marks off the distances, placing one
foot in front of the other. The base has to be broad enough to
withstand the wind, and the structure has to be set back on the
beach beyond the high tide mark.

Five, six, seven, eight, nine . . .

Sonny has decided on twelve. And he has decided to begin
with a square. That way he doesn't have to remember the length
of two separate sides.

Twelve, twelve, twelve, and twelve.

And he has already found the perfect spot among the seagrasses on a small rise that looks both ways along the beach.
Sonny begins stacking the gathered items—shells, bones, driftwood, ocean miscellany—along the lines of the foundation.

Twelve feet on a side. Twelve inches thick. That will be the
base. Keep things strong. Keep things simple. That's Sonny.
Strong and simple. Sonny's only concern is that he is building his tower on sand, and he remembers that Dad has warned
about building houses on sand.

Dig deep and lay the foundation on rock. That's what Dad has always said.

Before he left the motel, Sonny had knocked on Dad's door to ask if building a tower on sand was the same thing as building a house on sand.

But there had been no answer.

Sonny selects a turtle shell and hooks a bone through one of the openings. He attaches a piece of steel mesh to the bone and then another shell and more bones. He pounds a piece of driftwood into the sand for support and then begins again.

The work is very slow, and, after several hours, Sonny has made little progress. While he can use small pieces of everything for the base, he can see that he will have to find larger items for the sides of the tower or he'll be on the beach for all eternity. There are things at the motel that he can use. The broken lounge chair. The rake with the bent tines. The tire jack that someone left in the parking lot.

And there's the town.

Wham-wham!

The town will have many things that could be used for Sonny's tower, things people forgot when they ran away. Sonny gets excited, and he works faster.

The foundation is the most important part of the tower. Sonny knows this. Once the foundation is straight and true and well laid, he can be creative with his materials. He can be artistic. Sonny realizes that there is no reason that the tower can't be strong and functional and beautiful as well.

Sonny sits in the sand and pieces the foundation together.

The motel, the town, the beach. Each can contribute in its own way. Each can provide something for Sonny's tower.

And the reserve. Sonny is stunned that he hasn't thought of this sooner. The reserve. Surely there are things on the reserve that can be used for the tower. Maybe when he goes there, he'll find the ghost Indians. And once he explains what he's doing, once he explains what the tower is for, they will probably insist on helping.

Come be my hands, Sonny will say. Come join me in this my creation. Come and marvel at what I have wrought.

Perhaps they'll provide lunch.

52

MARA PLUNGED INTO THE FOG WITH ONE OF THE PAINTINGS and the hammer. She couldn't see a thing, not even the outline of the other buildings, but she knew the ground. Her feet could feel the paths that connected the houses. Her toes knew where the road came in and where it circled back out.

WHEN they were teenagers, she and Lilly had played a game that involved a blindfold, some spinning around, and lots of shouting. They called their game "Blind Bat."

"Blind bat, blind bat, find your way home."

That was the goal of the game. To find your way home blindfolded. The "blind bat" would be left to feel for the ground, listen for a familiar sound, search for a telltale smell, while the other player would yell out encouragement.

"Blind bat's hot."

"Blind bat's cold."

"Blind bat's very cold."

Originally, these encouragements were supposed to be of assistance. If the blind bat was moving in the right direction, the other player was obligated to let the blind bat know that she was on the correct path.

"Blind bat's getting very hot."

And if the blind bat was heading off in the wrong direction, the other player was duty bound to tell her that she was off course.

"Cold, blind bat, freezing."

Then, as Mara and Lilly got good at finding their way home, the rules were changed. The shouting continued, but now there was no requirement that the information be accurate, and the other person would generally do their best to confuse the blind bat. They even began to time each other, calling out intervals as well as instructions.

"Twenty-nine, thirty, thirty-one, thirty-two," Mara would yell. "Cold, blind bat, hot, hot, hot."

They must have looked like a pair of fools, stumbling around the reserve, disturbing the peace. But it had been fun.

MARA was almost to the next house when she realized that she had lost Gabriel. Or, more properly, Gabriel had lost himself.

Blind bat, blind bat.

Okay, not good. While the reserve wasn't that large, there were hazards to be avoided. If this Gabriel had gone east, he'd be fine. Eventually, he'd bump into the water tower or the community centre, or he'd stumble across the main road and work his way back.

But if he headed west, there was the chance he'd walk right off the cliffs and wind up on the rocks below. West was where the danger lay.

THERE was a second game that Lilly had shown her. It wasn't quite as much fun as Blind Bat, but it did involve the same level of shrieking. They never put a name to it, perhaps because it wasn't so much a game as something to do on days when strong winds came in off the ocean.

It was a game of timing and faith. Like the waves, the ocean winds came in patterns of seven, the big gusts blowing in at the end of a sequence. Mara and Lilly would stand on the headlands, their jackets held tightly to their bodies, and then they would run and count.

"One, two three, four, five, six . . . "

And at the instant of the big gust, they would fling open their jackets and leap into the air. If they had guessed correctly, the wind would catch them, lift them off their feet and sail them backwards, sometimes as much as ten feet. If they guessed wrong, they would simply crash to the ground.

Success was magic. Failure was pain.

And after a day of leaping and sailing and crashing, they would come home with torn knees and elbows, and the satisfaction that they were invincible. Breasts and boys would change much of that, but on the headlands in the wind, like the birds who rode the thermals, Mara and Lilly could fly.

MARA heard him before she could see him. He was breathing heavily, not from the exertion of walking—he hadn't come that far or that fast—but from worry. By now he knew he was lost, and the reality was probably distressing and embarrassing.

"Hello . . . "

Mara smiled as she listened to him call out and suck in air through an open mouth. Men. Embarrassment would be the stronger of the two emotions.

"Blind bat, blind bat!"

Mara was close enough now to see Gabriel jump. Lovely.

"You decide to give up on the Apostles?"

"What?"

Mara stepped in front of him. "The suicide thing," she said. "I'm just checking, because if you hold to your current heading, you'll walk off a cliff."

"How'd you find me?"

"You breathe through your mouth."

Mara was tempted to tell this Gabriel about the flying game, to see if he wanted to play. But the winds weren't strong enough, and that time had passed. It had always been a game for children with their skinny bird bodies and stick arms and legs and no fear that the world would harm them in any way.

A game for children who truly believed they could fly.

"Are you thinking about it?" she asked. "Because if you are, I'll take my paintings now."

"No," he said, "I was just lost."

"A lot of that going around." Mara twirled the hammer in her hand. "You think you can keep up this time?"

"Sure."

"That's what I figure." Mara shifted the hammer to her right hand. "Let's try it this way."

Mara had never hooked the claw of a hammer through a man's belt before. It seemed rather bold, but as she dragged Gabriel back to the townsite, any apprehensions were replaced with a warm glow of power. Towing a man through the fog by his belt might well be the adult version of Blind Bat.

"Am I going too fast?"

"No."

Mara found herself wishing that the fog would lift so the community could see her return from the hunt with her prey. Mara nails man. Film at eleven.

"How's the hammer?"

"Great idea."

She wondered how Gabriel felt about the matter, hoped that he didn't think this had anything to do with sex. Or worse, affection. But of course he did. What man wouldn't? Christ, but they were simple constructions.

"We're here."

Mara dragged Gabriel onto the porch before she rescued her hammer.

"Where are we?"

"Give me the red one."

Mara leaned the painting against the wall and held out a hand. "Nail."

"You want me to do that?"

Mara considered jamming the hammer back in Gabriel's belt and twisting it a bit. "Remind me again who was lost?"

"I can drive a nail."

Mara could taste meanness on her tongue. "Okay," she said. "Go for it."

Now it was a contest, and Mara had always liked contests. Gabriel and the nail. Could he hit the damn thing. Mara found herself hoping that he would miss, so she could say something pithy.

"You waiting for theme music?" It wasn't all that pithy. Tart. It was definitely tart.

"Maybe a drum roll."

"Rat-a-tat-tat." Now that was pithy. "Rat-a-tat-tat."

The first blow hit the nail squarely on the head, and Mara felt a pinch of disappointment. The second stroke missed the target, and, from the way Gabriel's neck disappeared into his shoulder, she guessed that it had found a piece of his hand.

"You okay?"

The sound seemed to come out of the ground.

"What was that?"

"What?"

Mara pushed past Gabriel and opened the door. There it was again. A low, rolling rumble. She stepped inside, could feel Gabriel step in behind her.

"I suppose," she said, because she couldn't think of anything else to say, "that you have a good explanation for this."

The fog floated into the room, but it was little more than a soft mist.

"Can't say that I do."

Mara took in the scene in front of her. "Shut the door," she said. "This is going to take a while."

53

THE HOUSE SHOULD HAVE BEEN EMPTY AND BARE.

All the homes, all the buildings, all the outbuildings had
long since been stripped and vandalized. Mara had walked
through them in turn on more than one occasion, searching for
reminders of the families who had once lived here.

There had been little left. Initials carved into a porch post.
A flyer from a big box store, forgotten on a high shelf. Thirty-
five cents lost in the sand at the playground. Nothing more
than that.

And now there was a dog on a blanket in the middle of the
floor. Along with a mattress, several chairs, a table, dishes, and
pots and pans. Nothing new. Everything with the look of having
been thrown away more than once. In one corner were the two
bench seats from the bus.

Soldier struggled to his feet and let loose another growl.

Mara waited for Gabriel to ask the obvious question.

"I thought you said the reserve was deserted."

"It is," said Mara. "What's your dog doing here?"

"He's not my dog."

Soldier continued to growl.

"Evidently."

Gabriel dropped to one knee and patted his thigh. "Soldier," he said. "Come on, boy. Good boy."

Soldier didn't move off the blanket.

"Where have you been, boy? Did you get lost?"

The growling stopped, and Soldier's back end began to quiver. Mara slowly walked the room.

"Someone's living here."

"More than one," said Gabriel. "From the look of it."

Soldier limped over and buried his face in Gabriel's lap.

"Where'd they go?"

"Heard us coming," said Gabriel. "Ran off."

"All the banging we were doing."

"Be my guess."

Soldier rolled over on his back and sighed.

"Who's living here, boy?" said Gabriel. "Folks from town?"

Mara picked up a pot and turned it over. There was the chance that some of the families had returned, but she knew better. If that had happened, the people would have come into town for supplies and to say hello. She would have known. Such a return would not have gone unmarked.

"Come on."

"Don't you want to stick around to see who shows up?"

"No one's going to return so long as we're here," said Mara, "and we'll never find them in the fog."

"Okay."

"I'll come back when I can see."

Gabriel got to his feet. "Come on, boy," he said. "Let's go home."

The dog stayed on the blanket.

Mara smiled. "Doesn't look as though he's going anywhere."

"He's just playing hard to get."

Mara stepped out onto the porch, hefted the hammer, and drove a nail into the wood siding. Whoever was living here needed to know whose house this had been, whose house it remained. They needed to know that they were not welcome.

Gabriel stood in the doorway. Soldier was at his side.

"You convinced him."

"He's hungry."

"Good a reason as any." Mara unwrapped the painting and looped the wire over the nail. "Does this look straight?"

Soldier whimpered and leaned against Gabriel's leg.

"Rose and Lilly Sampson," said Mara. "And Lilly's son."

Gabriel reached out and touched the frame. "This is where they lived?" He tilted the picture to the left. "This house?"

Mara nodded. "Lilly was my best friend."

Gabriel stood and stared at the portrait, his hands jammed deep in his pockets. Then he stepped off the porch and vanished into the fog.

Soldier began moaning, swaying back and forth, and when the man didn't return, the dog dove into the weather, howling as he went.

Mara stayed on the porch, listening for any sounds the land might be willing to share, waiting for Gabriel to reappear and explain himself.

Nothing.

Finally, she folded the butcher paper up and shoved the hammer into her jacket pocket. She checked the painting one last time. Okay. Enough was enough. She had saved this Gabriel once today. She wasn't going to do it again.

From now on he could save himself.

54

BY EARLY AFTERNOON, THE COLLAPSE OF THE SECOND DAM had made international news, with all the networks showing the same footage of dirty bronze tailings pouring into a glacial blue river. Along with music in minor chords and sombre voice-overs.

Dorian watched the spectacle for the first hour, before he hit the mute button and effectively turned the images into a screen saver. He wouldn't have guessed it, but watching the spill without the sound was quite soothing. He found himself drifting along with the effluence as it was flushed out of the holding ponds, and finding an unexpected peace in the chaos of the moment.

Nothing to be done about the spills. Shit happens. It would happen again. The Athabasca would shove the toxins into the Mackenzie, and the Mackenzie would dump everything into the Arctic. The river wasn't that pristine to begin with. For much of the last century, sawmills and farms along the way had been dumping furans, chlorinated dioxins, and phosphorus into the watershed. The river would eventually clean itself.

That's what rivers did.

Still, the spill was a public relations nightmare and an economic annoyance. Domidion would be mauled in the media.

Every past misstep that the corporation had made would be dug up and dragged naked through the streets. Stock prices, which were already unacceptably low, would go into temporary free fall, and any bonuses were now at the bottom of the Athabasca.

Along with the heavy metals from the tailing ponds.

All this before lawyers got their hands on the matter. Dorian had no idea what the legal ramifications might be, but he could hear a herd of class-action lawsuits stampeding over the horizon.

He had spent much of the day fielding questions from managers of large pension funds who were heavily invested in the corporation.

Yes, Dorian agreed, it was unfortunate, but now was not the right time to panic.

No, he had insisted, now was not the time to sell.

In between calls, Dorian would glance at the flat-screen. He had expected that the media would have come up with new and more dramatic images of the spill. But they hadn't.

Excellent. No fresh logs for the fire.

In a week, no more than two, the shock factor would wear off, the hysterics would run their course, and it would be time for a reasoned and civilized conversation.

Until then, it was Dorian's job to hold the blaze in check until it burned itself out.

WINTER arrived at a little after four, carrying a small box.

"Your new phone," she said. "We were able to retrieve all the information from the old one."

"What about the limo?"

"Zebras," said Winter. "A number of other corporations were affected as well."

Dorian was momentarily cheered as he imagined an angry pack of Bay Street barons standing at city curbs, trying to wave down cabs.

"What the hell is Security doing?"

"Everything they can."

Dorian turned the sound back on. Dramatic music filled his office. "You see that?" he said. "You see that?"

"I do."

"I want us to go on the offensive."

"Sir?"

"With the spill." Dorian hit the mute button. "I don't want us running for cover on this. I don't want us looking guilty, because we're not."

"It is our facility."

"Yes," said Dorian, "of course it is. But the occasional spill is the price we pay for cheap energy, and I think we should say this."

"Public Relations has suggested that we keep a low profile for the time being."

"No," said Dorian. "I think that's the wrong approach. We don't apologize. We educate."

"Educate?"

"You remember the shooting at that elementary school?"

"Sandy Hook, in Newtown, Connecticut."

"That's the one. How many people were killed?"

Winter closed her eyes for a moment. "Twenty children and six adults."

"Terrible," said Dorian. "And who got blamed?"

"The man who did the killing."

"No." Dorian could feel his calm slipping. "Everyone blamed the National Rifle Association and their policies on gun control. There was a huge outcry against guns."

"Yes," said Winter, "there was."

"And what did the head of the NRA do?"

"Wayne LaPierre."

"Yes," said Dorian. "He stood up in front of television cameras and had the courage to say that we needed more guns, that only a good guy with a gun could stop a bad man with a gun."

"According to the accepted studies," said Winter, "that's inaccurate."

"Inaccurate?" Dorian was shouting now. "Of course it's inaccurate. It's crap. Guns don't make the world safer. What did that ER doctor find?"

"Art Kellermann at Emory University."

"That's the one. Didn't he determine that guns in homes were thirty times more likely to be involved in the death of a member of the household than be involved in self-defence."

"Forty-three times."

"And yet LaPierre stood up with a straight face and said America needed more guns. You see where I'm going with this?"

"If you repeat a lie often enough, it becomes the truth."

"Exactly. Winston Churchill, right?"

"Joseph Goebbels."

"I should do an interview." Dorian sat back and took control of his breathing. "With that woman from *En Garde*."

"Manisha Khan."

"Let's set it up."

Winter adjusted her glasses. "We've received the psychological evaluation on Dr. Quinn."

"And?"

"No flags," said Winter. "Everything was inside the box."

"What about the writing on the walls?"

"Evidently Dr. Quinn was creating a list of man-made disasters."

"And that didn't strike our boys in white as odd?"

"They thought it eccentric," said Winter, "but evidently lots of people make lists."

Ms. Khan would be a formidable opponent. She'd want to squeeze concessions out of him. Responsibility. Sorrow. Remorse. A firm purpose of amendment. And she would get none of that. She'd be expecting a repentant company executive to walk onto her show, but what would arrive at the studio would be a corporate warrior, armed and ready. No retreat, no negotiation, no fear. Tell the truth. That's what Ms. Khan's viewing audience would hear. North America needs oil. The price of freedom is energy.

"Parliament is going to hold hearings," said Winter.

"Then we have nothing to worry about," said Dorian. "Do you know the fatal flaw of democracy?"

"People?"

"Democracy offers its enemies the means by which to destroy it." Dorian pushed back from his desk. "Anything else?"

"Your wife called," said Winter. "She'd like to talk with you when you have a chance."

"She wants to buy a house in Orlando," said Dorian. "As if Alberta isn't enough of a problem."

"And Dr. Toshi's office called again."

Dorian checked the television. Incredible. The networks were going to wear those images out. What the hell had happened to investigative journalism in the country?

"Look at that, Winter." Dorian stabbed a finger at the flatscreen. "Where's the pride?"

"Sir?"

"Strength," said Dorian. "That's what we need now. Strength and firm resolve."

"Yes, sir."

"I'm going to the gym."

Dorian flexed his abdominals and squeezed the muscles in his upper arms and shoulders. The more he thought about taking the offensive, the more he liked it.

"If anyone wants me, they can find me there."

Why be a lamb when you could be a lion? He tried to recall what John Wayne had said in one of his movies. Something about never apologizing, that it was a sign of weakness.

Good enough for the Duke, good enough for him.

55

BY THE TIME GABRIEL GOT BACK TO THE TRAILER, THE FOG was breaking apart along the horizon and patches of blue were pushing through. He eased himself into the rocking chair and stared out at the cedars.

So, he had finally found the house where his mother and sister had lived, where his nephew had been born. He had stood on the porch and waited for some fragment of emotion to overtake him.

Rage, sorrow, loss.

And all he had felt was the chill of a low-pressure system and a freshening wind off the ocean.

Soldier emerged from the trees and limped to the deck.

"The prodigal son," said Gabriel. "The return of the native."

Soldier lay down by Gabriel's feet, turning his back to the man.

"You're a fine one to complain. I'm not the one who ran off."

MINNEAPOLIS had been a world away from Lethbridge. Gabriel had never seen so many buildings, so much traffic. Joe had found a two-bedroom apartment near the University of Minnesota campus.

"When are Mum and Little coming?"

Gabriel hadn't cared for Minneapolis. He missed the open sky of the prairies. He missed the people on the reserve at Standoff. He even missed the wind.

That first weekend in the city, they had had breakfast at a hole-in-the-wall café called Al's, where you sat on stools at a long counter. Breakfast was good, especially the hash browns, and afterwards Joe had taken Gabriel for a walk on the campus.

"Place has over twenty libraries."

"No, it doesn't."

"Yeah, it does," said his father. "Guy in the Second Precinct has a son who goes to the U, and he told me that."

"Twenty libraries?"

"And there's an Indian centre over on Franklin. We should go there and pay our respects."

"I have a lot of studying to do."

"All you do is study."

"You want me to have good grades, don't you?"

"We can stop by this weekend. I've got the Saturday off. Maybe there's a drum group needs a couple of good singers."

They had walked across a bridge and looked down at the Mississippi. The river wasn't as impressive as Gabriel had thought it would be. It was muddy. That was the first thing he had noticed.

The water was the colour of mud.

GABRIEL watched the dog roll over and catch the slanting sun on his belly. With any luck, the evening sky would be crystal, and there would be stars. Gabriel slipped his shoe off and rubbed the dog with his foot.

"And nothing to look backward to with pride, and nothing to look forward to with hope."

Soldier let loose a long, deep sigh.

Late. That was his great sin. He had not acted in time, and it had been a grievous mistake. He knew that now. He should have known it sooner.

"Do you like poetry?" Gabriel pushed his foot under Soldier's chin. "Do you like Robert Frost?"

What else had the old laureate said?

"Home is the place where, when you have to go there, they have to take you in."

It was a lovely sentiment, but poets tended to overstate emotions, to play at the extremes of elation and depression, never spending much time mucking about in the middle. No one was obligated to take you in. Home wasn't a place. At best, it was a shifting illusion, a fiction you created to mask the fact that, in the end, you were alone in the world.

Gabriel wondered if Mara would stay on the reserve for the night or if she would go back to the yellow house. He shouldn't have walked away like that. He should have stayed. He could have spent more time in his mother's home.

Home.

Maybe Frost was right. After all those years, Rose had come home. The band had taken her in. They had taken his sister in as well.

~~~~~

THE Minneapolis American Indian Center was a multi-storey concrete and wood structure with dark windows that felt like the open mouths of caves.

"You see the wood designs in the facade?" Joe had asked Gabriel, as the two of them stood in front of the building. "George Morrison. He's a Chippewa artist. If we're lucky, we might meet him."

"Why are we here?"

"It's where the Indians are."

Gabriel was surprised to discover that he liked the overall effect of the patterns that Morrison had created. More than anything, the geometrical shapes reminded him of mathematics.

"I miss Mum. I miss Little."

"So do I," his father had said. "And they'll be here in no time."

IT had been waiting for him when he returned from India. The blank card with the photograph.

Little.

That was what he had always called her. Little. For little sister. The Little he had left had been a twelve-year-old girl. The Little who was smiling at him in the photograph was a grown woman with an infant son.

Gabriel found the stuffed puppy he had bought years before at the Calgary airport. It was in a plastic bag in a closet. He was pretty sure that babies liked stuffed toys, and he thought that he might buy a stuffed cat as well. Or a hippopotamus, or a penguin, or a duck. But first he needed to find his sister. And his nephew.

"Hi, Little," he'd say when his sister opened the door. "I'm back."

"Hi, baby," he'd tell the child. "I'm your uncle. Surprise."

THAT Saturday, they went to the Indian Center. Joe introduced himself to a woman at the reception desk and wound up in a conversation with one of the counsellors, a stocky man in a leather vest whose head bobbed about as though it weren't completely attached to his neck.

"Welcome to Anishinabe territory," the man told Joe. "You guys know any Black Lodge tunes?"

Gabriel was sorry he hadn't brought a book with him.

"This is my son," Joe told the man. "He's a real good singer."

Joe and the man settled into a long conversation about drum groups, and Gabriel wandered off in search of the Chippewa artist.

He didn't find him.

Instead, he found a gymnasium with a basketball game in progress. He leaned against the wall, while the teams raced up and down the floor, shouting, pushing each other, fighting for the ball. Gabriel had never had a strong interest in sports, but as he watched, he imagined that it might be fun to come down to the centre on a weekend and give basketball a try.

One of the better players looked as though he had just stepped off a movie set. He was lanky with dark skin and a long ponytail tied back with a red leather thong. Gabriel was impressed with the guy's skill, the way he could slide through traffic, get above the rim for a rebound, sink a shot with another player in his face.

Gabriel was about to leave to find his father when the guy took a shot from the top of the key. It was short. The ball rattled off the rim and bounced to where Gabriel was standing. He picked the ball up and stepped onto the court.

"You got a great shot," Gabriel told him, and tossed the ball back.

The guy caught the ball, bounced it a couple times, and said, "What the fuck do you want, white boy?"

When he found his way back to the lobby, Joe was waiting for him.

"So what do you think of the place?"

"Great," Gabriel told his father. "Really great."

THE envelope had had no return address, and nothing to indicate who had sent it. The heavy block letters on the envelope weren't Little's, and his sister would have written a note. The only clue was the postmark.

Samaritan Bay.

Gabriel had gone on the Internet that evening to find the place. And there it was. A small town on the coast, known for its turtle-nesting beach and natural hot springs. There were photographs of the annual turtle festival, photographs of a music festival, photographs of people playing on the beach.

At first, he hadn't noticed it. Just a mark on the map. Above the town itself.

The Smoke River Reserve.

Joe was from Leech Lake in Minnesota. Gabriel knew that. His father had talked about the place, had told stories of growing up in bogs and swarms of mosquitoes, had talked about brothers and sisters, cousins, uncles, and aunties. Not with any great longing, but with fondness. Listening to the stories, Gabriel understood that growing up in Leech Lake hadn't been all that easy, but his father's attachment to the place and the people had been enduring.

Rose had had no such attachment to Smoke River. Gabriel had asked his mother about the reserve on more than one occasion.

"What was Smoke River like?"

"Smoke River's got nothing to do with me, and it's got nothing to do with you."

"Do we have relations there?"

"We've got nothing there," his mother had said. "That place doesn't exist."

"Where is it?"

"It doesn't exist."

Why hadn't he thought of the reserve sooner? When he discovered that his mother and sister had left Lethbridge, when he discovered that they had packed up and disappeared, why hadn't he thought of Smoke River?

"My mother was from the reserve," Gabriel told the dog. "Did I tell you that?"

Soldier lay perfectly still in the sun.

"After my father was killed, they moved back here from Lethbridge and didn't tell me."

Soldier flicked an ear.

"She was angry with my father for taking the posting in Minneapolis. I guess she was angry with me as well."

Soldier opened one eye.

"You think it was my fault?"

Soldier opened the other eye.

"They knew where I was. They could have written. They could have phoned."

THE evening of his father's death, he had called his mother to tell her what happened. He expected that she would be devastated, and perhaps she was, but the voice on the phone had contained no emotion.

"What do I do?"

"Bury him."

"No, I mean when are you coming down?"

"Not," his mother had said.

"What?"

"Your father made his decision. You, too."

"You have to come for the funeral!"

"That's for you to do."

By then Gabriel was shouting. "You should have come with us! You were supposed to come with us!"

There was a long silence when neither of them spoke, when Gabriel wasn't sure if his mother was still on the phone.

"Mum?"

"Make sure you call his family. Tell them what's happened."

"We're his family! You and Little and me!"

"And you know where we are."

Gabriel had thrown the phone against the wall as hard as he could. Then he picked it up and threw it again.

~~~~~

SOLDIER pulled himself to a sitting position. The wind had picked up. There were small whitecaps on the water. Gabriel tried to remember the funeral. His father's fellow officers had come in force, and his father's relations had driven down from Walker in a tribal van.

And yet all he could recall of the occasion was sitting in the front row, alone, by himself, in an empty church.

56

THE GYM WAS EMPTY. DORIAN TOOK HIS TOWEL AND WATER bottle to one of the elliptical trainers. A hard thirty minutes on the random-hill program. Free weights. Grab a shower.

He'd call Olivia from the condo.

Toshi could damn well wait until tomorrow.

The price of freedom is energy? Had he actually thought that? Thank God he hadn't said it out loud.

Winter hadn't seemed too impressed with Dorian's insight on democracy. It was true, of course, but anyone with half a brain knew that democracy's enemies weren't the real danger.

It had far more to fear from its friends.

Dorian settled into a nice pace on the trainer and let his mind wander. A list of man-made disasters? Why would anyone do that? Such a list would be endless. More to the point, why would a sane man put such a list on the walls of a house? Kitchen and living room, bathrooms and bedrooms.

The front door.

Dorian closed his eyes and tried to retrieve the photograph that Security had taken of the front door.

Kali Creek.

That's what Quinn had written on the front door in capital letters.

Kali Creek.

Amazing how the past could find its way back to the present. Amazing how simple things could go so very wrong.

DORIAN had been in Spain—Valencia, to be exact—when the Kali Creek accident happened. Spain had been Olivia's idea. Neither of them could speak Spanish, so his wife had hired a young woman to come to the house two evenings a week to tutor them in conversational Spanish.

"We could just hire a guide when we get there," Dorian had offered. "Someone who speaks English."

"Where's the fun in that," Olivia had scolded.

Galiana Ruiz was from Barcelona, a short, slender woman with dark hair and a brilliant smile. It was the first thing that Dorian noticed. Galiana's smile.

"You will love Valencia," she told them. "It's not Barcelona, but it is a very artistic town, and right on the Mediterranean."

Dorian missed most of the evening lessons, but he was impressed by his wife's progress.

"*Dónde està el bañjo?* Do you know what that means?"

"No idea."

Olivia lowered her voice as though it were a secret. "Where's the bathroom."

Dorian had to admit that the phrase could come in handy. "How do you say, 'Where's the best hotel in town?'"

"Galiana says my accent is *muy buena*."

~~~~~

KALI Creek.

It had been a series of mistakes, each one compounding the others, Domidion had been building a pipeline across the interior of British Columbia. The work had been slow: trouble with environmental groups and First Nation communities, problems with the terrain and the thick underbrush.

Then a mid-level manager decided to try a shortcut. Instead of removing the undergrowth with chainsaws and machines as the crews had been doing, or using a standard herbicide that hadn't proven to be all that effective, this particular genius called main office and got another equally bright light to send Domidion's newest agricultural product into the field.

GreenSweep.

Everyone in the world knew about Agent Orange, the defoliant that had made its name in the 1960s during the Vietnam War, as part of the U.S. military's Ranch Hand program. It was a chemical combination of two phenoxyl herbicides that had been contaminated with dioxin.

GreenSweep was a bacterium. The only commonality between the two defoliants was the use of a colour in the names. Dorian tried to remember who had come up with "GreenSweep." Someone with a sense of humour.

ON the first leg of the flight, from Toronto to Zurich, Olivia had read sections of the guidebook to him. Dorian had wanted to settle back and watch movies, but his wife insisted that they needed to know what was waiting for them when they landed in Manises.

"Don't you want to be surprised?"

"I don't want to miss anything."

"We can't see all of Valencia in a week."

"We should stay for two weeks at least."

"I can't take two weeks off work."

"Las Fallas is in a few days," said Olivia. "And we have to see the Valencia Cathedral and the central market."

Dorian wasn't sure why seeing a cathedral was important, or a market for that matter, but Olivia assured him that it was.

"Valencia was founded as a Roman colony in about 138 B.C. Can you imagine that? Many of the buildings in the old town date back to the fifteenth century. That was before America was discovered."

"Not sure I want to be in a building that old."

"There's the Torres de Serranos, the Turia Gardens, and the Silk Exchange. Valencia is going to be fun," Olivia told him. "You'll see. We're going to have a great time."

On the third day of their Spanish vacation, just as they were heading off for breakfast at a small café recommended in the guidebook, Dorian had received the phone call about Kali Creek. Olivia had not been pleased with the situation.

"Surely there is someone at the corporation who can handle this," she said. "It's not the end of the world."

"I'm the CEO."

"You're also my husband, and I'd like us to spend some time together."

"They wouldn't have asked me to come back if it wasn't serious."

"What am I supposed to do?"

"You could come with me."

"What about Las Fallas?" Olivia had flashed Dorian a glance that drew blood. "And we haven't seen any of the shops in the Casco Antiguo."

"Then you should stay," Dorian had said. "If I can get back, I will."

"You won't." Olivia shook her head. "You enjoy disasters too much."

It wasn't true, of course. He didn't enjoy disasters. Disasters were disruptive. More than that, they were bad for business.

GREENSWEEP hadn't gone through any of the testing protocols. It wasn't supposed to have left the storage facilities.

The first mistake.

The recommended dilution ratio for GreenSweep was 1000:1. The GreenSweep that was loaded onto the plane in Terrace, British Columbia, was only diluted 10:1.

Yet another mistake. A mistake no one caught until after the plane had dumped its load into the Kali Creek watershed.

The effect had been immediate. Given the mountainous terrain of the area, the presence of streams and tributaries, and the impossibility of controlling the application, spraying *any* defoliant on such a landscape would have been an environmental nightmare.

And GreenSweep hadn't been just any defoliant.

Dorian had seen aerial photos of the area. Everything GreenSweep touched had died. Trees, undergrowth, animals, fish. Everything. It was only luck that the clearing crews had not been in the vicinity when the plane went over.

The damage might have been limited, but that afternoon, an unexpected storm had come out of the northwest, driving heavy rain in front of it, and the downpour had washed the bacterium into Kali Creek.

And from there, it found its way into the ocean.

DORIAN had not really enjoyed Valencia. The architecture was interesting, but the buildings were old and smelled of age. The streets in the old town were narrow and mysterious, but there was an air of danger to the shadows and the darkened doorways. The small shops were intriguing, but there was nothing in any of them that Dorian wanted. He had liked the central market best of all, with its triple-arched doorways and interior dome. There were large hams hanging on hooks, cheese wheels stacked on each other, an endless variety of seafood glistening on beds of fresh ice. Everywhere you looked, there were booths filled with spices, fruits, vegetables, and baskets of mushrooms.

But even here, the moment had been spoiled by vendors who recognized Dorian and Olivia for what they were—rich North Americans—and called out to them at every turn.

Olivia spent much of the time smiling and saying, "*No, gracias,*" over and over again. Galiana had been right. Olivia's accent was excellent. For all the good it did.

There was a mother-daughter team who caught them in one of the parks and insisted they each take a flower and then demanded payment. Dorian had given the flowers back, but the two women had dogged their heels all the way back to their hotel.

When they got to their room, Olivia had flung herself on the bed. "God," she had shouted at the ceiling, "but that was wonderful."

The morning that the call came, Dorian had hardly been able to smother his delight.

KALI Creek had been a catastrophe. GreenSweep had carved a path of destruction all the way to the coast. The surprise was just how virulent the bacterium had remained even after it had been diluted with salt water. It had destroyed all life in the bay and pushed the kill zone out into the ocean some twenty kilometres.

And it would have been front-page news had it not been for the earthquake in Japan and the resulting tsunami that destroyed the Fukushima Daiichi nuclear facility. The meltdown there might have been prevented if officials had acted sooner. But they hesitated, and, by the time they finally did open the valves and flood the exposed rods with sea water, it was too late.

For the next month, every news outlet settled on that single story, and when the anchors, the correspondents, and the on-site journalists finally looked up from their press kits, Kali Creek had been subsumed and forgotten in the more powerful images of nuclear Armageddon.

DORIAN increased the incline and leaned into the machine. The whirl of the mechanism and each breath he took echoed in the silence of the empty room. It felt good to have his heart pumping, his body sweating. Maybe he'd do a longer workout. Maybe he'd stay on the trainer for the rest of the evening. Turn the session into an overnight marathon.

How far could you go on one of these things? Montreal? New York? Valencia?

He picked up the pace. How hard would he have to push to break the trainer free of its moorings?

That would be fun.

Dorian Asher, executive extraordinaire, astride an exercise machine, chasing Thicke, Toshi, Khan, and a herd of Zebras along Yonge Street in the middle of rush-hour traffic; knight errant, bearing down on fools and felons alike.

Now, that would be something to see.

57

SONNY LIKES THE OLD YELLOW SCHOOL BUS. HE LIKES TO climb into the driver's seat and pretend to turn the wheel. Sonny presses on the gas pedal and works the shift. First gear. Second gear. Third gear. Fourth gear. When the bus is going too fast, Sonny steps on the brake.

Safety first. That's Sonny's motto when he's driving children to school. Safety first.

Sonny flips the turn signal on and looks to his left. If it were a clear day, he would be able to see the town from here.

Sonny flips the turn signal and looks to his right. If it were a clear day, he would be able to see the reserve and the top of the water tower.

Sonny, the bus driver.

Sonny, the tour guide.

Maybe the ghost Indians would like to take a ride with Sonny. He could show them the sights. The Smoke River, Canyon Falls, the turtle beaches, the Ocean Star Motel. Sonny could tell them all about Samaritan Bay and its history.

In the beginning, there was nothing. That's how Sonny would start. In the beginning, there was nothing.

Sonny would not point out the hot springs, even though

they are a local attraction. And he would probably avoid any mention of That One Bad Day. Tourists like happy things when they're on holiday. They like things that make them smile. They like to take pictures of bright business and magic moments.

Sonny is sure that the ghost Indians would enjoy such a tour. Wham.

And if they really liked the tour, they might give him a tip.

Sonny steps on the brake and brings the bus to a halt. Enough driving for the day. Everybody off! That's what Sonny tells the children. Everybody off!

Sonny checks the bus to see if there is anything left that he can use for his tower, but even the windshield wipers are gone. Two of the bench seats are missing, but the rear seat is still there. That is Sonny's favourite seat, especially when there aren't many people on the bus.

Like today.

From the rear seat, Sonny can watch the entire bus. When he's not driving the bus, he likes to sit here. Some days, if he is sleepy, he stretches out on the seat and takes a nap.

Today, Sonny is not sleepy. Today, there is work to be done.

Sonny steps off the bus, walks to the security fence, and hangs off the wire.

Wire.

That's what Sonny needs.

Wire.

If Sonny had some wire, he could weave it through all the pieces of the tower. Then the tower would be strong. Many of the towers in Dad's stories fall down or they burn or they're abandoned. Sonny doesn't want his tower to fall down, and if he had some wire, it wouldn't.

Sonny takes out his wire cutters, but the fence wire is too thick and rigid. He could cut the single strand of barbed wire that runs across the top of the fence, but that wire is covered with thorns. If he makes his tower with this wire, people might call Sonny's tower "The Tower of Thorns."

The Tower of Thorns.

It's an impressive name, but tourists might be wary of something called The Tower of Thorns. They might not want to have their picture taken next to something sharp and dangerous.

The Strong Tower.

The Tower of Power.

The Guiding Light Tower.

Those would be better names.

Okay, okay, now Sonny just has to find the right kind of wire. Not too strong. Not too weak. Not too thick. Not too thin. The just-right wire.

Wham-wham!

That's it! Of course! Sonny knows where he can find the wire he needs. He springs off the fence and tests the wire cutters on the thorn wire.

Snap.

Nice and sharp. Nice and sharp.

Sonny hangs on the fence, rocks himself back and forth, for in his mind, he can see the tower, can see the beacon lit, can see the fire's radiance slicing through the gloom.

And he trembles as he wonders what such a light might find in the darkness.

58

MARA SPENT THE REST OF THE AFTERNOON PROWLING THE reserve, searching the houses, lying in wait by the water tower. Several times she heard noises, saw shadows, and she had rushed forward to pounce on her prey. But, it was just the wind in the fog, and, when she finally left the reserve and headed down the trail, she had nothing in her jaws to show for her stealth and determination.

Nicholas Crisp was not at the hot springs.

Which was odd.

For as long as Mara had known the man, girl to woman, Crisp had seldom left his steamy domain. He had gone to town, of course, for groceries and a slice of community. And he had come to the reserve for the ceremonies and the feasts, had been a great favourite among the older women, who found his red beard, bald head, and booming voice an entertainment.

"Nicholas."

Mara followed the path that wandered through the springs. The man liked his water, and he could be relaxing in any of the pools.

"Nicholas! You here?"

The fog was beginning to break up now. Thick on the reserve. Feeble on the flats. Hide and seek. Having fun with her.

"Nicholas!"

The party had been a pleasant affair. Small, but pleasant. A hot soak and good food. With two naked men all to herself. Mara wasn't sure whether the men part or the naked part was the more problematic. Probably a little of both.

As she roamed the pools, she conjured up memories of the array of food that Crisp had set out on the table the night before. The hummus had been particularly good, full of garlic and finely chopped hot peppers. She had sampled the stuffed chicken breasts, the lamb orzo, and the seafood cannelloni.

All good.

And then there were the desserts. She could have spent the evening at that end of the table.

Mara was trying to remember just how many desserts there had been when she realized that she was hungry. Actually, she was starving. When had she eaten last?

Breakfast?

She hadn't eaten since breakfast? Thinking about food had been a mistake. What did she have to eat back at the yellow house? This Gabriel had used up all the eggs, and he had fried the last of the bacon. She wasn't even sure there was any bread left.

"Nicholas!"

THERE had been only enough money in the Tenderflake pail for a bus ticket to Toronto. Mara had put on a good face.

"I have to go to Toronto anyway," she told her mother and grandmother. "I'll get a job, work there a year, take some art workshops, and then I'll go to Paris."

"So, this is goodbye," her mother had said.

"I'll be back. I'm only going to Toronto."

"Your cousin Reedy went to Calgary, and he never came back."

"While you're in Toronto," her grandmother had told her, "you should look into nursing. A nurse would be a handy thing to be in case the painting doesn't work out."

CRISP'S single-wide was set back in the trees on a rise above the pools. Mara had always thought that, one day, the man was going to put his house up on blocks, remove the wheels, and throw a decorative skirt up around the perimeter, as most people with trailers would have done. But he had kept the wheels on the axles, and the hitch hooked to his pickup, rigged and ready for flight.

Mara could smell something simmering just inside the door, something hot and spicy. Surely the man hadn't gone off and left food unattended on the stove. A friend of her grandmother's had done exactly that. Bobbie Lake had been rendering bear fat when she discovered she was out of cigarettes. A quick trip to town turned into a stop at the Tin Turtle and more than one drink. By the time she got back to the reserve, the bear fat was long gone.

And so was her trailer.

Mara tried the door. She hadn't expected to find it locked, and it wasn't.

"Nicholas."

Mara had never seen the inside of Crisp's trailer, and she was surprised by the amount of interior space, which seemed somehow to exceed the exterior dimensions. She had assumed that he would be somewhat disorganized and cluttered in his housekeeping habits, but such was not the case. The place was clean, with none of the mustiness that Mara would have imagined of trailers and single men.

There were books along one wall, the works arranged alphabetically by author. Some of the titles she recognized: *The Book of Not* by Tsitsi Dangarembga; Eduardo Galeano's three-volume history, *Memory of Fire*; Melville's *Moby-Dick*; Oscar Wilde's *De Profundis*.

Others were ancient tomes, bound in embossed leather, softened by the centuries.

Red seemed to be Crisp's favourite colour. There was a red leather sofa, a red leather chair with a matching ottoman. The table was rose-coloured wood, while the curtains were a crimson variation of a William Morris pattern.

Mara wouldn't have imagined the man in this space. Maybe the trailer was his sanctuary, a second skin that Crisp slipped into at the end of each day.

A pot of what looked to be chili was bubbling on the stove. There was no danger that it would boil over or cook down any time soon. However, it did smell delicious, and now that Mara had come this far, she saw no reason not to go all the way.

She found a bowl and a spoon. A loaf of heavy multi-grain bread was sitting out on the counter, and she was able to locate the butter with little difficulty. Mara didn't think that Crisp would mind. He'd probably appreciate that someone had looked in to make sure nothing had burned or caught fire.

Mara gave the chili a stir and ladled a helping into a bowl.

Now that she thought about it, this was probably the same rationale Goldilocks had used to justify her raid on the three bears.

IT had taken a full day to get to Vancouver, and another four to get to Toronto. Mara hadn't imagined that any country could be that large. On a whim, she had written down the name of each town and city where the bus had stopped. Hope, Golden, Banff, Calgary, Medicine Hat, Swift Current, Moose Jaw, Regina, Brandon, Winnipeg, Wawa, Sudbury.

A young woman no older than herself had got on the bus at Gleichen, Alberta, and sat next to her all the way to Winnipeg.

"Mara."

"Celeste."

Mara had wanted to tell Celeste that she didn't need to use so much makeup. There were dried rivulets of mascara on the woman's cheeks, and the pancake around her eyes had shattered.

"What's in Winnipeg?"

"Boyfriend's in Gleichen."

Celeste smelled of smoke and old sweat. Her hair was black and coarse with red highlights. Her breath tasted of peppermint.

"You got a boyfriend in Toronto?"

"No."

"So what's there?"

"Don't know."

"Sometimes that's best."

By the time she reached Toronto, Mara had written the names of over 130 towns in her sketchbook.

THE chili was somewhat spicier than Mara would have liked, but she finished the bowl and had a second. The bread and butter helped. There was a kettle on the stove. Mara filled it and set it to boil. If Crisp came home in the next while, she'd make him a cup of tea and tell him about her plan. He'd probably want to help, but she didn't need it. She could manage on her own. She had always managed on her own.

Mara wandered the trailer with her cup of tea. There were old photographs in old frames, pictures of people at the hot springs, pictures of people on the reserve. Crisp was in some of them, and he didn't look as though he had aged a day. She found one of a group of young women and was surprised to find her grandmother in the second row.

Who had taken this? Certainly not Crisp. He wouldn't have been born yet. Or perhaps he had. Perhaps the man was ageless, a feature of the landscape, such as a tree or a rock, long-lived and constant.

Mara found a piece of paper and scribbled a note. She rinsed the cup and set it on the rack to dry. She was feeling good now, ready for the task ahead.

THE bus had been late, had pulled into Toronto at four in the afternoon, and Mara had stepped off the Greyhound into a Southern Ontario heat wave and a city that was melting.

Before the first week was out, she had found an apartment on Isabella near Church. By the end of the month, she was working at a deli on Queen and had signed up for two workshops at the Ontario College of Art & Design. She watched the bulletin board at the college and came away with a small table easel, a set of cheap brushes, a collection of used oil paints, and a six-pack of canvas boards that had never been opened.

The rest of that summer and fall had been spent going to every gallery opening she could find, looking at the paintings, studying the techniques, and watching the artists. What they wore. How they moved. What they said.

Breathless. It had all been breathless.

And she had wondered if this was how the woman who fell from the sky had felt as she tumbled through space and plummeted to earth.

Then one day, she looked up, and a year had become fifteen.

IT took longer than she had expected to raise the trailer hitch off the ball of the pickup. The crank was rusted and stuck, and Mara had to whack it with a piece of wood to break it free. The keys were in the ignition. The motor grunted and complained before it turned over and sent a billow of black smoke into the evening sky.

She sat in the cab, working the accelerator until the engine evened itself out, and then she pulled it into gear and let it roll forward towards the remaining lights of Samaritan Bay.

59

GABRIEL WOKE. HE WAS COLD AND STIFF, AND FOR AN INSTANT he wondered if he might have died when he wasn't paying attention. But he had simply fallen asleep in the chair on the deck, and what had been evening a short time before was now night. He tried to sit up, only to discover that Soldier had joined him and was lying across his lap.

It was a crowded arrangement, but not unpleasant.

Gabriel rubbed the dog's head and scratched him behind the ears. Soldier's body was warm, and Gabriel could imagine staying where he was and spending the night under the stars.

"You want something to eat?"

As soon as he asked the question, Gabriel realized that he was hungry. Very hungry. Starving in fact. He tried to recall what he had had for lunch, before he remembered that he hadn't had any lunch at all.

Breakfast.

Breakfast with Mara. That was all the food he had had the entire day.

"If you want to eat, you're going to have to move."

Soldier lifted his head. His eyes were soft and patient. His jowls were draped with drool.

"Lovely."

He should have told Mara, told her who he was and why he was here. Not that it would make any difference.

Hi, I'm Gabriel Quinn. I killed your family and friends. I killed my sister and her child. I destroyed the river and the forest and all life in the ocean for as far as you can see. Surprise, I'm the author of all that destruction. Are you attracted to me? How about we fall in love, have children, and live happily ever after.

Soldier barked and rolled off Gabriel's lap.

"Happens like that all the time in the movies."

Soldier crouched down and began growling under his breath.

"No, I'm not feeling sorry for myself."

And yet he was. Would his life have been any different if his father hadn't gone to Minneapolis? Would the family have stayed in Lethbridge and grown old together? What had driven Joe to leave? What had made his mother stay? Why hadn't he gone home when his father was killed? Why hadn't he stayed in touch?

How had he become such a monster?

Why do we ask the important questions *after* they've been answered?

GABRIEL opened the refrigerator and took out the boneless chicken thigh. He'd fry it up, turn it into a sandwich.

"What do you want to eat?"

Soldier banged into Gabriel's legs and began turning circles, moaning and groaning and shaking gobs of saliva onto the floor. Gabriel got a can from the cupboard.

"How about Kidney Surprise?"

The photograph on the refrigerator door had slipped. Gabriel gently lifted the tape and adjusted the picture. A sister. A nephew. And this glossy piece of paper was all that was left.

LETHBRIDGE was famous for its winds, but Gabriel had not cared much for the chinooks that rose off the eastern face of the Rockies and levelled everything standing. In the winter, they warmed the land, and this was a welcome relief from the profound cold that settled on the high plains in the dark months.

"Look at that," his father would say. "This morning it was twenty below, and now it's five above."

But the chinooks weren't just a winter phenomenon. They persisted during the spring and the summer, into the fall, and, each time you ventured outside, you had to lean and stand at angles to the land.

"Gabriel, you go out and play."

"It's too windy, Mum."

"Play with your sister," his mother would say. "Have her show you that flying game she does with her jacket."

THE chicken was spongy and coated with a suspicious slick. Gabriel set the thigh next to Soldier's bowl and went back to the refrigerator in search of something to eat. Eggs, frozen sausage, a withered apple.

There was always cereal. A meal for all occasions. Milk.

Raisins. Gabriel found half a peach at the bottom of the can. Soldier had already finished the Kidney Surprise. The chicken lay untouched on the floor.

Evidently the dog had standards.

THE family had had a small house on Lethbridge's west side. Gabriel's room was in the basement. It was his space. He was safe there.

Then one day his sister had come downstairs and marched into his room without knocking.

"I want to go to the coulees."

"You're not supposed to be in my room."

"I want to go to the coulees."

"So go."

"Mum says I can't go by myself, that you have to come with."

"I have homework."

"You always have homework. Caroline says there are pelicans in the coulees."

Gabriel had patiently explained that pelicans are ocean birds, and since there wasn't an ocean within a thousand kilometres, there couldn't be any pelicans in the coulees.

Little hadn't taken logic for an answer.

"Coulee, coulee, coulee, coulee," she had chanted, until Gabriel said okay, he'd take her into the coulees this once, and when they didn't find any pelicans, she could never ask him to do anything ever again.

~~~~~

GABRIEL had had any number of opportunities to tell Mara who he was. The hot springs, that evening in bed, at breakfast, the moment on the reserve when Mara was hanging the portrait on the door.

But he hadn't. Chances were, he wouldn't. There was no reason. He hadn't come back to find forgiveness or to start a new life. This wasn't his home. It had been his mother's, and, in the end, it had been his sister's.

It wasn't his.

And what exactly would he say? What would he tell Mara? How would he explain his role in the disaster that killed so many and destroyed so much? Where would he find the justification? "I was curious," he could offer. "I was curious."

Smart. He could blame it on being smart.

"You want to watch television?"

Soldier jumped up on the bed and buried his face in a pillow.

Gabriel put his bowl in the sink. Outside the night was clear, and the moon was full. It lit the tops of the trees and glanced off the breaking waves in the distance. This would be a night for a walk. He wondered if Mara was awake, if she might be interested in such a venture. Walk the beach in the moonlight. Forget about the world. Sit in the sand and wait for the water to come to them.

And when the time was right, he'd tell her the things he didn't even want to tell himself.

"Move over."

Instead, Gabriel crawled onto the bed and wrestled the covers away from the dog.

~~~~~

"IF there are pelicans," his sister had told him, "then you'll have to be my slave and do anything I want."

"There are no pelicans in the coulees."

They had been to the river bottom before with their parents, but this was the first time they had been on their own, and Little was impossible to contain. She raced up and down the trail, hiding in clumps of grass and jumping out to try to scare Gabriel.

"I saw you in the grass."

"No, you didn't."

"Yes, I did."

When they reached the big cottonwoods along the Oldman River, his sister signed for him to stop.

"Eagle!" she shouted.

"That's a magpie."

"Look, a coyote!"

"God, Little, that's a ground squirrel."

They spent much of that morning working their way along the bank of the river. There was a large pool with what could have been carp.

"Are those sharks?"

"No."

They saw a woodpecker, some ducks, and a small black snake. Gabriel showed her where a beaver had started chewing on a tree. By noon, they were hungry and exhausted.

"Come on," Gabriel had said. "Let's go back."

"Not yet."

"I'm hungry."

"We have to find the pelicans."

"There are no pelicans."

"Then what are those?"

Gabriel searched the sky, but he didn't see anything.

"On the water," his sister had shouted. "On the water."

And suddenly, there they were, flying in formation just off the surface of the river. "Pelicans!"

"Pigeons," said Gabriel. "Just big pigeons."

"Pelicans!"

"Or they could be . . . herons."

Little had watched the pelicans glide by, and she had reached out with her hand, as though she expected that she could touch them.

"Pelicans," she whispered, and she rushed over and threw her arms around Gabriel. "Now you're my slave."

When they got home, Gabriel's mother took him off to one side.

"You shouldn't lie to your sister."

"I didn't lie. They might have been pelicans, and maybe they weren't."

"She loves you."

"Sure."

Gabriel remembered how his mother had looked at him. "You're smarter than she is," she had said, "but she's got a better heart."

GABRIEL couldn't get to sleep. Soldier was banked against his body and had begun to snore, long, loud snorts that threatened to shake the trailer. Worse, the dog's damp breath was heavy on the back of his neck.

He wouldn't buy Kidney Surprise again.

The pelicans had been majestic. They had come down the river valley that day as though they owned the world. They hadn't flushed when they saw Gabriel and Little standing on that sand-bar.

They had held their course.

Even after they had passed, the birds stayed in a tight group-ing, riding the air, until they finally faded and vanished into the vastness of the prairie sky.

Gabriel adjusted the covers, so that his shoulders weren't exposed.

Maybe that's where he would start. If he decided to tell Mara who he was, he'd begin with the pelicans.

60

CRISP COULD FEEL THE FAILING LIGHT GLISTEN ON HIS BACK as he waded ashore. The swim out past the breakwater into the open ocean had been strenuous and exhilarating. And new. No matter how many times he had made the journey, it was always new.

Already there were signs of resurrection at the edges of the desolation. He had heard the rumours of marine algae and kelp in the sunlit shallows, and there had been a moment, between strokes and breaths, when Crisp imagined that he saw something large rocking gracelessly on the horizon, and he had slowed, rode the waves for a moment, and waited for it to reappear. It was just a swell, no doubt, but he had turned it into a whale he named Fred.

"Fred, you great heathen," Crisp had shouted across the water, "welcome home, lad, welcome home!"

Crisp plodded up the beach through the soft sand, letting the wind and the fading warmth dry his body. It was a fragile beginning, he had to admit, but it was a beginning. First Mara had returned and then Gabriel. The Ruin had pushed life away. Now life was pushing back, filling the vacuum as it has always filled the empty spaces in the world.

The plankton must have moved in when he wasn't paying attention. With any luck the small baitfish would begin to appear. Barnacles, urchins, crabs, and then the larger predators. He'd watch for the birds. The seagulls would be first. They always liked to arrive to a party early.

Perhaps even the turtles would return.

Crisp found his clothes where he had left them, laid out on a storm-tossed log. How he loved the drama of it all. The uncertainties, the surprises, the tragedies, the foolishness, the sacrifices, the greed.

People were endlessly amusing. And life? Was there a better game?

How would it be played today?

As he pulled his pants on, Crisp caught sight of a shape in the seagrasses, a shape out of place in this realm of liquid lines and soft edges.

"Well, well, well," he said. "So, whose little lamb are ye?"

It was a foundation of some sort, pieced together with shells and bones and assorted consumer waste. Crisp walked around the base, examined it from several angles.

It had to be the boy.

Sonny.

No one else would take the time. No one else would have imagined such a structure to be important. Inventive. The lad was inventive.

But what was it?

The boy had an original intellect, that much was known, but he never did anything without a reason, even if the understanding of the thing required a plough to bring it to the surface.

The light was gone now, and Crisp would have to find his way back to the hot springs in the dark. Hardly a problem. His feet knew the terrain as a child knows its mother's skin.

He wondered what Mara and Gabriel would do with the occasion, for such fortune was not easily gained and rarely realized. There would be decisions made in the coming days that would shape the match and put the sport in play.

He would have to be attentive so as not to miss a moment of the drama.

The sound filtered down through the trees and out onto the beach. Crisp turned his head to catch it. Someone was at the springs. Someone was at the springs, trying to start his truck. A visitor whom Crisp had not expected. He moved quickly through the sand to the harder ground, hoping he could arrive before they left. There was chili on the stove and bread on the counter, so no one would have to go hungry.

And then he stopped, turned back to the riddle in the sand and the grass.

A tower.

Of course, Sonny was building a tower. Crisp could see that now. A four-square tower. A beacon facing the sea. The boy had seen something on the water.

And he was raising a light to bring it home.

61

THE EXERCISE MARATHON HAD BEEN A MISTAKE.

He had stayed on the trainer far too long, had pumped his way up and down virtual hills until his left calf had cramped up.

Hard.

By the time he arrived at Queen's Quay and extracted himself from the limo, his back was stiff, and he could feel blisters forming on the balls of his feet.

DORIAN turned on the television as soon as he stepped into the condo. The top story was still the two breached dams, but the visuals had changed. Camera crews had spread out along the river and were documenting the waste matter as it floated past on its way to the next camera crew.

The road along the river was lined with trucks and vans and cars. Dorian could see people standing on the bank, shoulder to shoulder, cameras, cellphones, and iPads held over their heads.

He felt as though he were watching a rock concert.

Already the networks had lined up their resident experts in litters of three, all of them looking solemn and maintaining solid eye contact with the camera. Dorian recognized a number of familiar faces and was pleased to see that Corporate had not wasted any time.

He turned the volume down and took out his cell. The phone rang six times before a mechanical male voice repeated the number Dorian had just dialed and asked him if he wanted to leave a message. Dorian hung up and tried the number again. Just to be sure he hadn't made a mistake.

Same male voice. Same message.

Dorian checked his Rolex. Twelve-twenty. Olivia wasn't a night owl. She should be in her suite by now. What would be open in Orlando at this hour? No one played tennis at midnight. The restaurants would all be closed.

Disney World?

Nightclubs. That had to be the answer. Olivia had gone out with friends.

Dorian toggled the volume up. There was a map on the screen now with a moving red line and a sonorous voice-over that described the path the toxins would take and the timetable for the mess to reach important checkpoints.

Quickly the scene switched back to live coverage, and Dorian watched as the news crews and disaster groupies all piled into their vehicles and raced off down the road.

He had been wrong. It wasn't a rock concert. It was a moto rally.

Dorian turned the television off and went to the kitchen. He wanted a cup of coffee, but he knew that would be a bad idea. He'd be up all night, and tomorrow promised to be a busy and difficult day. Herbal tea would be the thing, something soothing. Camomile perhaps, or peppermint.

As he waited for the water to boil, he went back to that morning on Bloor Street. It wasn't just the purchases he had made. He had enjoyed the chance to get out into the world and talk with people who had nothing to do with work. Seeing Robert again, knowing that the man was still on the second floor of Rosen's was a comfort. Meeting Arlene at Royal de Versailles for the first time and chatting with Geoffrey in the cologne department of Holt Renfrew had delighted him more than he would have expected.

Geoffrey, in particular, had been a delight, letting Dorian sample scent after scent, explaining the chemistry of cologne as well as the etiquette. Dorian knew the basics, but Geoffrey had reminded him that relying on one cologne was always a mistake, that men, like women, should have a variety of aromas in their arsenal. A workplace cologne should be light and understated, something in the citrus family, while an evening out might call for a stronger scent with spice undertones or musky notes that would complement one's natural pheromones.

Men tended to over-spray, Geoffrey confided. A little behind the ears, around the face and chin were excellent choices, but the best location was the chest. There the cologne could mix with the body's warmth, and the fragrance would waft up and settle around a man's head like a halo.

"You don't need to use too much," Geoffrey cautioned. "And don't spray it down your pants. It's a waste and such a cliché."

Dorian tried to remember the colognes he already had.

"We've just started carrying Ambre Topkapi." Geoffrey had brought out a small but elegant bottle. "Very expensive. You might like it."

He had been comfortable inside the stores, behind the

glass, surrounded by the merchandise, pampered by the sales staff. Being back on the street had been a different matter. Every vehicle had a working horn. Every construction site had a jack-hammer. Every corner had a raucous contest of pedestrians and cars, all trying to get through the intersection at the same time.

People with clipboards, donation boxes, and surveys tried to accost and surround him, and there had been a white, bone-faced woman, stout as a stump with winter-kill hair, who had come down Bloor, waving a cigarette in the air and shouting something about "argo niggers."

Or maybe it was "cargo."

Dorian hadn't felt threatened by the woman, but the incident had made him appreciate the necessity of an executive car.

DORIAN decided on camomile, dropped the bag into the cup, and let it steep. He brought the tea to the sofa and tried calling Olivia again.

Dorian held his watch up to the light. The orange second hand was crooked, like a lightning bolt. Very distinctive. He'd have to go back to the store and ask Arlene for the story behind the design. He'd wear the Topkapi, see if she'd recognize the fragrance.

He lifted the tea bag out of the cup and tried the number again.

And again.

And again.

62

SONNY DID NOT GET HOME UNTIL VERY LATE. THANK GOOD-
ness the night had been clear and the moon and stars had been
out. Otherwise Sonny might have gotten lost. Dad has warned
Sonny about wandering in the wilderness, and now Sonny
understands what Dad was talking about, especially if you have
to carry a roll of wire.

Not just any wire. Copper wire.

Sonny is very pleased with his copper wire. It took him
much of the day and most of the night to strip the insulation off
the wire and put the roll together. The roll was heavy, and Sonny
had to set it down more than once so he could rest for a moment
and switch shoulders. It was especially difficult walking along
the beach in the sand, and Sonny is tempted to share this information on wandering and wire with Dad.

Wander not in the wilderness with wire.

But now it is morning. Now the day has begun anew. Now
Sonny is anxious to get started.

Wash.

Eat.

Copper wire.

Sonny goes to the bathroom and brushes his teeth. Now that

he has the wire, he'll be able to build the tower quickly, and, with the wire, the tower will be strong and beautiful. Sonny even likes the colour.

In the sunlight, the shells and the wire will shine and glow like alabaster and gold.

Wham-wham!

Dad has mentioned alabaster and gold any number of times, and Sonny is sure that Dad will be pleased when he sees what his son has wrought.

Sonny can't wait to start stringing the shells and the bones onto the wire and wrapping the wire around and around, weaving it in and out. And if he runs out of wire, he knows where he can find more.

Sonny wonders where the ghost Indians are and what they're doing and whether they would like to help him gather bones and shells. This would make the work go faster, and the sooner the tower is finished, the sooner Sonny can light the beacon.

The dining room is empty and cold. Sonny looks at the menu and decides on a waffle with patty sausages and a large glass of orange juice. Sonny is very fond of waffles, but he likes them plain, without all of the fruit and whipped cream that the tourists used to demand.

A waffle for Sonny, Sonny shouts to the kitchen. Plain. No compost. Sausage and juice!

As Sonny sits and waits for his waffle, he examines the blister on the side of his finger. He got it from cutting all the wire and now it hurts. After he eats, Sonny will find a Band-Aid to put on the injury.

Sonny stands up and walks to the kitchen. The room is dark,

and when Sonny turns on the lights, he can see that he'll have to settle for something other than a waffle.

Sonny taps the cupboard with his hammer, and the wood makes a hollow sound. He taps the next cupboard. Hollow. He taps the refrigerator.

Hollow, hollow, hollow.

How can everything be so empty? The cupboards. The refrigerator. The motel. The town. The beach.

Empty, empty, empty.

Thank goodness for the EverFresh vending machine.

Sonny takes a plate to the patio and examines the selections in the EverFresh vending machine. He is saddened by all the damage to the green plastic front and by the hammer marks on the dispenser doors.

Not good.

Perhaps Sonny was too enthusiastic when he was showing the dog how he could hammer things. Perhaps he should have shown more control and self-restraint.

A man without self-control is like a city broken into and left without walls.

This is one of Dad's sayings, and, while Sonny doesn't know what it is supposed to mean, he is sure that it applies to vending machines as well as cities.

Today the choices in the EverFresh vending machine consist of a peanut butter and jelly sandwich, a ham sandwich with tomato, and a banana. Sonny puts his money in the slot and makes his selection, but the machine doesn't make its *jingle-jingle* sound.

Sonny tries to open the door. Stuck. Sonny tries the door with the banana. Stuck. He tries the door with the peanut butter and jelly sandwich. Also stuck.

Stop being stuck! Sonny shouts at the machine.

Sonny tries to open the coin box so he can get his money back, but the box has a large dent in it, and now the key won't fit in the keyhole.

Wham-wham, hammer-hammer.

Sonny slides his hammer out of the belt and taps the plastic dispenser door.

Tap, tap, tap.

Nothing.

He taps it harder.

Tap, Tap, Tap.

The ham and tomato sandwich is bouncing about, but the door doesn't open.

Wham-wham, hammer-hammer!

Sonny smashes a hole in the dispenser door. The hole isn't very large, and Sonny has to pull the sandwich out in pieces. He smashes a second door and carefully rescues the banana. The sandwich and the banana are not a waffle, but when he closes his eyes, he can almost taste the warm butter and syrup.

Sonny checks the other vending machines. All broken.

Whatever your hand finds to do, do it with all your might.

Dad has offered this advice on more than one occasion, though Sonny isn't sure if hammers and vending machines are what Dad had in mind.

Sonny drops the banana peel into the trash can and casts his eyes over the beach in case something has come ashore when he wasn't looking. Then he loops the wire over his shoulder and heads for town.

63

MARA GOT UP AT FIRST LIGHT AND BEGAN PACKING THE
house. She had kept the cartons that had arrived with her, so
it was simply a matter of reversing the process. The books
went back in their boxes. The oil paints were arranged in their
Tupperware containers. The bedsheets, towels, and pillows
were stuffed into plastic bags and tied shut. Her clothes were
folded neatly in the larger of the two suitcases.

Her easel was going to be a problem. Mara could see that it
wasn't going to fit in the back of the pickup, that she was going
to have to take it apart and put it together later. It was a pain, but
she had done it before. She could do it again.

Mara hadn't thought this through. She knew that. Best just
to do it and work on the details and the difficulties later. There
would be plenty of time to find reasons why this was a bad idea.

Crisp's truck was waiting for her when she stepped off the
veranda. It was an old stepside Ford, red, with rusting wheel
wells and wood running boards. Mara slid behind the wheel,
pumped the gas pedal, and turned the key in the ignition. The
motor coughed and struggled to its feet. Mara pumped the gas
again, and the engine exploded several times before settling
into a rattling wheeze.

ANGELO Cosimo, who owned the deli on Queen where Mara worked, had let her hang four of her paintings just inside the front door.

"With a name like mine," Ange had told Mara, "I need something on the walls besides the flies."

The city had been expensive. The hard boards had had to be replaced with stretched canvases, the cheap brushes and paints put to one side in favour of boar bristles and quality oils. Mara had expected she would be able to save enough to fly home that first summer to see Lilly and her mother and grandmother, but when June arrived, Mara's chequebook showed a balance of $156.

"Good news," she said, when she phoned her mother. "It looks like I'm going to get a summer intern grant."

"So you're not coming home."

"I want to," Mara had said, "but if I get the grant, I'll have to stay here."

"No crime being broke."

"I'm not broke. It's the terms of the grant."

"Big city," said her mother. "I guess we look pretty old-fashioned."

"Mum . . ."

"You're not pregnant, are you?"

"No, Mum, I'm not pregnant."

"Your grandmother wanted me to ask."

"I tried calling Lilly last night."

"No one's home," her mother had said. "They had to take Rose to the hospital in Vancouver."

~~~~~

MARA had expected to find Gabriel sitting on the deck, enjoying the sun with Soldier lounging at his feet.

A Norman Rockwell moment.

She had not expected to find him inside the trailer, asleep, in bed with the dog. If she hadn't been anxious to get the move underway, she might have taken time to enjoy the tableau. Gabriel with an arm thrown over Soldier. Man and dog with the same expression on their faces. Both snoring.

Perhaps men and dogs had more in common than she might have imagined.

Mara opened the refrigerator door and sorted through the tenants. Eggs, some milk, butter, sausage, and an apple a little the worse for wear.

As she shut the door, Mara noticed the photograph. It took a moment for the image to register.

"Hey!"

Gabriel floated up out of a deep sleep and tried to focus. There appeared to be a woman in the trailer.

"Wake up!"

"Mara?"

"Sampson." Mara stabbed at the photograph. "This is Lilly Sampson."

"Sampson?"

"My best friend," said Mara. "What are you doing with a picture of her and her son on your fridge?"

Gabriel rubbed his face. "Sampson was her maiden name."

"What?"

Gabriel glanced around in search of support, but Soldier had disappeared. "My mother. Rose. Her maiden name was Sampson."

357

Mara stood in the middle of the kitchen, her hands on her hips. "You're Lilly's brother?"

Gabriel eased himself out of bed. His shirt and pants were badly wrinkled, but at least he was dressed. "Have you had breakfast?"

"You're Lilly's brother?"

"I can make pancakes."

Mara peeled the photograph off the refrigerator and thrust it at him. "Do I sound as though I want pancakes?"

THAT first summer in Toronto had been difficult. Business at the deli had fallen off, and Ange had had to cut her hours.

"Fancy schmancy French place on Bay is killing us," Ange told her. "Lots of glass. Gourmet hams from Italy. Twenty-two different kinds of olives. Who the hell pays a hundred bucks for a bottle of vinegar?"

By the time September arrived, Mara's bank balance was barely treading water and she had had to close the savings account. But she sold a painting. One day, when she had come to work, there was a blank space on the wall.

"Woman walked in," Ange told her. "Bold as brass. No questions. Took it right off the wall. Paid cash."

"Who was it? Did she leave her name?"

"Two hundred grams of Black Forest ham and three hundred grams of sliced provolone," said Ange. "That's all I can remember."

"Did she say anything about the painting?"

Ange shrugged. "Must have liked it," he said. "Who buys something they don't like?"

~~~~~

OKAY, so this Gabriel could cook. Mara would give him that. The pancakes were fluffy and golden.

"You were all she talked about. Riel this. Riel that. How smart Riel was. How Riel looked after her."

Gabriel nodded. "When she was little, she couldn't say 'Gabriel.' The best she could manage was 'Riel.'"

Mara turned the photograph towards Gabriel. "That was his name."

Gabriel stopped eating.

"Her son. Your nephew."

"What?"

"Riel." Mara pushed her plate to one side. "Lilly named him after you."

Gabriel sat back in the chair. Then he pushed away from the table, got up without a word, and stepped through the door of the trailer, letting it swing shut behind him.

Mara stayed seated.

Hell.

He hadn't known.

Well, that had certainly been tactful and considerate. She waited, hoping Gabriel would come back inside. She still had questions, and she wasn't about to let his feelings get in the way of answers.

And when he didn't reappear, she picked up her fork, reached across the table, and finished the food that was left on his plate.

64

SOLDIER WAS ON THE DECK, WAITING FOR HIM. GABRIEL
hoped he might find some sympathy in the dog's eyes.

"So, you think it's my fault."

Of course it was his fault. He should have gone home. He
should have looked after his mother and sister. He had been
angry. Angry that his father had been killed. Angry that his
mother had stayed in Alberta. Maybe if she and Little had come
to Minneapolis with them, his father wouldn't have died. She
hadn't even come down for the funeral.

She'd thrown Joe away.

She'd thrown him away as well.

That was how it had felt. That was where the fault lay.

So, why should he have gone back to Lethbridge? There was
no promise there. Just high prairie winds and small town cruel.
Except for the people on the reserve. The Blackfoot had been
generous. But that hadn't been enough.

His mother and sister had been the only family he had left,
and that hadn't been enough either.

Gabriel heard the screen door bang behind him.

"Your sister loved you."

"I loved her."

"But you never came home. What happened?"

"Nothing."

Mara tried to remember when Rose and Lilly had come back to the reserve. Mara had been what? Twelve? Thirteen? That would have made Lilly eleven? Eleven years old with a sick mother, a dead father, and an absent brother.

That wasn't quite right. Lilly's mother hadn't been sick then. Not at first. That would come later.

"And now, here you are."

Gabriel tightened his mouth. "Here I am."

Lilly had liked to drag Mara into the woods and for long hikes along the shore. She could name every bird, every animal, every fish, and if she found something new, something she didn't recognize, she would name it herself.

"She made a bet with you once." Mara watched Gabriel's face. "A bet about . . . seagulls?"

"Pelicans." Gabriel nodded. "Pelicans in the coulees."

"You told Lilly that they were . . . "

"Large pigeons." Gabriel turned and faced Mara. "Why are you here?"

"I'm moving back."

"Back?"

"To the reserve." Mara spread her feet and anchored them to the deck. "I could use some help."

Gabriel shot a glance at the truck. "You're going to move everything in that?"

"I rented the house furnished. The furniture isn't mine. All I have is the easel and a bunch of boxes."

Gabriel walked to the edge of the deck. He could see the motel from here. He could see the beach and the Apostles. Higher on the side of the hill, steam was rising off the hot springs.

How could the sun be this cold?

"Okay," he said. "I'll help. If you'll tell me about my mother and my sister. And my nephew."

"Why?"

Gabriel shrugged.

"Sure," she said. "And you can tell me why you never came home."

LOADING the books and the boxes and the bags took no time at all. The easel was another matter. Gabriel walked around it several times, trying to see how things went together. It looked simple enough.

"You've taken this apart before, right?"

Mara balanced a box on her hip. "Is there a problem?"

"Maybe we should make two trips. Boxes and bags in one load and easel in the other. That way we won't have to break it down."

"It won't fit through the door."

"Here or on the reserve?"

"Both."

Gabriel ran a hand along one of the wood uprights. "Did my mother ever say anything to you?"

Mara set the box on the table. "Thought we were going to do this after the move."

He nodded. "You got a screwdriver?"

"In the drawer by the stove."

"And a wrench?"

"Same place."

Gabriel sat down next to the easel and began working the screws loose. Did my mother ever say anything to you? There was no purpose in asking that question, no salvation in knowing the answer. There were only so many things his mother could have said. That she had a son. That she had a son who had run off. That she had a son who never came home.

Or maybe his mother hadn't said anything at all. That was always a possibility. She had changed her name. She had left without a word. Maybe, by the time she found her way back to the reserve, she had been able to erase him from her memory as well.

65

DORIAN'S DREAMS—WHEN HE DREAMED AT ALL—WERE disturbing, non-sequential chase fragments in which he was beset by enormous dogs. Sometimes they were friendly, sometimes they were murderous. There were people who claimed to be able to analyze dreams, but Dorian had never seen the point. First, he was sure that such individuals were frauds, playing on the insecurities and vanities of the gullible. Second, he didn't need anyone to tell him what his dreams were about.

He didn't care, had no interest whatsoever in an explanation.

When he was in his early teens, he had had dreams about mermaids. Mermaids were most likely about sex. That didn't take any clairvoyant abilities. A pack of murderous dogs was about the anxieties and pressures of life.

The lead hound was closing on him, its jaws snapping, its eyes blazing. And then there was a sudden shriek, and the dogs vanished. Dorian rolled over, turned off the alarm, and buried his head in the pillow. Maybe he could conjure up a mermaid or two before he had to get up.

The second time the alarm went off, he realized that the sound was the phone. He looked at the bedside clock. Five-thirty? Only one person would call him at this hour, and the news wasn't going to be good.

"Tell me."

"Pardon?"

"Olivia?"

"Dorian?"

What the hell? His wife? At this hour? She didn't get up before nine on a good day.

"It's five-thirty."

"I know," Olivia said. "I couldn't sleep. I was afraid, if I called later, I would miss you."

Dorian sat up and rubbed his eyes. "You didn't miss me."

"I saw the news. It's terrible."

Yes, yes, Dorian thought to himself. It's terrible, horrific, shocking. Every distressing adjective you could find in a thesaurus and more. Blah, blah, blah.

"They had a picture of you on CNN." Olivia sounded more upset than Dorian would have expected. "They made you sound like a criminal."

"It's a spill," said Dorian. "Unfortunate, but it happens."

"Are you okay?"

"I'm fine." Dorian paused and took a deep breath. "I called you last night."

"You did?"

"I called late, and you weren't in."

"I must have been out."

Dorian lay back on the bed and tucked a pillow under his head. "So, when are you coming home?"

For a moment, he thought he had lost the connection.

"Olivia?"

"I'm here," she said. "Dorian, that's why I'm calling."

~~~~~

DORIAN stood under the shower for a very long time and let the warmth seep into every part of his body. Now that he was up, he might as well make the most of the early start. Treat himself to a good breakfast, arrive at the office early, get prepared for what promised to be a very busy day.

Dorian laid out the dark blue Kiton with the chalk pinstripe. It was the perfect suit for the crusade ahead. Something with *gravitas*. *Gravitas*.

He had always liked the word. He had heard Morgan Freeman use it in an interview about acting, and he was sure the same principle applied to business.

Dorian sorted through his shirts. The soft yellow Zegna with the colour-on-colour texture would go well with the suit, but he went for the silver grey Brioni instead.

It had the look of armour.

The tie was more of a problem. Bright colours might be read as insincere or smug. Sombre colours could be misinterpreted as repentant and apologetic. Dorian wanted something that said "powerful and in control of the situation."

In the end, he settled on the navy blue Stefano Ricci with a grey stripe, white dot details, and a gold shadow line. It was a gleaming presence knotted at his neck. If the tie had had a hilt, it might have been mistaken for a sword.

Mark Twain had said that clothes make the man. But what most people didn't know was that Twain was being satiric. The complete quotation is "Clothes make the man. Naked people have little or no influence on society."

Still, Dorian was sure that the writer would have been impressed with today's attire.

Dorian considered turning on the television, to see if anything untoward had happened overnight. Instead he stood at the windows, stared at the lake in the early light, and regretted, once again, that he hadn't bought the condo near Avenue Road and Bloor. He hadn't seen the problem until he moved in and discovered that the area around Queen's Quay was a tourist magnet, discovered that each time he stepped out of the building, he would run into families from Medicine Hat, Alberta, or Moose Jaw, Saskatchewan, or Dildo, Newfoundland.

With three kids and a camera.

All the way down in the elevator, he debated where he was going to eat. Not the Bluebird. He didn't think he could ever go back there. But there were two places he had been meaning to try. The Stock restaurant at the Trump Tower on Bay and Toca at the Ritz-Carlton on Wellington. Both had been recommended by friends at the country club.

Dorian was tempted by the Stock at the Trump, but he had never felt much affection for, or kinship with, "The Donald," as Trump's first wife had referred to him at a press conference. The man was extravagant and arrogant. A loud-mouthed egotist who gave wealthy people a bad name. Trump might have been nicer, Dorian speculated, if he had made his fortune on his own rather than having it handed to him by his parents.

On the other hand, narcissism was not an intelligent reason to dismiss good food.

There was a cab at the curb. Dorian climbed in the back.

"Do you know where the Trump Tower is?"

"You want to go to the Trump Tower?"

"Perhaps," said Dorian, "I may want to go to the Ritz-Carlton."

"You want to go to the Ritz-Carlton?"

"Which one do you think is the better place for breakfast."

"Trump Tower," said the driver. "You go to Trump Tower."

Dorian checked the time. Six-thirty, and no call from Winter. That was good news. With any luck, he might just be able to have breakfast in peace.

"Let's go to the Ritz instead."

"You like the Trump."

"No," said Dorian. "I wish to go to the Ritz."

"The Trump is just there."

"The Ritz. Take me to the Ritz-Carlton."

TOCA opened for breakfast at 6:30. Dorian was surprised by the number of people already in the restaurant.

"For how many?"

"One," said Dorian. "Someplace quiet."

Toca was a collection of connected rooms and alcoves. It felt somewhat disorganized and, at the same time, intimate. Dorian was shown to a corner table at the back. Water, coffee, a glass of freshly squeezed orange juice, along with a copy of *The Globe and Mail*. There should be more moments such as this in a life, when you were allowed to sit back, relax, and have someone else do all the work.

What was that proverb they had learned on their trip to Spain? *Qué bueno es no hacer nada y descansar después.* "How beautiful it is to do nothing and then rest afterwards."

So Olivia wanted a divorce. *Qué bueno es no hacer nada*, indeed. Now there was someone who knew how to sit back and let someone else do all the work. There was someone who knew everything about doing nothing and resting afterwards. All this time in Orlando, all the talk about a place in Florida. A divorce. In the middle of a major business crisis, and she wanted a divorce.

Dorian was surprised how calm he felt. He knew men who saw marriage as a fashion statement rather than an institution, men who changed partners with the same frequency as they changed their wardrobes.

Dorian didn't think of women that way, but he could see where one might.

"Have you had a chance to look at the menu?"

The menu was not extensive, but there were some interesting choices.

"I'm torn between the Salmon Benedict and the Lobster Vol au Vent."

"Both are excellent," said the server. "You can't go wrong with either."

"Tell me about the Lobster."

"Puff pastry," said the young man, "with Yarmouth lobster, mushrooms, and egg."

Dorian ordered the fruit selection as well. It would probably be too much food in the end, but a little indulgence never hurt anyone.

He had finished the juice and was enjoying a second cup of coffee when his phone rang. This time it was Winter.

"I'm at the Ritz-Carlton having breakfast. Could you have the car sent around."

"Certainly," said Winter. "Half an hour?"

"Any new problems?"

"No, sir. The holding ponds have been drained and the dams repaired."

"Where do we stand on the PR front?"

"As well as can be expected," said Winter. "You have an interview with Manisha Khan this evening. I'll have a briefing for you when you get in."

"I'm looking forward to the interview."

"Yes, sir," said Winter. "I'm sure you are."

THE lobster was fine, though not excellent, the puff pastry somewhat soggy. But the dish had been a pleasant and interesting combination of textures and tastes. The fruit filled in the gaps nicely.

He was finishing his coffee and getting ready to pay the bill when he noticed that he was sweating. The front of his shirt darkened in ragged patches, and his face was wet and flushed. The trembling started in his hands and fell upon his body with a vengeance.

"Are you all right, sir?"

"Yes," said Dorian, trying to hold himself together. "Late night, early morning."

"Would you like some more coffee?"

"No, just the bill. And another napkin please."

The tremors slowly passed. Dorian leaned forward on his elbows, feeling cold and drained.

This was Toshi's doing. The man had pricked and probed him enough to know what the hell was going on. And if he knew, he should have fixed it by now. What if this had happened during the Khan interview? The CEO of Domidion breaking out in a sweat and shaking on camera? He was going to have to change specialists again. And this time, he'd have to be firm with the man—or woman—as to his needs and expectations.

Dorian took the bottle from his pocket, shook out a pill, and held it up to the light. The side effects would probably kill him more quickly than any disease.

A divorce.

Dorian hoped Olivia didn't expect to get rich from this adventure. That wasn't going to happen. Any division of their property was going to leave her holding the short straw. Now that he thought about it, she was probably having an affair. The extended stay in Orlando. The late nights. The distance in her voice.

An affair? Whom had she found to sleep with in Orlando? A washed-up tennis coach? A sleazy real estate agent?

A cartoon mouse?

THE car was waiting for him, and he was pleased to see that it was a Mercedes, rather than a Lincoln Town Car. The Mercedes was the classier of the two, and it also had the more comfortable back seat.

The traffic was heavy, and the limo had to creep its way down University and onto the Lakeshore. Dorian settled in the seat and let his mind float. The mermaids were nowhere to be found, but neither were the dogs. And for the first time in a long while, there was nothing waiting for him when he closed his eyes.

66

MARA BACKED THE TRUCK UP, SO GABRIEL COULD WALK THE boxes onto the porch and straight into the house.

"Just put everything in the living room."

The easel had not been as difficult to dismantle as Gabriel had feared, but, as a precaution, he had marked the matching joints, in case there was any question as to how it went back together.

"What are you going to do for a table?"

Mara looked around the room. "I'll manage."

Gabriel did a quick inventory. No stove. No fridge. The only parts of the house that were still in place were the roof and the walls.

And the kitchen sink.

Gabriel tried the faucets. Dead dry.

"What were their names?"

"Who?"

"Your mother. Your grandmother."

The question caught Mara off guard. Mum. Granny. Those were their names. Those had always been their names.

"My father's name was Joe," said Gabriel, bailing Mara out for the moment. "My mother's name was Rose. But you knew that."

"June," said Mara, now that her memory had caught up with her mouth. "And Muriel."

THE easel went together well enough, but when Gabriel stepped away to admire his handiwork, he discovered he still had two screws left. He checked the easel carefully, but he could not find where they were supposed to go. Mara was busy arranging the books and her paints, and didn't notice as he searched for the mistake that had left him with extra parts.

"Everything okay?"

"It is," Gabriel said, and he slipped the screws into his pocket.

Even with the books, the paints, and the bedding strewn about the living room, the house felt bare and depressing.

"You know, you don't have a refrigerator."

"I know."

"Or a stove."

"I know that, too."

"You can't live here like this."

"I can do whatever I please."

Gabriel did another circuit of the easel, checking the supports, making sure the metal straps had the right amount of tension. He didn't think that two screws would make a big difference, but he wasn't familiar enough with easels to be sure. He didn't want Mara to be working on a large canvas and have the painting come crashing down because of his negligence.

Gabriel patted the easel. "The last time you took this apart," he said, "did you wind up with extra screws?"

"No." Mara came over and pushed the easel closer to the window. "Did you wind up with extra screws?"

"Nope," said Gabriel, "but I can see where you could."

The house looked worse than it had before. Empty, it had had the illusion of First World possibilities. A little paint, a new kitchen, tile in the bathroom, hardwood floors, stainless steel appliances, and suddenly you'd be looking at a centre spread in *House & Home.*

Instead, with Mara's bedding and clothes piled on the floor, the place had the feel of a refugee camp.

"Can you take the truck back to Mr. Crisp?"

"Sure."

Mara held out the keys. "Maybe you could put some gas in it."

"I can do that."

SOLDIER was waiting on the porch. Gabriel knelt down and rubbed the dog's neck.

"You going to stay or come with me."

The dog dropped down and flattened himself against the planks.

"She hasn't got any food," Gabriel told him.

Soldier ran his tongue around his muzzle.

"Zip. Zero."

Soldier stood up and trotted to the passenger side door.

"Good choice."

Mara came through the door. "You're still here," she said.

"You want me to make you a sandwich? I could go back to my trailer and find something."

"No."

"Egg salad?" Gabriel opened the door, and Soldier jumped in. "I make good egg salad."

Mara's stomach was beginning to complain. Nothing serious. Just a reminder.

"Ball joints are loose," she said. "Brakes pull to the right."

MARA stayed on the porch. So, here she was. Home. Against all good sense, she had come home. She went inside, lay down on the floor, and pulled the blankets around her. The sun was streaming in through the window, and there was a gentle warmth to the light.

In that moment, in her mother's house, she was at peace. But she knew as she lay there that coming home had been the easy part.

67

GABRIEL WAS SURPRISED BY THE NUMBER OF CARS IN THE
Co-op parking lot. Soldier had spent the entire trip with his
head hanging out the window and now his face was covered with
drool. "Okay. You get to stay here."

The store was busy. And there was food on the shelves. More
than Gabriel had noticed in the past. Eggs, flour, milk, cheese,
bread, several cereals. They were all here. Even tomatoes and
bananas.

Gabriel was trying to decide between Cheerios and Shredded
Wheat, when he heard a voice explode behind him.

"Master Gabriel!"

Nicholas Crisp was blocking the aisle with a shopping
cart.

"Stocking the galley, are ye?"

"Ran out of food."

"A great sin that," said Crisp, "for there's no predicting the
hour when folks might call and needs to be fed."

"I've got your truck."

"Indeed ye do." Crisp scratched his beard, and his eyes
brightened. "There's a good story to the theft, I'll warrant."

"I didn't take it. Mara borrowed it."

"I know," said Crisp. "I know. For she left a note informing me of her intentions."

"She's moving back to the reserve."

"Yes," said Crisp. "High time, too."

"I'm just giving her a hand."

Crisp took a bag of oats from the shelf. "Your mother was from here."

Gabriel stiffened.

"Be that a secret?" said Crisp, his voice full of concern. "For I'm a poor vault with regard to such valuables."

"You knew my mother?"

"Aye," said Crisp, "and your sister as well. But let's talk as we shop, for there's hardly world enough and time for both."

Crisp led the way, plunging up and down the aisles, as though he were navigating a ship through high seas and dangerous reefs.

"Your mother left the reserve when she was young. Some say she ran away, and there's pocket change in that to be sure. Samaritan Bay were a cruel place for the People in those days, and Rose wished to escape the shoals of a small town. Tell me, did she succeed?"

"No."

"No good anchorage anywhere in this world." Crisp wrestled a large bottle of ketchup off the shelf. "All boats run against the tides."

CRISP pushed the cart to his truck and set his groceries in the bed. "And what of yourself?" he asked, his voice soft and gentle. "Are ye moving home as well?"

Gabriel handed him the keys. "I can walk back."

"Indeed you can," said Crisp, "but I've a proposition that requires your presence. Will ye ride with me awhile and hear me out?"

"A proposition?"

"Fresh and wet it is," said Crisp, tapping the side of his head, "and will require a league or two to dry it out."

Gabriel couldn't keep the smile off his face.

"Laughter being a form of consent," said Crisp, "I'll take it ye approve."

"I can hardly say no."

"Excellent," cried Crisp. "And while we wait for things to thicken, we'll tour the cradle of our misfortune."

Gabriel was still smiling. "The what?"

"Let me show ye where it all began," said Crisp, his voice suddenly old and cracked. "And where it came to an end."

68

SONNY WALKS INTO TOWN ALONG THE BACK STREETS AND through the alleys. He sets the wire down in the shade at the edge of the Co-op parking lot and watches people go in and come out. Sonny recognizes each person, and as they disappear into the store, he whispers their names to the trees.

Peter Canakis, Carol Miller, Judy Webb.

Sonny sees Mr. Crisp go into the store. When Sonny sees Mr. Crisp, Sonny ducks down and doesn't say a word. Best the trees don't know about Mr. Crisp.

An old pickup pulls into the lot, and the naked guy who likes to die on Sonny's beach gets out.

What is going on at the Co-op?

Is Sonny missing something?

Are there free samples?

Is today a holiday that Sonny has forgotten?

Sonny counts up the number of people he has seen go into the Co-op. Sixteen. So far, Sonny has seen sixteen people.

The next car that pulls into the lot is a blue van. Sonny likes blue. It's one of his almost favourite colours. His other almost favourite colours are red, green, orange, and purple. Sonny's two favourite colours are black and white, because they are

379

easy to remember and because you can't go wrong with black and white.

Sonny watches a thin man get out of the van, and before Sonny can stop himself, he says the man's name.

Mark Vigneux.

But Vigneux's Hardware is closed. Sonny has gone past the store many times, and the windows are always dark, and the doors are always locked. Maybe Mr. Vigneux has returned and is going to reopen the store. Sonny would like that. He remembers wandering the aisles and looking at all the tools and the paints and the plumbing fixtures.

If the hardware store is open again, Sonny will buy a tape measure for his tool pouch, just to let Mr. Vigneux know that people care.

Right then, Leigh Taylor rides up on his bicycle. Taylor's Butcher Shop. Organic ducks and rabbits, fresh eggs and stewing chickens. When the shop was open, Mr. Taylor had let Sonny go into the backyard to pet the animals. He especially liked to pet the baby bunnies before Mr. Taylor made them into sausage.

Mr. Taylor's shop has been closed for a very long time, but now he's back in town. Mr. Vigneux and Mr. Taylor have returned.

Wham-wham.

Maybe after all this time, people are coming home. Maybe they have missed their Sonny. Hammer-hammer.

Sonny is enjoying watching all the people. It's almost like the old days, he tells the trees. Soon the tourists will come back and rent rooms at the Ocean Star Motel. Soon they'll swim in the pool and lose things on his beach.

He steps out of his hiding place and steals across the Co-op parking lot and into the alley behind the Tin Turtle, the roll of copper wire over his shoulder. There are treasures in the darkness and wealth in secret places.

That's what Dad says.

And he's right.

As Sonny searches the empty lots and rummages behind the vacant buildings, he finds an old harrow disc half-buried in the ground. Near the Petro-Canada station, he discovers four lengths of rebar, along with a plastic hubcap that looks like a shield.

The hubcap is quite light, but the harrow disc is heavy, the rebar long and awkward, and Sonny finds it difficult to carry everything at once.

Who will help Sonny?

Sonny holds his hands up to the heavens.

Who will help Sonny in his hour of need?

Then Sonny has an idea. He holds the hubcap parallel to the ground and flings it towards the beach. It sails off, glistening in the sun, floating on the breeze. He hefts the rebar as though it were a spear, and tosses each piece as far as he can. The harrow disc he carries.

Fling the hubcap. Toss the rebar. Carry the disc.

Fling the hubcap. Toss the rebar. Carry the disc.

Sonny is certain that the people at the Co-op would enjoy this game, especially the part with the rebar.

Fling the hubcap. Toss the rebar. Carry the disc.

Fling the hubcap. Toss the rebar. Carry the disc.

Until he finally reaches the tower.

Sonny takes the copper wire off his shoulder and sits down in the sand. He has just begun unrolling the wire and laying each strand next to the rebar when he catches sight of something in the distance, gliding above the swell of the ocean.

A bird.

Sonny can't believe his eyes. He jumps up and rushes into the surf.

A solitary bird, small and fast on the wing. A bird where there had been no bird the day before. Or the day before that. Not since That One Bad Day.

Sonny will have to hurry now. The tower must be finished. The beacon must be lit. And then everything will be as it was before, everything will be as it was in the beginning.

69

DORIAN CAME OUT OF THE ELEVATOR IN FULL STRIDE. WINTER
hurried to keep up.

"Tell me."

"Athabasca, Khan, Quinn," said Winter, reducing the conversation to code.

"My wife wants a divorce."

"The situation in Alberta has worsened."

"She's staying in Orlando. Says we've grown apart, says she
needs to find herself."

"PR is putting a television campaign together that highlights
North America's continuing need for energy and Domidion's
commitment to a healthy environment."

"Needs to find herself? Who talks like that?" Dorian stopped
in the corridor and turned back to Winter. "Are you married?"

"No, sir."

"Very astute. Why buy the cow? Right?"

Winter was an excellent assistant, and Dorian had chosen
her himself, but there were times when he would have preferred
a man in the position.

"Sorry. Inappropriate."

"The fish kill is massive," said Winter. "There are dead

383

animals as well—fox, raccoon, deer, moose, bear, coyote—along the banks of the river for seventy-five kilometres downstream from the breach."

Dorian continued down the hall.

"And we have reports of human casualties."

"Casualties?"

"Eight confirmed. An additional thirty-five in hospital. Those figures are expected to rise."

"Christ. What's the stock doing?"

Winter checked her tablet. "Down nine points."

"The woman has no sense of timing."

"Khan?"

"No." Dorian sat down in his chair as though he were trying to hammer a nail through steel. "Olivia. The stock is in the shitter, and she wants a divorce? *Now* she wants a divorce?"

Dorian could feel the sweat beginning to form on his upper lip. He closed his eyes, and there was his pack of wild dogs with Goofy in the lead, chasing Olivia around the Epcot Center.

"Anything on Quinn?"

"The mother and sister," said Winter. "When they left Lethbridge, they went to a place called Samaritan Bay."

"Samaritan Bay?"

"It's a small town on the coast of British Columbia."

The tremor was unexpected. It started in his fingers, and Dorian had to press his hand down hard on the desk to hold it in place.

"Unfortunately," said Winter, "there is no record of any Quinns in that town or the immediate area."

"Keep looking."

~~~~~~

DORIAN waited until Winter was at the elevators before he fished the bottle from his pocket.

Lucror.

Why did all medications have such bizarre and unfathomable names? Pantoprazole. Creon. Allopurinol. Prednisone. Levothyroxine. Why couldn't the major pharmaceuticals just match the name to the function?

Happy. Sleepy. Calm. Horny.

Dorian swallowed the pill and then went back to his computer. He brought up *VisitOrlando.com* and spent the next while scrolling through the gallery.

All the houses in the photographs were buff or tan, earth colours with some pastels thrown in for contrast. Everywhere he looked, there were swimming pools and tennis courts, with people in golf shirts and shorts, sandals, straw hats, and dark glasses, everyone basted with suntan lotion and bug spray.

Boredom and anonymity.

What did Olivia see in the place? Dorian was sure that Q hadn't run off to Florida, but all things considered, if the man had wanted to disappear and not be found, Orlando had much to recommend it.

70

"MASTER DOG ALWAYS SITS IN FRONT," CRISP EXPLAINED, AS he eased the truck out of the Co-op parking lot. "He'd be better served in back where there's more sky and wind and room to roam, but he'll have none of it."

Gabriel tried to find a comfortable position between Crisp and Soldier. The dog had his head out the window again, and Gabriel had to lean forward to avoid the blowback.

"Says he don't want to miss none of the conversations." At the intersection, Crisp turned the truck away from the town. "A day it was, much like today. That's how it all began."

Soldier quickly pulled his head in and began humming.

"Right you are, Master Dog," shouted Crisp over the wind. "I've messed the story up again, for she don't start on a day like this at all. She starts as life herself starts. In the water."

Soldier settled against Gabriel's shoulder.

"Aye," said Crisp. "It's somewhat nervous in the prologue, with a happy middle and a tragic ending. Do ye know your Jacobean drama?"

"No."

"Everyone dies in the last act," said Crisp. "That's all ye needs know."

Soldier's ears came up.

"Yes, yes," said Crisp. "I'm easily distracted. What I want to say is that it began on a day such as this. And it began in the ocean. I'd gone for my swim, and I went too far. I let my pride rule my prudence. There it is. The fatal flaw."

Crisp passed the Ocean Star Motel and turned into the hills.

"So, there I was, with the edge of the land but a thin line floating on the belly of the sea, when a spasm catches me, cramps me hard and quick, and down I go."

Soldier raised his head and began a low keening.

"But, up I come," cried Crisp, "for I've the strength of giants. Yet, truth be told, I'm in dire straits for me legs were chain spliced and sheep shanked. And then, when I think that all is lost, I touches something in the water and something touches me. At first, I think it's a stub of a log torn loose from the land by a storm, and I grabs it like a baby might grab a breast."

Soldier dropped his head onto Gabriel's lap, and the keening turns to a soft whimper.

"But it weren't a log. No, not a log at all. It were Master Dog, adrift in the great salty, same as me. And that's how it was done. The two of us hurrying on the other with encouragements and threats, him stroking and me floating for a while, and then me pulling for dear life while he reposed on my back like a child in a cradle. All that morning and afternoon we argued with the colossus, until she turned around and tossed us ashore, shipwrecked and busted."

"You found Soldier in the ocean?"

"And he found me," said Crisp. "It were a mutual discovery, with credit enough for both."

The road narrowed and steepened. As it wound into the mountains, Gabriel caught glimpses of a stream in a deep canyon.

"There." Crisp steered the truck into an opening on the shoulder. "There is where it began."

Crisp opened the door, and Soldier leaped out, ran howling to the edge of the chasm.

"One day was all it took."

Gabriel walked to where Soldier was waiting and looked over the edge.

"It's the rare man what gets to see the results of his genius."

Below, Gabriel could see the path of destruction that followed the stream, could see the grey and brittle silence that rose up the sides of the canyon in all directions.

"So," said Crisp, "what think ye of your handiwork?"

71

COMING HOME HAD DEFINITELY BEEN THE EASY PART.
Packing up her stuff, throwing everything into the back of a
pickup, driving to the reserve, and unloading the lot.

Easy peasy.

Now what?

Here she was, in a shell of a house without a stove or a
refrigerator. At least she had remembered to bring a roll of toilet paper. For all the good it would do her. Neither the toilet nor
the sink had water.

Lovely.

What had she been thinking? This Gabriel had volunteered
to bring her food. She could have sent him to the Co-op to get
some essentials, things that wouldn't spoil right away. Bananas,
apples, dry cereal, bread, butter, jam, cheese. Even milk would
last one night, probably two.

All she had had to do was ask.

But no. Cut off her nose to spite her face. Pride. One of life's
lessons, her mother had told her. Some people learn it, and
some don't.

PROGRESS had been slow. In her second year, Mara had a painting accepted in a student exhibition. She had donated another to a charity auction for cancer research, had watched as the bidding stopped at half the value she had set on the piece. There was an honourable mention in a juried event, five paintings in a group show, and an unexpected grant from the Ontario Arts Council.

Business at the deli recovered. Ange was able to give her as much work as she could handle, and, when the workshops finished in May, she was able to fly home.

"Rose ain't doing so good," Mara's mother told her.

"She don't talk much," her grandmother said, "and Lilly's got to feed her."

"A stroke?"

"Probably should talk to Lilly."

"Day comes you have to feed me, just dump me in the woods."

"Not going to dump you in the woods, Granny."

"You'll be in Paris," said her grandmother. "You won't even know it happened."

Mara had spent most of the time with Lilly, walking the reserve, visiting the town, wandering the beach.

"They're not sure what's wrong with her," Lilly had told her. "So they're not doing anything."

"What's going to happen?"

"Guess we'll find out."

In the end, the trip home had been somewhat unnerving. The reserve had been smaller than she remembered, the town slow and boring. Even more disturbing, Mara's mother and grandmother had seemed distant.

"So, how you been?"

"Fine."

"You're not sick or anything?"

"No."

"Bet that Toronto don't have a view of the ocean."

"It's not on the ocean."

"Don't know if I could live someplace where you couldn't see the ocean."

Lilly hadn't smiled much, and there had been none of the laughter that had been so much a part of their lives.

"How come you came home?"

"To see you."

"Nothing much to see. I'm still the same."

"So am I."

"You still going to go to Paris?"

"One of these days. What about you?"

"I got Mum," Lilly had told her. "I'm not going anywhere."

Maybe this was what happened as you got older, but more than once during the visit, Mara found herself wondering if she should have stayed in Toronto.

MARA found a piece of paper and a pen and began a list of things to do. Sure, the house looked desperate right now, but all it needed were a few adjustments. She'd get Crisp to help her with the electricity and the propane tank. The septic should still be working. The Co-op could order a stove and refrigerator. Two weeks to get everything in. Three tops.

Mara paced out her old room. Six feet by eight feet. It had

seemed larger. Her bed had been under the window, her dresser against the wall. There had been a small bookcase and a smaller desk with a lamp.

And that had been it. That was all she had needed. Perhaps it was all she had ever needed.

Mara walked through every room several times, making a list. Besides the obvious, she'd have to find a table, several chairs, and a sofa of some sort. Dishes, glasses, silverware, a kettle for boiling water, a broom, a mop.

A bed.

She'd definitely need a bed.

And a wood stove.

Her grandmother had had a cast iron stove in the living room that had kept the house warm. The stove was gone, of course, but the hole in the ceiling, along with the trim collar and part of the stovepipe, was still there.

HER first solo show was at a small second-floor gallery on Dundas West that doubled as a yoga studio. Mara had stood nervously in the far corner of the long room, with a glass of wine, trying to look intriguing in the way artists were supposed to look intriguing, watching the people dutifully file past her paintings. It had been a good turnout, but consisted mostly of fellow students, their partners, and anyone they had been able to drag along on the promise of hard cheese and cheap wine.

Halfway through the evening, an older couple had arrived. The woman looked to be in her seventies. She was short with steel-grey hair and a soft face. Her companion was taller, thinner, had a cane, and staggered slightly when he walked.

After they had made one circuit of the room, the woman came over to where Mara was standing.

"Are you the artist?"

"I am," Mara had said.

"I'm interested in your paintings."

"She likes the blue one," said the man. "It'll match the sofa at the cottage."

"Don't mind him," said the woman. "He thinks he's funny."

"I am funny," said the man with a grin. "Everyone says I'm funny."

"I'm going to buy those two," said the woman, pointing to the far wall. "I hope you intend to be famous."

That night, Mara had rushed back to her apartment to call her mother and Lilly, to tell them about the show, about the woman and her husband, about being able to put red dots next to each painting.

She got as far as picking up the phone before she realized that she didn't know what she would say, how she would describe this new life, what difference any of this would make in the world from which she had come. That world, the world of the reserve, was concerned with the river at dawn and a neighbour who could only stare out windows while her daughter sat with her, patiently, waiting for the morning sun.

In the end, she set the phone by the pillow and curled up on the bed. Maybe her grandmother had been right. Maybe she should have been a nurse.

~~~~~

MARA had forgotten about the stove. It had been a lovely thing, and for reasons she could not explain, this was the keenest loss. Of all the material things that had no real value beyond memory, this was the keenest loss.

Mara lay on the floor and pulled a blanket over her shoulders. So, here she was. Home. After all this time, she was home.

She didn't know whether to laugh or cry.

Mara had just decided on a good cry when she realized she was not alone. Standing in the doorway, frozen in the light, was a young woman with long black hair and almond eyes.

72

DORIAN WORKED HIS WAY THROUGH A FINAL DRAFT OF Domidion's annual report, and when he was blind from reading enthusiastic income projections and staring at multicoloured pie charts, he called Toshi's office. The receptionist put him on hold, and he had to suffer through a violin version of the Beatles' "In My Life." That gave way to an instrumental with pan pipes, followed by someone, other than Leo Sayer, singing "When I Need You."

Then the woman was back. "Mr. Asher."

"Yes."

"Dr. Toshi has arranged for a bed at Toronto General. Do you know where that is?"

Dorian tried to keep the annoyance out of his voice. "A bed?"

"Dr. Toshi would like you to check in to the hospital this evening before eight. Is that a problem?"

"I wish to speak with Dr. Toshi."

"The tests require that you fast," said the woman, jogging right along. "No food or water after nine tonight."

"Dr. Toshi?"

"You'll be in the hospital overnight, so you might want to bring some toiletries and any clothes you feel you'll need."

"And Dr. Toshi?"

"If all goes well, you'll be released by noon," said the woman, keeping the same steady pace. "We'll call and arrange an appointment when we have the test results."

SO, Toshi wanted to put him in a hospital. Well, that wasn't going to happen. Dorian wasn't about to spend an hour in a hospital, let alone overnight.

At least not without an explanation.

What was it the man didn't understand?

If Toshi thought it might be cancer, then he should say so. If he suspected something such as Parkinson's or some variation of Hodgkin's, then Dorian had a right to know. Instead, Dorian had been reduced to listening to Marathon Woman and her robotic instructions.

Asian reticence.

It was only cute in movies.

Of course, one obvious answer was stress. The tremors, the sweating, the dizziness, the loss of concentration, the vivid metaphors. All stress. Dorian had raised this possibility with Toshi on a number of occasions.

"What about stress?"

"A contributing factor to a great many health problems."

"So, it could be stress."

"We'll know more when we get the test results."

This was Toshi's mantra. Test results. Dorian wasn't sure how many more tests there could possibly be. Dorian had already endured MRIs, CAT scans, X-rays, a muscle biopsy, a colonoscopy, and tests for ALS, CVD, and HIV, for West Nile, tuberculosis, Lyme disease, and diabetes. Every time he went to see Toshi, there was another round of tests waiting for him.

Stress.

Toshi was probably reluctant to say stress, because that was akin to admitting that he knew no more about the patient's condition than did the patient.

Stress.

Dorian was sure that he didn't need any more blood tests. He certainly didn't require an overnight stay in a hospital or another assault on his orifices. It was common knowledge that the body was very efficient at healing itself.

If it was left alone.

Dorian leaned back in his chair, closed his eyes, and tried to think of nothing.

Meditation.

That might just be the answer. Dorian remembered a movie where people sat around with their eyes closed and their legs crossed. They had sat there with their arms hanging freely from their sides, the tips of their thumbs and third fingers touching.

Had they been humming?

Yes, they had.

Eyes closed. Arms at your side. Thumb to finger. Hum.

Eyes closed. Arms at your side. Thumb to finger. Hum.

"Sir?"

Dorian opened one eye. Winter was standing in the doorway. She had a thick, dark green manila folder in her hand.

"I was meditating."

"Excellent activity for reducing stress."

"Was I humming?"

"Yes," said Winter, "you were."

Dorian looked at the folder. "Good news would be appreciated."

"Security found this at Dr. Quinn's house."

Someone had written across the face of the file in large block letters, "The Woman Who Fell from the Sky."

"I believe Dr. Thicke mentioned such a file."

"He did."

"Internal Domidion documents," said Winter, placing the folder on Dorian's desk. "They appear to have originated from our archives."

"Wonderful."

"Copies of site reports, risk assessments, confidential memos, requisition records. All of them classified. Along with a series of newspaper articles."

"Copies?"

"Yes, sir," said Winter. "All the documents in the folder are copies."

"The originals?"

"We don't know."

"And the newspaper articles?"

"Local coverage of the Kali Creek mishap," said Winter. "Photographs, eyewitness accounts, obituaries."

Olivia was probably playing tennis at this moment. Dorian pictured her standing on a clay court under the Florida sun, tossing balls into the air. Ridiculous. No one could spend that amount of time hitting a stupid yellow ball over a stupid green net and call it a life.

"GreenSweep?"

"Yes, sir," said Winter. "Evidently 'The Woman Who Fell from the Sky' was the name that Dr. Quinn originally gave the GreenSweep project."

Dorian opened the file and looked at the first page. "What's this?"

On the inside of the folder, the word "Kousoulas" had been written in block letters and underlined.

"I believe it's a name," said Winter. "Greek."

"Do we have any Greeks named Kousoulas working for us?"

"No, sir," said Winter. "We don't."

Dorian ran his hand across the file. It had the feel of old felt. "So," he said. "What do you make of all this?"

"Dr. Quinn?"

"Yes."

Winter paused as though she were waiting for the question and the answer to find each other. "Exceptional biotech mind. Anti-social tendencies. Eats lunch in front of an empty aquarium. Writes on the walls of a rented bungalow."

Winter ticked off each item as though she were reading a list.

"Limited family life. No long-term relationships. Trauma as a young adult."

Dorian nodded quietly to himself. "Let's have coffee and sandwiches sent up."

"Yes, sir. Coffee and sandwiches."

"This may take a while."

"Shall I have Dr. Thicke keep himself available, in case we need him?"

"Tell me, Winter, what do you know about tennis balls?"

"Sir?"

Dorian lay the folder open and spread the documents out on the desk. "Tennis balls," he repeated. "How many do you think you could hit before you got bored?"

73

"YOU'VE KNOWN." GABRIEL TURNED TO CRISP. "YOU'VE known all along."

"Guessed," said Crisp. "With a small certainty here and there for good measure."

Gabriel ran a hand along Soldier's flank. "Nicholas Crisp," he said, "Finder-Minder."

"Aye," said Crisp. "That be me, all right."

"Little asked you to try to find me."

Crisp sat down next to Soldier. "She did, for she loved ye desperately."

"And my mother?"

"She was sick by then. 'Dementia' is the name they gave the thing in her brain. And soon there weren't a shim thin enough to slip between truth and fiction."

"I didn't know she was sick."

"Lilly told me how ye didn't come home after your father died, how they lost track of ye and ye of them. Is that what happened?"

Gabriel shrugged. "What does it matter?"

"No juice in half a story," said Crisp. "No matter how hard ye squeezes."

Gabriel kicked at a loose rock and sent it clattering over the edge. "It was you."

"Blamed for much." Crisp lowered his eyes. "And guilty of some."

"You sent the photograph."

Crisp nodded. "I only found your scent on the eve of The Ruin. After that unbearable day, there weren't much left to offer but the image of her and the boy."

"I was in India." Gabriel stood on the rim of the canyon and looked down. Below he could hear the sound of rushing water. "Kali Creek?"

"Aye," said Crisp. "This be the place."

Riel, she had named her son Riel.

"Is there a way down?"

Soldier scrambled to his feet, the fur at the back of his neck fanned forward.

"No profit in seeing what can't be changed."

"Is there a way down?"

Crisp took a breath. "Aye," he said. "There be such a thing. A trail starts just there by that dead tree. A narrow snake it is, steep and dark, full of twists and slips.

"Where does it go?"

"Creek follows the canyon till they both find the Smoke," said Crisp. "Master Dog knows of such things and can show you the way."

Gabriel walked to the tree and put his hand on it. The trunk felt dry and hollowed out. "No," he said, "I want to go alone."

Crisp nodded.

Gabriel looked back at the truck. "The groceries are for Mara."

"Master Dog and I can see that they arrive in good order."

"She knows who I am," said Gabriel. "You might as well tell her the rest."

Crisp returned to the truck, Soldier at his heels. "Mind the first drop," he shouted back. "Ye slips there, and ye rides the shale to the bottom."

THE trail was wet. The ground curled and slid under his feet, and he had to grab the vines and roots and drive his heels against the rocks to keep his balance. Here the earth was dark brown and alive, but as he sank into the canyon itself, the colour shrank away and died.

The creek was running clean and cold. He set his hand in the water, let it run past his fingers, and watched for a time, hoping to catch a glimpse of something moving below the surface. Once, he thought he saw a shadow, a fish, perhaps, or a turtle.

Or wishful thinking.

He hadn't expected the bones. Almost everywhere he looked, everywhere he walked, there were bones. He hadn't thought about that. There had been the turtle bones on the beach and bleached shells stuck to the Apostles, but these bones were different. They hadn't been buried in the sand or crushed by the waves. They lay out on the ground where the creatures had died, one minute alive, the next minute dead, the fall of the creek drowning out the weeping.

Gabriel moved quickly along the trail, stumbling, falling at times, his pants and shoes damp and muddied. Once he came upon a cluster of bones that might have been a family of rabbits.

Another time he found what looked to be a deer and a fawn lying at the water's edge.

But he couldn't be sure. In the end, the only thing that the bones resembled were bones. If there was a memory of an animal hidden in the skeletons, Gabriel couldn't find it.

Much of the time was spent in half-shadows. At moments, too few to mark, the sun would find its way to the bottom of the canyon and form pools of light. In one of the pools, he found two tiny skulls. Twins perhaps.

He hadn't intended this.

Yet this is what he had done.

HE had come home. Once he had come home.

In his second year at Stanford, he had flown to Calgary, and, on the bus ride to Lethbridge, Gabriel had tried to think what he was going to say. He hadn't spoken to his mother since his father's death, hadn't seen Little since the day he and Joe had left for Minneapolis. He wanted to see his sister, wanted to surprise her, wanted to tell her that she had not been forgotten.

He was sure she would be thrilled to see him, too.

He wasn't sure what he would say to his mother.

It was evening when he stepped off the bus. He could have taken a cab. Instead, he had started walking. He and Lilly had been born to this place. It was home. At least that's what it said on their birth certificates. But, as he walked through town, Gabriel hadn't found any sense of belonging. Even as he stood at the top of Whoop-Up Drive and looked across at the lights of the west side, he hadn't found any reason to be here.

The walk down to the river bottom, across the bridge, and up again was longer than he had remembered. At one point, he stepped off the path to stand in the stiff prairie grass. They had played here as kids, had chased each other up and down the coulees. There in the distance was the High Level Bridge. Off to the left was the stand of cottonwoods and the bend in the river where they had seen the pelicans.

There had been a moment when he thought that there might be a bond in the blood, that he would remember the land, and the land would remember him.

So he had waited.

But there was just the sky and the wind rising out of the west.

Their house had been on Princeton Crescent, a grand name of a street for an ordinary run of small homes on narrow lots. The place looked even smaller now. His father had planted a Russian olive in the front yard. The tree was still there, looking as fatally thin and grey as it had the day Joe had dug the hole.

Gabriel stood on the sidewalk in front of the house, hoping that Lilly would see him and come rushing out. That was how he had imagined the reunion. Lilly running out of the house and throwing her arms around him.

He had bought a stuffed dog with floppy ears at the Calgary airport, before he remembered that Lilly would almost be a teenager by now. And he had found a box of chocolates for his mother, the same brand his father had bought Rose for special occasions.

Lilly didn't come running out, and Gabriel finally went to the door and rang the bell. A young woman he didn't recognize answered it. The woman did not look happy to see him, and he was clumsy in his explanation.

I used to live here.

My family used to live here.

I thought my mother and sister still lived here.

I've been gone, but now I'm back.

My father planted that tree.

The woman watched him closely, her left hand on the door. No, she didn't know a Rose Quinn. "I'm cooking dinner," she told him. "Check with the neighbours."

He did.

Up and down the street he went, knocking on doors, hoping to recognize a familiar face, asking the same questions, getting the same answers. Until evening turned to night, and a police car came along and angled up on the sidewalk beside him.

GABRIEL picked up the skulls and turned them over in his hand. He had missed all of it. His mother's funeral. Lilly's marriage. The birth of her child.

He placed the skulls on the ground where he had found them. Now he was cold, and he wanted to be rid of this place. But the path forced him deeper into the canyon. The walls rose far above his head, until the sky was a jagged sliver of light in the tops of the trees. The only sounds were the creek and the silence of the land, and they followed him as he made his way through the desolation.

THE police constable was a woman, and she was understanding. A concerned neighbour had called in. A man was in the area, knocking on doors, trying to find lost relatives. Or so he said.

Gabriel showed her his driver's licence and his Stanford ID.

The officer was smiling by then, and Gabriel had to admit that the situation had a certain comic aspect.

"The caller thought you might be a criminal."

"No," Gabriel said, by way of a joke, "just a university student."

He took his time walking back down to the river and up the other side, and every time a car flashed by, Gabriel tried to catch a glimpse of the driver. He got a room at the Lethbridge Lodge, overlooking the courtyard and the pool. He had a light meal, ate the chocolates while he watched television, and went to bed.

In the morning, he caught the bus back to Calgary.

On the plane to San Francisco, he looked around for a child who might like the dog, but in the end, he propped it under his head, leaned against the window, and went to sleep.

THE path left the creek and began to rise. The Smoke was farther on, but Gabriel had seen enough. He began the climb, hiking along in his wet pants and ruined shoes, as the trail made its way out of the canyon and found the light. When he reached flat ground, he picked up the pace, weaving his way around the trees, crossing small creeks on the wood planking. And then the path turned to asphalt, and the asphalt ran into a small parking lot.

There, on the far side of the lot, in the shadow of a large cedar, was an old truck. Next to the truck was a bald man with a flaming beard, and standing beside him was a scruffy dog with an honest face.

74

"THE WOMAN WHO FELL FROM THE SKY."

It was a rather prosaic title, borderline romantic, but Q's notes and the documents he had compiled made for disturbing reading. How in hell had the man been able to put the pieces together?

Winter had had sandwiches and fruit brought up, along with coffee. Dorian hadn't touched any of the food. Neither had Winter. She had quietly taken up a position in one of the wing-backs and waited while Dorian made his way through the papers.

"Several years ago, we looked at the possibility of genetically modifying the SDF 20 variation of *Klebsiella planticola* for use as a commercial defoliant."

"GreenSweep."

"Yes," said Dorian. "GreenSweep. Dr. Quinn and Dr. Thicke split the project between them. Dr. Thicke's team was tasked with increasing the virulence of SDF 20, while at the same time limiting its life cycle. Dr. Quinn's team was responsible for extending the bacterium's environmental range, while preventing horizontal gene transfer."

Dorian could hear the energy seep out of his body. A tire with a slow leak. What he needed was a patch and a nap. The Lucror didn't seem to be doing much, which probably meant that Toshi was running out of options.

Or didn't know what he was doing.

"The two teams were able to increase the bacterium's virulence, and they were able to extend its environmental range by splicing in genetic material from thermophiles and psychrophiles."

"Very ambitious."

"However," Dorian continued, "they were only partially successful in limiting the bacterium's life cycle, and neither team was able to eliminate the risk of genetic transfer."

"Chaos theory."

"At the time, Dr. Quinn recommended that we terminate the project. He was concerned that GreenSweep had the potential to become an event horizon."

Winter blinked once. "An environmental black hole."

"That assessment was considered excessive," said Dorian. "It was felt that if we could find a way to control life cycle and horizontal transfer, we would have a potent and commercially valuable defoliant."

The watermelon looked particularly good, and Dorian helped himself to several pieces. The coffee was still hot.

"GreenSweep was not supposed to leave our facilities."

"Kali Creek."

Dorian sipped at the coffee. "Mistake on mistake on mistake. In the end, we shut the project down and disposed of the remaining stock."

Winter cocked her head. "But?"

Dorian pulled several pages from the folder and handed them to Winter. He waited patiently while she read.

"It's probably not an issue," he said, "but I'd like you to verify that the proper protocols were followed."

"Yes, sir."

"And, Winter," said Dorian, "do it quietly."

DORIAN spent the rest of the afternoon reviewing the Athabasca spill. Domidion had acted swiftly enough. The ponds had been drained, the breaks repaired, collection booms had been strung across the river at various points, and the surface effluents had been sucked up into storage tankers that the corporation had rushed into service.

Dorian knew that the equipment and the trucks were mostly for show, knew that the dioxins and the heavy metals were already on the bottom of the river, where neither the booms nor the vacuums could reach them. Still, it was a good show, and Public Relations had sent footage of the cleanup operation to CBC, insisting that *En Garde* give the corporation equal time to tell their side of the story.

Dorian looked at the clock. He'd have to eat and clean up a bit before the show. He thought about calling Olivia to tell her that Toshi wanted him hospitalized. It sounded rather dramatic, "hospitalized," though it might be more effective if Winter made the call.

Your husband has been hospitalized.

Of course, there was no reason to suppose that Olivia would rush to his side. And there was no telling how the Board would react if they discovered that their CEO was sick. Best to leave that dog lie.

"Nothing serious," he could tell Olivia. "Nothing to worry about."

And suddenly he was angry. Angry about the divorce. Angry about Florida. Angry that they had bought the condo on Queen's Quay. Angry with Toshi.

Angry that he had settled for the Rolex instead of getting the Jaeger as well.

Dorian looked at the clock. Time enough for a steam. Perhaps even a massage. Relax. Gather his strength. Tonight he'd settle with Manisha Khan.

Tomorrow he'd go shopping.

75

GABRIEL COULD FEEL THE MUD SQUISH ABOUT IN HIS SHOES as he walked across the parking lot. It was a disagreeable sensation and reminded him of baby diapers.

"The hound's uncanny," shouted Crisp. "I wagered you'd find a captain's share of inconvenience and bother on your journey, but Master Dog said ye would be along shortly and none the worse for wear."

"I appreciate your waiting for me."

"Nay, we didn't wait," said Crisp, "for as ye can see, we've been engaged in some measure of toil."

The back of the Ford was filled with appliances and furniture.

"Are you moving?"

"Nicholas Crisp. Finder-Minder." Crisp moved to the side of the truck and gave a large cast iron stove a pat. "This be the grandmother's," he said. "Her pride and joy. Many's the time I stood before it and warmed my blood to the boiling."

"Mara's grandmother?"

"The same."

"I thought the stove had been stolen."

"Stolen?" Crisp thought on this for a moment. "There was thievery, to be sure. Enough to raise the hackles and sour the milk, but much was moved into storage for safekeeping. For when the People return."

"I don't think Mara knows that."

Crisp slapped his head with his hand. "Have I done it again? Forgot to mention the matter to Mistress Mara?"

"She'll be happy to have the stove back."

"And there be the reward, certain sure," said Crisp. "Still, the omission's a worry-weight on my faculties."

"Are those the appliances from the house, too?"

"They are indeed."

"And the table and the chairs? The bed?"

"Matching cuffs and collars, near as I can remember," said Crisp. "I marked the lot so I could put them back as needed, but some of the sign has faded, and a measure of speculation is in play."

Soldier came around the truck, snorting and mumbling to himself.

"Yes, yes," said Crisp, holding up his hands. "I do talk too much, though it's no great mischief, for I loves conversation and the company that comes with it."

Soldier waited for Gabriel to slide to the middle before he jumped in. Crisp climbed behind the wheel.

"Keep an eye," shouted Crisp, "for she's heavy at the topsail and likely to capsize in a rolling sea."

Crisp took the turns slowly, keeping the truck flat and level, but when the road began to rise, he pulled over and stopped.

"I was optimistic," he shouted. "She'll tip on the next tack for sure, unless we brace the cargo."

"How?"

"Master Dog is of no use in this matter, for he's all brain, and I must tend the tiller. Which leaves yourself and your strong back."

"So Soldier is the brains, and I'm the brawn."

"Control the top," said Crisp, "and the rest will follow."

There was no room to stand in the back of the truck.

"Ye needs ride the bumper," said Crisp. "Both feet here. One hand on the tailgate, the other on the fridge."

"Stand on the bumper?"

"Keep her upright, and the rest is clear sailing."

The bumper was flat and corrugated. Gabriel tried to angle his feet, but there was little room.

"I don't think this is going to work."

Crisp didn't help the situation. He wasn't as careful as he had been before. Gabriel's standing on the back end had given Crisp an unwarranted confidence, and he careened up the road, diving into the bumps and potholes and heaving out the other side. Gabriel bolted his feet to the bumper as best he could, took a death grip on the tailgate, and set his whole body against the white enamel box that wanted to tip on him like a chainsawed tree.

All the way up the road to the reserve, Crisp shouted instructions from behind the wheel, while Soldier sent sheets of slobber flying out the passenger window.

"Brace! Damn your eyes! Brace!"

When they got to calm ground and the houses were in sight, Crisp stopped the truck and came back to check on Gabriel.

"Brilliant!" shouted Crisp. "For we thought we'd lost ye to the last wave."

Gabriel couldn't feel his fingers, and the muscles in his legs were locked. He pulled his hand away from the refrigerator and discovered it was cramped in position.

"Are ye in need of assistance?"

"I'm okay."

"For ye appear to be somewhat sprung."

"Maybe some help getting down."

The ground felt strange, and he had to take a few steps to correct for tilt and balance.

"Hop in," said Crisp, "for she's a smooth sea, now, and a deep harbour."

The passenger door handle was covered in drool.

"I think I'll walk," said Gabriel.

"As ye wish," said Crisp. "Master Dog and I shall disembark the cargo, while we awaits your arrival."

GABRIEL'S legs were still stiff from the ride up the hill on the bumper, and he didn't stop limping until he got to the water tower. It was probably the sunshine, but, as he walked through the townsite, the reserve didn't feel quite as lonely and abandoned.

Crisp and Soldier were waiting for him on the porch. They had been busy. The only things left on the truck were both stoves, the refrigerator, and a mattress.

"I could have finished it myself," Crisp sang out. "But Master Dog insisted I wait, so ye might have a hand in the ordering of this new world."

"Where's Mara?"

Soldier grumbled and chased his butt around the porch.

"Not answering the flags or pipes." Crisp jammed the tongue of the dolly under the refrigerator. "Might have gone to town on foot and been missed by us going and coming."

"Then why didn't she go with me?"

"Thought about it later perhaps," said Crisp. "Or she might have gone back to the house for something forgot and needed."

"She'll be surprised when she gets back."

"Lend a hand, now," said Crisp, "for there's no surprise but at the finish."

IT didn't take long to get the truck unloaded. Putting the bed together took more time than it should have, and both men had to wrestle with connecting the stovepipe to the venting collar in the ceiling.

"The electricity will have to be arranged," said Crisp, "but the water should be little more than an obliging valve and a long wrench."

"You can get the water working?"

"The main's at the community centre. It were turned off when the People was removed."

"So, we can just turn it back on."

"That would be the plan," said Crisp. "Course, the pump might be in the scuppers or the valve froze up, but if all's well, we'll have water by evening."

Soldier led the way. He was off the porch at the run, dancing across the ground. Crisp and Gabriel followed.

"Did your mum ever talk about the Smoke?"

"I don't think she had any good memories of the place."

"There's truth in that," said Crisp. "Her dad ran off, you see. Mother died hard. She herself was badly used by some of the boys in town."

"But she came back."

"Salmon, birds, turtles. They all come back." Crisp began walking again. "Humans ain't no different. Don't need a reason."

THE community centre was white clapboard with green trim, raised out of the ground on a cinder-block foundation.

"Many a feast were had here." Crisp opened the door and stepped across the threshold. "Singing, drumming, dancing, eating. All the fine things in life."

"Sounds a little romantic."

"Aye, so it does, for there were drunkenness as well, with hard words exchanged over money and women, and hot blood leading to altercations. It were no paradise, if that be the question. But it were a community."

Gabriel looked around. The room was a long rectangle, with a basketball standard at either end. One of the rims was missing. It had been pleasant in the sun. Inside the building was chilly and damp.

Soldier appeared at the doorway, sniffed once, and then raced away into the warmth of the day.

"They would set the drum up here and the tables with the food over there. There were folding tables and folding chairs, a microphone for the announcements, the storytelling, and the bingo." Crisp rubbed his hands together. "I once won a mountain bike in a blackout game."

"The water shutoff?"

"Nostalgia," said Crisp. "It will surely lead a body astray. Come now, for there's more to do than listen to windy tales."

The basement of the centre was dark and gloomy. The only light came from the narrow windows set high on the wall, where the foundation broke ground. Crisp made his way to the far corner, wrench in hand. Gabriel moved closer to one of the windows and looked into the rafters.

"Here's a puzzle," Crisp shouted to Gabriel.

"Another one over here," Gabriel shouted back.

Crisp appeared out of the shadows. "The water's already been turned on."

"Mara?"

"Perhaps," said Crisp. "Perhaps. What have ye found?"

"The wiring," said Gabriel, pointing to the heavy beams that ran the length of the basement. "Much of the wiring has been cut away."

76

CRISP TOUCHED THE END OF THE WIRE THAT WAS STILL attached to the ceramic insulators. "Clean cuts," he said. "Bright and recent. I was wondering how he was to bind it all together."

"Bind what together?"

"Why, the tower," said Crisp. "Have ye not seen the tower the boy's building on the beach?"

"Sonny?"

"You must admire the lad's ingenuity."

"He took the wire?"

Soldier appeared at one of the windows and began scratching at the glass.

"It seems that Master Dog would like a moment of our time," said Crisp. "Come along, for he's not one to be kept waiting."

"He's a dog."

"And what better thing is there to be?"

Soldier was waiting for Crisp and Gabriel when they emerged from the basement. He skipped off the steps, ran out for fifty yards, and then came back on the fly. He began groaning and throwing himself at Gabriel's legs.

"Yes, yes," said Crisp, "we can see that ye has an important matter to put before us."

Gabriel watched the dog as he took off on another rambling loop. As Soldier turned to come back, Gabriel saw it.

Smoke.

There was smoke coming out of one of the chimneys. Smoke the colour of fog.

"Your sister's place," said Crisp. "And that's smoke true enough."

"Mara?"

"If it's not," said Crisp, "then it must be a surprise. And life don't have enough of them."

This time, Soldier didn't come back. He kept going, striking a straight line to the house with the smoke. Crisp raised his head and expanded his nostrils.

"Do ye smell that?" Crisp licked his lips and drew a hand down his beard.

Gabriel sniffed at the air.

"Put your lungs into it," said Crisp.

"Food."

"Food, indeed," said Crisp. "And let's hope we're not too late."

Crisp hurried off towards the house, leaning forward, his nose on point. Gabriel had to hurry to keep up. When they got to the porch, Crisp held up a hand.

"Best to come in quietly, so as not to frighten dinner," said Crisp, and he opened the front door gently and stepped inside. Gabriel stayed at his shoulder.

The scene was unexpected. Mara was sitting on the floor, surrounded by plates of food. And she wasn't alone. Soldier was curled up by the fireplace, next to the trunk from the beach.

And sitting around the room on the floor and on makeshift beds were a dozen other people.

Mara waved a hand at him. "I think you two know each other."

It took Gabriel a moment, and then he recognized the young girl he had pulled out of the water.

"Company," boomed Crisp, and he whacked Gabriel on the shoulder. "Ballast and barnacles, but we've got company!"

The girl smiled and got to her feet. She stood with her hands clasped in front of her, and she began to sing the song that Gabriel had sung on the rocks that foggy morning.

And one by one, the other people stood and sang with her.

77

DORIAN ARRIVED AT THE TELEVISION STUDIO EARLY, SO HE would have time to relax in the green room and go over the talking points that Winter had prepared for him.

Athabasca River? Tragedy.

Oil extraction? National priority.

Safety protocols? The best in the industry.

Environmental damage? Minimal.

Legal liability? Unfortunate accident.

It was all a waste of time. North American Norm didn't give a damn about the environment. Cancel a favourite television show. Slap another tax on cigarettes. Stop serving beer at baseball and hockey games. That was serious.

Spoil a river somewhere in Humdrum, Alberta? Good luck getting Norm off the sofa.

Of course, Dorian wasn't going to say any of that on national television. He was going to smile his charming smile, plump up his voice, drop it into a soothing octave, and look regal. No one was going to listen to the interview. It would be his appearance that carried the day, his manner that set the agenda.

Was he well dressed? Did he look honest? Did he sound trustworthy?

"Mr. Asher?"

The woman had a clipboard in one hand and a stopwatch in the other.

"Ready, are we?"

"Ms. Khan has to do the top of the hour news," said the young woman, "and then the two of you will talk. Do you need any coffee, water?"

"No, I'm fine."

"Then if you would follow me."

MANISHA Khan was on a set made up to look like a model living room in an upscale furniture store, talking about a murder-suicide gone wrong, in which the perpetrator had died and his intended victim had escaped with only minor injuries.

Dorian watched Khan work. The woman was sincere and efficient. She exuded power and compassion, with a strong sensual undertone. And she knew how to dress. Tonight Khan had selected a simple business suit with a dark skirt, a plum blouse, and a soft grey jacket with black and green flecks.

Franco Mirabelli perhaps. Or Vivian Shyu.

They would look fantastic together on the set.

"Mr. Asher." Manisha was up from her anchor seat and on her way to where he was waiting. "I really appreciate your agreeing to be on the show."

"Always happy to chat with our friends at the fourth estate."

Manisha put her hands on her hips. "I do believe you're trying to charm me."

"Just a simple businessman."

"Who happens to be the head of one of the largest and most powerful corporations in the world."

"You can't believe everything you read at the checkout counter."

"We have about twenty minutes, and I want to cover as much territory as possible."

"You ask," said Dorian, practising his smile. "I'll answer."

A large man, who looked as though he stocked shelves at a big box store, stepped onto the set.

"On in ten, nine, eight, seven . . . "

As the man counted down, Dorian closed his eyes and reminded himself who he was. A warrior. A scholar. The Regent of Domidion, Protector of the Realm.

"Good evening," Manisha began, "and welcome to *En Garde*."

Dorian drew in a long breath and opened his eyes.

"Tonight we're talking with Dorian Asher, CEO of Domidion International. Thank you for coming tonight, Mr. Asher."

"Dorian, please," said Dorian.

"Not one of the company's better days."

"Energy extraction has its difficulties."

"I'm not sure the word 'difficulty' quite describes the destruction of the Athabasca River and the Mackenzie River system."

"We have crews on the river right now. We expect that it will take several weeks to clean up the discharge. And we will be there until the cleanup is complete."

"We've talked to experts in the field who say that the damage is already done, that the cleanup is simply for show."

Dorian flashed a smile and shook his head sadly. "Let me assure you that Domidion doesn't spend millions of dollars simply for show."

"Well," said Manisha, "this *was* Domidion's fault."

Dorian held up a hand. It was something that politicians did to cut off debate, and he liked the gesture. "It may not be quite that simple. As you know, Domidion has been the subject of a series of cyber attacks by a terrorist group known as the Zebras."

Khan leaned forward. "Are you suggesting that the holding ponds were sabotaged?"

"At this time, we have no evidence to suggest sabotage." Dorian paused to let everyone catch up to the idea. "But I can tell you that we have an investigative team on site and that we're co-operating with provincial and federal authorities."

"Feels like a smokescreen."

"Due diligence, Manisha," said Dorian. "Due diligence."

Khan turned to one of the cameras. "We're told that the Athabasca may never recover. What do you say to people whose health and livelihoods have been destroyed by the spills."

"The modern world runs on energy, Manisha. Domidion can't change that. The spills are unfortunate, but our first priority has to be the security of the nation and the protection of our children's future."

Dorian was getting bored. If the questions didn't present any more of a challenge, he might fall asleep.

"That all sounds brave and responsible, Dorian," said Manisha, "but Domidion's track record with regard to disasters such as the Athabasca River is not all that sterling."

Dorian ran a hand through his hair. "I'm afraid," he said, his voice full of fatherly concern, "you'll have to be a bit more specific."

Khan sat back in her chair. "Let's talk about Kali Creek."

Suddenly, Dorian was awake. Wide awake.

"I beg your pardon."

"Kali Creek," Khan repeated slowly. "March 9, 2011."

Dorian held up a hand, but Khan continued.

"An experimental defoliant known as GreenSweep was used near Kali Creek in British Columbia to clear undergrowth for pipeline construction. The crew spraying the defoliant made a mistake with the concentration, and the result was a massive environmental disaster."

Dorian managed a smile. "Defoliants are used for many applications."

"GreenSweep was developed and manufactured by Domidion during your term as CEO, wasn't it?"

"I'd like to talk about our cleanup efforts on the Athabasca. I've brought some footage that I'm sure your viewers will find interesting."

"A storm put the defoliant into Kali Creek, and it was washed into the Smoke River and then into the ocean at Samaritan Bay. One hundred and thirty-seven people lost their lives. Over three hundred were hospitalized."

"Manisha . . . "

"A Dr. Gabriel Quinn headed the GreenSweep project, and, according to Dr. Warren Thicke, Dr. Quinn has gone missing. Would you like to comment on that?"

DORIAN didn't stop at the green room to gather his overcoat. He'd have someone pick it up later. Khan wanted to get a photo, and her assistant asked Dorian to sign the guest book. Instead he walked straight from the set to the Front Street entrance, where the limo was waiting for him.

It was only after the car had crossed University that Dorian realized he had no idea where he wanted to go.

78

SONNY SITS IN THE SAND BY HIS PILE OF BONES AND SHELLS and stones, and he sings as he strings each piece on the copper wire.

Turtle bone, clamshell, clamshell, clamshell.

Turtle bone, clamshell, clamshell, stone.

Sonny hammers the lengths of rebar into the sand and wraps the wire around the iron. Around and around. Sonny can't remember when he's enjoyed himself so much.

He presses the bones and the shells and the stones together so that there is no space in between. The wire glows in the sunlight, the bones and the shells burn bright. The darker stones anchor the pattern with grace and solemnity.

Turtle bone, clamshell, clamshell, clamshell.

Turtle bone, clamshell, clamshell, stone.

Up and up it goes, until the tower is above Sonny's head, and he has to reach to anchor the last layer. Then, he sets the harrow disc on top and loads the bowl with wood.

Sonny stands back and looks at his creation. Beautiful. The shells and bones sparkle, and the copper wire flashes in the evening light. The tower leans a little to the right, but if Sonny leans a little to the left, the tower looks straight.

Now all Sonny has to do is light the beacon and wait.

Just not yet. Sonny wants to wait for the right moment. He doesn't want to waste fuel.

Waste not, Sonny tells himself, want not.

Sonny takes out his handkerchief and polishes the copper wire, and when he does, he notices something moving down a sand dune behind the tower. A large something. At first, Sonny doesn't believe his eyes. He rubs them. He rubs them again.

Rub, rub, rub.

Wham-wham!

A turtle!

Wham-wham, hammer-hammer!

It's a sea turtle, just like the turtles who used to arrive on Sonny's beach during tourist season. A ragged turtle with worn flippers and a wide indentation in its shell, as though it has been carrying a heavy weight for a long time. At first, it appears that this turtle has cut its head, but when Sonny looks more closely, he can see that it's just a colourful marking.

Big Red. That's what Sonny will call this turtle. Big Red.

Sonny tears some seagrass out of the sand and holds it out, in case Big Red is hungry.

Come on, Big Red. Come on, Big Red.

Sonny can see that Big Red wants to get to the ocean, so he quickly gets behind the turtle and sights the water over her shell. There are several large sticks in Big Red's way and Sonny removes them. There is a log in her path, and Sonny piles sand on both sides so Big Red can slide over.

Come on, Big Red, Sonny yells. Come on, Big Red.

The ocean is still two hundred yards away, and Big Red

begins to tire. She stops for a moment and raises her head to find the smell of the sea. And then, slowly, she continues on.

Sonny dances around her. He wants to pick her up and carry her to the surf line, but Big Red is much too large for that. And Sonny knows that she has to make the journey on her own. Sonny remembers telling the tourists to leave the turtles alone.

Don't touch, he used to tell the tourists who came to the beach to watch the turtles. Don't touch.

So Sonny doesn't. But there's nothing wrong with encouragement. There's nothing wrong with singing. There's nothing wrong with dancing. There's nothing wrong with telling jokes. These are entertainments that might encourage Big Red and help her along her way.

Two bears go into a bar.

A duck walks into a pharmacy.

Sonny gets down on his belly and uses his elbows to pull himself through the sand. Come on, Sonny whispers to Big Red. Let's have a race. You and me. A race to the sea. Bet you can't beat me. Bet you can't get there before me.

Go, Big Red!

Up and down the sand dunes they go. Sonny and Big Red. Out onto the flats to where the sand turns wet.

Come on, Big Red. Sonny is winning.

As soon as the turtle feels the wet beneath her shell, she revives and pulls herself along with powerful strokes of her flippers. Sonny's elbows are beginning to hurt. He lifts one up and he can see that it's beginning to bleed. When the race is over, he'll have to get Band-Aids for his injuries.

But that's okay. Dad has mentioned sacrifice more than once, and Sonny isn't going to stop because of a little blood.

And then the surf breaks over Big Red's shell, and the surf breaks over Sonny's back, and the race is over.

Big Red is the winner!

Sonny leaps out of the surf and dances in the rapid water.

Big Red wins!

Sonny's whole body is vibrating. His elbows sting. There is sand in his shirt and his pants. And Sonny is happy. Big Red has made it back to the ocean. Big Red has come home.

Sonny stands on the beach and watches the turtle disappear into the waves. Then he walks back up the beach to the tower, singing as he goes.

And in the weakening light at the edge of the world, Sonny lights the beacon fire.

79

EVERYONE SAT IN A LOOSE CIRCLE AND PASSED THE FOOD around. Mara handed Gabriel a deep bowl. Inside were round balls.

"This is Mei-ling," Mara said. "She's the one you pulled out of the water."

"I pulled them all out of the water."

"She says she was the first."

Gabriel picked up one of the balls. He sniffed it but couldn't place the flavour. Mara nudged him.

"Just eat it."

"What is it?"

Mara looked at Mei-ling. "*Yu wang?*"

Mei-ling nodded.

"Fish balls," said Mara. "They're very good. And they're fresh. The Chins have found a beach north of here that has fish."

"What's that?"

"*Tsa bi hoon*," said Mei-ling. "You would call it . . . spaghetti?"

"Vermicelli."

"Yes, vermicelli. With pig."

Gabriel brought the noodles to his mouth. "This is pork?"

"Very sorry," said Mei-ling. "No pork. We use fish."

432

Gabriel took a mouthful. "It's good."

"Good?" boomed Crisp. "This is a feast for any man, and more than most could hope for. Ye must try the *jiao zi*. Is that pronounced correctly?"

"Yes," said Mei-ling. "Very perfect."

"Dumplings," said Crisp. "Melt in your mouth."

"Two families," said Mara. "The Chins and the Huangs. That's Mei-ling's father, Chi-ming, and her cousins, Jia-hao, Guan-ting, and Jun-jie. They're Taiwanese."

Mara went around the room, introducing everyone.

"Mei-ling speaks good English. Her cousins do okay. The rest of the families not so much."

"I spies a good story on the horizon," said Crisp. "But perhaps we should postpone the telling, so as not to confuse the tale with the tucker."

GABRIEL searched each face and tried to remember the order of the rescue, but it was hopeless. He had shared a bleak rock in a savage sea with these people. He knew them no better than he had known his own sister, and yet here he was, having dinner with the lot as though they were family.

"We work on ship," Mei-ling began. "Chin family, Huang family. But the ship is old. Nothing works well. My father fix this, and my cousins fix that, and then everything is good."

"But a fox can only chase so many rabbits," said Crisp.

Mei-ling stopped. "Fox?"

"What he means," said Mara, "is that more things broke than you could fix."

433

"Yes," said Mei-ling. "We try very hard, but things break, and then more things break. Soon we can no longer fix the things that are broken."

One of the younger men said something to Mei-ling in Taiwanese.

"Jun-jie asks that I tell you about the storm."

"A storm?" growled Crisp. "Splendid."

"Don't mind Mr. Crisp," said Mara. "He gets excited easily."

"Indeed, I do," said Crisp, flinging his voice about the room, "for I'm a pirate's dog with a bone, when it come to a good story."

Mei-ling's father began moving his hand up and down. The other men nodded their agreement.

"My father reminds me of the size of the waves," said Mei-ling, "for they were . . . formidable. Is that correct? Formidable?"

"Formidable," roared Crisp. "Yes, yes, it's a fine word. Yet all manner of mercy and mayhem may come out of a storm."

Mei-ling paused a moment to let Crisp's words fly by. Then she continued.

"The storm was very bad. Water was everywhere. And when it passed, the ship was broken. Neither my father nor my cousins could fix it. At first we thought someone would come, but no one did."

Gabriel's butt still stung from having tried to sit on the orange chair. "You had no means of communication. No radio?"

"No," said Mei-ling. "No radio. No steering for the ship. There was computer for navigation, but it would not work properly."

"They were trapped on board," said Mara. "Can you imagine?"

"Yes," said Mei-ling. "Trapped."

434

Mei-ling's father reached out and patted the floor.

"Then we see land and think we are safe." Mei-ling's eyes filled with tears. "But the land disappears."

"A woeful tale, indeed," said Crisp, his voice wavering. "For to see salvation and have salvation denied is a great sorrow."

"But it comes a second time. The land. Closer now, and my father says we must try to reach the shore."

"A wise man," said Crisp. "A most wise man."

"We get into a small boat. Enough room for all of us, but when we are near the shore . . . "

Crisp ran a hand across his head. "The waves put the boat upon the rocks."

"Yes," said Mei-ling. "We are in the water, and we are dying, until the singing man pulls us out of the sea. Until the singing man saves us."

Mara smiled and touched Gabriel's hand. "His name is Gabriel," she said. "Gab-ri-el."

Mei-ling quickly translated and the faces of her family and relations brightened.

"Gab-ri-el," they all said in bits and pieces.

Mara turned to Gabriel. "The singing man," she said. "I like that."

MEI-LING told about coming ashore, how the families lived in the woods and out of sight, fearful that they might be arrested, how they had found the reserve and the empty homes.

"We are sorry," Mei-ling said, "but we are cold and hungry."

"Yet welcome, nonetheless," said Crisp.

Mei-ling hung her head. "In the town. My cousins took things that did not belong to us."

"Nothing that wouldn't have been shared had the need been known." Crisp's beard danced on his face. "I'll settle all matters with the folks and leaves ye with free passes to the hot springs, where ye can throw off the trials of your old life and warm yourselves in the new."

"That is most kind."

"Not at all," said Crisp, "for good company's a rare thing and everyone else in this kingdom has heard my stories at least once. Tell me, do ye like stories?"

"Oh, yes," said Mei-ling, "we like stories very much."

"Excellent," said Crisp.

"And we have dessert," said Mei-ling. "Jun-jie has made *feng li su*."

"Dessert!" Crisp gave his belly a great whack and threw an arm around Gabriel. "What say ye?" he bellowed. "Can we find the room?"

"I should be getting back," said Gabriel.

Crisp leaned against Gabriel and whispered in his ear. "Look around," he said. "This is the back to which ye needs be getting. Look around. Ye are already here."

80

DORIAN SAT AT HIS DESK, FIGHTING THE NAUSEA THAT HAD decided to make a return engagement. Winter and the woman from Public Relations sat on the sofa.

"Who wants to go first?"

"It might actually work to our benefit," said Lustig.

"Having Kali Creek and GreenSweep splashed all over the national news might work to our benefit?" Dorian paused to let the concept hang in the room. "That's PR's spin on this?"

"Not spin," said Lustig. "Strategy."

"I'm waiting."

"We're expecting the situation in Alberta to worsen in the next few days. There have been several communities along the Athabasca adversely affected by the spill."

"And by 'adversely affected,' you mean . . . "

"A higher than expected mortality rate."

"People are dying."

"Fortunately," said Lustig, "most of these are Native communities where the mortality rate is already higher than the norm."

"Higher than the mortality rate in . . . white communities."

"Making it difficult to determine whether the additional deaths are the result of the spill or lifestyle."

"We're talking about poverty."

"Along with alcoholism, drug use, and irresponsible behaviour."

The nausea was threatening to turn into diarrhea. Dorian could feel his gut twisting around itself.

"Kali Creek and the threat of a rogue scientist might give us some breathing room," said Lustig. "Properly managed, it could take the edge off the Athabasca."

"Dr. Quinn is hardly a 'rogue scientist.' I'm not sure we want to suggest that he's deranged."

Lustig's smile was just short of patronizing. "He writes on walls."

"That makes him eccentric." Dorian drew in a deep breath and tried to force the pain out of his abdomen. "What I want to know is how Manisha Khan knew about Kali Creek, how she knew about GreenSweep. Just how did that happen?"

"I'm afraid that at this point we'd only be guessing."

Dorian could have gone straight from the studio to the condo and just called it a night. There was nothing he could do about the interview, and a good night's sleep might have been the better course of action. Instead, he had called Winter and Lustig, summoned them to his office after hours. It was a small pleasure, something that the CEO of Domidion could do.

And he had.

"Guess away."

Lustig took the lead. "According to Security, the documents found at Dr. Quinn's house were all copies. It's possible that Dr. Quinn sent the originals to *En Garde*."

"To what purpose?"

"To embarrass the company," said Lustig. "Or we may have an internal leak."

"Zebras? At Domidion?"

"A possibility."

"So, we don't know anything." Dorian was on his feet and moving around the room. "We have no idea who leaked the GreenSweep file. We don't know where our genius scientist has gone. We don't even know if there are any good movies on television tonight."

Lustig frowned. "Pardon?"

"Something I haven't seen more than once." Dorian struck the desk with his hands. In the silence of the office, it sounded like a shot. "All right. Let's release the hounds."

"Yes, sir," said Winter. "Release the hounds."

"Who was responsible for spraying GreenSweep at Kali Creek?"

Winter tapped at the tablet. "Independent contractor out of Prince George."

"What about the company responsible for the construction of the holding ponds at our tar-sands facility?"

"Somosi Construction."

"One of our subsidiaries?"

"Yes."

Dorian turned to Lustig. "Use PR's usual sources to leak Domidion's intention to sue the former for negligence and the latter for breach of contract, and I want you to start a serious conversation on the possibility of sabotage."

"We can do that."

Dorian turned to Winter. "Go back ten years. Don't we have other misadventures besides Kali Creek and the Athabasca?"

"We do," said Winter.

"Let's lump everything together. All our sins. Accidents, disasters, gross negligence, major miscalculations. Work up some plausible conspiracies. Toss out the t-word if you have the chance. Park the mess on the doorstep of a couple of the more annoying environmental groups, and be sure to mention the Zebras as many times as possible."

"That could work," said Lustig.

Dorian enjoyed the warmth that spread across his face. "It doesn't have to work," he said. "'If you can't convince them, confuse them.'"

"Harry Truman," said Winter.

"Yes." Lustig's face was suddenly animated. "The conspiracy theorists will run with it all on their own, and we can work with the talk shows to organize discussion forums on energy extraction and domestic terrorism."

"That's the spirit," said Dorian. "Yellow, red, blue, green, purple, orange. You mix them all together and what do you get?"

Dorian waited to see which of the women wanted to step forward.

"Grey," he said. "You get grey."

Lustig was on her feet. "We better get mixing."

WINTER waited until Lustig had reached the elevators. "Your wife has phoned several times. She sounds upset."

"Good."

"And Dr. Toshi's office rang. They sound annoyed."

"Excellent."

"And I looked into that other matter."

Dorian wondered if Winter had a boyfriend or a lover. Not that it was any of his business. She could well be lesbian. Or celibate.

"Dr. Quinn's notes were accurate. Before GreenSweep was cancelled, Domidion had produced 10,000 litres of concentrate."

Not that Dorian was attracted to Winter, though he could see how she might be attracted to him.

"The concentrate couldn't be incinerated. Too toxic. Landfills, impermeable clay caps, and injection wells were also out of the question."

Perhaps after he and Olivia had taken care of their business, Dorian would ask Winter out to dinner. A business dinner, where the two of them could relax and talk about the corporation's recent expansion into bottled water.

"So it was put into drums and shipped to our storage facility in Tadoussac."

"Quebec?"

"Yes."

"At least we know where it is."

Olivia had been fish and Chardonnay. Dorian guessed that Winter would be meat and Merlot. Not that you could tell such a thing just by looking at someone.

"In fact," said Winter, "we don't. Shortly after the drums arrived in Tadoussac, they were loaded onto one of our barges for disposal at sea."

"What?"

"There appears to have been a mix-up."

"GreenSweep is on a barge?"

Winter always managed problems with a quiet competence. It was this ability, Dorian conceded, that made her good at her job. And attractive as well.

"The *Anguis*?"

"Yes, sir," said Winter. "All of our stock of GreenSweep is on board the *Anguis*."

Capable assistants were rare, Dorian reminded himself, while lovers and wives were easy enough to find. Always best to maintain the line between the two.

"Well," he said, "then there's not much to be done."

"No, sir," said Winter. "There's not."

Still, Dorian would have liked to have been able to ask Winter if she found power intoxicating, if she was aroused by authority. The question would have been completely inappropriate, of course, and easily misconstrued.

He was simply curious.

81

TODY IS A VERY GOOD DAY. IT IS SUCH A GOOD DAY THAT
Sonny doesn't even think to check for salvage as he walks along
the beach.

Big Red has returned.

Halfway up the slope to the motel and the neon star, Sonny
looks back at the water. He can't see the tower anymore, but he
can see the glow of the beacon fire burning bright.

Sonny. Keeper of the flame.

Sonny. Turtle master.

The sand and the dirt roll under his feet, but he leans into
the hill and climbs all the way to the top without stopping.
Tonight is going to be a special night. Perhaps he and Dad will
go for a swim. They haven't done this for a long while. Not since
the pool heater stopped working. Or maybe the two of them will
sit on lounge chairs under the stars.

Together.

And Sonny will tell Dad what he's done. He will tell him
about the tower and the turtle and all the exciting things that
have happened in the last little while, things that Dad may have
missed.

Wham-wham.

They could even buy a frozen pizza from the Co-op. Pepperoni with extra cheese. They could sit on the patio by the pool and eat pizza together.

Can you see the light on the beach, Sonny will ask Dad. Your Sonny built that. All by himself. See how it lights up the dark.

Sonny hurries past the EverFresh vending machine and the Lava Java machine, and stands in front of Dad's door.

Dad.

Sonny knocks softly on the door.

Dad.

Sonny knocks on the door again, his knuckles snapping against the wood.

It's your Sonny.

But there is no answer. Perhaps Dad is sleeping. Or maybe Dad's gone to town to pick up the pizza.

Dad.

Sonny slumps down next to the door and presses his face against the frame. All the light is gone from the sky now, and just as Sonny settles in to the darkness, the electric eye turns on the courtyard lights, and the patio is bathed in a soft yellow blush. Sonny curls up in the doorway and begins to sing quietly to himself.

Turtle bone, clamshell, clamshell, clamshell.

Turtle bone, clamshell, clamshell, stone.

And little by little, he sings himself to sleep.

82

GABRIEL STOOD ON THE PORCH AND IMAGINED THAT HE could feel the world swell as it prepared to welcome the spring tide.

Inside, Crisp and Mara and the two families swapped stories. Crisp was telling everyone how, as a young man, he had worked his way to Australia on a tramp steamer, how he had been chased by a pig in the outback, how an emu had tried to kick down an outhouse while he was in it.

The spring tide.

It would arrive tomorrow, well before dawn, and Gabriel would follow it out to the Apostles. From the saddle high on the rocks, he'd watch the sea retreat, would watch it pause to take a breath before it turned and rushed back to the beach, drowning everything in its path. Tomorrow he would watch the sun break out of the mountains for one last time. Tomorrow the water would do the rest.

GABRIEL heard the door open behind him.

"Mr. Crisp suggested that I come out here and keep you company." Mara stuffed her hands inside the sleeves of her sweater. "He said you were thinking of taking advantage of the spring tide."

"Why do women do that?"

"Do what?"

"Put their hands in their sleeves. My mother and sister used to do the same thing."

"What do men do?"

"We put our hands in our pockets."

"Then there's your answer."

SCIENCE was supposed to have been the answer. World hunger. Disease. Energy. Security. Commerce. Biology would save the world. Geology would fuel the future. Physics would make sense of the universe. At one time, science had been Gabriel's answer to everything.

Love. Friendship. Family.

He had loved the quiet calm of numbers and symbols, had been fascinated with the way in which molecules arranged themselves in orderly patterns, had been driven to see what was behind each of nature's doors. Who wouldn't be? Who could resist such questions? Who would want to?

How had he come to such a fantasy, that there was a benign purity in scientific inquiry? He had mistaken the enterprise completely, had seen only the questions and had ignored the obvious answers.

What was the proper goal of research?

Profit.

What was the proper use of knowledge?

Power.

He could see his errors now, could see all his illusions in stark relief. Too late, of course. Very much too late.

"NICHOLAS said you walked the canyon."

"Needed the exercise."

"No one walks the canyon for exercise."

Inside, Mei-ling was telling a story about an uncle who had gone to California and got a job driving ambulances up and down the hills of San Francisco.

"Tell me a story."

"What?"

"A story," said Mara. "Tell me why you came home."

"This isn't home."

"Then why come? Why come to this place?"

"You wouldn't understand."

"Sure I will. You don't want to tell me, because you're afraid that I *will* understand." Mara drove her hands deeper into her sleeves. "Besides, if you're going to kill yourself, my knowing isn't going to matter."

"I'm the reason for all of this." Gabriel spread his arms, as though he were trying to embrace the world.

Mara leaned against the porch post. "Rather ambitious, don't you think?"

"What?"

"Responsible for all of creation? Yes, I can see how such a burden would drive a body to Samaritan Bay."

Gabriel lowered his arms and let them hang dead at his sides.

"I'm going home." Mara stepped off the porch. "You want to walk with me?"

"Sure."

"Try to make it interesting."

"What?"

"The truth." Mara fashioned a smile. "If you're not going to tell me the truth, at least try to make the story interesting."

83

IT WAS WELL AFTER TWO IN THE MORNING BEFORE DORIAN
took the elevator to the garage and eased himself into the back
seat of the limo. He wasn't particularly tired, was wide awake in
fact. And hungry.

Tension would do that. So would excitement. The leak of
the Kali Creek file should have enraged him, but strangely
enough he felt calm and in control. The warrior was back. Turn
a setback into an advantage. That was the way of the warrior.
The media liked blood. Fine. He'd give them blood enough to
choke on.

Athabasca. Kali Creek. The other large and small misfor-
tunes that Domidion had been a party to over the years. Taken
as a whole, they could be seen as the environmental wreckage
left behind by a callous corporation that valued expediency over
morality, profits over ethics.

Or they could be understood as a concerted assault by
shadow extremists on one of the world's most successful and
innovative conglomerates.

Corporate malfeasance or international conspiracy. The
trick was to control how the matter was read.

Dorian made a mental note to caution PR against using the term "terrorist." Now that he thought about it, television and politicians had already sucked all of the power out of the word.

An environmental collective.

Now there was a good catchphrase. Attacked by an environmental collective. No need to mention Marx, Lenin, or Mao. Some eager journalist would do that job for him.

"Am I taking you home, sir?"

Dorian hadn't been paying attention. "Kip, isn't it?"

"Yes, sir."

"You've driven me before."

"I have."

"I don't suppose there are any decent restaurants open."

"Just fast food."

Dorian tried to picture himself at the drive-through of a McDonald's or a Tim Hortons or some other fat-on-a-bun establishment. He was hungry, but he wasn't *that* hungry.

"There is a place you might wish to consider."

Dorian leaned forward.

"A hotel. Five stars. On Cumberland near Avenue Road."

"The Hermes?"

"Yes," said Kip. "That is the one. I am told the room service is excellent and available twenty-four hours for hotel guests. But you must take a room for the evening."

"I had considered buying a condo in that building."

"Very expensive," said Kip. "Very exclusive."

Dorian sat back and straightened his tie. "You're an exceptional driver, Kip."

"Are we to go to this hotel?"

Dorian put his face against the window and watched the city lights flash by. "Drive by Toronto General."

"The hospital?"

"Yes."

Kip shook his head and glanced in the rear-view mirror. "That is not where you wish to go. My auntie went there, and she did not come out."

"I have a friend there."

"Ah," said Kip. "I sincerely hope your friend is in good health."

"No," said Dorian. "It appears that he might be dying."

"This friend," said Kip, "is he wealthy?"

Dorian sat up straight. "What difference does that make?"

Kip turned onto University and came to a stop behind a panel van. Even at this time of the morning in the city, there was traffic.

"Dying wealthy is harder than dying poor."

"Really."

"Oh, yes. Assuredly," said Kip. "The wealthy may buy anything they wish. Anything at all. But they may not buy their way out of dying. This is most frustrating, is it not? To have all that money and power, and no control over one's mortality."

"Everyone dies."

"Yes, yes," said Kip, "but having lived in such luxury and security for so long, the wealthy must feel cheated by the equality of death."

The traffic lightened as the car crossed Richmond.

"Is this friend a good friend?"

"Yes," said Dorian, "a very good friend."

451

"Then you should not tell him he's dying. If at all possible, keep this truth from him. He will be happier if he doesn't know."

"I'm not sure that's a good idea."

"It is an excellent idea," said Kip. "For if your friend does not know that he is dying, then he will continue to enjoy what he can purchase with his money and not waste his time cursing what he cannot."

TORONTO General looked like any number of generic office towers in the downtown core. Dorian had remembered something a bit more grand, something more architecturally distinct, but it was a hospital after all, not a world-class hotel.

"You should bring your friend some chocolate."

"Chocolate?"

"Yes," said Kip. "My mother says that people who are dying enjoy chocolate."

Dorian stepped out of the car. The building looked deserted. The lights were on, but he couldn't see anyone inside. He wondered if people got sick this early in the morning or if heart attacks and strokes waited until the sun was up.

The woman at the reception desk was reading a book.

Dorian closed his eyes for a moment and concentrated on the idea of authority. "Good evening."

The woman closed the book reluctantly.

"Admissions?"

The woman kept a finger stuck between the pages. "They're closed."

"Oh dear." Dorian flexed his jaw muscles. "That's awkward."

"Can I help you?"

"Toshi," said Dorian, filling his voice with generosity and privilege. "Dr. Benjamin Toshi. I need to check on one of my patients."

"Toshi." The woman checked her computer screen. "Internal medicine?"

"That's right," said Dorian. "The patient's name is Dorian Asher. He's booked for a procedure tomorrow morning. I wanted to know if he has been admitted."

The woman hit several keys. "No," she said. "He hasn't been admitted."

Dorian ran a hand through his hair for effect. "How do patients expect us to help them?"

The woman shrugged. "You'll have to reschedule."

"I think Mr. Asher is concerned about the procedure."

"Don't blame him." The woman glanced at her monitor. "Angiograms aren't exactly a giggle."

DORIAN startled Kip when he opened the back door.

"That was a very quick visit," said Kip. "Were you not able to see your friend?"

"He died," said Dorian. "Quite suddenly."

"Sometimes this is a blessing," said Kip. "Though most distressing for the living."

"Yes." Dorian fastened his seat belt and sank back into the assurance of leather. "Most distressing."

"Am I to take you home?"

"No," said Dorian. "Take me to the Hermes."

84

THE NIGHT WAS A PLEASANT SURPRISE. THE SKIES WERE clear. The stars sparkled overhead. A full moon lighted the tops of the trees and brightened the trail.

An evening to savour.

But as Gabriel trudged down the hill, he couldn't find much to enjoy.

"I'm a scientist. I developed a defoliant called GreenSweep. GreenSweep caused The Ruin. I'm the reason your mother died, the reason your grandmother died, the reason my sister and her son died, the reason the reserve is a graveyard.

"I am Death, the destroyer of worlds."

Well, he hadn't said that. There had been no need to say that. By the time they got to her grandmother's house, Mara was in no mood for confessions or forgiveness.

"GreenSweep? Is that your idea of a joke?"

"I didn't name it."

"No, you just invented it."

"You don't really invent bacteria. You sort of . . . rearrange the DNA."

"And they paid you for this."

"Yes."

"To kill people?"

"It wasn't supposed to kill anyone."

"Look around."

"It wasn't used properly."

But by then, Mara had lost any sense of generosity, and he couldn't think of any good way to explain his role in the destruction. Not that there was anything to explain. He was responsible.

He would always be responsible.

So the story had ended, almost before it had begun. Mara had mounted the steps and disappeared into the house. Then she had reappeared, and Gabriel had, for a moment, hoped that she wanted to continue the conversation, hoped that she might have found a reason to forgive him.

Okay. Not forgive him. That would have been too much to expect. To understand. Maybe if he could take her through the intricacies of the story, she might understand. Maybe the telling would allow *him* to understand.

Instead, she had handed him the drum and his jacket.

"These are yours," she said.

"Actually," said Gabriel, hoping to slow the moment, "they were my father's."

"Low tide is at five," she said. "Don't be late."

And she walked back into the house and shut the door.

GABRIEL stood outside the house for a moment and considered his options. He could go back to the trailer and put his things in order. Bag the garbage, pack his clothes, tidy the place up, so Crisp wouldn't be stuck with a mess. But he had done most of that already.

"You might as well stay," he told the dog, as he headed down the trail. "She's not angry with you."

But Soldier dashed off, bugling as he went. At least the dog seemed happy, though Gabriel had no idea what gave dogs pleasure. Maybe they just liked being alive. If they did, they could teach humans a thing or two.

And then Soldier was back, weaving himself around Gabriel's legs.

"At least someone is having a good time."

Gabriel didn't see it until the trail broke out of the trees. A light. On the beach. A light where there should be no light. He stroked the dog's head and drew him close.

"Curious."

Soldier rubbed his face on Gabriel's leg.

"What do you think it is?"

Soldier took several steps forward and waited.

"All right," said Gabriel. "Let's find out."

The trail wound its way back into the forest, and Gabriel was only able to locate the glow in fits and starts. But as he cleared the trees for the last time and stepped onto the beach, he could see the light clearly.

"Look at that."

It was a tower. Someone had built a tower on the beach. Shell and bones and stones. All held together with copper wire and rebar.

So this is what Crisp had been talking about.

Sonny.

All in all, the boy had done a good job. As Gabriel walked around the tower, he was impressed with the artistry and the workmanship. He wouldn't have thought that Sonny had such a thing in him.

Soldier flopped down in the sand and waited.

"You know what's going on?"

Soldier closed his eyes.

"Did you help him?"

In the distance, the motel sign on the bluff blinked on and off, and Gabriel found himself wishing that the stupid star would stop working altogether.

Soldier's head snapped up. He scrambled to his feet, circled around the tower, and began a low whimper.

"What is it?"

As Gabriel reached out to stroke the dog, to calm him, Soldier exploded out of the sand.

"Soldier!"

But the dog kept running, his body flat to the ground, his ears laid against his head, as he raced along the shore and vanished into the night.

"Soldier!"

The wind picked up, and the flames crackled angrily. It would be dawn soon. Gabriel sat in the sand next to the tower and waited for the tide to complete its retreat. The fire didn't offer much warmth, but the light it gave off was unexpectedly comforting.

85

CRISP EASED HIMSELF INTO THE POOL AND HELD HIS BREATH. Nothing like heat for tired muscles, he reminded himself, but, blistering bunnies, the hot did rip your breath away.

He had enjoyed himself. The food. The company. He and the two families swapping stories and neither side crying hold.

Glorious.

He had noticed Gabriel slip out and then Mara after him. Neither had been in sight when he climbed into his truck, and he imagined that they had gone off to sort the misdemeanours from the felonies.

Crisp was curious just how Gabriel was going to explain himself, curious as to how Mara would react. She was a smart girl. She'd see the complications, resist the easy reactions and the simple answers.

Or she wouldn't.

Still, the man had a great deal to justify, for recklessness and pride were difficult treasons to defend.

Crisp waded to the edge of the pool and hoisted himself out of the water with just his arms. He stood naked, glistening in the starlight, his head turned to the side to catch any sounds that were blown his way. He could hear the ocean, could hear the tidal cycle organizing itself for the morning ahead, and, beneath that, the faint crackling sound, as though eggshells were being crushed underfoot.

Strange.

The night was clear. Crisp climbed to the top of the rock. From here, he could see all the way to the beach, and, in that moment, he found the fire flickering in the dark, a guttering candle set at land's end.

"So, the boy's done it. The beacon lit." Crisp slowly stretched out his arms, arched his back, and cried out to the stars. "Is not my word like fire?"

And now on the freshening wind, he could taste the smoke. It had been a long time since he had savoured such a smell or taken pleasure in such a sight.

A blazing tower. At last. A blazing tower.

But the evening was not his to enjoy. Crisp got dressed quickly. There was much to do. Cheese, meat, fish, fruits, vegetables, bread. Beverages for everyone. And something sweet for the coming celebration.

He was almost to his trailer when he heard it. A distant screech that ran across the waves like a knife on steel. At first, he thought it might be the scrape of a raven come back to the bay after all this time, but the sound was too hard, too sharp for a bird.

Crisp waited for it to come a second time, but all he found in the darkness was the sound of his own breathing.

86

THERE ARE THREE REASONS WHY SONNY DOES NOT SLEEP through the night.

One. On account of the sharp scraping noise that sounds like the time a long-haul trucker rubbed his trailer against the concrete abutment in the motel parking lot.

Two. On account of the chilly night air that forces Sonny to huddle against the door to Dad's room for warmth.

Three. On account of the snoring.

Sonny is not really sure about the scraping noise. When he wakes up the first time, the sound is only a memory. Still he did hear something. The cold is more of a problem, but then he is warm and cozy as though someone has covered him with a quilt.

It is the snoring that is the problem.

Be quiet, Sonny tells the quilt. Sonny is trying to sleep.

But the quilt continues to wheeze and snuffle and snort, and finally Sonny rolls over to discover that he is sleeping next to the dog.

The dog from the beach.

Sonny isn't sure if sleeping with a dog is a good idea, but Sonny likes the warmth, so he tries putting his hands over his ears. He tries humming the turtle-bone song in his head. He tries patting the dog gently to calm him down, in case the snoring is the result of bad dreams.

Nice doggy. Good doggy. Quiet doggy.

Sonny has almost fallen asleep again, when the dog wakes with a great snort and scrambles to his feet.

Good morning, doggy.

And then Sonny feels the dog's soft, warm tongue on his face. He has watched television shows about animal babies and animal mothers, where there is a great deal of licking, and Sonny wonders if the dog thinks he is a puppy.

That would be okay. Sonny, the puppy. Someone's baby.

Nice doggy.

And then the dog stops licking and starts growling. At first Sonny thinks that the dog is angry. Maybe he wanted to sleep longer, but now that Sonny is sitting up, he can see that the dog is not growling at him. The dog is growling at the door.

The door to Dad's room.

Not so loud, doggy, Sonny tells the dog. You'll wake Dad.

But the dog doesn't listen. He growls louder and then begins to bark and scratch at the door.

Quiet, doggy, says Sonny. Quiet.

Suddenly, the dog charges the door and hits it with his shoulder, and Sonny wonders if the dog knows something he doesn't. Perhaps Dad is sick in bed and can't get to the door. Perhaps Dad has fallen in the bath, because he doesn't have the special tub that Sonny has seen on television.

Perhaps Dad is hurt.

Sonny knocks on the door.

Dad!

He knocks harder.

Dad, Dad, Dad!

The dog keeps jumping against the door, and now Sonny jumps with him.

Wham! They hit the door together.

Wham! They hit it again.

Hammer-hammer!

They crash into the door as hard as they can, and this time the frame splits and the door flies open.

Dad!

Sonny and the dog fall into the room.

Dad!

When Sonny gets to his feet, he is covered in cobwebs and dust. So is the dog. Both of them are covered in cobwebs and dust.

Dad.

Sonny can see that Dad is no longer here, that Dad has not been here in a very long time. Sonny sits on the bed, and a cloud of dust floats off the covers and hangs in the air. No wonder Sonny has been so lonely. No wonder Sonny has been so hungry.

Cobwebs and dust.

The dog comes over and licks Sonny's hands. He lays his head on Sonny's lap and sings gently. Then he takes Sonny's shirt sleeve in his mouth and pulls on it.

No, doggy. Sonny does not want to play.

The dog pulls harder.

No, doggy. Sonny is sad.

But the dog does not stop, and it occurs to Sonny that the dog might be trying to tell him something. The dogs on television do this all the time. Drag people out of the woods. Drag people to anxious relatives. Drag people to safety.

Drag people home.

This dog wants to drag Sonny out of Dad's room.

Do you want to show Sonny something, doggy? Is that what you want to do?

The dog yanks and tugs on Sonny's sleeve and pulls him out the door.

All right, doggy, Sonny tells the dog. Sonny will follow you. Maybe we can play together. Maybe we can find some food.

The dog releases Sonny's sleeve and lopes on ahead. Sonny looks back at the open doorway for a moment, and then he follows his friend down the hill to the beach.

87

MARA LAY IN HER BED WITH HER EYES CLOSED. SHE WAS NOT asleep, had not been asleep, was probably not going to get any sleep. She should have been happy and at peace. The stove, the refrigerator, the kitchen table, her grandmother's cast iron stove. All returned. Mr. Crisp was an enigma, to be sure. What else had the man put into storage? What else had the man rescued?

But Mara wasn't happy. The fury had been overwhelming, and it had not subsided. So that was why this Gabriel was trying to kill himself. He wasn't unstable. He wasn't depressed.

He was guilty.

GreenSweep? That's what he had called it. As though it were a handy household cleaning product. Who does that? Who makes such a lethal concoction simply because they can? What had he been thinking? He had destroyed a community, devastated an ecosystem, and what had been his reason?

Science.

That's what he said when she had asked.

Science.

Mara couldn't think of a single intelligent question that had science as the answer.

Shit!

Shit, shit, shit!

So, she was awake, and she wasn't going to get to sleep, and if she wasn't going to sleep she wanted to talk. She wanted to talk with this Gabriel, wanted the hard facts, whole and complete, not just the self-indulgent fragments of remorse and shame.

She wanted the truth.

Well, not the truth. The truth was useless. She knew what had happened. She knew who was responsible. What more was there to know?

And what of this Gabriel? He hadn't wanted forgiveness, wasn't seeking absolution. He had wanted confirmation of his transgressions. He had sought out condemnation.

Well, it wasn't going to be as easy as all that.

Shit.

Mara threw off the covers and stepped onto the cold floor. She stood there for a moment shivering, debating whether this was as good an idea as it had seemed when she had been warm in bed.

Probably not.

But she got dressed anyway. She grabbed the yellow slicker from the closet, laced up her boots, opened the door, and walked out into the night.

88

THE LOBBY OF THE HERMES WAS SMALL BUT ELEGANT. ART DECO ironwork framed the doorways and the windows. The walls were patterned with dancing figures that reminded Dorian of the Etruscan frescoes he and Olivia had seen when they were in Rome. The floor was covered with a series of thick Persians, the air scented with the faint aroma of rose.

Yes, they could accommodate him.

Yes, the twenty-four-hour concierge service could provide him with a meal.

Yes, they understood the stresses that captains of industry had to endure.

"We have a junior suite available. Do we need parking?"

"No," Dorian told the young man. "We don't. My limo will pick me up in the morning."

He had thought that the food would relax him, but after he finished his meal—an Algerian lamb shank with seared baby bok choy and couscous, along with a glass of the house red—he was still awake.

The room was spacious, and he tried walking from one end to the other, weaving his way in and out of the bathroom, with its separate shower and tub and an alcove with a door for the toilet.

He turned on the television in the hopes of finding a movie, but there was nothing on the networks, and he had seen everything on the pay-per-view channels.

In the end, he got dressed and took the elevator down to the lobby.

"Is everything all right?"

"Everything is fine," Dorian told the young man at the desk. "I'm just restless. I think I'll go for a walk."

"It's a lovely night for a walk," said the young man. "Should I call you a cab?"

"That wouldn't be much of a walk now, would it."

"Of course," said the young man. "Do you require a map of the area?"

"I live here," said Dorian, his voice warm and generous. "This is my city."

IT was four-thirty when Dorian stepped out onto the street. He had already decided on a route. East on Cumberland to Bay, south on Bay to Bloor, and west on Bloor to Avenue Road.

Bloor was the quandary.

If he walked on the north side of the street, he'd pass Harry Rosen, Williams-Sonoma, Burberry, and Louis Vuitton. If he crossed with the light to the south side, he'd be able to look in on the merchandise at Cartier, Royal de Versailles, Coach, and Prada.

North or south. In the end, he might have to flip a coin.

The walk did not start well. In the dark, the shops along Cumberland seemed somewhat mingy and reduced, a little too common, a little too tawdry. Travel, eyewear, sushi, hair and skin care, lingerie, gelato, luggage, cosmetics, a parking garage, all anchored by a statue of an overweight businessman in hat and overcoat.

The bronze man had his mouth open, one hand raised in a startled expression as though he had just received word of an unexpected downturn in the market.

Dorian strolled past the small park with its ornamental grasses and wooden walkways. There were tables and chairs set in a pebble clearing, trees growing inside concrete doughnuts, a water wall, and an enormous granite boulder that had been brought south in pieces and reassembled next to the TTC station.

Without the sounds of the business day, without the annoying wrangle of traffic and the garbling jangle of shoppers, the street was a dead thing.

So this was Toronto, when no one was looking.

DORIAN should have checked himself in to the hospital. The problem wasn't going to go away. The nausea and the pain were more frequent now, the flights of fancy more pronounced. He should have sat down with Toshi, should have listened as a stranger told him that his life was coming to an end.

How did you tell someone that? How did you start?

Six months, eight months, a year? Did you get to spin a wheel?

Dead man walking in a dead town. The difference was the city would come back to life, would rise out of the grave each day and open at nine.

Saturdays and Sundays, ten to five.

Of course, there would be options. There were always options. Toshi would have brochures that outlined the available choices. An operation. Chemotherapy. Radiation. Diet and alternative herbal therapies. A new, cutting-edge risk-reward protocol.

A limited engagement at a hospice.

Or nothing.

There was always nothing.

Dorian stayed on the north side of Bloor. Here, the stores were better lit. Harry Rosen had the spring collection on display.

Teal. The colour for this season appeared to be teal.

There was life on Bloor. Cars were moving, their lights glittering off the glass of the store windows. Dorian could feel his body relax as it soaked up the shifting colours and the liquid reflections.

He was enjoying the moment and didn't see the woman huddled in the doorway, wrapped in a sleeping bag.

"You got a cigarette?"

"Sorry," said Dorian. "I don't smoke."

"Twenty dollars."

"Pardon?"

The woman unzipped the sleeping bag and stood up. She was taller than Dorian would have expected and older, with a tangle of black hair and blue eyes that were crisp and startling.

"I'll read your fortune," she said. "Twenty dollars."

Dorian smiled. "You read fortunes?"

The woman stepped in against him. "Did you know that a fortune may be read on a face and a fate found in a query?"

Dorian could feel the heat bristle off her body, could taste her breath on his face. The whole affair was somewhat disconcerting, but oddly enough, Dorian found that he was enjoying himself.

"Twenty dollars."

"All right," he said. "Twenty dollars."

"You get one question."

"One?"

"You're already rich, so you don't need to ask about that. Your wife doesn't love you anymore, but you know that already. Don't waste my time with the stock market."

Dorian took the money clip out of his pocket, removed a twenty-dollar bill, and handed it to the woman.

"Shouldn't I get three questions?"

"There's only one question worth asking."

Dorian felt an unexpected chill snatch at his body.

"Go ahead," said the woman, her voice soft and low. "Ask."

Across the street, Dorian could see Tiffany's rose-speckled stone facade and its alcoved entrance. From a distance, the two windows on either side of the doorway looked like gun ports guarding access to a fortress.

"Why don't you just keep the twenty."

The woman reached out and touched his face. "Ask the question."

"There's nothing I need to know."

The woman was smiling now. Her eyes flashed in the night, and her lips curled away from thick, yellowing teeth.

"Ignorance will cost you another forty."

Dorian looked at the money in his hands.

"Deal," he said.

The woman picked up her sleeping bag and stepped out into the lights of the city. She looked older now, and her hair wasn't black, as Dorian had thought. It was dark red, more the colour of old blood.

"I am well," she said, as she took the twenties, "if you are well, too."

Dorian watched her walk away, the sleeping bag bundled in her arms.

Will I be remembered?

That's what he should have asked her. Dorian considered running after the woman. For sixty dollars, she could surely answer that question. But now he was cold from standing in one spot, depressed by what he already knew.

Will I be remembered?

He continued west, walking past Williams-Sonoma and the rest of the shopfronts, hoping to recapture his good cheer and optimism. At his back, the sky was beginning to lighten, and for a moment, he was tempted to turn around and walk into the rising sun.

Instead, he made his way to the Hermes, where the hotel staff knew who he was and were waiting to welcome him home.

89

IT WAS TIME.

The spring tide had arrived, the highest and lowest water of the season. And all around, for as far as Gabriel could see, there was sand where there had been sea.

Life as a circle.

Not that his life had had any such shape. Lethbridge. Minneapolis. Palo Alto. Toronto. Samaritan Bay. Not a circle. Not a straight line. Something less precise. Something broken.

Gabriel stood and shook the beach off his pants. He would have liked to have said goodbye to someone. To Mara especially, not that that was going to happen. To Crisp, for Gabriel had come to enjoy the man and his passions. Even Sonny would have been welcome company.

And where in the hell had Soldier gone?

THE walk across the sand flat was uneventful, but as Gabriel started the climb up the side of the Apostles, he was surprised by the flashes of colour against the darker rock. And movement. Tiny crabs scuttled about. An orange starfish tucked itself away in a deep crevice. He was still climbing on brittle

472

shells and bones, but now there were living creatures to avoid.

The ocean was coming back to life. In spite of everything, it was coming back to life.

Not that Gabriel could claim any credit.

He found the saddle. The wind was sharp, and he gathered his jacket around him for warmth. He wouldn't take it off this time. Fully clothed or naked, it wouldn't make any difference.

He fished the marker out of his pocket and tried it against the rock, but the surface was too damp and cold to leave any sign. What he needed was a sharp knife or, better yet, a piece of caulk.

Church Rock.

He had almost forgotten about that. He touched the basalt, slowly using his finger to spell out each word. New Mexico. 1979. The Navajo reservation. A large nuclear waste spill had destroyed the Puerco River a few months after the Three Mile Island disaster.

Gabriel picked up his drum and wiped the head against his jacket. He hadn't intended to bring it with him, but Mara had made it clear that she wanted all of him gone. He tested the hide. Soft. But the sound was still good, and he began a steady rhythm, matching the beat to the ocean, pitching the song against the wind as it drove the waves onto the rocks.

He turned to face the shore. In the distance, he could see the burning tower and was cheered by the light. The drum sounded good. He sounded good. He could almost hear his father singing with him.

"A crow hop?"

Gabriel reared back and lost his balance. The drum banged against the rock.

"Damn!"

He whirled around and came face to face with a large yellow sea creature that had clambered over the side of the basalt and was slithering towards him.

"Suicide?" shouted the yellow creature. "Suicide? And you sing a crow hop?"

"Mara?"

Mara's face was obscured by a slicker. It had slid over her head and bunched up in a wedge around her shoulders. More than anything, she looked like a movie-monster crab with a lumpy dorsal fin.

"You can't be here."

"Sure I can." Mara pushed the slicker off her head.

"The tide's coming in. You need to get back to the beach."

Mara looked over her shoulder. The early surges had already found the base of the Apostles. "You don't get to kill yourself."

"What?"

"I have questions."

"Questions?"

"And I want answers."

"We don't have time for this."

"Make time." Mara braced herself against the side of a column. "I'm not going anywhere."

"This is crazy." Gabriel wiped the salt spray out of his eyes. "I killed your mother. I killed your grandmother."

"I know."

"I killed my sister and my nephew." Gabriel's voice was a whisper now. "I killed them all."

"Yes," said Mara. "You did."

"I couldn't save any of them."

"Maybe you can save yourself."

"I don't want to save myself."

Mara moved forward along the rock face until their shoulders were touching. At her back, she could feel the waves slam into the pillars.

"All right," she said. "Then you can save me."

90

THE DOG IS FAST. SONNY IS FAST, TOO. BUT NOT AS FAST AS the dog.

Slow down, doggy.

The dog runs ahead and waits, runs ahead and waits, runs ahead and waits.

Slow down.

By the time he gets to the beach, Sonny is out of breath. But the dog doesn't wait. He runs on ahead, and every so often he runs back to make sure Sonny is still following and has not become discouraged and given up.

Now there is no doubt. The dog is trying to show him something.

Wait for Sonny.

Sonny checks the ocean. The night was brighter when the moon was up, but even in the early-morning darkness, Sonny can see that it is low tide, and Sonny doesn't like low tide.

There is too much land at low tide. The world is strange and frightening at low tide. Low tides are sneaky. It is easy to get lost in a low tide.

Today the tide is very low and very sneaky, and as Sonny follows the shore, he makes sure he keeps both feet on dry sand.

Sonny is no fool.

Low tide, he shouts after the dog. Be careful like Sonny.

Suddenly the dog breaks away from the ocean and the low tide, and runs up into the soft sand and the grass.

Good listening, doggy, Sonny shouts. Good listening.

Suddenly, there is a low flicker in the gloom, and now Sonny knows where the dog is taking him.

The tower.

The dog is taking Sonny to Sonny's tower.

The flame is weak. That's the problem. The dog is trying to warn Sonny that the beacon is about to go out.

Sonny pumps his arms and charges through the sand.

Clear the way. Clear the way.

Sonny quickly lays pieces of driftwood on the harrow disc and watches as the beacon flares, hot and powerful again.

Situation saved by Sonny.

Situation saved by Sonny and doggy.

The pile of wood is smaller, and Sonny knows he will have to find more, but for now, he needs to rest. He'll look for wood later.

And then Sonny smells it.

Sonny stands up and looks around, and when he does this, he sees the blanket spread out on the sand and he sees the wicker basket. He sees the dog lying on the blanket next to the basket.

The doggy is having a picnic.

Sonny knows that smell. Sonny would know that smell anywhere.

Toasted cheese sandwiches!

Good doggy, Sonny tells the dog. Toasted cheese sandwiches are Sonny's favourite.

"Aye," says a voice that makes Sonny jump. "I remember ye have a tooth for a soft melt."

Wham-wham!

Sonny reaches for his hammer.

"Easy lad," says Crisp, "for I mean ye no harm. This be your tower? A fine piece of work it is."

Crisp sits down on the blanket, opens the lid of the basket, and lets the aromas spill out.

"I thought you might be hungry from your exertions."

Sonny looks at the tide. Then he looks at Crisp.

Tide. Crisp.

Crisp. Tide.

"Toasted cheese with Dijon mustard. There's fruit and juice. Scrambled eggs and sausage, and tea in the Thermos, if ye have an inclination."

Sonny looks at the dog.

"Yes," says Crisp, "the dog will vouch for me, for we saved each other upon a time, and if ye have an inclination, I'll tell ye the story while we eat."

Sonny comes to the edge of the blanket. He is very hungry, and the food smells very good.

Is it safe? Sonny asks the dog. Is it safe?

The dog rolls over in the sand and farts.

Good doggy, says Sonny. Good doggy.

"Eat what ye will." Crisp holds out a sandwich. "For there's more things in heaven and earth than can be imagined."

Sonny takes the sandwich. It is still warm and soft, but with a crunchy crust. Just the way he likes it. Sonny gives part of the sandwich to the dog.

478

"His name is Soldier," says Crisp, "though he's not opposed to a new name now and again, and perhaps ye can find something to please the both of ye."

Sonny chews on the sandwich. He can taste the cheese and the mustard, the bread and the butter.

Salvage, Sonny tells the dog. I name you Salvage.

"A fine name," says Crisp, wiping the grease from his beard and licking his fingers. "And when ye have done your fill, there's something I must show ye, something ye will want to see, for it is creation itself and not to be missed."

Sonny sits in the sand at the edge of the blanket and eats his sandwich. Somewhere behind him, he hears the sharp scraping sound he has heard before, and he turns to find it.

"Aye," says Crisp, "I hear it, too. But ye must eat first and gather your strength, for we've a long day ahead of us."

The tide has turned. Sonny surveys the ocean, watches it swell and rise up, marks the fog as it tries to steal its way back across the water. He smells salt on the wind now, tastes it on his tongue.

And in the distance, out on the Apostles, Sonny catches sight of two figures huddled together on the rocks.

91

DORIAN SAT IN THE HOTEL RESTAURANT, ENJOYING A LIGHT breakfast while he watched the street come to life. He had been tempted by the sausage and waffle pairing, but had resisted, had ordered the yogurt and fruit with a whole-grain bagel instead.

As a single man, he would have to watch his figure.

The server had just cleared away the dishes, when Dorian's cellphone began to vibrate.

LAST night had been intriguing. And revealing. The hospital, the tour of Bloor Street in the dark, the woman in the doorway. He had spent the rest of the night and early morning sitting in bed with his clothes on, watching television with the sound off, and coming up with questions he could have asked.

Sixty dollars.

Will I be remembered?

God, but he was glad he hadn't asked *that* question. The woman had frightened him. He didn't like to admit it, but she had. Her red hair. Her blue eyes. Her yellow teeth. He had been thrown off, had lost sight of who he was.

What had she said? Something about being well?

~~~~

THROUGH the window of the restaurant, Dorian watched a Mercedes SL65 AMG drift by. "I am the master of my fate," he said, letting his voice roll across the table. "I am the captain of my soul."

"Sir?"

The server was standing at his shoulder.

"'Invictus.'" Dorian took the napkin off his lap and considered the man. "Tell me, how long have you worked here?"

"At the Hermes?"

"Yes."

"Since it opened," said the man. "Is everything all right?"

"Yes," said Dorian, "everything is fine. But I was curious. If you had one question you could ask, what would it be?"

"About the hotel?"

"No," said Dorian. "About life. Life in general. Your life."

"I'm sorry, sir," said the man. "We're not allowed to ask such questions."

Dorian's cellphone began vibrating again.

HE had called Olivia's suite after he had returned from the walk. He expected he would get her answering machine. And he had. He waited until he heard the beep.

"We don't need no stinking questions." That's the message he had left. "We don't need no stinking questions."

And then he had hung up.

~~~~

481

THE server circled the table. "Will there be anything else?"

"Do you have pie?"

"Pie?"

"Cherry," said Dorian. "Apple, if there is nothing else."

"I'm afraid we have no pie."

"No pie?"

"We have some excellent lemon pound cake with a raspberry compote," said the server. "Shall I bring you a portion?"

"No," said Dorian. "We don't need dessert all the time, do we."

A heavy-set man in a dark suit hurried into the restaurant. He looked remarkably like the bronze statue on Cumberland.

"Mr. Asher?"

Dorian smiled generously and waved the man to the chair across from him. "Mr. Knox, I presume."

"I'm sorry to be late, but it was somewhat short notice."

"Coffee?"

"Please."

Dorian raised a hand, but the server was already on his way.

"Gordon Knox," said the man, and he handed Dorian a card.

"Dorian Asher."

"The head of Domidion."

"Just the CEO," said Dorian, pleased that the man had done his due diligence.

Knox waited until the server had poured the coffee. Then he opened his briefcase and took out a large brochure.

"Are you staying here?"

"Last night."

"It's a very exclusive property."

"Yes," said Dorian. "It's why I called."

Knox cleared his throat. "In addition to the hotel, the Hermes has seventeen residences. There are two currently for sale."

Knox turned the brochure so that Dorian could see the pages. "The Miliken and the Leeson."

"The residences have names?"

"The names can be changed of course," said Knox. "Depending on the owner."

Dorian ran a finger down the page. "Does either of these have eastern and southern exposures?"

"Yes," said Knox quickly. "The Leeson. It has 3,587 square feet, two terraces, and a private elevator, all on two levels."

"Price?"

"Asking 7.5."

"Offer 6.5. Settle at 6.8."

"Wouldn't you like to see it first?"

"No need."

Dorian glanced outside. The limousine was at the curb. Dorian hoped that Kip was at the wheel. He wanted to tell him about the woman and the sixty dollars. The man would enjoy that story.

"Have the papers sent to my office. Tell the courier to ask for Winter Lee."

DORIAN finished his coffee and paid the bill. He was sorry there was no pie, and he would mention this to the management after he moved in. As he walked through the lobby, he could feel the phone buzzing in his pocket like an angry insect.

He could check the screen, but Dorian was sure that it was Olivia. She had come to her senses. She was calling to tell him it was all a misunderstanding, that she didn't want a divorce, that she had just been annoyed with him and his reluctance to consider a property in Orlando.

"I am the master of my fate. I am the captain of my soul."

The doorman saw him coming and moved effortlessly to open the door.

"Have a good day, sir," said the man.

"The Asher," said Dorian out loud, as he stepped through the door and into the first day of his new life.

What will I do with my new beginning?

Now there was a question he could answer.

92

TOASTED CHEESE, TOASTED CHEESE, TOASTED CHEESE. Sonny has never seen so many toasted cheese sandwiches. Every time he finishes one toasted cheese sandwich, Mr. Crisp reaches into the basket and finds another.

"Ye needs consume the veggies as well."

No, says Sonny. Toasted cheese.

"Scurvy's no chuckle."

Toasted cheese.

Crisp watches Sonny eat. "I'm sorry, lad. I didn't know ye had hard-hammered the vending machines, for I'd packed the dispensers with provisions enough."

A gust blows the napkins into the air. Crisp snatches at them, catching two before the rest get away. The tide is running hard, and the soft fog begins to blunt the edges of the world.

"Finish up, lad," says Crisp. "For we mustn't be late."

Sonny leans against the dog. Is it a surprise, doggy? Is it a surprise?

"Bring the dog with ye, if ye wishes, but ye both must be quiet and reverent."

Dad has warned Sonny about the hot springs, and Dad has warned Sonny about Mr. Crisp.

"It's just over there," says Crisp. "And when we gets back, I believe that there's cherry pie and ice cream."

Cherry pie and ice cream! Cherry pie and ice cream!

Wham-wham!

Sonny doesn't remember Dad ever having any prohibitions on cherry pie and ice cream. Sonny thinks hard. If toasted cheese sandwiches are good and if cherry pie and ice cream is good, how can Mr. Crisp be bad? And if Mr. Crisp is good . . .

"Are ye coming, lad?"

Come with Sonny, Sonny tells the dog. Come with Sonny.

Crisp strides through the sand and the grass, and when he gets to where the beach starts to slope up to the bluffs, he stops and drops to his knees.

"There," he says in a low whisper. "She be there."

Sonny and Soldier crawl forward. Crisp reaches out and pushes the grass to one side.

"Do ye see? Did ye ever think ye would see such a thing again?"

At first, Sonny doesn't see anything. Just the grass and the sand.

"There," says Crisp. "Just there."

Sonny crawls closer to Mr. Crisp and is surprised to find that Mr. Crisp smells very much like Dad. Now that he thinks about it, Mr. Crisp has the same deep voice that Dad has. But Mr. Crisp is not Dad.

"A thing of beauty, it is."

Still, Mr. Crisp is here, and Dad is not.

"She comes ashore early this morning."

Sonny raises up on his elbows, and now he can see what Mr. Crisp sees.

It's Big Red!

"Easy lad, for she's laying her eggs."

Big Red, Big Red, Big Red, Big Red! Go, Big Red!

Sonny watches closely, and suddenly he sees an egg roll into the hole. And then another. And another. Now the eggs are pouring out of Big Red, and Sonny tries hard to keep count.

Twenty-two egg, twenty-three egg, twenty-four egg.

All the eggs are white and round, and look like large Ping-Pong balls.

Forty-six egg, forty-seven egg, forty-eight egg, forty-nine egg.

"Look there," whispers Crisp. "She's done and is coming out."

Very slowly, the turtle climbs out of the hole and begins filling it in with her flippers. Sonny pushes a little sand into the hole.

"Don't be helping her," says Crisp, "for there is a way it must be done, and it's she what must do it."

Sonny can help. Sonny is a good helper.

"You are indeed." Crisp rubs Sonny's back. "But she don't need our help. It's us what needs hers."

Sonny likes the toasted cheese sandwiches. He likes cherry pie and ice cream. He likes the feel of Mr. Crisp's hand on his back.

Sonny reaches out and runs his hand across the indentation in the turtle's shell.

Good turtle. Good Big Red.

Little by little, the turtle fills in the hole.

Crisp backs away from the hole. "With me," he says, "for she's done and will be heading back to open water."

The turtles have returned. Soon the eggs will hatch. Soon the baby turtles will dash to the sea.

As it was in the beginning.

"Hurry, lad," Crisp shouts. "For the rest of the faithful have arrived."

Sonny shuffles through the sand, digging his toes into the loose beach, and kicking it up in front of him.

Turtle bone, clamshell, clamshell, clamshell.

Turtle bone, clamshell, clamshell, stone.

Sonny stops and turns his face to the wind. He listens to the sea crash into the land, and as he watches, he sees shapes emerge from the scuttling fog.

Two figures.

Two figures stolen from the water and carried to shore, like salvage on the incoming tide.

93

GABRIEL WAS QUITE SURE HE HAD NEVER MET A MORE STUB-
born woman.

"You can't stay here!"

"The hell I can't!"

"You need to go now!"

"I'll go when I feel like it!"

Gabriel was afraid they had waited too long. By the time
they made their way down the sides of the shafts and reached
the base of the Apostles, the flat had vanished. The water here
was already up to their knees, and the rip was strong. It pulled at
their legs and sucked the sand from under their feet.

And then another wave would come in and break over them.

"Hold onto me!"

Gabriel leaned into the tide, as though he were hiking up a
steep hill. Mara gripped his belt as they floundered in the roil.
The white water yanked them backwards, tossed them forward, sometimes sideways. As he struggled towards the beach,
Gabriel could hear the surf pounding the sea floor behind him.
It smashed into the rocks and drove the wind against them, as
the ocean tried to run the fugitives down.

That's how Gabriel imagined the scene. Fugitives. Escapees from an island prison. The count of Monte Cristo. Papillon. Napoleon.

Gilligan.

"What?"

"Nothing!"

"You said, 'Gilligan'!"

"Don't let go the belt!"

Once, a massive wave caught them from behind, knocked them off their feet, and then sucked them backwards. Gabriel had clawed at the sand, had felt Mara ripped away by the surge, felt himself being dragged off.

"Mara!"

"Gilligan!"

"What?"

"I'm right here!"

And so she was. Somehow it had been Mara who had kept him from being swept away.

"That was a good one." She stood waist deep in the water, wiping the hair out of her face. "You feel like doing that again?"

"No."

Another wave broke on their backs.

"You're not the only one who didn't come home."

"What?"

"Home!"

"What?"

Gabriel began timing the waves, driving forward with each surge, trying to hold his place in the undertow.

Drive and hold.

Drive and hold.

And then he was on his hands and knees in quiet water.

"You okay?"

"Fine!"

Mara helped him to his feet.

"You're going to love the next part."

Gabriel didn't hear the cheering right away.

"Look at that," said Mara, and she started walking towards a large group of people standing by the tower.

"What are they doing?"

"Waving," said Mara. "Cheering us on."

Gabriel straightened up. His pants were soaking wet. His shoes were gone, and he only had one sock. He tucked his shirt in and succeeded in driving more sand into his crotch.

Mara picked something off his forehead and straightened his jacket. Then she headed up the beach towards the people and the dry sand.

"Fix your hair," she called back. "It looks as though someone tried to drown you."

94

GABRIEL DID NOT FOLLOW MARA RIGHT AWAY. INSTEAD, HE stood on the shore with the surf snaking about his feet and watched the waves explode over the Apostles. It was an impressive show of force, and he had to admit that the view of this natural cycle was better from where he now stood than from where he had just been.

It was only after he turned to join the people by the tower that he saw the turtle.

A sea turtle. Dragging itself towards the water. A turtle with a depression in its shell and a blood red slash across its neck.

It couldn't be the same turtle from the tank in the lobby at Domidion, the turtle with whom he had shared his lunch all those years. Surely there were other turtles with indentations in their shells, other turtles with red markings.

That turtle had disappeared in Toronto.

This turtle had appeared on a beach in Samaritan Bay.

"You catch a train or something?"

The turtle was moving slowly, coming right at him. She looked tired. Her fins were ragged and scarred, as though she had crawled a great distance.

"Walk?"

Gabriel found himself hoping that it was the same turtle. There would be a good story in that. Turtle escapes corporate prison, eludes capture, still at large.

"Seat sale?"

Gabriel squatted down and waited for the turtle to reach him. He wanted to get a good look at this turtle, to see if he recognized her, to see if she recognized him.

"You ever spend time in a tank?"

It couldn't be the same turtle.

"What about it?" Gabriel lay down, so the reptile wouldn't see him as a threat. "You can tell me."

The turtle slid along, pulling and pushing herself forward, leaving a long drag mark in the sand.

"I won't tell anyone."

The surf had caught him again. Small waves broke over his back. Larger waves would follow.

"It's pretty rough out there," he said, getting to his feet. "If I were you, I'd wait."

When the turtle was level with him, she stopped. But it was just to catch her breath. She didn't look at him, and she didn't vary her line. She paused, raised her head, and then began moving again, straight into the surf, seeking the very waves that Gabriel and Mara had escaped.

And as he watched, she sank into the water and turned on her side, pulled hard once with her flippers, and vanished.

95

GABRIEL SAT IN THE SAND FACING THE OCEAN AND ATE everything Mara put in front of him. He couldn't believe all this food had come out of the one picnic basket.

"The man knows how to pack," Mara told him.

Gabriel helped himself to a ham and cheese sandwich. "Is there a kitchen in there somewhere?"

Crisp and Sonny, along with the Chins, the Huangs, and a number of people Gabriel didn't recognize, watched the waves. The larger ones brought cheers from the crowd.

"That's the guy from the Co-op."

"Folks in town saw Sonny's tower," said Mara, "and came down to see what was up."

"And Crisp is feeding them?"

"Mr. Crisp is a man of substantial talents."

Gabriel tried to peer into the basket. "Is there any roast beef?"

Sonny had found a long stick, and, as each wave receded, he and Soldier would race after it, would plant the stick in the sand as far out into the ocean as possible. And as the wave turned, the two of them would scamper back up the beach, yelping and shouting, the water hard on their heels, Sonny's face bright as the sun.

Crisp had joined in for a while, but after several of these sprints, the man had come back to the blanket, awash in sweat and breathing hard.

"The lad's a demon for fun."

"And you're not as young as you used to be, Mr. Crisp."

"Indeed, Mistress Mara," said Crisp. "Not by an eternity."

"Is it true about the motel?"

"True enough," said Crisp. "The Chins have experience on cruise ships, as it turns out, and you knows that Jun-jie can cook. They're going to help the lad with the motel, and it's expected that the business will support the lot."

Crisp poured himself a cup of tea. It came out of the Thermos, hot and fragrant. "As well, two of the cousins are mechanics and have plans to fix the old bus and offer tours of the environs."

Crisp blew at the steam.

"And Mr. Collins has installed the Huangs in that empty lot behind the Tin Turtle. Master gardeners they turn out to be, and will be supplying the town with fresh produce."

It had been unexpected. The tears. Mara tried to fight them back, but without success, and her shoulders began to shake.

Gabriel had been slow to see what was happening, but then he quickly tried to gather her in his arms.

She slapped his hands away, her eyes flashing through the tears. "Do I look like I need to be held?"

Gabriel glanced at Crisp.

"Don't be looking at me for starboard or port," Crisp said quickly, "for I've no compass in such matters."

"I'm fine," said Mara. "I was just thinking about the reserve."

"Aye, the reserve," said Crisp. "No need for tears on that

account, for the word's already on the wind. They'll come home. Ye mark my words, they'll all sail home."

Two of the Huang boys had joined Sonny in his stick game. Soldier sat at the water's edge and watched the ocean move. The sun had held. The fog bank had come to the breakwater, but no farther.

"Do ye see?" Crisp waved a banana at the fog. "It's an ancient wall what holds the sea in check and dams the land. Not a sound it makes. Comes and goes without a word, it does. Ye may thrust your hand through it and breathe it in if ye have a mind."

Crisp pushed off the sand. "Not even a proper colour, but all the hues at once. Ash. All ash. The sun burns it. The wind moves it. It has neither fangs nor claws."

Soldier shifted nervously and bent his ears forward.

"Yet no one can catch it," said Crisp, taking a step towards the water. "No one can hold it. And ye cannot reason with the creature."

Mara looked at Soldier. "The dog hears something."

Soldier growled and began moving down the beach, the muscles along his back and neck bunched and hard. Sonny was running into the ocean with his stick, laughing as he ran down the slope of damp sand, when the dog began to bark.

Crisp was on his feet. "Sonny!"

Down into the belly of the ocean the boy ran, his stick held high, delight bubbling off his body. Soldier chased after him, howling as he went.

"Sonny!"

And in an instant, Crisp was sprinting through the sand, throwing up showers and sparks.

"Sonny!"

Gabriel hadn't believed anyone could move that fast. One moment, Crisp was standing by the blanket, the next he had caught Sonny, snatched him up, and was racing back up the beach, Soldier at their heels, as the scream came slicing through the fog.

A long, terrible, scraping screech that ran out along the shore as though the world had been ripped open.

Soldier spun about, began barking and snapping at the crowd, began driving everyone from the edge of the water.

"Get back." Crisp was shouting and waving an arm, as he carried Sonny to safety. "Get back."

And then something dark and impossibly large pushed its way through the fog, rose up and slammed into the beach like an axe into flesh.

Crisp put Sonny down on the blanket, took a deep breath, and turned back to the ocean. "Ye surely don't see that every day."

It was the prow of a ship, a huge and dented hulk, corroded and blackened, with fresh, bright tears on its side where it had smashed into the rocks on its way to shore. Half in the fog. Half out.

Crisp turned to Mei-ling.

"That be the vessel?"

Mei-ling shivered and put her hand to her mouth. "Yes," she said, her voice no more than a soft whisper. "That is our ship."

Crisp was the first to move. He walked down the beach, circled the bow, stroked the metal flank of the monster, as though he thought it was in need of affection. Sonny followed in Crisp's footsteps, walking where Crisp walked, touching what Crisp touched.

Salvage.

Crisp smiled and rubbed Sonny's head. "No lad," he said. "There be no salvage here."

Mara took Gabriel's hand. "Come on," she said. And the two of them made their way to the water's edge.

"There," she said. "Near the top."

The upper reaches of the ship were hidden by the fog, but Gabriel could make out letters and then a single word.

Anguis.

The rest of the people from town slowly moved to the ship, Mei-ling and the two families hanging back. Crisp banged on the side of the hull to get everyone's attention.

"I'll be needing your help," he said. And he placed both his hands on the bow and bent his back into the ship.

Gabriel couldn't believe Crisp was serious. He expected the man would give up the joke, and they would all have a good laugh. One individual wasn't going to move this ship. It was stuck fast in the sand. Even if everyone on the beach helped in the pushing, nothing was going to happen.

"Come on!" shouted Crisp. "For we've not much time."

Gabriel shook his head. "You're kidding."

Mara punched him on the shoulder. "Come on," she said. "When are you going to get another chance to push a ship off a beach."

"You're never going to move it."

"It's not about moving," said Mara. "It's about community."

The hull was cold and hollow, and great rivers of rust ran down its sides, as though the beast had been wounded and bled. Gabriel had not considered how death might feel, but he supposed it might look like this.

"You will sing?"

Mei-ling and the rest of the Taiwanese crowded about Gabriel and Mara.

"You will sing that song?"

"A stupendous idea," shouted Crisp, and he began to beat out a rhythm on the hull.

"It's a bad idea."

"Least you can do," said Mara. "Seeing as you're not dead yet."

And so he started, singing the lead weakly, trying to find the right pitch. He was well into the first push up when a second voice joined his.

Mara.

By the time he got to the honour beat, Crisp and Sonny had joined in, their voices fighting each other. And then Mei-ling and the families. By the second verse, the people from the town had come to the song as well.

It wasn't pleasant, but it was loud.

Not that the ship was moving. It hadn't moved. They could sing and push until they were hoarse and sore, and it wasn't going to move.

Then Crisp raised his voice above the surf.

"Sonny!" he cried. "Lend us your hammer!"

Wham-wham!

"That's it, lad," Crisp roared. "Hit it again!"

Wham-wham, hammer-hammer!

Sonny's hammer rang against the hull, and slowly, by degrees, the sound of the strikes and the voices came together, until Gabriel could feel the vibrations running through the steel, could feel the song in the ship itself.

But now there was something else. Not a voice. More a tremor that Gabriel could feel in his feet. Thunder perhaps. That was it. Spring thunder.

"Away!" Crisp moved through the singers, pushing them away from the ship. "For the high ground," he shouted.

Gabriel staggered in the first few steps. Mara grabbed his arm as they ran up the beach.

"If you could do it over."

"I can't."

"I know. But if you could."

"Higher," shouted Crisp, as he drove everyone out of the sand and onto the face of the slope. "There be the push and the shove what's needed."

The first wave smashed into the ship's flank and sent a shiver through the structure. And, as Gabriel watched, the *Anguis* moved.

"Again!" cried Crisp.

The second wave was larger. It lifted the vessel by the stern and slammed the bow down into the sand.

"Again!"

The next four waves came in a rush, welled up under the *Anguis*, and broke the ship's hold on the shore.

"There she be!"

The seventh wave was enormous, taller and more massive than anything Gabriel had ever seen. It slammed into the hull, set the *Anguis* afloat on the tide, and sucked the ship into the fog.

Everyone stood on the slope and waited. Gabriel was sure that the ship would reappear on the next wave, was sure that the *Anguis* would rip through the fog and bury itself in the beach once again.

THE BACK OF THE TURTLE

But it didn't.

Crisp was the first to break the silence. "Well," he boomed, "that surely worked up an appetite." And he went to the basket, lifted the lid, and began laying the food out on the blanket. "Eat up, eat up!"

Gabriel tried to find the Apostles in the fog and high water, but it would be hours before the tide would raise them up again.

Mara appeared at his side. "You're thinking you should have stayed on the rocks."

"This doesn't change anything."

"Maybe not," said Mara.

"I'm still responsible."

"All right," she said. "Then do something about it."

Crisp came striding through the sand with Sonny in his wake.

"That was a powerful song," he said, "to have conjured up such a wave."

"It wasn't the song."

"Aye," said Crisp. "The song and the lad's hammer."

"And I don't think it was the hammer, either."

"And yet the song was sung, the hammer struck, and the wave came."

"You knew it was coming."

Crisp shrugged. "I'll admit to a possibility. But patience, for the boy's got something of yours."

Sonny was holding the drum.

"He found it on the beach. Ye must have lost it when ye and Mistress Mara was out frisking about on the rocks."

The drum was wet, but there were no tears in the hide. Gabriel turned the drum over in his hands.

"Here," he said, handing it back to Sonny. "You keep it."

"That's kind of ye," cried Crisp, "for the boy's fond of such things."

"Then he should have this, too." Gabriel slipped out of his jacket and brushed off the back so that the tipis shimmered in the sunlight. "Consider it today's salvage."

IT was late afternoon by the time the people began to leave the beach. Sonny had spent the time in his new jacket, running up and down the sand with Soldier at his heels, hitting the drum and singing something about clamshells.

Mara stayed in the grass next to Gabriel.

"I still want to hear that story."

"Which one?"

"The one you don't want to tell."

A flock of seagulls passed overhead on their way to town, arguing as they went, and on the bluff near the old motel, a raven shouted abuse at anyone who would listen.

"There." Mara put a hand on Gabriel's arm. "Look there."

The sun had cleared the mountains and was lighting the face of the waves, driving the fog away from the shore.

"Look!" Mara shaded her eyes.

"What?"

"Do you see them?"

Pelicans. Coming in low, gliding across the water, following the line of the shore, with the sun on their wings.

"Are those the ones you and Lilly saw?"

Gabriel watched the squadron work its way north towards the headlands and the reserve.

"The very ones," he said.

Mara and Gabriel stayed on the beach until the tide turned and the fog lifted, until all that was left was a beacon on a line of land and a silent horizon on an endless ocean.

96

DORIAN SHOULD HAVE BEEN TIRED. HE HADN'T GOTTEN ANY sleep, but by the time he arrived at the office, he felt positively electric. The nausea and the pain were gone, and for the moment he was able to imagine a future that did not include doctors and hospitals.

The condo papers would be signed later in the week, and, as soon as everything cleared, he planned to move in. No sense wasting time. He'd put the Queen's Quay condo on the market immediately. There would be some legal issues, but he wouldn't deal with them until Olivia returned from Orlando.

If she did return.

And he had stopped off at Royal de Versailles, had bought the Jaeger, to celebrate his new life.

"A very fine watch," Kip had said, when Dorian got into the back seat.

"Yes, it is." Dorian slipped the Rolex off his wrist and weighed it in his hand. "What kind of watch do you have?"

"A dependable watch." Kip had held out his arm. "Very inexpensive. Very accurate. It runs on solar energy. No winding. No batteries."

"Have you ever wanted to own a Rolex?"

"A Rolex?" Kip had grinned. "What would I do with a watch such as that."

"What if someone gave you a Rolex?"

Kip filled the car with laughter.

"You are a funny fellow," he told Dorian. "Very funny indeed. I must watch you very carefully."

WINTER was waiting for him by the elevators in the garage.

"Good news would be appreciated."

"Someone tried to kill the prime minister."

Dorian waited to see if Winter had decided to start his day off with a joke.

"Half an hour ago," said Winter. "It's all over the news. CNN, Fox, CBC, CBS, NBC, ABC."

"Shot?"

"A knife."

"That's terrible."

"Wounded," said Winter. "Not serious."

Dorian waited for the doors to close. "Have PR send flowers."

"Already done."

"And the Athabasca?"

"Gone."

"Gone?"

"The prime minister is the only thing on the networks."

"Kali Creek? Dr. Quinn? GreenSweep?"

"All gone," said Winter.

As soon as Dorian arrived at his office, he turned on the television.

"White male. Middle-class. From Northern Ontario." Winter worked her tablet. "No word yet on why he did it."

Dorian flipped through the major channels.

CNN was airing an interview with an expert on combat knives, who was describing how such a knife, in the hands of a skilled assailant, could be as deadly as any firearm. CBC was showing images of the outside of a restaurant, just blocks from Parliament Hill, where the attack had occurred.

"The blogs are the same," said Winter.

"God bless the media."

"Amen," said Winter.

"Stock prices?"

"On the rise."

"What do you think?" said Dorian. "Quite the *deus ex machina*."

"Yes," said Winter. "It certainly is."

Dorian stuck out his wrist. "I bought a new watch."

"Very handsome."

"And a condo. They're sending the paperwork over this afternoon."

"Mrs. Asher called," said Winter. "Several times."

Dorian relaxed in his chair. He couldn't get over how marvellous he felt. "Anything else?"

"Two items," said Winter. "I did a search for the word "Kousoulas."

"And?"

"It appears to be a proper name."

"But?"

"I found a D.G. Kousoulas who wrote a number of books on geopolitics, but he's dead." Winter consulted her tablet. "I was also able to locate a photographer, a veterinarian, a media consultant, an account executive, a lawyer, and a basketball player."

"Quinn circled that name in stars. It must mean something."

"That would seem to be a valid assumption."

"Keep looking." Dorian checked the Jaeger against the clock on the wall. The clock was two minutes fast. "What's the second item?"

"The *Anguis*."

"Again?"

"Another possible sighting," said Winter. "Three weeks ago. Off the coast of Northern California."

Dorian sat back and folded his hands across his stomach. "It's at the bottom of the ocean."

"Yes, sir."

"I can feel it in my bones."

Dorian swivelled about so he could see through all the glass partitions at once.

"We need to do something about the tank in the lobby."

"Yes, sir."

"Let's fill it with fish. Lots of colour. Something to perk the place up."

"Salt water?"

"And maybe a turtle."

Winter straightened her glasses. "I'll talk to Maintenance today."

Dorian touched his pocket. "Tell me," he asked Winter, as she got to the doorway. "Have you ever wanted to own a Rolex?"

97

CRISP LOWERED THE TRAILER HITCH ONTO THE BALL OF HIS truck. "And where will I be mooring Master Gabriel?"

"Near me, I guess," said Mara.

"Near enough for the eye," said Crisp, "or for the conversation?"

"Conversation," said Mara. "But no closer."

Soldier sat down outside the door to the trailer and began whining.

"Master Dog appears to have a concern," said Crisp.

Gabriel squatted down and rubbed Soldier's neck. "He's nothing but concerns."

"Someone must do the job." Crisp set the chains. "Carry the valuables what might break, and I'll drag the rest ashore."

Soldier whined louder and scratched at the door.

"He wants in," said Mara.

Gabriel looked at the dog. "He can't ride in the trailer."

"Why not?" Mara opened the door, and Soldier quickly pushed past her. "He seems to know how to take care of himself."

"All he does is sleep and fart."

"Dangerous thing," Crisp shouted back, "to argue with a woman what's smarter than oneself."

Gabriel was about to say something to Crisp about sexism and clichés, when Soldier popped out of the trailer, a stuffed dog in his mouth.

Mara arched her eyebrows. "Didn't take you for the cuddly-toy type."

Soldier dropped the dog at Mara's feet and stood poised at the ready.

"Long time back."

"Girlfriend?"

Gabriel nudged the stuffed dog with his foot. "I bought it for Lilly."

Mara picked up the dog and shook it gently, so that its ears flopped up and down. "Now that's a story I want to hear."

Soldier began whining again, more loudly this time, his body trembling as though he were going to shake himself apart.

Mara smiled. "I think he wants the puppy."

Gabriel shrugged.

"So, we're set, are we," said Crisp, popping up from behind the truck and climbing into the driver's seat. "It's the trail for the two of ye and the road for me."

The trailer groaned and snapped as Crisp dragged it off the pad. Soldier carefully took the puppy in his mouth and followed the truck as it headed to the reserve.

"It's a nice day," said Mara. "Why don't we take our time."

"Sure."

"And you can tell me the story of the stuffed puppy."

Gabriel checked the horizon. No fog. No ship. No enormous waves.

"Where do you want me to begin?"

"Start where all stories start."

"All right," said Gabriel. "There was a woman who lived in a sky world. And she was curious."

98

THE ATHABASCA WAS MONTHS IN THE PUBLIC'S REAR-VIEW
mirror now, and, while there was the occasional outcry over
new studies that documented the continuing damage to the
Mackenzie and the Arctic, the newspapers had consigned such
revelations to the back pages of the "Life and Arts" section.

The networks ignored them altogether.

The prime minister continued to be front-page news, the
attack, the stitches in his arm, his return to the House. A month
after the incident, he played in a celebrity golf tournament,
where he had swung his driver with vigour for the television
cameras and the supermarket tabloids.

It had taken most of that time for Domidion's share prices to
recover. But recover they did. Olivia had finally returned from
Orlando. With a tennis pro. A younger man. It had been such a
cliché that Dorian would have put it on his Facebook page.

If he had had such a thing.

The tennis pro lasted exactly two months. Olivia put the
Bridle Path house up for sale and moved to Vancouver. It was
strange, but Dorian didn't miss her, didn't miss being married,
whatever that meant.

What had they seen in each other? Thank goodness they had never had children.

He wasn't sure he liked being alone, but he was enjoying his new life at the Hermes. He especially appreciated having a private elevator. Each time he stepped inside and slid his security key into the card reader, he felt valuable, as though he were being put away in a vault for safekeeping.

Even the hospital procedure had not been as bad as he had imagined. But the results had been inconclusive. That was the word Toshi had used. "Inconclusive."

"We'll continue to monitor the situation," Toshi had told him.

"What situation is that?"

"We'll probably want to do another biopsy."

After he was discharged, Dorian stopped off at Rosen's, and Robert helped him with three new suits, a casual jacket in dark teal, and a cashmere overcoat.

DORIAN looked up to see Winter on her way to his office. Today, she was wearing a dark charcoal wool skirt and jacket with a silver-on-silver silk blouse. Elegant and efficient. He wasn't going to ask, but he was curious what she might say if he were to suggest a drink after work.

"Good morning, Winter."

"Good morning, Mr. Asher."

"Good news would be appreciated."

"Six items," said Winter. "The Zebras have begun releasing the confidential health records of Toronto's top business leaders."

"Mine?"

"Not so far."

"Should I be insulted?"

"Second. Uruguay's General Assembly has voted to ban all Domidion agricultural products."

"Again?" Dorian shook his head. "What's three?"

"The pipeline."

"More delays?"

"We're encountering stiff opposition from local communities and First Nations."

Dorian wondered if the knife attack was going to serve the prime minister in the next election. People tended to be partial to wounded heroes.

"Have a word with Legal," said Dorian. "Let them know we're displeased."

"Yes, sir."

"Next?"

"Dr. Quinn and Dr. Thicke," said Winter. "We've still not been able to locate Dr. Quinn. Nor have we found the mother or sister."

"Does the Board feel we need to find Q at this point?"

"No."

"Then let's not bother." Dorian rubbed his eyes. "And Thicke?"

"Dr. Thicke has submitted his resignation and is taking a position with Syngenta."

"The Swiss conglomerate? They're a competitor."

"Yes," said Winter, "they are."

"Doesn't Thicke's contract contain a non-competition clause?"

"It does," said Winter. "Should we enforce it?"

"God, no," said Dorian. "With any luck, Thicke might set Syngenta's research back a few years. What's the last item?"

Winter tapped her tablet and handed it to Dorian. "This was taken by a passenger on a cruise ship."

The image was a low-resolution photograph of a dark ship with rust stains running down its sides, sitting low in the water.

"We've had the photograph enhanced. It's the *Anguis*."

"What's that?" Dorian squinted at the screen. "The white smear near the bow."

"According to the reports, the *Anguis* scraped the side of the cruise ship."

He and Olivia had taken a cruise once. Seventeen days across the Atlantic, from Barcelona to Miami, with stops in Málaga, Cádiz, Gibraltar, Agadir, Lanzarote, Tenerife, and La Palma. There had been an outbreak of an intestinal virus, and the ship had been put under a sanitation regime that consisted of staff members spraying copious amounts of bleach on handrails, tables, and the insides of all the elevators.

He and Olivia had gone to two floor shows and left in the middle of the second one when a large man in a tuxedo began singing "Send in the Clowns." There had been a daily art auction where you could buy art no one wanted, a casino that was designed to depress the most ardent gambler, and several wine-tasting events where the vintages had arrived in plastic sacks.

And the food.

Everywhere you turned there had been food.

By the time they had reached the Azores, Dorian was prepared to kill someone to get off the ship. On that trip, he would have given anything to have been hit by a garbage scow.

"Damage?"

"Minimal," said Winter. "According to the passenger postings on Facebook and Twitter, it was all quite exciting."

"And the *Anguis*?"

Winter took the tablet from Dorian and ran a finger across the screen. "The captain of the cruise ship gave the authorities a projected course for the *Anguis*."

"The Gulf of St. Lawrence?"

Winter nodded. "If it stays on course."

Dorian put his head in his hands and squeezed his temples. "So, it's coming home."

"It would appear."

"I don't suppose we can just sink it."

And for the second time that Dorian could remember, Winter smiled.

99

CRISP AND SOLDIER LOUNGED IN THE SAND AND WATCHED Sonny run up and down the beach. The boy had Gabriel's jacket on. It was too big for him, and, when he moved, it flapped about his thin body like a great set of wings.

"Easy, lad," Crisp called out. "Ye mustn't scare them."

Each day since Big Red had laid her eggs in the sand, Crisp had brought Sonny to the beach to check on the nest. The boy would sit in the sand for hours, banging the drum, singing his turtle-bone song.

"The boy has scant talent for melodic renderings," Crisp told Soldier, "but he has a honeyed heart, and on that account we needs put up with the excruciations."

THE ocean had come back first. On the days when Crisp swam out to the horizon, he found more and more signs of life. Small fish darting about the seaweed, urchins and anemones huddling together, crabs and starfish patrolling the rocks and sandy bottom, larger fish moving in from the depths.

Early one morning, Crisp had spotted movement in a kelp

bed just off shore. "Look, lad," he said, grabbing Sonny and turning him about, "that be an otter!"

The birds were not far behind, the gulls leading the way. Noisy and combative creatures they were, ready to take all sides in an argument. And later the oyster catchers, the petrels, the sandpipers, the grebes, and the scoters.

Last week, the ravens had returned in force, forever unsympathetic.

And now the turtles were hatching. It had started in the night, and, when Crisp and Sonny had reached the nest early that morning, the baby turtles were already making their run to the sea. Sonny had been unable to contain himself. He ran back and forth between the nest and the surf, banging the drum and yelling encouragements.

Crisp sat in the sand and watched Sonny dance in the air and walk on the water. "Easy, lad," he yelled to no avail.

Back and forth Sonny went, his arms flying, the jacket flapping, the drum floating over his head like a balloon.

Go turtles!

CRISP had dragged the trailer onto the reserve, set it behind Mara's house so as to keep the two of them close without blocking the view. And he had watched her coax the story out of Gabriel piece by piece, and so far, he had heard little in the telling to recommend the man.

Crisp and the dog had spent many a night debating the prospects for that relationship, with nothing to show for their time but the argument itself. It was Lilly that had brought them together, the sister and friend that Gabriel and Mara shared, and there was no particular promise in that bond.

Kindness perhaps. Even affection.

Crisp had seen a spark or two, but nothing bright enough to kindle combustion.

Soldier had been more optimistic.

But then dogs were known to favour happy endings.

SONNY stood in the surf, the jacket rattling in the wind, as he drummed the last of the turtles into the water.

Crisp stroked the dog's neck. "Look after the lad," he said, "for our Gabriel don't need ye anymore."

Soldier rolled up against Crisp's leg and began licking at his paw.

"Aye, Master Dog," said Crisp, and he leaned back, enjoying the sound of the waves on the beach, and the warmth of the sun on his face. "I am well."